BEYOND THE CALL OF DUTY

"Marriage is out of the question, Gabriel."

"Ah, well," he said with a quiet sigh. "We shall fight our own private war then, won't we? I won't have it any other way. Perhaps you need time to think it over. You can give me your answer next Saturday night. Be ready by eight o'clock. I'll arrange our transportation."

"You'll need directions to my home—" she began, but he interrupted with a wave of his hand.

"By the time we meet again, my beautiful compatriot, I'll know everything about you down to the size slippers you wear. *Au revoir, mademoiselle.*"

By the same author

Dancing in the Dark

Available from
HarperPaperbacks

Surrender the Night

Susan P. Teklits

HarperPaperbacks
A Division of HarperCollins*Publishers*

HarperPaperbacks *A Division of* HarperCollins*Publishers*
10 East 53rd Street, New York, N.Y. 10022

Cover illustration by Diane Sivavec

First printing: October 1994

Printed in the United States of America

HarperPaperbacks, HarperMonogram, and colophon are trademarks of HarperCollins*Publishers*

❖ 10 9 8 7 6 5 4 3 2 1

I dedicate this book to every spirit broken by the cruel hand of domestic violence. May love find you, soothe you, and heal you.

1

Vanessa Davis took a seat in the dining room, primly arranged her pink brocade gown and laid a lace napkin across her lap.

The table was exquisitely dressed, polished, and spread with a white linen cloth. Beneath the pale light of the chandelier, cutlery gleamed, crystal sparkled, champagne bubbled. Every dinner plate seemed to glisten as fashionably as the guests. Despite the glaring red coats of British soldiers, the war seemed to fade into the glamour of the surroundings. For now, the world was restored to elegance.

Colonel William Smith, the Commander of this newly arrived British company, remained standing at the head of the table. When he reached for his glass of champagne, everyone quieted to hear his toast.

"I wish to express my sincere gratitude to the Borden family for providing me with these comfortable quarters and such a fine meal of welcome . . . " he began, and everyone interrupted with a round of applause.

"You deserve to be saluted for your bravery in the face

of your Patriot neighbors who so foolishly expect to overthrow the most powerful kingdom on earth. Tonight we share our friendship the way we will soon share a victory in this rebellious land! To the King!"

"To the King!" they all cried and Vanessa feigned an equal amount of enthusiasm, a vivacious smile on her lips as she glanced around this table full of Crown sympathizers. Dressed in their Sunday best, they represented whatever Tory stronghold the British army could find in this area. Vanessa knew Colonel Smith had had a terrible time finding that support.

When Smith had arrived yesterday, he'd camped his men in the woods overlooking the village and spent hours searching for a friendly household to shelter his officers. Doors were slammed in his face, children bombarded him with rocks and crabapples, a hidden sniper took two shots at him. After having marched here from friendlier New York City, Colonel Smith was astonished at the hostility he found in Pennsylvania. By the time they'd arrived here, his men were already exhausted from the long march through the great forests of this colony where they were twice ambushed by a hidden detachment of the famed Pennsylvania riflemen. Lives were already lost and not a single battle was waged.

Colonel Smith was not the first British officer to be duped by his own intelligence sources who claimed most of America was teeming with Loyalists. Vanessa could clearly hear skepticism in the voices of the soldiers here tonight; some were clearly angry.

"Those cursed riflemen picked us apart out there! And they hid in the trees all the while so we couldn't get off a good shot!"

"If Howe wants Philadelphia, why not send a few battalions here instead of dribbling companies into this colony? In such small numbers, we're defenseless against those cursed riflemen . . . "

"I'm sure the General has a plan of some sort . . . "

"I'm not so sure! He spends more time with his mistress than his army! While we're out here dying he's lying abed with Miss Lizzie! If he wants Philadelphia so badly, why doesn't he decide when and how to take it?"

Vanessa sighed at her plate, pretending to be bored by all the war talk like the other women at the table. She would have attempted a more genteel conversation, but few of these proper Millbridge ladies would dare converse with Vanessa Davis. They believed her to be a Tory whore, although none had any proof. They didn't need any. The Davis family had long been the scandal of Millbridge and Vanessa was accustomed to walking in the shadow of its dark history.

"My dear Lieutenant, you're overanxious for battle," she heard the Colonel say as she let her attention drift to the head of the table. "When the General feels his forces are strong enough, he will take Philadelphia at once, you can be sure."

"I'm not sure about anything since Ticonderoga fell to a parcel of mountain boys from Vermont," the Lieutenant replied, drawing a secretive smile from her as he added in disdain, "And our ranking officer dragged off in the middle of the night without being granted the decency of putting on a pair of britches!"

Vanessa laughed outright, her humor blending into the drunken gaiety at the table.

Colonel Smith looked momentarily embarrassed as he quipped, "What can be expected from the likes of Ethan Allen, eh? Green Mountain Boys indeed!"

"A stroke of luck, I'm sure," the Lieutenant snorted, and the Colonel laughed haughtily.

Vanessa watched the Lieutenant lean aside as a servant filled his plate. It wasn't the first time she had noticed this particular officer, how rugged and virile he seemed in comparison to the other soldiers. Broad shouldered and tall of stature, he wore his distinguished uniform very well. The crimson shade of his coat highlighted the deep tan of his complexion and the big brown hands that poked from beneath the carefully pressed ruffles of his white blouse. Any woman could see he was every inch a man. The other men at the table displayed an almost feminine elegance, but this one moved with the agile grace of a young lion.

"We mustn't bemoan our few losses and remember our glorious victory in New York City instead," the Colonel was advising. "Besides, I'm sure Burgoyne will soon retake Ticonderoga."

"Are his forces large enough?" The Lieutenant seemed to be asking himself the question.

"He has ninety-five hundred men and Colonel St. Leger is mustering more at Fort Oswego to join him in a push toward Albany."

"These forces seem sufficient," the Lieutenant drawled in his deep, husky voice. Vanessa watched him wash down a mouthful of beef Wellington with the Colonel's fine champagne. For a moment, his dark eyes wandered, and Vanessa wondered if this might be the right time to catch his attention.

She leaned forward, into his line of vision, and reached for her glass of champagne.

He saw her at once, the fork in his hand poising in mid-air. Vanessa deliberately remained in his view, letting the candlelight illuminate the blue sheen in her raven black hair and the delicate peach hue in her creamy complexion. In profile, her features appeared very delicate and aristocratic. Her high-boned cheeks and proud brow announced their lovely lines, softened only by the sensuous fullness of her lips.

When the Lieutenant's interest was completely caught, Vanessa teasingly disappeared back into her seat.

"I see you've noticed Vanessa Davis," she heard the

Colonel whisper. He gave the Lieutenant's arm a tap and said with a naughty chuckle, "She came unescorted tonight. Her father's a Tory but he couldn't attend because of some unnamed malady. She chose to come alone, which is not entirely proper of her, is it?"

"A gentleman is likely to get the wrong idea, eh, William?"

They snickered privately and resumed eating.

Vanessa allowed a servant to refill her glass and watched a million bubbles dance inside the crystal stem, then froth upward into a replenished pool of the sweet, sparkling liquid. She should refuse another helping, this being her fourth glass. Her lips were already numb.

She wasn't much of a drinker, but tonight was a special occasion. Vanessa never had the opportunity to sport with real British soldiers, only Tory civilians. The mere thought of toying with a man like the Lieutenant made her feel a need for extra courage.

The dessert service interrupted her thoughts. Each guest was presented with a Tipsy Squire Truffle baked in its own glass dish. They applauded the beautiful confections. Vanessa lifted her spoon and sampled the rich creme topping, leaning forward just enough to be seen from the head of the table.

The Lieutenant was watching her, noticing the way her full pink lips curled around the spoon. His complete attention fueled her nerve. Yes, she could do this, play with this big virile soldier until he was reduced to telling her anything and everything to get what he wanted.

These thoughts excited her, renewing her courage until she was filled with a cold, hard vengeance. Yes, the Lieutenant would be her next male victim, joining the ranks of so many other men whom Vanessa had left broken, humiliated, and ashamed. It was the way she had always been treated by the hand of the opposite sex. Let them all pay for the demon who sired her.

To be sure her inhibitions were completely washed away, she took a last sip of champagne, set the glass down, and turned toward the Lieutenant.

Her violet eyes met his orbs of midnight blue.

The Lieutenant's spoon halted in mid-air. Except for the Colonel, none of the other inebriated guests noticed the way she stared at him, startling him with a bold and unmistakable acknowledgment of his interest in her. He sat enchanted, unable to look away from the uncanny shade of her eyes. They were the color of lilacs, fringed by sooty lashes as dark and sensuous as the invitation she extended from the far end of the table.

The Lieutenant's loins gave a sudden, fierce tug. The spoon slipped through his fingers and fell into the truffle dish with a messy splatter. Colonel Smith threw back his bewigged head and laughed until the curls above his ears danced. The Lieutenant looked at him, somewhat embarrassed, then abruptly straightened his cravat.

"Sir, are you finding humor at my expense?"

"I certainly am," William chortled merrily. "I enjoy watching our stiff and battle-weary young men be lured into a night of soft play. Drink more champagne and let the war be damned tonight!" William followed his own advice and promptly swallowed another glassful. "Listen to how my guests are enjoying themselves and the dancing has yet to begin!"

Vanessa realized William was quite correct in his assessment of the party's intoxication level. Champagne was rare during wartime and everyone was taking advantage of its abundance tonight.

"Is there no end to your stores of champagne?" the Lieutenant inquired smoothly, his eyes continuing to seek Vanessa out.

"None! And we shall enjoy it tonight, then set ourselves aright before Colonel Swanson arrives with our orders."

"That won't be too soon," the Lieutenant said with a grin.

William gave his shoulder a reassuring pat. "Not until next week. Think of it! We've plenty of time to sleep this one off!"

Someone tapped her on the shoulder and Vanessa jumped, losing the napkin on her lap as she turned around. It was Malinda Borden, her plump and dimpled face discreetly hidden behind the silk pleats of a fan as she leaned down and whispered, "Are you getting tipsy?"

"Of course!" Vanessa laughed. She put up her own fan and added, "I should stop but I was so upset when I arrived tonight I just can't seem to care . . . "

"Another row with your father?"

Vanessa nodded. She didn't want to discuss it, or even think about it.

Malinda's blue eyes fell sadly. Not a citizen in Millbridge was more aware of Vanessa's horrendous domestic situation than "Mally" Borden. In fact, she was one of Vanessa's few real friends in the community and the only one she confided in.

"Did he hurt you, Vanessa?"

"No, but he tried. I got away." Vanessa could feel the fear tighten her face until she knew Mally could see more than her words revealed.

"If you're in danger, let me go to my father for help," Mally offered.

"Nonsense. He shouldn't be asked to shelter a woman of my reputation."

"You always say that, Vanessa! You should know by now that no one blames you for the life you've had to endure."

"Please . . . " Vanessa implored, snapped shut her fan and whispered, "Let's not talk about it now. I just want to forget . . . have fun . . . "

"Of course you do!" Malinda soothed. She patted her

shoulder and suggested slyly, "Perhaps that handsome gent with the Colonel can help you forget your troubles. He's been watching you all night."

The guests were adjourning for coffee and Vanessa accompanied Malinda into the crush of happy people in the parlor. The pitch of laughter rose until it was almost shrill. Faces blurred past, a steady parade of familiar neighbors interspersed with red-coated soldiers and servants in starched white pinafores.

They found their way to the confection table, which was lavishly spread with an assortment of sweet treats. It was standing just inside the French doors that opened into the garden. One of the doors was ajar and the cool air felt refreshing on their flushed faces.

"Father is not pleased with the Colonel," Malinda divulged quietly. "He knows this is a Quaker household . . . that Friends do not approve of drinking . . . "

"How rude of him," Vanessa remarked, then gave her friend a teasing nudge in the ribs. "So why is your nose so red, Mally?"

"Say it isn't! I've done my best not to let him see me."

Malinda pretended concern as she searched the crowd for her father, but her vivid eyes were alive with humor. "I'm having so much fun!" She giggled, reaching for a colorfully iced bon-bon. "But mother is so upset she's gone upstairs in a vapor!" She laughed then, as if her mother's prudish behavior was funny, but the humor made her hand unsteady. The cake she selected promptly slid through her fingers and dropped into the punch bowl with a gay little splash. "Oh dear!" she gasped.

"Clumsy!" Vanessa teased, grinned at the cake. "Hand me the ladle and I'll fetch it out."

Just then a gentleman approached the table, picked up the ladle and stopped short when he saw the cake on the bottom.

"What the devil is that?" he asked no one in particular.

"A bon-bon," Vanessa answered soberly and had to squeeze Malinda's arm to keep her from laughing.

"Well, if that's all it is . . . " the man slurred, filling a cup and walking away with a lopsided grin on his face.

They looked at one another and burst into a fit of hilarity that made everyone around them smile, although they hadn't the slightest idea what was so funny.

"You have the most delightful laugh," a man's voice drawled just behind her.

Vanessa quieted, felt the back of her head nudge into something very hard and broad. She stopped, her senses suddenly alert to the pleasing scent of tobacco and leather tinged with a subtle fragrance of fine European cologne. A pair of strong brown hands came around her then, lightly holding her arms as a deep throaty chuckle sounded against her ear. "Shall I rescue the bon-bon or would you like to do it?" Without turning around, Vanessa knew exactly who he was—the dashing young Lieutenant.

Malinda hid her blushing complexion behind her fan, her pretty eyes gazing at Vanessa's captor as if she'd never seen a man before.

"If you would be so kind," Vanessa began just as Malinda lost her courage and excused herself to dash to the powder room.

The Lieutenant released Vanessa then, moving around her to the table. From behind, Vanessa admired the sturdy width of his back, the way his jacket tapered around a narrow waist. With one capable scoop, the disintegrating bon-bon was removed from the bowl, set on a plate and handed to a servant. She smiled her thanks, and the Lieutenant dipped into a graceful bow that ended in a most chivalrous kiss to the back of her hand.

"Allow me to introduce myself," he said, standing up and looking at her with eyes that sparkled with genuine humor. Not only was he handsome, Vanessa surmised, but likable besides. "Lieutenant Paul Graves . . . of His Majesty's Fourth Mounted."

"Vanessa Davis," she demurred, letting her gaze linger on his a bit longer than was proper in so crowded a room.

For some reason, she didn't really care who was watching just then. There was something about this man that she found exciting, not only because of her nefarious plans but because he didn't seem to be the kind who easily fell into traps. Through her mind roved a hundred ways of doing what she intended to him and, quite surprisingly, she felt her pulse quicken. He seemed to sense her warmth, the color of his eyes darkening ever so slightly.

"Come," he said quietly, his voice a full octave lower as he extended his arm. "Walk with me . . . in the garden."

She looked away, broke the heady spell of the moment and lightly laid her hand on his. It was too proper a gesture for the instant reaction it caused between them, a subtle jolting of the senses in deep, intimate places. She was as aware of the rugged texture of his skin as he was of her velvet softness. By the time they paused inside the garden door to have their glasses refilled, they both knew exactly what they would do together before this night was through.

They stepped outside, strolled across the flagstone balcony where other couples mingled while waiting to dance. It was a cool night, a new spring season still young on this clear and bright evening of May 15, 1777. Another campaign of warfare was about to begin, wintering soldiers bursting out of camp at the same time that this beautiful Pennsylvania countryside bloomed toward another ripe harvest. What an irony, Vanessa thought, " . . . so much new life amid so much death."

"Not only are you beautiful but profound besides," the Lieutenant remarked.

Vanessa looked up, startled to realize she'd spoken aloud. It was the alcohol. She'd had far too much to drink, and should spill out her glass at this very moment and refuse another sip.

The Lieutenant paused beside a hedge of lilacs, tugged a blossom free. He held it up to her cheek. "The color is a perfect match," he said, his voice as soft and thoughtful as his gaze. For a moment, with those dark eyes focused entirely upon her face, Vanessa felt like the only woman in the world. "I've never seen eyes the color of yours before . . . as strange as they are magnificent . . . " He slid the stem through the hair at her temple. So gentle was his mood, his touch, Vanessa stood there feeling oddly transfixed by him.

Momentarily bereft of words, she just blinked up at him, suddenly wishing he'd engage her in the usual small talk that men waged with women they thought they were about to bed.

"You're too free with your compliments," she finally managed to say in a small voice.

He started to walk with her again and she took the opportunity to catch her breath, to stop feeling so disturbed by what should have been a normal night's work.

Damn this champagne! It was making everything seem so lopsided and odd. Even the landscape seemed queer, the silver incandescence of the moon driving the hedges into deep shadows while illuminating the flowers until they looked like bright white pompons. The garden was blooming gloriously, but its beauty seemed somewhat unnatural; or was it just the liquor affecting her vision?

"From where in England do you hail, Lieutenant," she asked casually, hoping conversation might straighten her teetering mood.

"Leeds . . . in Kent. Have you ever been to England?"

"Heavens no! I'm a farmer's daughter, born and raised right here in Millbridge. We've not the money for such grand excursions. So tell me, do you share England's opinion that we colonists are hopelessly barbaric?"

The Lieutenant laughed, a soft and airy sound that seemed to start somewhere in his belly and rumble up into his throat. She liked the sound of it, how spontaneous and genuine it was, so completely bereft of any pretense.

There was a sparkle of good cheer in his eyes when he looked down at her. "My dear lady, if you must know, my opinion is that England has become hopelessly self-righteous and over-impressed with itself. Half the soldiers in my battalion are having the time of their lives over here . . . and most will probably stay on."

"You don't say!"

"I do," he insisted, stopping on the path. He stood there looking so tall and elegant in the moonlight as he lifted his glass. He studied every sparkling crystal edge for a moment before he said, "Barbarians who drink from crystal. Imagine it! Why, I expected crude earthen pots and tents and pies made of mud."

She giggled at his jest, lifted her own glass and clinked the edge against his. "To the barbarians . . . "

"Here! Here!" he toasted, flashing her a mischievous grin before enjoying a healthy swallow.

More relaxed now, he took her hand and they strolled along the twisted stone path where other couples meandered and whispered and stole chance embraces behind the foliage. He was in no hurry and Vanessa admired his dignified control. After all, his manhood was as starved as that of any other soldier; most wouldn't think of wasting this much time before grabbing at her.

"We picked a perfect evening for a soirée, Vanessa," he said, stealing a quick glance at the canopy of stars overhead. "The stars of a spring night can somehow block the memories of cold winter camps . . . make me relieved that at least the snow is past, if not the war."

They were crossing the lawn now, leaving the garden behind, moving toward the white picket fence in the distance that separated the Borden home from Fleece

Downe Road. Vanessa sighed as the cool night breeze swept across the treeless expanse of green turf, the first chords of a minstrel's minuet dancing on the light winds.

"Ah! the music has begun," the Lieutenant announced. "Shall we dance?"

"What?" She looked up at him, saw a flash of bright white teeth against the ruddy darkness of his skin. "Here?"

"Why not?" He shrugged, still smiling.

She giggled, amused by such a reckless proposition from such an elegant man. "We're drunk . . . "

"Yes, but on what, the champagne or one another? Come, let us see . . . "

He promptly tossed his glass over his shoulder. Vanessa gasped, laughed, watched him snatch her own goblet and send it off to the same dark fate.

A moment later, she was in his arms and they were twirling across the grass like a pair of playful children. He was so tall and strong and purposeful that she found it oddly easy to dance on the uneven surface of the lawn, her slippers barely skimming the surface while she spun with him in a whirl of billowing pink silk and red wool coattails. Expertly, faultlessly, he turned her, waltzed her, glided her until she was thoroughly caught in his uninhibited mood, caring as little as he did about who might see them out here in the middle of the front lawn. And all the while he watched her, enjoying every expression of girlish delight that crossed her face.

Vanessa could not remember a time when she'd had so much fun. Especially not with a man. They were the enemy, all of them. She knew better than to let any get close to her, even those she was about to seduce for the sake of the Cause.

But this one was different. The way he looked at her with those dark eyes, so full of animation and admiration, every sparkle seeming to rain praise upon her uplifted face. And the way he touched her, his fingers so warm and gentle as they brushed a curl out of her eyes or smoothed her cheek, made her feel strangely adored.

Some impulse made her lean closer, deeper into his arms. Beneath the scarlet wool of his coat, his arms felt like blocks of iron, stiff with muscle yet carefully tender. A white wool jerkin seemed barely able to contain his broad chest, the metal buttons straining against his thick physique every time he took a breath. His long legs moved with an athlete's grace, so swift and sure, his powerfully muscled thighs intermittently grazing her own in between the steps of their private little dance. Closer and closer they danced until their bodies were touching more intimately, more boldly, more hungrily.

Their gaiety was slowly consumed into headier emotions as each contact of their bodies seemed to pronounce the intensity of their physical attraction to each other. Laughter became just a whisper on their lips as their eyes met in the darkness of this night. Passion was slowly mounting between them like a pot left to simmer on an invisible fire. They didn't speak of it, didn't feel a need to acknowledge what was so evident between them by the time they reached the fence on the edge of the property.

She wanted him, wanted the way he looked at her, touched her, made her feel like some rare and special prize. She was appallingly excited by him, not just in a physical way, but somewhere else, in a place where she had only known pain and hurt from the hands of a man.

Her spirit.

His back grazed the fence and he stopped dancing then, standing very still and straight as he held her in his arms and stared into her eyes.

"Look up at the stars," he whispered breathlessly. She blinked at him strangely but did as he asked. "There . . . your eyes . . . they're almost translucent in the moonlight . . . if only you could see them as I do." He caught her chin with just his fingertips, made her look at him again, seeing the way his eyes caressed every line and curve of her face. "And it makes your skin shine like white velvet. I daresay, you are magnificently beautiful, Vanessa Davis, as breathtaking as the land that bred you."

He pulled her closer, until their bodies met and she could feel the full length and breadth of him, how ample was the manhood he wore so proudly. The shock of her own arousal made her breath catch in her throat.

"Paul . . . " she breathed, too astonished at his effect on her to think of anything witty to say, anything that might restore some sense to the blissful confusion of her mind. This wasn't the way it was supposed to be! He should be the one aroused beyond reason!

His hand slowly slid up the length of her spine, disappearing into the mass of curls that hung down her back, disheveled now by the wind and the fingers that artfully snaked through her glossy black mane. He tilted her head back, those mysterious midnight eyes of his skimming over every curve of her throat, her half-bared shoulders, the ripe swell of her breasts that were scantily hidden beneath a daring neckline. The intensity of his gaze made her tremble in deep and private places, rendering her limp and pliant in his powerful arms like an artist's clay ready to be formed into whatever he wanted.

His lips scampered up the front of her throat, warm and tender on her delicate skin. She shuddered wickedly.

But then he released her, abruptly, took her hand and started striding alongside the fence, his long legs swift and purposeful now. She stumbled after him, one hand on her throat where she could still feel the touch of him as if it was burned into her skin. "Where are we going?" she gasped, her voice weak, winded.

He didn't answer, just asked in a thick and throaty voice, "What road is this?"

"Fleece Downe Road . . . "

"Do the rebels control it?"

"Why . . . er . . . the rebels control all of Millbridge."

He laughed then, his voice raspy. She liked it, liked everything about this stranger whose calm confidence brought out a side of her that Vanessa never knew existed.

Her womanhood.

Every crooked plan she'd had for him was now abruptly displaced, floating away.

"With a thousand British soldiers camped on the Poquessing Creek, the Continentals still waltz the countryside . . . " he muttered, stopping at the main gate and quickly removing his scarlet regalia. A waistcoat, vest, and British-issue spatter dashes were all tossed into the shrubbery until he stood clothed in only a white blouse and britches and knee-high black leather boots.

What a stallion he was, so tall and sleek, his narrow hips wrapped in a decorated scabbard that housed a shimmering silver sword. No evidence of his loyalties remained on his person by the time he scaled the rails in one smooth swing of his long legs. From the other side, he motioned to her, his gaze mirroring her own excitement.

She came to him, let him lift her high into the air until the hem of her dress brushed the top rail. She felt his hands tighten around her waist, the muscles of his forearms bulging with the effort to bring her down safely to the other side. He lowered her slowly, let her body slide along the full length of his own in an unspoken ceremony of physical play. And all the while he let her stare into his face where his hunger was now completely unguarded.

Between her legs grew a tremor, then a pulse. His unwavering eyes were direct, demanding, full of a fire that spread rapidly.

Her slippers touched the ground just as his lips found her skin again, scampering up her neck, along her shoulders, underneath her chin. The touch of him, scent of him, strength of him, made her shiver with delight as he expertly aroused her, without those clumsy, awkward advances she was familiar with from the local boys she'd played with. This was no dim-witted farmhand who'd tell her anything about his family's loyalties after a few kisses. No, this man handled her with the grace of an artist, every stroke of his lips painting her with new and vibrant shades of desire.

"The rebels won't take me prisoner tonight, Vanessa," he whispered against her throat, "only you . . . and I shall revel in you as I haven't enjoyed a woman in a long, long time."

"Paul . . . please . . . " she whimpered in a soft voice that didn't sound anything like her own. She had to put a stop to this! It was already out of control, but what woman could resist the way his lips were caressing her cheek, her brow, her chin, everywhere but her lips. He made her desperate to taste him, discover him, know him in ways not meant for strangers.

Instead of resisting, her hands were sliding across the broad lines of his shoulders, up the back of his neck until her fingers slid under his wig and pulled it away. The piece fell to the ground in a flash of white, a puff of powder. Her hands filled with thick glossy waves of his natural hair. It was dark, streaked with auburn lights, as clean and fresh-smelling as the rest of him. She was kissing his face, every broad and angular curve of it, barely aware of her own sigh of pleasure as his mouth finally slid over her own.

Their lips glanced once, then met and clung to this first taste of each other. She quivered at how warm and delicious he was, how the faint trace of tobacco nipped into the flavor of expensive champagne. She wanted more and let her lips boldly explore every inch of his own. It excited him, made his arms close around her, holding her tight as their embrace deepened and their mouths were drinking with an uninhibited thirst. For just a moment, their kiss became numbing, almost bruising.

But then he lifted her up, started carrying her down

the road. "Where can we go . . . " he groaned against her lips. "Tell me a place . . . "

"The barn . . . down the road . . . it's not far . . . "

He pressed her face against his breast where she could hear the wild thump of his heart and his panting breaths. He held her close, so very possessively, as he followed her directions. She barely remembered reaching the old abandoned barn that stood in the middle of an acre-wide green.

They were inside. It was dark, musty. Slivers of light pierced the interior where the wood was rotted and split.

The place was familiar. She'd been here many times before but never like this. The other times, her companions were aroused and throbbing and aching, not herself.

"You're too beautiful to be taken in a barn." He was murmuring against the top of her head. "Isn't there a better place?"

"Don't be silly," she scoffed, stroking her fingers through the thick waves of his dark copper hair, "I'm just a whore . . . "

"No," he sighed, sinking to his knees in the hay. His face drew close enough for him to sample from her as if she was some rare and exotic confection. "The skin of whores is not as soft as silk . . . nor is their scent so fresh and sweet."

He laid her down, the hay sticky and prickly against her back. He was hovering over her, the sweat of unchecked passion gleaming on his face. Big strong hands moved from her waist, slowly glided over the swollen curves of her breasts. His touch was breathtakingly tender, so subtle and adoring as if he was savoring each and every centimeter of her body. It made her feel utterly exquisite, like the most beautiful woman ever created.

"Tonight you'll be my queen," he said and his words only made her feel more beloved. He leaned down, kissed her long and hard on the mouth. "And I'll adore you as you deserve, Yankee beauty."

None of this was real. Not the way his hands held her head and demanded every angle of her lips. Not the way he made her body want to lift from the hay and melt into his own. Not the way she clung to him as his lips careened around the back of her neck and shoulders while his fingers deftly separated the buttons of her gown.

The garment fell away, her naked breasts tumbling into his hands like a pair of ripe spring blossoms bursting from a pod. The sight of her own nakedness caused a shock wave of alarm to course through her but she couldn't react to it, not when his mouth was ravishing her in places where no man had ever touched her before.

Oh! he was a master, a champion, showering her with the most tremendous physical delights she had ever felt from the hands of a man. This was a dream, all of it, some kind of wicked lie. Men had brought only pain and destruction to her life. Never pleasure. Not like this.

It must stop. Now! She should never have let it get this far. Her whole reputation in Millbridge was at stake. They believed her to be a Tory whore, a woman who frequented the parties of loyal Crown families, usually leaving on the arm of a man. While they thought she was bedding him, Vanessa would play on his passion, make him talk, then turn him over to the Whigs who would drive him and his family out of town. It was a calculated ruse, always risky, but somehow she had managed to escape intact every time. No man could resist his own banal instincts and when she promised to give him all the next night, each one always agreed, duped by her clever excuses as to why she had to leave him unsatisfied for one more night.

Why did she feel so different this time, so strangely out of control?

Perhaps it was the way this man was looking at her, so directly, so completely, seeing all of her and wanting her all the more. She had never felt so wholly desired in her life.

This must stop but it couldn't, wouldn't, unless she made it happen. Impossible! A woman so long abused could not resist this chance to feel so loved and worshipped, so worthy of a man's adoration. It was a fantastic, unbelievable dream.

Far from mind faded the sight and smell of the barn, her original intentions, the time of night and her place within this hour of her life. She saw only the two of them, tumbling and straining and writhing in a passion so fierce and commanding that neither could control it.

Pain burst through a place deep inside her body, sharp and sudden. Vanessa gasped, her eyes popping wide open.

The dream vanished.

The Lieutenant's face poised above her, his body falling suddenly motionless as he stared at her in complete astonishment.

"Virgin?" he rasped, his voice deep and rough. "No!" Suspicion washed all the passion from his molten gaze, his handsome face turning hard and cold. "Who are you?" he demanded.

An icy chill rushed through her, seemed to freeze her in place. She didn't move or speak, just lay there staring at him in complete confusion.

What had she done? The Lieutenant would tell everyone the truth about her, destroy her cover of a Tory whore. It would get back to her father. Dear God! He'd kill her for this if he found out.

"Why?" the Lieutenant was demanding, his tone of voice so crisp and harsh it made her suddenly terrified of him, of what damage his rage could cause to her person.

Ever so slowly, without daring to take her eyes from him, she rose on her elbows and began to inch away from him.

He followed her. "Why? Tell me why you did this. Answer me!"

"I don't know," she gasped up at him, her eyes wide with terror.

He saw her fear, realized how frightened she was and made an attempt to calm himself. He sat back on his heels, took a long drink of air. When he spoke again, his voice was much softer, more controlled. "I'm not going to hurt you, Vanessa. I just want to talk to you."

Talk? Ha! She had stopped falling for that ploy at about the age of ten when it finally occurred to her that every time her father "talked" to her, it ended in another beating.

He reached down to stop her retreat and the motion made her jump like a spooked rabbit. She jerked out from under him, grabbed her dress and scrambled to her feet.

"No! Don't run!"

She backed up against the barn wall, her hands trembling violently as she hurried into her dress, all the while watching the man who stood tall and naked in the middle of the shadowy barn.

"Stay . . . stay away from me . . . "

"Vanessa," he began but she didn't listen; her eyes were darting between his hulking figure and the open barn door. "Please don't run off . . . just listen to me . . . I wouldn't have done this if I knew you were chaste. Why? Why did you let me . . . "

"I was drunk . . . I forgot myself," she said, desperate now to get around him and reach the door. "I just want to go home."

He saw her intentions, put up a hand to stop her flight. "Alright . . . but at least tell me where I can find you . . . "

"I don't want you to find me," she cried, bolted off the wall and leaped through the open barn door.

"Vanessa! Stop!"

He was coming after her, his giant strides no match for her own even though she ran for her life. He caught her, grabbed her arm in a tight grasp and whipped her around to face him.

Her fist launched against the side of his face, hard enough to stun him and force him a step backward. His dark eyes widened in shock at the force of her blow, at the rage in her voice and on her once beautiful face as she spat venomously, "Keep your hands off me! And pray you never see me again!"

He just stood there staring after her like a dumbstruck man, unable to believe what was happening. She was running away, this woman with whom he'd shared such a fierce and compelling passion, now fleeing across the green as if it all meant nothing.

He started after her, still hitching his britches, his bare feet moistening in the wet grass. From the back of his mind a dark memory tried to surface, remind him of what had happened the last time he was involved in an indiscretion with a woman.

It was the day his twin brother Michael was gunned down.

For an instant, images of that horrible day raced through his mind. Michael's face, a mirror image of his own, stiff with fear as he faced the accusations from the front lawn of their father's estate.

"Who bedded her? Which one of you did it? I can't tell you bastards apart!" The accuser's flintlock caught the light of the sun, flashed and streaked through the sky as it leveled at a pair of twin boys sporting blades on the lawn.

The gun cocked with a sound that still echoed in his head and brought with it a rush of gruesome memories from the blackest recesses of his soul.

Michael jumping in front of him, momentarily blotting out the bright orange flash of flame as the gun exploded. The impact of the ball lurched him backward, sent a spray of warm wet blood up his arms as his brother toppled into them. And all the while, as if from far away, his father's voice screamed, "No! No!"

Then his father was upon him, nearly breaking his wrist to wrest away the sword that was slashing at his brother's killer like a machete in the fist of a demon. His father sent it hurtling out of his reach and he could still see it spiraling across the blue sky, end over end, its bloody edge sparkling gaily in the sunlight.

Now he groaned aloud, let his face fall into his hands, tried to shake away the memories that left his whole body shuddering in a black and bitter grief. It had been a long time since he remembered Michael's death so clearly.

An indiscretion with a woman. That's how it all happened, the taking of a chaste maid. It was the same sin that stole a brother who was at his side from the moment life found a pair of seeds in a woman's womb. Until the day he died, he would never recover from the loss of his twin brother. Never.

He blinked at the night, realized he was standing petrified in the middle of the green. His eyes scanned the dark timberline until he saw a flash of white disappear into the woods.

"Vanessa!"

He sped after her, his long legs easily consuming the space between them. He entered the woods where she did, saw the vague outline of a woman as she zigzagged between the trees.

"Leave me alone!" she screamed over her shoulder. "Go away!"

The back of her dress was open, flapping wildly in the wind of her flight. He grabbed hold of a piece, heard her cry out as she tried to spin away from his grasp. A moment later, she was in his arms, her small white fists pummeling uselessly at his chest, his arms.

"Stop it!" he panted, clamped her tight in his arms and whispered fiercely against the top of her head, "I'll not leave you like this . . . to bear the mark of my sin. I'm not that kind of man! Take me to your father . . . I'll tell him what happened . . . make him understand . . . convince him to let me restore your honor in holy vows!"

For a split second, she stopped fighting, as if his words temporarily took away her panic. "What," she gasped, looking up at him as if he had just gone mad. "Marry you? You must be out of your mind!"

"No! I've stolen your dignity. Your honor must be restored!"

She jerked out of his arms, stumbled backward a few steps, and stared at him as if he was some kind of two-headed monster. "Honor? Ha!" She laughed then, a wicked little sound that echoed through the damp woods like a dark spirit flitting in a macabre dance. "My honor was stolen a long time ago."

"Don't say that."

She only laughed again, the sound hollow and cold.

Dear God! what kind of soul had this woman? It was downright chilling to watch her, hear her, look into the soft and sensuous beauty of her and see such a cold and ugly hate.

"You don't understand, Lieutenant. My dignity is beyond retrieval. Just be away from me and forget we ever met."

With that, she turned on her heels and flew away, an angel of heaven running back into whatever unspeakable hell she'd come from.

2

Two young Captains stood before a parlor window in the Army's New York Headquarters and quietly conversed. No one noticed them, not the soldiers who came and went from the house nor the family who opened their home for the army's use. Everyone was too busy, caught in the multitude of tasks demanded by a major military encampment. Like a pair of predatory birds, their minds focused on the prey they were ordered to find somewhere in the turbulent theater of the American Revolution.

"We should be honored to be chosen for this mission," one of the Captains whispered. "The General must have great confidence in us."

"I'd have more confidence in us if these passes weren't so ambiguous," the other Captain complained. "We're liable to be hung as spies behind our own lines!"

"Come now, we'll never catch the likes of the Archangel without being able to pass through any lines we must . . . British or Continental. He's out there somewhere, so deeply undercover, so flawlessly obscure, we've no choice but to do the same in order to catch him."

"Do you really think anyone will ever discover him?" They looked at each other then, one doubtful, one hopeful. "In all my years of intelligence work, I've never come across anything like this. His own General doesn't know who he is yet he takes counsel from this master spy as if his every word came from the Great Book itself."

"Amazing, isn't it?" The Captain looked away, into the frosty glass window where he watched the reflection of his face fill with an expression of marvel. Under his breath, he began to recite the popular Whig poem written in honor of the Archangel that was known even to the children in this rebellious land.

Speak not a word for he can hear,
No lengthy range can fool his ear.
Creep silent, swift, a whisper's tread,
Shadows fall o'er the Archangel's head!
Thundering wings, hooves of steel,
A golden edge does his rapier wield.
Enemy sleep while he strikes this night,
Angel of freedom, with him we fight!

The less confident Captain shifted in his boots, momentarily intimidated by the huge reputation of the man they were assigned to find. "The man's a bloody folk hero! How the devil does he do it?"

"No one knows," the other soldier replied. "And to date, he's foiled every mission to find him. I daresay, the Continentals have no more lethal weapon than this invisible spy who seems to know what the British will do even before the British do! That's why I want to be the one who catches him at last!"

This Captain grinned through the window, his vision slowly sweeping along the green ripples of land in the panoramic Mohawk Valley. He could see the river from here, the mighty Hudson, broad and deep and dark, rumbling between the deciduous foothills. The river commanded the valley, carved whatever path it willed with its magnificent liquid power. Nothing could challenge its majesty, not the density of the forested slopes nor the sky that hung so low and mean above the valley. It was about to rain, and this early in the season, one never knew if it would be snow or water.

"Think of it! If we find him, we'll be heroes!"

"And if not?"

The more confident Captain looked at his partner and decided not to answer. He wasn't about to discuss the ramifications of failure before they'd even begun the search. Besides, he wasn't in the mood to think about dying. "Let's get on with it," he said cheerfully, giving his partner a cuff on the arm and turning away from the window.

"God be with us," his partner muttered darkly, then followed him out of the room.

3

The noonday sun cast a welcome warmth across the cobbled streets of Millbridge. Vanessa noticed many women without shawls strolling through the shops of the village, only aprons covering their shifts and white cotton mobcaps protecting their heads. Children leaped after their mothers with the peculiar energy that seemed to infiltrate everyone at the onset of spring. It was as if winter's cold could impede the spirit until the first peep of spring came along to liberate the heart.

She sighed dully, turned away from the window of Joshua Stone's apothecary shop and returned to the pretense of shopping. It was Monday, the day when Joshua's secret legion of Whigs collected in his shop after he closed for the mid-day meal. Two others were already there, milling around the room, poking through cupboards, feigning great interest in the fine collection of spices and medicinal herbs.

Vanessa avoided them. She should have so much news to tell them after the Borden dinner party on Saturday night, her first opportunity to sport with a genuine British soldier. Had she done her job she would now have news about the size of the Lieutenant's company, how long they would stay, what their orders were. Instead, she could only relate what she had heard at the dinner table, about a Commander named Swanson who would arrive in a week with the army's orders. When she'd told Joshua all this at church yesterday, he had seemed pleased enough and hadn't noticed her shamefaced retreat from further conversation.

Her body still ached from the Lieutenant. Every time she felt the soreness it made her think of him, taste him, remember how wickedly alive and adored his touch had made her feel. If only it was just a dream, a wonderful dream that turned suddenly terrible, one from which she could awake without having to wear the mark of it for the rest of her life.

Joshua closed the shop door. He went to the window, looked outside for a moment before drawing the drapes. All the while he brushed his hands across his rotund belly, adding more grime to his shirt, then sniffed allergically at whatever scene in the street happened to catch his attention.

A pair of redcoats meandered down the opposite side of the street.

Vanessa looked after them, her breath catching in her throat until she saw that neither man sported a Lieutenant's braids.

Two boys trailed after the soldiers and perfectly imitated their pompous strides. A woman saw the boys' antics and chuckled aloud.

The soldiers turned around.

"Lobsterbacks!" the boys hollered, heaving fistfuls of crabapples at the soldiers, then flew into the alley, screeching hilariously as they ran.

Every person in the street stopped and laughed aloud. Embarrassed, the soldiers stalked away angrily while the people began to slowly move on. Those least committed to the cause left the quickest, Vanessa noticed, the stauncher Whigs lingering to chuckle with one another. She sighed, aware of how the war was tearing this small town apart, forcing people to choose between love of the motherland and love of the continent they called home. For the most part, people did what any reasonable person would: join the majority and take whatever side was winning at the moment.

"Damned British!" Joshua muttered, dropping the drapes and walking to the cellar door, behind which a few loyal Whigs were waiting. He opened it, didn't bother to watch them file into the room, just cleared the counter of potted herbs and sacks of medicinal powders.

Vanessa took a deep breath, mentally rehearsing the lies she planned to tell them about Saturday night.

A half-dozen citizens slumped around the counter, talking about their fields, their children, the war and their neighbors. They came to the shop every Monday at noon to hear Joshua's plans for the week and to discover which Millbridge resident was getting too close to taking up arms for England. Between the six of them, volunteers would be found to frighten off the offenders, to burn a barn, axe a wagon wheel, or drive off a few head of cattle. They did whatever they must to lessen England's formidable chances.

For the purpose of secrecy, Joshua gave each of his devoted Whig friends a code name. Because of his business he chose herbal names for all. When he began to address them in this private way, they knew the meeting had begun.

"Basil, stop leaning on that crock . . . you're crushing the mint . . ."

"Sorry, Josh . . ."

"Gather round, neighbors, and listen good. I've got news today."

Vanessa looked up in surprise, not expecting Joshua to

have his own announcement. Perhaps it would keep the attention away from her and the dinner party. She leaned closer, eager to hear while feeling suddenly and wonderfully redeemed.

"You all know about my famous cousin, Francis Stone," he began and everyone nodded.

Of course they knew Surgeon Stone. He served the First Squadron of the Philadelphia Light Horse, a Continental reconnaissance company wholly responsible for the victory at Trenton. Ever since that triumphant day, all of Pennsylvania revered the First Squadron and the daring young Lieutenant Colonel who commanded this crack corps, Gabriel St. Claire.

Joshua grinned broadly as he continued, "Francis got word to me yesterday that his company has moved into the area."

"Really?" Rosemary gasped in surprise. She looked around as if expecting to find a Continental scout hiding behind a stack of crocks. "Where are they?"

"On the other side of the Creek somewhere."

"The First Squadron . . . here in Millbridge?" Vanessa exclaimed, delighted that this news would keep everyone more than occupied today. There would be no questions for her to squirm out from under. "St. Claire himself!"

"That's right, Lavender," Joshua said. "Now I don't know exactly where because men of this caliber don't let *anyone* know of their whereabouts, not even local Whig relatives like me!"

"I'd love to see St. Claire," Rosemary piped up. "I hear he's very handsome . . . that he's from France and still speaks with an accent that makes the ladies swoon—"

"Oh for God's sake," Thyme scoffed. "Who cares for these romantic notions about him, eh? What matters to us men is that he's the best spy on the continent."

"And what matters to me is that we all shut up and listen so we can get on with our day," Joshua demanded and everyone instantly obeyed for fear they might miss more news. "Francis has asked that we lay low for a week or so and don't cause any trouble in these parts until their business is done. We can't be getting underfoot."

"General Howe must be serious about an attack on Philadelphia," Thyme concluded intelligently, "otherwise, Washington wouldn't spare his best surveillance company."

"If he's sending his best, I wager it won't be long until the Archangel drifts into town as well," Spearmint added, her eyes glittering in genuine excitement.

Joshua rolled his eyes. "You wouldn't know the Archangel if you fell over him," he said. "Now then, Lavender, you're to go to the abandoned barn on Fleece Downe Road at midnight tonight. Francis wants to talk to you."

"What?" Vanessa wasn't sure she had heard him right. "Me? What the devil does he want with me?"

"He wanted to know how I knew about Swanson and I told him you got the information. So he wants to talk to you."

"Did I do something wrong?"

"How the hell should I know? Just be there tonight and do as he says."

"If you help them," Rosemary encouraged her with a brief hug, "it'll make us all look good and maybe St. Claire will recruit us!"

"I've enough nerve for our sort of business but not theirs, Joshua!" Vanessa was genuinely stunned by this request for an audience. "What if I do something wrong and spoil their plans?"

"Oh for the love of God!" Joshua groaned. "Please don't embarrass me in front of my cousin!"

"But all I did was sit at the table and listen to the soldiers talk!" Vanessa insisted, desperate to diminish her importance.

"Stop leaning on those hibiscus plants!" Joshua snapped at her, moving aside the crock she was perched against. "Look! You broke the stalks! Now get a hold of yourself!"

"Easy for you to say," she muttered under her breath.

"Do you want to do it or not?" Joshua demanded with an impatient sigh.

A long and anxious moment passed while Vanessa considered her answer. Finally she murmured, "Of course I'll go if your cousin wants me to . . . "

Rosemary and Spearmint let out a whoop of delight, linked their arms and promptly danced a jig around the room. Joshua rumbled after them and demanded that they lower their voices.

"We'll be famous!" Rosemary crowed. "We helped the Philadelphia Light Horse! Imagine it! The Millbridge Whigs! Surely one of us will be recruited!"

"I'm not so sure I could join a Continental regiment right now," Basil said, frowning at the notion as if he was already asked to volunteer. "Who would tend the farm?"

"Let your son do it," Spearmint suggested. "He's old enough to work a hoe."

"If I join the army," Thyme thought aloud, "I would definitely volunteer for Light Horse duty. Aside from the Archangel, whoever he is, the spying of our mounted men is the only effective weapon we have against England."

Joshua realized he no longer had control of the group. His cousin, Surgeon Stone, had asked a simple favor and these Whigs were already decorating themselves with future glory. "Alright, this meeting is adjourned . . . now get out . . . all of you . . . and don't be blubbering this kind of gibberish all over town."

No one responded. They didn't hear him; they were all too busy laughing and patting Vanessa's back for good luck as they disappeared through the cellar door.

No wonder the Continentals had so many problems.

The only person who could control a Patriot was the Lord God Himself. Ah well, Joshua thought as he opened the shutters and unlocked the door, better God than the King.

The officers who gathered inside the Lieutenant Colonel's tent gave not the slightest regard to army regulation. On a cot against the far wall lay Gabriel St. Claire, his long legs dangling over the edge, an arm tossed across his eyes as if to blot out the world. On the spare cot sat the company Surgeon, Captain Francis Stone, his legs clamped around a pair of glass vials to hold them steady as he carefully mixed the ingredients of a smallpox vaccine. At the desk was perched Major Robert Blaire, second in command, not at all concerned with duty as he wearily studied the silhouetted tree limbs that hung against the roof of the tent. The Quartermaster, Lauren Stuart, sat across from him, contentedly napping, his head nestled upon a pile of requisition sheets.

They were just passing another dull evening, trying not to think about how close they were to their Philadelphia homes and how long it had been since they last saw their families. Eighteen months. And here they were, just a few hours' ride away, without permission for even a visit. They were officially assigned to the Northern Department in New York, only sent here to perform the critical covert mission of discovering the British intentions for Philadelphia.

It was wearing their nerves very thin, being forced to camp here on the Poquessing with a largely inactive British company stationed a few miles away. They were supposed to be spying on the enemy, but the British were dawdling, as usual, while their Commander had not yet arrived from Manhattan with their orders.

They were, consequently, bored beyond reason.

The flap of the tent moved. Gabriel opened his eyes and saw a familiar face poke through the opening.

Sergeant Benjamin Cooke squinted at them, his tiny, intense black eyes resting atop a perpetually red nose. At six feet four inches in height, the man was built like an ox and perfectly suited to his much flaunted position as the Lieutenant Colonel's personal sentry and the musterer of troops. No one would wrestle with this greasy, black-haired bull of a man who was as crude as he was loud and, even worse, drunk from dawn to dusk.

"This tent ain't never been so quiet! Why, I thought the only way to shut you up was to hit you over the head with a sledgehammer!" Benny roared at his own humor, crawled half inside the tent and took a swig from the flask of rum he always had hidden on his person.

"When Colonel Stephen Moylan takes charge of us, he won't allow you to hide rum anymore, Benny," Gabriel said and fought to keep a straight face while watching the Sergeant's reaction.

Benny hadn't thought of this before. He put a dirty hand to his mouth and gazed at his Commander as though he was having a beatific vision. He choked on his mouthful of rum. It spit through his fingers and dribbled down the length of his hairy arms.

Major Blaire studied Benny with an aloof roll of his soft brown eyes. Robert Blaire had a lazy face, usually blank of expression, his appearance not at all marred by a receding pate that slowly robbed him of his thin brown hair. Short and stockily built, he seemed too young for his distinguished air.

"Aren't we permitted a moment's peace?" the Major inquired.

Benny just shrugged and wiped his mouth on his sleeve. "You want some rum, Bobby?"

"Can't you think of anything but drinking?" Francis asked, giving Benny a good-natured sneer.

"Nope! Why the hell do you think I joined the army, huh? My wife won't let me drink is why!" As usual,

Benny got caught up in the tale he was about to tell. He knelt on the floor and drew picturesque symbols in the air with his hands. "She's a fine looking woman, understand, but there ain't a thing between her ears. Why, a man can stick his hand clear through her head! I swear! She ain't nothing more'n finely shaped acorn squash!"

Gabriel erupted in a burst of laughter that was hearty enough to nearly topple him from his cot.

"I'm trying to sleep!" the Quartermaster grumbled, lifting his head of curly red hair and glaring at Benny. Lauren Stuart didn't realize there was ink all over his round and freckled cheeks, nor did he understand what Gabriel found so amusing. The Lieutenant Colonel just looked between them and laughed all the harder. "I'll never get any sleep so long as this war continues," Lauren snarled. He got up and pushed Benny aside as he stomped out of the tent.

"One day I want to meet this *charmant amour* of yours, Benny," Gabriel chuckled in his husky, accented English.

"My what?" Benny looked at him stupidly.

"Never mind, Benny," Francis said, corking his vials and putting them aside. He leaned forward, held his head in his hands and sighed. The pose made his shock of frizzy blond hair stick out in every direction, his faded blue eyes showing far more intelligence than the rest of him. His tall and lanky appearance was almost too comical to project the kind of unshakable devotion this learned physician had for the Cause. "You know he always lapses into French when he's tired."

"Allez au diable!" Gabriel quipped, grinning mischievously.

"Humph!" Francis snorted back at him. "You think I don't know you just cursed me to hell?"

The Lieutenant Colonel finally sat up. "Speaking of France, where's my bourbon?" He used the toe of his boot to lift a few nearby objects and look under them.

"Drinking will be the death of this army," Robert said,

starting to pluck the dirt from beneath his fingernails. "Drinking and no respect for the officers."

"I've no complaints, Robert," Gabriel said, still poking through the paraphernalia on the floor for his bottle. "So long as they fight well when they must, who cares what else they do, eh? That's why the British are such lousy combatants. They're more worried about the regulation shine on their buttons."

Francis snorted. "Well said."

"Here, Gabe . . . have some rum instead," Benny suggested. Gabriel took the flask and gulped down a few mouthfuls.

"Burns, don't it? Just do what I do and swallow it quick," Benny coached. "Makes your eyes tear, don't it? I'm getting real low on the stuff, Gabe. Shouldn't we be ordering more soon?"

"See what I mean," Robert continued to voice his complaints about Continental conduct. "This is the only army in the world where Sergeants give orders to Lieutenant Colonels."

"You've gotten pompous since Trenton," Gabriel retorted, reminding the Major of how narrowly they had attained the title of heroes after that particular mission.

Their job was to police American lines while Washington traveled toward the Hessian encampment across the river in Trenton. They had done so, in the cold cruel elements of that Christmas night, but the better organized British intelligence department managed to sneak a warning through to Rall, the Hessian Commander at Trenton. By some stroke of what was certainly divine intervention, Rall never read the note while he continued to celebrate the holiday. It was found on his person the next morning, the seal unbroken, never read by the Hessian who lay mortally wounded on the field.

"Does that mean you're going to get me more rum, Gabe?" Benny's mind traveled in one direction at a time.

"My dear Benny," Gabriel sighed, urging Benny to his feet, and slung an arm around the sentry's hefty shoulders. "Do you know how many letters are sent to Congress by officers of this army? Thousands." Gabriel slowly turned Benny around, leading him toward the front of the tent. "In order to be a good officer, a man must content himself with writing a letter every day, asking for more of everything, knowing he'll get nothing. Nonetheless, we write the letters, hope for the best and scavenge for supplies in the meantime. Of course, the Light Horse get special preference. We're only seventeenth in line for necessary goods!"

"Who's first?"

"Whatever officer has the most political power at the moment."

"I'll bet that she-rabbit Schuyler gets whatever he wants!" Benny said with genuine distemper. "Humph! He's up there dawdling on his rump, pretending to be busy, while his nit-wit aides run around looking for the right thing to do."

"Like I said," Robert reiterated. "No respect for the officers—"

"'Cos there's only three good ones, Bobby!" Benny declared. "That's right! There's only three men in this whole damned army who have a right to wear a uniform . . . if they're lucky enough to git one . . . Washington, Arnold, and St. Claire! If that ain't the truth, I'll eat my legs right out from under me!"

"A truly gifted speaker you are, Benny," Gabriel drawled, graciously ushering him out of the tent.

Francis chortled as a flicker of a grin played across Robert's tight, thin lips. "At last! The Major smiles!"

"Oh go to the devil, Francis!" Major Blaire finally got off the desk, stretched, yawned, then asked in a very disinterested voice, "You don't need me at the meeting in Millbridge, do you, Gabe?"

"No. Francis will come along after he gives the farrier that vaccine."

"I hope he's asleep," Francis said with a puzzled shake of his head. "I've never seen a man so afraid of a scratch that could save his life. The mild fever he'll get from this is like a child's cough compared to the real disease."

"I want it done tonight, Francis."

"I know, Gabe. If I have to tie him down, I'll do it."

"Good luck, Surgeon," Gabriel said, started to smile, then yawned instead. "I don't have the energy for this meeting, but it's been arranged so I'll see it done."

"You don't really expect to find more than a patriotic Tory hunter, do you?" Robert watched the Lieutenant Colonel thrust an arm through his ammunition belt and locked it into place.

"Not really, but who knows, eh? That demonic Archangel could be a mere Tory hunter for all we know. Damn him. I'm tired of looking for him, but I aim to put a stop to what he's doing to me. No matter where I go, he shows up. Why? Here we are in the middle of nowhere and once again the General returns my intelligence information with a note, 'Sorry, but I received the same information about Swanson just hours ago. Good try, Gabriel, keep up the good work!' Damnit! I'm tired of it!"

"I know, Gabe. It's not a bit fair to you."

"I don't care about fair, Robert. I just want him out of my life so I might be recognized for what I do and not because the Archangel is in my constant shadow."

"That's not true, Gabriel," Francis tried to soothe. "Everyone knows you're a better spy than any the British have. Even their notorious John Andre tips his hat in your direction . . . if he can find you!"

"Bah!" Gabriel snarled, never so easily incensed as when he spoke about the Archangel. This invisible spy seemed to know every move of the First Squadron, following their missions, using their skills only to jump ahead and steal the enemy secrets just as Gabriel managed to discover them. The Archangel stole his glory time and again. Although the officers jokingly referred to this anonymous spy as "Gabe's Ghost," it was no laughing matter to the Lieutenant Colonel. It was an embarrassment to him, a humiliation that stabbed at his heart.

"Enough of this talk . . . it infuriates me . . . "

Francis stood up, put the vials in his pocket and joined Gabriel at the flap of the tent. "When this mission is over, we should request leave for the men. It's been eighteen months now."

The change of subject soothed Gabriel. "I've already requested it," he said as he slid his hands into a pair of regulation leather gauntlets. From beneath the shade of his stark brow, those eyes that could make the ladies swoon smiled at Francis. "I haven't been home in so long I forget how to get there. Ah well. Such is the price of glory."

"Fun, isn't it," Robert said.

"Things could be worse," Francis offered. "We could be assigned to the main army."

Robert grimaced at the roof of the tent. "I hear the rank and file average just a meal a day now. Something must be done about provisions or we're doomed."

Gabriel just nodded, slapped a decorated, tri-cornered hat on his head, and swung into his cloak. "I've spent half my life doomed to die, Robert, first by the guillotine, and now here. Given this choice, however, I'd rather die for something right than live for something wrong."

With the breath of that noble comment left to linger in the air, he disappeared through the flap of the tent.

4

The abandoned barn on Fleece Downe Road hulked against the midnight sky like a crippled beast. The structure leaned at a precarious angle, its torn and dilapidated walls appearing too injured to support their own weight. Wide louvered gates dangled on broken hinges and squealed miserably in the spring winds. It was a rotted and musty place now, the only evidence of a useful past found in the streaks of dull red paint still clinging to a few panels of wood and the rusted farm tools that lay discarded in the shadows of its sagging walls.

Vanessa paced the grassless barnyard, old chicken feed crunching underfoot. She plucked at the lint in the pockets of a cloak that felt too warm for the season.

Or was it just her nerves?

Every time she looked at the barn, that unholy hovel where she had lost what was left of her innocence, she flushed with shame. Just to remember what she'd done in there, mindlessly, recklessly, with a passion more fierce than any she'd ever felt before, made her want to fall to the ground in repentance.

The distant rhythm of hooves sounded through the stillness of the night. They were coming. She listened to their thumping progress through the woods, her stomach knotting the instant a pair of soldiers materialized on the far side of the green.

Dragoon sentries they were, sitting tall upon mounts decorated with the accoutrements of war. Carbine buckets, saddlebags and holsters, heavy metal stirrups meant to support a man while he fought for his life. Unlike the ragtag appearance of most American regiments, these men sported clean uniforms, blue coats with red lapels that matched their underlying red wool jerkins. Their leather accessories were highly polished: black breast straps, thigh high riding boots, the handsome brass-chaped scabbards that hung from their hips.

The first rider to reach her reined his beast hard enough to make it whinny in annoyance. A deadly carbine leveled at her solitary figure.

"Lavender?"

Vanessa nodded.

"Open your cloak and turn around."

She obeyed instantly even though she was somewhat awed by these stringent security measures. While her back was turned, she heard the men murmur something among themselves, laugh, then ride to opposite corners of the barn where they sat and waited. One of them issued the call of a crow that brought a second pair of riders out of the woods.

One rider came forward, but she noticed the other one stop, abruptly yank on his reins hard enough to make his mount partially rear. She couldn't see the face of this stalled rider in the dim light, but she noticed the silhouetted angle of his tri-cornered hat. He was definitely watching her.

The other rider loped into the barnyard. "What is this?" he asked, dismounting and walking up to her. "A woman?"

This man was tall and narrow of build. He had a long thin face, wiry blond hair, dull blue eyes that seemed miles away from his mouth, connected only by the sharp and narrow streak of his nose.

"You must be Captain Stone," Lavender said and extended her hand. She hoped her palm wasn't too sweaty. He whipped off his hat and kissed her fingertips. His lips were cold. "I'm honored to make your acquaintance, sir."

"Please drop the formalities, my lady," Captain Stone said and hurriedly stood up to have another look at her. "My name is Francis." His keen blue eyes rushed over every elegant curve of the face that peered up at him from within the soft hood of her cloak. "Forgive me for staring, but I was hardly expecting a woman tonight—"

"There are many women in Millbridge who are deeply committed to our cause," she said in a clear and steady voice.

"I'm sure there are," Francis quickly agreed while glancing over his shoulder at the man who was still sitting motionless in the middle of the green. Francis looked momentarily puzzled.

"Will you be needing my services?" Vanessa asked, wanting to get down to business and not stand here being perused by men, even if they were the Philadelphia Light Horse.

"Well . . . er . . . " Francis' attention came back to her. "I arranged this meeting for the Lieutenant Colonel, not for myself."

"St. Claire?" Vanessa asked and could hardly suppress the sudden jitter that ran through her. This was most unexpected. "But Joshua said you were the one who wanted to talk to me about Swanson."

"For obvious reasons, Gabriel's meetings are never disclosed in advance."

"Of course," Vanessa agreed, secretly designing a plan

to bash Joshua's head over this. She was hardly presentable and wished she'd taken the time to fashion a more glamorous coif than the plain braids coiled around the back of her head. Before meeting such a venerable man as Gabriel St. Claire, a person should have time to prepare.

Francis was looking over his shoulder again. "Yes, well . . . I'll be just a moment to fetch him." He stuck his hands in his pockets, tried to appear nonchalant as he sauntered up to the man on horseback. "What the devil are you doing up there?"

"Arriving at a most startling conclusion," the rider said in a resonant voice that carried an unmistakable French accent.

St. Claire. It was him.

Vanessa immediately corrected her posture and tried to impress him with her professionalism even though he was still too far away to be seen.

"What conclusion? What are you talking about?"

"It's private," the Lieutenant Colonel evaded, finally looking away from her long enough to catch the attention of his sentries. With a brisk jerk of his head in the direction of the woods, he dismissed them.

One rider instantly obeyed. The other one paused.

"You too, Benny."

"Aw Gabe . . . I ain't leaving you here uncovered."

"The woman is harmless. We've met before."

What? Surely she didn't hear him correctly. She had never laid eyes on Gabriel St. Claire. Whatever was he talking about?

"Go on back to camp, Francis. I'll explain this later."

Francis was still confused when he returned for his mount, bid her a pleasant adieu and gave the sentry named Benny a sharp glance. "You better do what he wants."

"Aw! Francis . . . this don't feel right to me—"

"Benny!" The Lieutenant Colonel's voice didn't sound

so elegant this time. Benny instantly spurred his mount and thundered away with Francis trailing behind.

Only when they were out of sight did he swing a leg over the saddle horn and jump to the ground. He moved toward her, a stealthy and athletic grace in his movements that she found oddly familiar. But then he was swaggering into the faint light of the barnyard and Vanessa saw who he was. At first, her mind refused to accept it. Not until he removed his tri-cornered hat and bent into a most chivalrous bow did she clearly recognize the auburn-haired Lieutenant Graves.

All the blood rushed down to her feet. Without being aware of it, she backed into the barn wall and slumped so weakly against that scant support that she thought the whole building would collapse.

"Oh no . . . " was all she could utter, watching the man resume his lofty height until his massive frame completely blotted out the surroundings. She was alone with those mysterious blue eyes that seemed to pierce her very soul, seeing every scintillating memory of their indiscretion. Something so private and sensual passed between them just then that it made her want to shrink in shame. Even the Lieutenant Colonel seemed momentarily dumbstruck as he shifted in his boots and awkwardly cleared his throat.

"Very good, Vanessa," he finally murmured in that unforgettable masculine voice that sounded even more intriguing because of his elegant accent. "I would never have known."

"But I . . . you were . . . this is—"

"Quite a surprise, isn't it?" Gabriel finished for her. He couldn't take his eyes off the sight of her, how those magnificent lavender eyes reflected the pale moonlight like a pair of giant mirrors. She shifted in her slippers, leaned one way then the other, as if trying to decide whether to run, hide or dig a hole and bury herself. "Lavender . . . what an appropriate code name."

"Dear God," she murmured, feeling humiliated beyond expression. To think of what she had done with this honorable man was enough to make her blush so deeply she was sure her flesh would melt from the bone. "But I didn't know who you were!"

"You weren't supposed to. After all, I was spying on Smith the same way you were."

"But you sounded . . . acted . . . so . . . so convincing!"

Exactly what was she referring to, his prowess as a spy or as a man?

"You were quite convincing yourself," he said huskily, obviously making his own choices about what to compliment.

Her cheeks flamed at just the idea of what he might be recalling right now, anything from that silly dance on the lawn to the baring of their bodies in the hay of the very barn she was leaning against. To save what was left of her pride, she moved away from the barn wall and promptly presented him with her back. It was easier if she didn't have to look at him.

"I don't blame you for being angry," he said more soberly now. "When I first realized who you were, I felt the same way."

"I can't imagine how sore your opinion of me must be—"

"Quite the contrary. Although I'm a bit embarrassed to have been so outwitted by a woman spy—"

"Outwitted?"

"My dear woman, I never allow myself to be distracted from a mission . . . at least not until you seduced the wits from me—"

"But I never did anything like that before!" she cried and covered her face with a hand that shook so violently she nearly poked herself in the eye.

"You're obviously distraught . . . otherwise you would realize how unnecessary it is to make that particular point with me."

Even though they were not facing each other, they certainly shared the same thought just then. That first startling moment of penetration.

Now she really felt like a fool, an inexperienced virgin fool.

"I will not be mocked by you, Sir!" she snapped, hefted her shoulders and stomped off with a great show of injured dignity to which she had not claim whatsoever.

He caught up with her at the corner of the barn, his gloved hand easily grasping her arm to check her flight.

"I was merely stating a fact. Forgive me, but I neglected to mention that in civilian life, I'm a lawyer, which makes me overconcerned with facts."

"Is that so?" she fumed, flinging off his hand with dramatic fury and facing him with a venomous courage. "Well that does not give you the right to assail my virtues, Lieutenant Colonel! Put *that* in your collection of facts!"

She stormed off, only to be caught again, gently but firmly stopped in her tracks. "Let's not forget who ran off and gave me no chance to render your virtues proper justice, *Miss* Davis!"

"I don't want your justice!" she snapped.

"Well, I do want justice for you, *mademoiselle,*" he said from so close behind her she could feel his breath breezing through her hair. The scent of him, nearness of him, made her body respond in ways that only incited more of her misguided anger. "And I'll have it," he stated flatly. "But I have something else to talk to you about . . . something that concerns our country and our mutual politics. In the interest of our Cause, won't you at least hear me out?"

She could feel him staring at the back of her head, waiting for her nod of compliance. It came, but not without a very dramatic sigh. He released his grip, urged her to sit on the ground, next to the sneezeweed, and allowed her a moment to compose herself. She didn't look at him, just drew up her knees, hugged them tight and stared into the woods.

"My company was sent here to intercept information concerning the invasion of Philadelphia. As you and I discovered on Saturday night, Colonel Swanson will be the key in this affair."

Out of the corner of her eye, she watched him fold his hands behind his back and quietly pace the green. She could almost read his thoughts as he sank into deep concentration. The intensity of his pose gradually affected her until it was impossible not to respect this master spy when he was at work. The St. Claire enigma was a powerful one.

"A study of the man has revealed his weaknesses. One of them is in regard to women. Without telling you too many details, I believe my strategy against him can work with the right woman playing a convincing role. You've proven yourself to be a faultless actress. Tory hunter or not, you have the talent to serve me well."

He stopped talking and Vanessa knew he wanted some kind of answer. "What would I have to do?"

"Arrange an invitation for us to Swanson's dinner party next Saturday night. This shouldn't be too difficult because of your friendship with Malinda Borden."

"I see no problem with that. What role have you in mind for me?"

"The same . . . a Tory prostitute. You must seduce Swanson as effectively as you seduced me."

"I did not seduce you anymore than you seduced me!"

"Allow me to take that as a compliment, my lady," he said with a smug arrogance that effectively relit the flame of her anger.

"I am *not* your lady!"

"No, but you will be."

"I beg your pardon?"

"Don't change the subject . . . we'll discuss our personal business in a moment. Now then, you and I shall arrive at the Bordens together. We have a perfect cover. The guests saw us leave together last Saturday night and when we never returned, I'm sure we were gossiped about. Don't look so mortified, Vanessa. Nothing could be more perfect than to convince Swanson that you and I are passionately in love . . . "

His choice of words unnerved her, though she wasn't quite sure why. "I don't understand—"

"I'll tell you more when I pick you up on Saturday night."

"Why can't you tell me now?"

This drew a sigh from the handsome young Commander. Apparently, his patience was thinning. He took off his hat and slowly wiped his brow with a cloth. "It's much more effective if individual participants in a mission know only the details concerning themselves. Matters can get clumsy otherwise," he said quite intelligently, replacing his hat in such a way that it shaded his deep-set eyes and made the line of his jaw look very fierce and dashing. "Trust me. I've had plenty of practice."

His arrogance made her grit her teeth. "So I've heard," she snapped.

"I was going to try something else, but after I saw you here tonight I'm quite confident this new strategy will be far superior. I could find another woman, I suppose, but I wouldn't have the necessary confidence in her."

"And you have enough confidence in me?"

Again he sighed, put his hands on his hips and struck a cocky pose directly above her. "You're surprisingly naive for a woman who takes such dangerous risks with her chastity. Have you any idea what effect you have on a man?" She didn't say anything, just stared at the top of her knees. "I would speak more plainly, but I've already done enough damage to your virtues. Let my own behavior speak for itself, eh? Not only did you lure me from my work, but you've left me tossing and turning every night since . . . unable to forget you . . . forget what you did to me right here in this barn."

"Don't . . . " Her cheeks instantly flamed and she wanted to rail at him, but couldn't.

He was suddenly squatting before her, his gloved hand holding her chin with the same gentle power that had haunted her ever since that fateful night. He looked at her squarely, directly, so that she could see that he was not mocking her at all. He was perfectly serious. For some unknown reason, she felt compelled to hear him out.

"I'm not trying to embarrass you. In truth, I praise you for possessing every powerful trait of womanhood that men can only dream of. By the end of the night, you'll bring Swanson to his knees! If I can discover his orders, through you, a whole city could be spared!"

She gulped, felt the coldness of her anger melting in the sincerity of his argument. "But I'm just a Tory hunter . . . " she said in a small voice, suddenly aware of the way their eyes were roaming all over each other's faces. "I have no proficiency in your ranks."

"You needn't do anything different," he was saying, his voice dropping into a whisper. "Just do as you always have and leave the rest to me."

One of his eyebrows rose as if in final question. He released her chin but not her gaze and stood up, his long cloak fanning out in the wind, erasing the rest of the world until it was just the two of them, like before, alone in the night.

"Alright," she whispered up at him. "I'll do it."

He smiled and his white teeth seemed to slash across the ruddy tan of his cheeks. A sparkle of victory temporarily brightened his dark eyes.

If only he weren't so damned handsome! She looked away and feigned sincere interest in his boots.

"As for the other affair, I'll not treat you as some whore and forget what we did together. When my assignment in this area is over, we shall be married with all haste."

Vanessa's jaw dropped open. "What?"

"You heard me."

"Are you out of your mind?"

"No, I'm quite sane."

"But you can't marry me!"

"I can marry anyone I want."

"Oh, for heaven's sake!" She got off the ground, dusted off her cloak and completely dismissed such a ludicrous suggestion. "I have no intention of getting married . . . ever."

Gabriel looked at her sharply, finding her remark strange, especially from such a desirable young woman. Other maids her age spoke of nothing but marriage, yet this one seemed to utterly dismiss the idea of it, as if nothing could matter less to her.

For some reason, it made him remember how their misbegotten tryst ended the other night, with his cheek stinging from her blow, his senses stunned by the cold rage that flashed across her face in that single storming moment.

There was something very dark and ugly inside this woman, hidden under what he found to be a warm and sensual beauty, a kind of seething anger that motivated her rejection of him that night the way it was inspiring her comment now. It was directed at him, he knew, but not caused by him. No, it was there before, put there by someone else.

He kept his thoughts to himself. "If you must know, I felt the same way about marriage until our . . . er . . . indiscretion the other night. I always thought I'd be a bachelor forever. Ah well. Such is life, eh? It changes like the wind."

"Good night, Lieutenant Colonel . . . " She started heading for home.

Of course he followed her, being utterly dauntless. "Vanessa, surely you know how obsessive the French are about their personal honor. What I did to you was wrong and can only be set aright through marriage. Besides, we're not the first couple to marry for no better reason than honor's sake. Our reservations can be overcome in time."

Vanessa just laughed, cold again as she quipped, "If you don't want to marry me and I don't want to marry you, what's the point?"

"The point is your honor must be restored . . . as well as mine."

"On the basis of such an intangible principle—"

"My brother was killed because of such an 'intangible principle,'" he interrupted with no small amount of feeling. Vanessa stopped walking, sensing that he had just said something he hadn't meant to. "I have no intention of repeating that mistake. I only need one time to learn a lesson." Whatever possessed him to tell her this personal secret seemed to suddenly vanish. He turned away abruptly and headed for his horse. "You are a fine woman and do not deserve to be left marked for life because of me."

"We were both drunk," she said and watched him mount.

With one foot in the stirrup, he turned and said, "We were more than just drunk and you know it."

She opened her mouth to argue but thought better of it. He was right but she certainly wasn't about to admit it.

Not even to herself.

"I'm unable to reckon with this, Lieutenant Colonel—"

"My name is Gabriel."

"I find it difficult to assume such familiarity with you."

"Do you now?" He walked his mount over to her, leaned down to cup her chin and draw her face up to where he could see her. An amused chuckle escaped his lips. "You are indeed a maid, Miss Davis. We were intimate and I can hardly name a more familiar pose between a man and woman."

She swatted his hand away, her anger rising again. Some foul curse sat on the tip of her tongue, but it was difficult to hurl it while her eyes were straying across the wide spread of his thighs, how rigid and proud he sat atop his mighty steed.

"Marriage is out of the question, *Gabriel.*"

"Ah well," he said with a quiet sigh. "We shall fight our own private war then, won't we? I won't have it any other way. Perhaps you need time to think it over. You can give me your answer next Saturday night. Be ready by eight o'clock. I'll arrange our transportation."

"You'll need directions to my home—" she began but he interrupted with a wave of his hand.

"By the time we meet again, my beautiful compatriot, I'll know everything about you . . . down to the size slippers you wear on your feet. *Au revoir, mademoiselle.*"

With that, he spurred his prancing steed into a quick gallop across the green, leaped the hedges and disappeared into the forest.

5

"Shut the drapes and get out of here, Vanessa."

"I'm nearly done, father . . . just another moment."

Fred Davis rolled onto his side, pressed his face into the cushions and tried to shut out the noise of that damned brush of hers. Scratch. Scratch. Scratch. He clenched his eyes shut. There was too much light in the room. He liked the parlor dark, the drapes drawn, no candles lit, just the shadows and his jug and himself.

She started humming to herself, scrubbing at the blackened hearth bricks and rinsing out her brush in a pail of water.

"If you don't stop that racket, I'm going to box your ears, girlie—"

"But the Lieutenant's coming tonight and you've not let me clean the parlor all week," she said, her voice light and airy, the way it always got when she was trying to placate him. "Why don't you take a nap and rest while I finish?"

"Because I just woke up from a nap. I don't want another nap. I want you to stop scratching that brush around here—"

"I'm almost finished."

He'd had enough. He rolled off the divan and affected a grim expression as he stalked over to her.

As usual, she saw the menace on his face and backed away, her eyes large and round with sudden fear. "Alright, father—"

"Give me that thing."

She obediently handed him the brush.

He snatched it out of her hand, clenched the thing in his fist and gave her a good hard pelt across the mouth. She gasped, her head banging into the bricks, her hand clinging to the place where he'd struck her.

"Next time, you do what I say *when* I say it, girlie. Now get out of here."

She scrambled off the floor and ran away.

The Davis farm had a long, steep driveway that seemed to climb straight into the sky. The narrow lane was lined with tall oaks that hadn't been pruned in years, the branches heavy and sagging over the middle of the road like a giant leafy umbrella. The place was sadly neglected, Gabriel determined, as he took notice of the overgrown fields and weedy meadows. If it had once thrived as a farm, it now lay in waste.

Like the family who owned it.

Gabriel had not been prepared to hear the violent and tragic history of Vanessa Davis. Benny Cooke spared no details when he reported his findings, acting characteristically glib when he related Fred Davis' long association with the bottle. The town physician had recently warned Vanessa that her father's mind was deteriorating as rapidly as his health and staying alone with him on the farm was downright dangerous. He was an extremely unstable man.

Gabriel's concern turned serious when he heard about the controversial death of Vanessa's younger brother, Daniel. Only two years ago the boy was found dead in the barn by his sister. The sorry end met by this twelve-year-old boy had caused an uproar in a community that had long wrestled with what to do about Fred Davis' violent drinking habits.

It was no secret in the community. Fred had always been a man of dangerous passions and his youthful marriage to the beautiful Vivien Davis was often cause for gossip. He sometimes fought with her publicly and it was not unusual for Vivien to be seen around town with bruises on her face and neck.

When Vanessa was born eighteen years ago, many hoped Fred would change and, for a few years, he seemed to genuinely soften. But then a son was born, Daniel, and this child was sickly, colicky. The stress of his care wore on Fred, who was soon heard to blame his wife for the boy's poor condition, accusing her of doting on Vanessa to the neglect of Daniel. Fred started drinking again and Vivien began sporting enough bruises to keep her away from town for long periods of time. At this point, no one knew what Fred was doing to the children, only that Vivien was known to send them away, to an aunt in Erie.

Years passed. The frail but cheerful Danny Davis contracted influenza, scarlet fever, and had a bout with the pox. The doctor was a constant visitor to the house, but Fred was careful to hide his poor habits whenever the physician was near.

Danny was eleven when another bout with the flu brought the doctor. But this time, he found more than just an illness and was stunned to see the extensive injuries on the boy's frail body. Not only was the child sick, but Fred had given him a thrashing that his weak body would never quite recover from.

Thereafter, Danny walked with a limp, seemed crooked of back and, even worse, began to have convulsions. It was one of those convulsions that caught him alone in the barn and caused him to swallow his tongue. The boy suffocated to death by the time his sister came to call him for dinner.

Vanessa should have been the one who became unhinged, but it was Mrs. Davis who finally succumbed to her years of torment. She became hysterical, uncontrollable. The woman never regained her wits and was taken away soon after. No one had seen her or heard from her since.

Vanessa changed rapidly, becoming distant and quiet. She kept few friendships in Millbridge and no one knew how she managed to live there with no protection from Fred. Her own personal history with her violent father was completely unknown. She never discussed it. Instead, she seemed to live on a cold and bitter hate, an emotion that turned to vengeance at the onset of the war.

Already scandalized by the community, she allowed her reputation to be further compromised by posing as a Tory whore. As only Gabriel and a few others knew, she was completely aligned with Joshua Stone, the leader of the Millbridge Whigs, and took an active role in routing Loyalists. No one had more reason to embrace the cause for personal liberty than the brokenhearted daughter of Fred Davis.

Gabriel walked across the porch, noticed the house was in far better condition than the property. The floorboards were swept, the two windows flanking the door clean and clear. The setting sun reflected itself in the panes, a vibrant golden light that contrasted with the kelly-green shutters and snowy-white paint of the house.

He knocked on the door.

* * *

Vanessa heard the knock and frantically applied one last dab of powder to the bruise on the side of her face. He was here. She had to stop crying, get a grip on herself. This was not the way to approach such a critical evening, so nervous and shaken, her head smarting and her cheek aching.

Vanessa cringed, clenched her eyes against a rush of humiliation just to remember that violent episode in the parlor. It wasn't the physical pain that mattered now, it was the spiritual disgrace. Nothing was more degrading than to be struck like that, when she was so unprepared and defenseless, able to do nothing but whimper for mercy and scramble away like an errant dog yelping against a cruel master's lash. Powder could cover the cut on her mouth, a compress could soothe the lump on her skull, but nothing could heal the pain in her spirit, the place where her personal dignity was ripped away.

Gabriel.

"Think of it! With your help, a whole city could be spared!"

His voice rumbled through her memory, its rich deep tones as soft as distant thunder, warning her of a new menace, one she had never encountered before.

The tears stopped as a much different kind of disturbance trembled through her. It was powerfully pleasurable in those secret hidden places of hers that hadn't existed before he came into her life. Gabriel. What kind of man was he who could so effortlessly unsettle her in the exact place where her hatred of men kept her safe and secure. Yes, he put a nick in the wall of her rock-hard convictions with his noble and genuine ways. How bold and proud and elegant he was, even in his most intimate moments.

She shivered, picked up her puff and started dabbing

at the cut again. Any moment now those dark eyes of his would be focused entirely upon her, and he would see what no one was supposed to know. Oh, but how he could discover her secrets with those big worshipping hands that made her burn with a strange new fire when he unleashed his magnificent male passions! She'd known only pain at the hands of a man until this one who made her feel so completely and utterly adored, as if she was the most beautiful creature on earth. And in those scant few moments in his arms, Vanessa was beautiful again, unscarred by violence, unknown to pain.

Just the thought of who he was, the notorious St. Claire himself, and to have known him in such a private way, as a man and a lover, made her body warm with a queer and contrary excitement. It was a kind of terrifying thrill, a flush of embarrassment mixed with the heat of an irresistible arousal.

These thoughts were unnerving but enchanting enough to momentarily dispel her pain. She stared at the face in the vanity mirror, looked for some trace of what had made her feel so different ever since the day that man walked into her life.

Nothing looked different. It was the same face, one that reminded her of another woman with the same violet-eyed features.

Her mother.

Vanessa felt a sudden pang of yearning for her, for the maternal guidance a girl would need now as she changed from maid to woman. It would be so comforting to be held in those arms now, so close and secure, to be told how pretty she was even after an ugly beating, how one day their lives would be better.

Mother always blamed herself for being too weak to protect her children from Fred, but Vanessa never faulted her mother. In her own gentle way, the woman had provided them with a safety net, a soft place to fall and weep.

Vanessa glanced at the back of the bedroom door, took a deep breath, knowing she'd have to face that angry bear in the parlor once again. Without her mother and Danny, she felt so alone and afraid, like a person caught in a house of horrors with no way out.

Gabriel's knock wasn't immediately answered. He knocked again and heard a shuffling sound from inside, like someone wearing loose shoes and scuffling across wooden floorboards.

The door opened, the threshold filled with the tall rumpled figure of a man wearing a red flannel shirt and loose blue britches. He had thick white hair, unkempt and wild, his dingy skin mottled with patches of pink and yellow.

Fred Davis. "What do you want?" the man growled, blinking as if he had to focus his eyes before he could see Gabriel.

"I'm Lieutenant Graves. I'm calling for your daughter."

"She's busy primping herself. You'll have to wait."

The door slammed in his face.

Outrage bloomed through his insides. He grit his teeth against it, grabbed the doorknob and twisted it open.

He let himself inside. The room was dark, not a single lamp lit.

"I said wait on the porch, man!" Davis snarled from where he was reseating himself on the divan, next to a clay jug of spirits.

Gabriel ignored him, slammed the door shut and arrogantly searched out the tinderbox beside a small stone hearth. He lit a candle, lifted it off the mantle and held it aloft where it could effectively destroy Fred's cover of darkness.

It was a tidy parlor despite its unseemly occupant, clean and simply furnished. A large oval rug covered the center of the floor, braided in colorful yarns. There was fresh linen on every table, the shelf over the corner hearth was neatly dressed with china figurines and a black enamel music box. A brass spittoon sat near Fred on the blue brocade divan, the metal highly polished.

Gabriel settled himself on a cane rocker, put the candle on the table next to him and propped his feet on an ottoman. He looked directly at Fred.

The man's face grew very red and bloated, until his eyes seemed to disappear into the flesh under his downy white brows. He seemed on the verge of exploding and Gabriel hoped for an eruption, an excuse to relieve himself of the barely suppressed ire he felt since hearing of the horror this man had caused in the life of his kin. No one deserved a beating more than this man, this liquored monster who felt he had the right to batter women and children.

"Father, please let the Lieutenant in and be neighborly!" Vanessa called from somewhere in the back of the house.

"Little tramp!" Fred cursed under his breath and continued to glare at Gabriel. "What are you staring at, soldier?"

"Am I staring?" Gabriel asked, his tone of voice deep and menacing. "How rude of me." He clucked his tongue at himself and watched Fred's face turn a deeper shade of red. It was a deliberate taunt, one that provoked a higher and more dangerous level of tension in the room.

"I side with the British in this war, which is the only reason why I'm letting you sit here, soldier."

"How fortunate for me."

Fred knew the man was deliberately mocking him. All the while, his eyes continued to dissect Gabriel from across the room. Quickly, he sucked down a mouthful of whiskey and enjoyed the heightened feeling of anger that sped through his body. It made him feel very alive. Under normal conditions, he would unleash his wrath upon anyone as arrogant as this young soldier, but something warned him away.

Fred didn't like the looks of this man, the mean glint in his dark eyes that watched him with an animal-like alertness. He was big, formidable, his movements smooth and confident. Fred watched him casually cross his legs, then reach into his breast pocket to withdraw an expensive gold case that housed a collection of carefully rolled tapers. He took one and placed it in the corner of his slightly grinning mouth.

"Vanessa! Hurry up!" Fred boomed.

Gabriel heard her footsteps beyond the parlor door. He came to his feet, watched her glide into the room like a fairy princess flitting through the halls of hell.

She was clothed in voluminous folds of lavender silk, the fabric dancing around her long legs like swirling water. Her narrow waist was sheathed in a broad pink-satin ribbon matched to the lining of a snug-fitting bodice with a daring neckline. Her full round breasts swelled above it like frothing snow, pure and white and soft. Her glossy black hair was arranged in a fashionable assemblage of curls that hung halfway down her back and spilled lazily over one bared shoulder. It was artfully woven with thin strips of lavender and pink ribbon.

He found her to be strikingly beautiful, so tall and aristocratic yet so softly sensuous, more than enough woman to make a man's blood warm just looking at her. Whatever reservations he had about using Vanessa Davis in this mission vanished without a trace. By evening's end, she'd have Swanson groveling at her feet.

She saw his approval, the barest smile whispering across her plush pink mouth when he took her hand. He bowed low, awarded a warm kiss to the tips of her delicate fingers as if it might somehow heal the broken places hidden inside this ravishing young beauty.

"I'll be the envy of every man tonight," he declared,

standing upright and looking into those pale lilac eyes that were so thickly framed by long black lashes. What a brilliant contrast, he thought, darkness and light, just like her life.

"Are you always this free with your compliments, Lieutenant?" she was asking, handing him a white lace shawl that he immediately draped over her shoulders. Obviously, she had no desire to linger here with her father.

Fred watched the soldier escort his daughter outside, then stop in the doorway. He leaned back to grab the knob with his gloved hand, looked at Fred and smiled. It was an evil grin, like an ugly mask on his handsome face.

"I'll see you again, Davis," the Lieutenant said in that growling voice of his.

Fred didn't doubt it. He took a long swig from his jug and listened to the man's determined footsteps as he led Vanessa to the coach on the drive. The soldier would definitely be back, Fred knew, and next time he might not control what Fred sensed about him the moment he walked into the house.

The Lieutenant wanted to kill him.

Gabriel was unusually quiet as he settled her into the coach and took a seat beside her. Vanessa glanced at him several times as they rode down the drive and maneuvered through the stone gates, then turned onto the main road into town. He had his hat back on, the brim pulled low enough to hide his eyes. All she could see of him was the stiff set of his jaw. Perhaps he was contemplating the night's business, she told herself, deciding not to bother him although her jittery nerves could hardly stand the silence.

If he were any other man she would demand the details of this mission instead of sitting here straightening the seams of her gloves and pretending interest in the scenery. But this was no common military man, she reminded herself and continued to leave him alone with his thoughts. Gabriel St. Claire was too proven a master in espionage, a fearless field Commander, an expert in Light Horse reconnaissance and combat maneuvers. Surely this was why she respected his silence now, not because he was the only man she had ever submitted to.

Orchard Road began its descent toward the Poquessing Creek and the curves in the road became sharper and more treacherous. Gabriel slowed the team and cautiously maneuvered the winding hillside. Fifty feet below, she could see the sparkling current of the creek, the water glimmering beneath a soft green blanket of woods. The air smelled like spring, the rich fragrance of pine sap and honeysuckle blending into a sweet, delicate aroma. She took a deep breath of air, let it remind her of the way she used to scale these cliffs as a child, barefoot and nimble and too young to be afraid of anything.

Except her father.

The glaring light of the setting sun suddenly disappeared behind a thick outcropping of rock. Gabriel slowed the team into the bend, then brought them to a halt. He glanced around once as if to be sure this section of Orchard Road was deserted. For the first time since they had left the house, he looked at her.

She was instantly startled by the intensity of his gaze. It was piercing enough to explain his silent mood.

Gabriel was angry. Very angry.

She froze, stared at him warily but when his voice emerged, it wasn't angry at all. It was soft, as light and calm as the breeze.

"Your role in this mission is very simple, Vanessa. You're to encourage the flattery of Colonel Swanson . . . permit him to preoccupy your evening, presumably at my expense. Be conspicuous about it. I want the guests to notice what's happening. They should expect me to challenge Swanson for your favor."

"You intend to duel with him?" Vanessa wondered if a Colonel would accept a challenge from a subordinate. "What if he doesn't comply?"

"He will. Swanson has a fetish for sporting his honor on the dueling grounds. He enjoys flirting with women at these social events in order to draw out the valor of their escorts. They duel for her favor in traditional British fashion . . . a fight to the death with no spectators."

"What?" Her attention was caught. "What if he kills you?"

The barest grin fluttered across his lips. "I'm encouraged by your concern for me."

"Really!" she sighed in exasperation. *Men! Maybe this one wasn't so different after all.*

He chuckled at her dry expression. "You can spare my life tonight by giving Swanson no chance to challenge me first. English tradition dictates that the man who strikes the gauntlet must choose the weapon of the duel. This choice must be mine. If I can keep a gun out of his hand, he'll be dead by first light."

Death. The reality of what she was doing came over her with a splash of real danger. It sprinkled up her spine like a spray of cold water. This was no innocent Tory-hunt. She wanted to shiver but didn't, looked down at the back of her hands and feigned great attention to a crooked glove seam.

"I assume you'll force him to talk about his orders on the dueling grounds." She tried to sound more intelligent than afraid.

"Correct. He just arrived last night and has yet to address his men with their orders. He plans to do so on Monday."

Vanessa nodded, satisfied that she knew enough about the mission to perform her assigned role. "I think I can hold his attention. How should I signal you when the moment to challenge is at hand?"

"There's no need for a signal," he reassured. "Just perform your own role in this mission and let me do the rest. I'll know when to move. Remember, this is no different from what you've been doing for Stone . . . just a bit more deadly."

She grimaced. "I'll do my best," she murmured.

"Very good. Now then, would you kindly look up here at me?"

"What?" Startled, she looked up, surprised to find her chin suddenly trapped in a set of gloved fingers. An effort to pull away was stifled by the unexpected return of that icy stare of his, only now it was focused squarely on her face.

The bruise. He saw it. Panic fluttered through her belly along with a sinking sensation of shame.

Gabriel saw her embarrassed dread and felt his anger return in a sudden hot flush. She'd covered the injury well, he noticed, only faint traces of tiny pink scratches were visible through the powder. He could tell by the nature of the wound that it was caused by something coarse, probably wooden. There was no doubt in his mind who had inflicted it.

For a moment, he was so utterly outraged he couldn't speak, just sat there gritting his teeth and trying to control the kind of male distemper this woman would only recoil from. Having heard her tragic history was bad enough, but to see ripe evidence of abuse on her face added a fierce bite to his anger. It was sharp enough to make him momentarily consider returning to the Davis farm after this mission was done for the sole purpose of killing Fred Davis.

It had been a long time since Gabriel felt this kind of reckless rage, this driving compulsion to mete out punishment. Not since Michael was killed.

He let go of her chin, looked away so as not to frighten her with his fury and whispered through clenched teeth,

"For such a long-legged woman, you wear a very small slipper."

It took a moment for her to comprehend the meaning behind his words. When she did, Vanessa immediately covered the spot with her hand and recoiled against this unexpected probe into her sordid private life. He knew the worst, this honorable man, and her cheeks flamed in unbearable shame.

"You're a man of your word." She had to struggle to keep her composure. With her eyes riveted to a crack in the wall of rock beside the coach, she asked, "What else did you find out about me?"

Gabriel couldn't stand to see the way her lustrous raven curls quivered in her attempts to save her pride. It made him ease the rottenness in his own mood just for her sake. "I know it all," he sighed dismally.

She didn't say anything for a long moment, just sat there staring at the rocks. Finally, in a small, bitter voice she said, "I can just imagine what an ugly picture the ladies of Millbridge painted about our family."

"No . . . only about your father." he corrected gently. "And when I see ripe evidence of his abuse on your face, I'm inclined to believe what I've heard."

"Such as?"

"He beat your mother . . . probably you as well. But even worse, this town believes he killed your brother, Danny."

"That's not true!" she cried, whirling around on the seat as if he'd just scraped a raw nerve. Her eyes were filled with a wild denial when she declared, "He didn't kill him."

"Then who did?" Gabriel asked, sincerely wanting to know.

"We don't know."

She was kidding herself. "Oh for God's sake," he snapped, clenching his teeth against a throat full of rising rage, "the physician said your brother died from convulsions caused by injuries to his spine . . . injuries wrought by the hand of your father."

She whipped around on the seat, once again glaring at the rocks. "I don't want to discuss this any more," she said tersely. Rage was a natural reaction, her only weapon to warn people away from the raw wounds in her soul. Besides, it was powerful enough to swallow the shame. "It's none of your business."

"The hell it isn't," he growled. "We've private matters between us that make this very much my business. For God's sake, the man killed your brother! Aren't you afraid he'll do the same to you one day?"

"I said . . . Father did *not* kill Danny."

"Then who did? Who could beat the tender spine of a child so badly it renders him bent and convulsive and lame? A goddamn monster is who! Your father! *He* caused those injuries. You can't deny it!"

"*Stop it!* I won't listen to any more!" she cried out while the painful memories ran through her brain. Images of a little boy lying on the floor of the barn, his fists full of hay, his skin a deadly blue. Oh Danny! Dear sweet Danny! Always so ready to laugh, so cheerful despite a life of sickness and pain. He was an angel, too good for this world, a black-haired cherub who deserved so much better than he ever got from life. And so he died, all alone, with nothing but the hay to cling to when death came to snatch him away.

She covered her face with her hands, the mere memory of Danny's pain making the strength rush out of her like a breeze through a crack in a wall. "Just leave me alone . . . " she moaned, cringing against the first sob to spill out of her throat.

"Damnit!" Gabriel cursed himself as she burst into tears. He rooted through every pocket in his jacket until he found a clean cloth. He offered it, tried to sound soothing as he said, "I didn't mean to do this . . . I was just trying to understand why you refuse my offer of marriage when it could very well save your life."

She couldn't answer, was crying too hard to speak now. He hated himself for doing this, upsetting her so badly, pressing this delicate subject much too far for such a tender heart to endure. For that matter, how could a man so experienced with women possibly be so inept with this one? Where this raven-haired beauty was concerned, he couldn't seem to do anything right. First, he let her seduce the wits from him, and now, instead of charming her with a sympathetic marriage proposal, he had managed to make her weep in misery.

Vanessa could not remember the last time she had let herself cry like this for Danny or why the bottled agony in her soul chose this moment to erupt. But it did, sweeping out of her like torrents of rain, deep black waves of anguish that left her feeling totally broken and shattered inside. She didn't even try to resist Gabriel's arms when they came around her. It was useless, she was too weak to do anything but hang limp against his rock-hard chest and cry until his blouse was damp from her tears.

"No wonder you're so damned angry inside. Your rage is probably what kept you alive all these years . . . like a shield around what's left of your heart."

She started listening to what he was saying, his words slowly beginning to register. Her sobs diminished, becoming breathless sniffles as she huddled against his chest and felt the soothing vibration of his voice. It was deep and smooth, so very relaxing.

"Tragedy is the greatest killer of youth, isn't it? Just like me . . . always wishing he hadn't jumped in front of me when he did . . . that it was my head that took the ball . . . not his . . . not Michael's . . . "

She didn't know what he was talking about, but it didn't matter because his tragedy somehow distracted her from her own.

"I was about your age when it happened . . . and never so young again . . . " He stopped, sighed, seemed momentarily lost in his own mournful thoughts before his words once again breezed through her hair. "But you've survived, Vanessa, learned how to live with horrors unknown to most. It's incredible how you managed to protect yourself behind this wall of hate. You've won a fine victory . . . outwitted him . . . still beautiful despite the beast who sired you."

She felt his hand touch her hair as if admiring those parts of her that he praised aloud. Bewildered now, she just hung in his arms and listened, unsure if she should move away or stay near him. All the while, she listened to the steady thump of his heart in his chest, soothed by its steady rhythm and the steely strength in the arms that held her.

Silence. It washed over them as soft and light as the spring breeze that swept up the road. For a long moment she lay against him, too drained to move, to do anything but listen to his breathing and the rustling melody of dancing treetops. From a distant field, a red-winged blackbird rifled the quiet with a long bloated song that soared above the crackling rush of life within the surrounding forest.

"I've been careless with you again, haven't I?" Gabriel asked himself more than her.

The spell was broken. She sat up, looked away, dabbed at the salty water on her face.

"I'm sorry I upset you before the mission."

She didn't say anything, just kept her eyes pinned to the woods and took a deep breath of air, all the while aware of the way he was watching her. They weren't strangers any more but neither was completely comfortable with the way they had just breached that distance.

Gabriel picked up the reins, snapped them, set the coach in motion.

Vanessa was enormously relieved.

He didn't say anything, his face steeped in concentration as he tried to make some sense out of this increasingly complicated relationship of theirs, this liaison that never should have happened in the first place.

After a long moment, he muttered, "I can't stop thinking about you."

"What?" She looked up at him, startled at what he had just said.

He stopped the coach again, looked directly into her eyes and said solemnly, "This whole affair disturbs me and I just can't rest until it's been honorably concluded . . . until you agree to marry me."

"But I—"

"No," he interrupted, putting up a gloved hand to silence any further protest. "You don't understand . . . no man on earth is more suited to a bachelor's life than I. Believe me when I say this proposition of mine is not lightly presented."

He stopped, waited for her to say something, but she couldn't think of a single word to utter. His revelation only made his proposal seem all the more preposterous.

"I know how shocking this idea must seem to you."

She nodded mutely.

"I swear on my brother's grave that I'll never pressure you for anything more from this marriage than what you're willing to give. Trust me."

This finally brought a reaction, found her tossing a dry laugh into the wind. "I'll never trust any man."

"I don't blame you but it doesn't quiet my conscience one bit. It's the truth that bothers me . . . how I wronged you . . . took what did not belong to me . . . hurt you the way he's done."

She tried to look away but he wouldn't allow it, ever so gently cupped her cheek in his palm and made her face him again. "The truth is I admire you for what you've been through . . . respect you too much to turn away and just forget it."

He meant it. The man was perfectly serious.

Vanessa just sat there staring at him in a kind of appalled rapture. No one had ever spoken to her like this before. Not Vanessa Davis, the beaten daughter of an alcoholic, a woman people chose to avoid rather than confront. Yet here this valiant young champion sat and praised everything about her that was dark and ugly.

"I . . . er . . . don't know what to say . . . " she stammered in a trembling voice that sounded very undistinguished to her ears. "I have to think about all this . . . "

"*Très bien* . . . that is enough for me . . . to know you'll at least consider it."

He let go of her cheek and went back to driving, not stopping the coach again until they arrived at the Borden residence.

She was still badly shaken when he helped her out of the coach; he could feel the nervous tremble in the hand he took. Just before they reached the stoop he stopped her, using the glow of the porch lanterns to determine her condition.

"Let's put this other affair behind us for now," he said in a thin whisper, then leaned closer and added, "Try to absorb yourself in the identity you wear tonight. It will calm you . . . to be someone else."

There was a strange wisdom in his words, made her wonder if this was why he chose such a shadowy profession, so he could be someone other than who he was. "I'll try," she murmured.

"Good. And remember, it's just a mission, probably your last because I won't allow my wife to run around seducing the enemy. If I think Swanson is really charming you, I'll be very jealous."

"You're out of your mind—"

"Promise."

She looked at him skeptically, "You bedevil the wits from me."

"Promise."

"Oh alright."

He flashed her a victorious smile. It was dashing but irritating at the same time. "That's bloody good of you, little doxy," he teased and finally managed to wring a laugh out of her, even if it was full of scorn. He led her up the path, swung open the door and whispered, "May liberty prevail."

"Amen," she breathed and slid inside.

Nothing could have boosted her shaky confidence more than watching the mastery of Gabriel St. Claire at work. The man seemed to disappear right before her eyes, vanishing into the identity of Paul Graves and becoming a British soldier as casually as a man changed his cloak. By the time they crossed the lobby floor and joined a group of officers in the parlor, he was speaking proper English, discussing war movements pertinent to England, speculating about Howe's spring campaign just like everyone else. In fact, he became Lieutenant Graves with such fluidity it made Vanessa begin to feel like the woman who left the dinner party on his arm a week ago, confident of her seductive powers, ready to use them in the fight for her country's freedom.

Colonel Swanson was much older than she had expected, quietly mannered with tired, woeful brown eyes that lent him the look of an aged buck. His complexion seemed unusually red against the stark white color of his wig, especially his tiny dot of a nose. It was the sign of a drinking man.

Her courage soared. No woman on earth was more familiar with men who over-imbibed. Just to see the drink in his hand brought a cold wind rushing over her heart, freezing it into a tough, hard shell. She suddenly felt enormously capable.

Careful not to be too bold, she allowed him to look into her eyes for just an instant after he kissed her hand. The Colonel's eyebrow raised in surprise at her mild indiscretion. But she put up her fan, smiled behind it, wickedly enjoying this first notice of his and the satisfaction of knowing she'd caught his interest so soon.

"Won't you have just one more drink before dinner?" Gabriel asked for the third time.

"I've had enough," she replied firmly, handing her empty glass to a passing servant.

"Is that so?" her escort inquired, an auburn brow arching in question.

She looked up at him, feigning a flirtatious smile while her eyes remained hard and direct. "It is."

"Are you on a temperate whim for reasons of faith or because you're afraid we might get reckless again?" She didn't answer, gave him a scathing look behind the pleats of her fan and wondered who she was glaring at, St. Claire or Graves. At the moment, she couldn't tell the difference. "Your temper's showing, my beauty," he said and chuckled in amusement. "And you know how inviting I find your fires."

Something dark flashed through his eyes just then, something she'd seen before, a kind of private storm only seen when his passions were aroused. He drew her close enough to make her feel the physique beneath his uniform, catch the manly aroma that exuded from him, and see the spy so well hidden behind the midnight blue of his eyes.

Gabriel. He was there for just a brief flashing moment, an instant that gave her a vivid glimpse of exactly who was inside the uniform tonight. The man who made love to her in the barn, coveted her every inch, desired her like no one ever wanted her before.

Desire. It raced between them just then, quick and bold and very much alive. It made her remember everything that was going on beneath the surface of their contrived personalities, from the lust they shared on a barn floor to her heart-wrenching sobs in his arms only an hour ago. This man had a way of touching her in places no one else could find and she felt suddenly, overwhelmingly threatened by him.

She pulled away from him, her whisper a warning, "Keep your mind on business."

A servant's bell tinkled, announcing dinner.

Once again, she was trapped in his clutches, forced to allow him to escort her to the dinner table.

Thankfully, they weren't seated together and Vanessa was grateful for the broad expanse of table between them. Despite how many times he glanced her way, she refused to look at him, refused to see the personal messages he conveyed beneath the perfect veil of his disguise.

She was completely unnerved by him and more than a little awed as she listened to his involvement in the table conversation. He knew a wealth of military information, could discuss the strengths and weaknesses of British units with amazing fluidity. There was no doubt in her mind that Gabriel spent a good deal of time in enemy units because no one but a true redcoat could know what he knew. He must surely have nerves of steel to indulge in such a dangerous occupation. And all the while, he managed it so brilliantly, so flawlessly. No one at the table tonight had even the slightest reason to doubt him, to even guess who was sitting there among them. The infamous St. Claire himself! And there he sat, as calm as any other soldier on a night's leave, while absorbing every bit of sensitive military information spilled so glibly over a plate of food.

He made her feel very proud of their Cause just then, of the many brave men who took such enormous personal risks to fight for it. Respect welled within her but this was just another emotion to add to the already jumbled mix. She felt like she was reeling in some crazy dance with steps she couldn't quite master, locked in the arms of a partner who aroused both her best and her worst defenses.

Bewildered, she forced her concentration away from St. Claire and planted it firmly on easier prey.

Swanson.

He'd been watching them throughout dinner, his glances discreet but watchful. Just as she'd done two weeks ago with the Lieutenant, she caught one of Swanson's discriminating glances and rewarded him with a vivacious smile.

The Colonel pretended not to notice it, reached for his wine glass and nearly knocked it over.

Gabriel saw the exchange, his private grin reflected in the gleaming dessert service at his fingertips.

Vanessa felt smug, not sure if it was because she was succeeding with Swanson or impressing Gabriel.

They adjourned to the parlor for dancing. While they waited for the minstrels to prepare their instruments, Gabriel led her to the table of confections where she found a tray of the same brightly iced bon-bons served by Martha Borden two weeks ago.

"Do be careful with the sweets tonight," Gabriel said and chuckled at the way she rolled her eyes.

"I wish you hadn't seen—"

"I saw everything about you last week," he murmured, his voice as warm as his suddenly attentive gaze. "But what I enjoyed the most was the way you laughed. You don't laugh very often, do you, Vanessa?"

Why was he doing this, flinging these personal comments at her, making her wonder how much of this exchange was from Gabriel and how much was from the Lieutenant? Confused, she didn't say anything, just shook her head at the plate of confections and selected one. "I was tipsy that night."

His hand once again snuggled her waist in a very possessive manner. "The evening was indeed intoxicating," he said and she could feel the breath of his words sliding down the side of her face like a soft, caressing wind. "And most unforgettable for me. Did you know I once vowed to my friends I'd never marry until I found the woman who could seduce me?"

His choice of words brought back memories that made something warm and pleasant quiver very deep inside her. It brought a flush of color to her cheeks, a reaction she despised in herself. She didn't answer, didn't even look at him, just stood there feeling trapped between wanting to flee and knowing she couldn't. This mission depended upon acting infatuated with him yet it wasn't the night's business he made her contemplate now.

No, it was a far different image of him that bloomed from her memory, his intimate side, what he looked like when stripped of all his clever disguises. She would never forget the splendor of his nakedness, how long and sleek and brown was his body, so full of manhood, so rigid with want inside her seeking hands.

Her body was aroused and she suddenly hated it, the way it betrayed her, made her pulse with heat in secret, private places. She had never felt so vulnerable in her entire life.

He seemed to read her thoughts, catch the intensity of her mood as he led her onto the dance floor and into the first steps of a popular minuet. They couldn't take their eyes off each other, moving across the floor with their gazes locked as firmly as their hands.

Even the melody seemed to work against her. The tune was slow and romantic, the dim light in the room making her feel as if no one could see how they were staring at each other. With every brush of their bodies, their attention became deeper, more intimate.

The noise in the room faded away. Those eyes of midnight beckoned her into his thoughts, made her want to remember every hypnotic moment in his arms. Excitement coursed between them like the unexpected flash of a flint, the power of their attraction seeming to stun him as much as her. Last time she could blame the champagne but tonight, she had no such excuse, no easy escape from what was happening between them.

"I need to be alone with you," he said when the music stopped and she knew it was Gabriel speaking in that moment, not Paul Graves. "Come outside with me."

"I don't want to—"

"The hell you don't."

Arrogant bastard! she wanted to scream, barely able to resist an urge to snatch her hand away, run out of the room, the house, his life.

Instead, they were passing through the verandah doors, stepping into the garden, her breath as fast and hard as his own. She saw where he was heading, behind a tall stand of lilacs, the same bushes he fetched a blossom from last week. But this encounter wouldn't be so innocent.

"Please . . . I don't want this . . . " she whimpered in a last attempt to save herself.

"Oh, for God's sake," he growled, spun around, the look in his eyes raining down on her like a shower of fire. She gasped, pushed against him almost frantically as he snatched her into his arms and lifted her feet clear off the ground. "I want you so much I can't even think," he hissed, cupped his hand around the back of her head and forced her to see his smoldering eyes just before his face blended into hers.

Their mouths met so hungrily it sent a great shock of energy charging through her belly, making her gasp into the crush of his kiss, the burning bruising passion he was suddenly pouring into her. It overwhelmed her, stole away her wits, her will, her need for anything but the enormous pleasure blooming through her veins.

No man ever wanted her like this, so adamantly, so fiercely, with so much of himself. He seemed barely able to control it and this only encouraged her to be as reckless as he, to drive her fisted hands from his blouse and send her fingers plunging into the dark hair hidden beneath his wig. Her touch only emboldened him more, made him clench her tight in his arms, close enough for his fire to rage into her, fast and furious and full of a glorious heat.

She was suddenly clinging to him, pouring her fever into him, kissing him like some starved and thirsty whore. A tiny and desperate sigh escaped her lips as he parted them and ravished her with a longer, deeper drink, one that made her whole body shudder and her mind fill with thoughts of nothing but him, only him.

But then he pulled away, suddenly, abruptly, his face buried in her hair as he cursed, "Damnit, work your wiles on him tonight, not me." Even while he protested, his mouth continued to devour her, nibbling at her neck, under her chin, along the side of her face. "If it wasn't already too late, I would run to the opposite end of the earth to be away from you . . . from what you do to me."

"It's not too late!" she panted, clenching her eyes against the mere sight of his desire. "We'll never see each other again . . . after tonight . . . never again."

Gabriel glanced through the twisted shrubbery and saw the Colonel's silhouette in the verandah doorway. He was standing just inside the drapes, talking to someone while his eyes followed their every movement behind the bushes.

"Our fate is sealed as sure as my mark on your body," he whispered hoarsely and for some reason, in spite of the sensual chaos between them, she noticed that his British accent was still firmly in place.

Suspicions raced through her brain. It was a ploy! If his emotions were truly involved, no man could maintain an alias so well!

Abruptly, she pulled away from him, fixed him with a stony look. "I don't want you," she said, wanting to prick his ego the way he had just pricked hers.

He chuckled, his handsome lips still reddened from the passion of her kiss. "Your body affirms what your lips deny, young maid. About certain things, a woman can't lie to her man."

"You are *not* my man!" she breathed in a cold whisper. "And don't think I'm fooled by this ruse of yours. You're playing with me—"

"Am I?"

"Don't . . . "

She turned away but he checked her flight with one reach of his hand. "Think what you want, believe what you will, but what I took I now claim as my own. You belong to me, Miss Davis, as sure as the sun will rise tomorrow."

How dare he assume so much! She swung around, let every bit of the hatred in her heart flow into his face like a rush of winter wind. "I swear I hate you."

"No you don't. You hate *him,* but instead of punishing the one who deserves your wrath, you make *me* pay the price for his sins!"

"Get out of my life and you won't have to pay any price!"

"Damn you, Vanessa!"

He was genuinely angry, snatching her hand and stalking toward the house. She stumbled after him, trying to straighten her hair and her clothes as if that might help put in order everything that was awry with this night. Beneath the surface of this mission there was a wild and dangerous undercurrent, one she didn't understand enough to fight.

He was in control, not through brute force but because of the disturbing mystery within this multi-faceted and brilliant young spy.

Oh! How did she ever get involved in something like this?

A moment later, they were twirling across the dance floor again, an upraised fan her only device to hide the bright flush on her cheeks. Her heart was hammering in her breast, her nerves drawn as tight as the set of the Lieutenant's jaw.

Gabriel wasn't surprised to feel a tap on his shoulder. He turned around and saw Colonel Swanson.

"May I, Lieutenant?"

"Of course, sir." Gabriel politely moved away.

The game had begun.

Vanessa's spinning emotions came to a screeching halt. She was suddenly very aware of her real role tonight, of how much was at stake, of how many lives rested upon the successful completion of her work.

"The Lieutenant is quite smitten with you," the Colonel said, his round brown eyes soft and gentle with understanding. "Did you have a row with him in the garden, my dear?"

"He's pressing me too much," she sighed, not really knowing why she said this.

Think! she commanded herself.

"Oh?" Miraculously, the Colonel seemed sincerely interested in hearing more. The reaction surprised her, brought her back to her senses. "Surely he's not pressing you for favors unbecoming of a gentleman."

"Oh no!" she said at once. "It's marriage he's after."

"I see," the Colonel said with a fatherly nod of his head. "You must understand what war does to a young soldier . . . makes him face his own mortality. He becomes suddenly hurried about such things as marriage and family . . . afraid to die before he has the chance . . . "

She affected a proper blush, watched the edges of the Colonel's mouth twitch into an affectionate smile.

"But on the other hand, these men don't realize how easily frightened a maid can be at the prospect of marriage."

"Indeed!" she breathed, feigning delight at his understanding. It worked. He looked suddenly pleased with himself. She dove a bit further into the moment. "What a relief to be so well understood! I tried to tell him as much, but he wouldn't listen! He kept telling me about his orders and the campaign and . . . oh! I'm boring you with my personal affairs!"

"Nonsense," the Colonel said quickly, giving her gloved fingers an affectionate little squeeze. "My late wife, Jenny, was a young girl, timid and shy . . . but how beautifully she blossomed with me!" The Colonel's eyes turned sad, distant.

"I'm so sorry," she said gently. "When you first proposed, did she hesitate like I have?"

"Of course!" His attention came back to her. "I was nearly twenty years older than she. This gave her good reason to pause."

The music stopped but their conversation didn't. They shared a glass of punch and continued to discuss her imaginary troubles. "A friend of mine married an older man and she seems quite taken with him," Vanessa contrived. "She claims he's more sure of himself than the younger men who've come calling."

Just for effect, Vanessa cocked her head and pretended to be comparing him to the tall soldier across the room. Gabriel was watching her with a very stoic expression on his face but he made no move to reclaim her.

The Colonel became bolder now that he had struck a genuine chord with her. He leaned toward her, cast a wary eye at the Lieutenant while saying, "When I first saw you tonight, I thought to myself, now there's a woman who could grace a General's arm. You are startlingly beautiful and your carriage is like that of a queen!"

"My goodness!" Vanessa breathed, blushed prettily and fanned herself.

"Have I been too bold?"

"Perhaps," she whispered demurely, then feigned a worried glance in Gabriel's direction. "I should rejoin him . . . he looks upset . . . "

"Nonsense! I'm a Colonel. I outrank him!" Swanson chortled playfully, promptly leading her into another dance.

He'd start flirting more outrageously now, Vanessa knew. They always did when they thought they'd won her.

Around the floor they sped, talking easily, laughing gaily, thoroughly enjoying the attention they were receiving from the other guests.

Gabriel was prowling the perimeters of the room now, his expression becoming angry.

This time, when the song ended, he approached Swanson and gave his shoulder a tap. "I would like to reclaim her for the next dance, Colonel," he said a bit too stiffly. Swanson bowed away gracefully.

Gabriel maintained the angry look on his face as he leaned down and whispered in her ear, "You're doing very well. I'm sure the man's blood is roaring in his veins . . . perhaps not as fast as mine."

"I wish you wouldn't add these personal comments of yours to everything you say tonight," she said in a withering tone. "You're making me nervous."

He nodded his head and for a moment, Vanessa believed she had finally put him at bay. Until the music began to fade and he was once again drawing her close, whispering in that deep, husky voice of his, "If I win the duel, will you be mine?"

She was about to hurl a nasty remark at him when she noticed Swanson approaching. For the benefit of both men, she said aloud, "You're much too persistent, Lieutenant."

Gabriel stopped chuckling when the Colonel tapped his shoulder. There was genuine irritation on his face when Swanson requested another dance with her.

Gabriel refused.

Vanessa held her breath.

"I shall have the next dance, soldier, and that's an order," Swanson insisted.

"We're off duty, sir," Gabriel countered.

"The hell we are," the Colonel said with a slightly drunken laugh, sweeping an arm around Vanessa's waist and spinning her out of the Lieutenant's reach. She watched Gabriel march off the dance floor to join a group of soldiers, where he let his bitter complaints be heard. They all turned around to watch Vanessa and the Colonel. Other guests began to notice. Gabriel made a move to come forward and Vanessa's heart leaped in her breast. She was almost relieved when a soldier grabbed his arm and attempted to calm him. When the next song began and Swanson made no attempt to return her, Gabriel finally made his move.

Her pulse quickened, a sense of danger falling over her like a sudden chill. Gabriel was coming across the floor. There would be a scene. She held her breath, mentally rehearsed those words of his from earlier tonight, *"Don't let him challenge me first. If I can keep a gun out of his hands . . . he'll be dead by first light . . . "*

She mustn't let Swanson see him. She tossed some witty comment at the Colonel, made him laugh and pause in his dance step just long enough to make their next turn veer directly into Gabriel's path.

They swung around, collided with the steely expanse of Lieutenant Paul Graves.

They jolted to a halt.

Every couple on the dance floor stopped moving.

All eyes were pinned to the two men.

Vanessa stepped away, put a hand to her lips and looked around as if in search of someone's aid.

Malinda Borden rushed through the crowd, grabbed her arm and held it while she watched Gabriel launch into his deadly game with the mastery that made him famous.

"You are deliberately preoccupying her evening, Colonel. I brought her here. She belongs to me."

"Is that so? Then why are we having such a delightful time together?"

Several gasps sounded from the crowd. Every face was filled with excited anticipation as they secretly enjoyed this shocking spectacle.

"Vanessa, you will cease dancing with him at once," Gabriel said in that commanding voice of his.

"But Paul—"

"Very well!" Gabriel snapped, withdrew a gauntlet from his belt and snapped it against the Colonel's cheek. Vanessa shrank in relief, never imagining that she could be so glad to see a gauntlet tossed. "I challenge you to a duel for the lady's favor, Colonel Swanson."

The older man's eyes lit like a child's when gazing upon a tempting dessert. "Your challenge is accepted, young man." Everyone applauded as Swanson bent and nobly picked up the gauntlet. "Choose your weapon."

Victory. It sparkled from the dark recesses of Gabriel's eyes. She barely saw it before the look of triumph vanished, devoured by another emotion when he looked at Swanson.

Malice.

Pure and so ruthless she was certain no expression on a man's face could convey such a deadly message as Gabriel's did the moment his lips formed that single, fateful word.

"Rapier."

The shine went out of Swanson's eyes. He looked genuinely startled. "Rapier?"

"Yes, on the green at the abandoned barn on Fleece Downe Road. I will await you at dawn with my second. Come along, Vanessa."

He made a great show of escorting her from the room, possessively wrapping her shoulders in a shawl and hurrying her outside.

They were halfway down the steps before she summoned the nerve to look at him, then found herself astonished to watch his rugged cheeks split with the broadest grin she'd ever seen from this elegant man.

It occurred to her, then, exactly what had happened tonight, every aspect of the evening jelling into perfect logic.

Gabriel had orchestrated everything. He had arranged it all, from their heady embrace in the garden to the flustered state she was in when first delivered into Swanson's hands.

"Nothing could be more important," he once said, "than to convince the guests that we're madly in love."

Yes! He had indeed played upon her feelings to be sure she wouldn't falter in the plan, then let Swanson's fatherly manner lead her from there.

By the time the Borden coachman delivered her into their carriage, Vanessa was positively livid.

"You bastard!" she hissed, the moment they cleared the Borden property. Gabriel looked at her in surprise. "I could slit your throat for the way you played with me tonight!"

"What are you talking about?"

"You know exactly what I mean! You took liberties with me in the garden, *sir!*"

A secretive smile twisted across his mouth just before he turned his attention back to the dark road. "I wouldn't be so sure of that if I were you, *Miss* Davis."

"And why not?"

"Because a good spy never tells his secrets."

She was about to launch another curse at him when the message behind his words struck her.

Who could know if he played her false or not? Even with her, his cover was perfect.

The man was brilliant.

She decided not to say anything for fear she might mistakenly compliment him. Instead, she kept her eyes pinned to the road ahead and wished with all her might that he'd disappear from her life tonight and never come near her again.

6

The two men sat alone in a vacant parlor in their New York headquarters and quietly conversed over a late night service of tea.

"The Archangel is not in New York. He's left . . . gone to another theater of the war."

"I agree. If he was here, he would have found that phony information we sent out."

"Damnit! How the devil can we find him now . . . on a continent this large? He could be anywhere!"

Frustration flashed between them, momentarily silenced them. One man took a gulp of tea, the other sat drawing lines on the butler with the sweat on his fingertip.

"He was here two weeks ago. This much we know. We'll have to track him somehow."

"Yes, like bloody hounds!"

"We'll go underground," he said, ignoring his partner's chagrin, "infiltrate a Continental scouting party. Someone out there must be connected to him. Random surveillance might lead us somewhere, maybe not to the Angel himself, but at least to the new field he works."

"Yes, but the Continentals claim they don't know who he is."

"I'm not sure about that."

"What?"

"Did it ever occur to you that Washington might be lying about the man's anonymity?" His partner didn't say anything, just sat there looking stupefied. "I've always found this entire situation to be somewhat preposterous . . . that Washington could receive such a wealth of military information from a man he doesn't even know! If he doesn't know him, how can he trust him . . . actually base the movements of his army on whatever intelligence the Archangel sends him? No. There's something very wrong here."

"Like what?"

"Like Washington might know more than he's letting on, is what."

"Then why don't we infiltrate his headquarters?"

"Because it's already been done and no evidence was found. What strikes me odd is that the Archangel always seems to be in the center of the action, like he knows where to go. The only way he can do this is if he is somehow connected to one of Washington's regiments."

"A mounted company . . . "

"Of course. If the Archangel follows anyone, it would be the cavalry corps . . . Washington's only reconnaissance personnel. I say we discover which mounted regiment recently left New York and follow them."

An unspoken agreement glanced between them. "Very well. It's a start, isn't it?"

"Humph!" the officer snorted at his empty cup. "As good as any, I suppose. The man's good . . . the best I've seen. Even John Andre respects him and they say Andre's the greatest spy who ever lived."

"Not anymore. His ego's smarting since he came to this continent, eh? Between the Archangel and that Bourbon rogue, St. Claire, he meets his match no matter which way he turns!"

"Ah yes . . . St. Claire . . . the Great Imposter! Guts of iron, that one. Why, I hear he collects uniforms the way other men collect . . . " He stopped, sat upright in his chair and hissed, "Hold on a minute! Didn't St. Claire and his First Squadron just leave New York?"

"About a week past. So?"

"Think, you fool! There's our mounted company!"

They both shot out of their seats at the same time, abandoned their tea, the room, the house. Five minutes later they were on horseback, flying down a country road that wound along the Hudson like a snake in a gully, following its winding path until they found the road they wanted.

The Road to New York. They leaped upon it, headed south.

To Philadelphia.

7

Vanessa couldn't sleep. Hours after snuffing her candle she was still tossing and turning, her mind refusing to rest after such a harrowing evening. When sleep did come, it was brief, merely sprinkling some rest across her bare nerves and titillating her mind with bizarre images of the day's events.

The wooden scrub brush flying into her face. How the parlor spun when she cracked her head against the hearth. Swanson's tender eyes warming with affection over her girlish troubles. Disconnected phrases whispered in her ears, *"The light hurts my eyes . . . "* her father whined. *"War makes a man face his own mortality . . . "* Swanson counseled. *"I want you so much I can't think . . . "* Gabriel groaned.

Gabriel. Gabriel. Her last view of him was burned into her memory, the way he looked while sitting on the coach seat tonight, his tall figure cloaked in the dark, only a thin line of moonlight illuminating the outside edges of his face.

"It would be better if we never saw each other again," she'd said to him just before they parted ways tonight.

"Better? Better than what . . . your living alone in that house with the likes of your father?"

"Good night, Lieutenant Colonel," she'd snapped, inwardly stung by his remark, hoisted her skirts and prepared to get out of the coach.

"I'm determined to change your mind," he had said so casually, so matter-of-factly, it made her pause on the chaise seat.

She looked back at him, where he sat so calm and straight in the dark, the shadows of night draped around him like a well-made cloak. No matter how exasperated she was with his persistence, she'd had a sudden sinking feeling that no amount of resistance would be enough to stop him. He was, after all, a rebel warrior, accustomed to fighting enormous odds, even in the face of constant defeat.

"Good-bye," she'd said and hurried out of the coach, aware that he didn't answer her, that he was watching her every footfall until she disappeared inside.

That was hours ago. It was four o'clock in the morning. She had to get up, get out of this bed, stop thinking about him, the duel, how every wrinkle in the sheets seemed to irritate her.

As if to mock her shattered nerves, her father's loud, nasal snore raked through the halls of the house. He was content to sleep in the alcoholic bliss that destroyed everyone who had ever lived in this house.

She decided to get some air, draped her plain cotton nightdress in a shawl and headed outside. For a long moment, she stood alone in the abandoned barnyard and looked toward the woods in the direction of Fleece Downe Road. Gabriel's soldiers would be there soon.

She started into the fields, her bare feet padding across the damp deadness of the earth, nothing but the moon to light her way. It was a quieting walk, with the land ensconced in the queer serenity of pre-dawn. Not even the crickets chirped and the mosquitoes were lazy in their swarms. She found the path that led through the woods to the old barn on Fleece Downe Road, not knowing or caring why she chose to come here, just that she felt compelled to see the outcome of the duel. There was an old pile of rocks on the timber's edge and she climbed them swiftly, found her favorite notch and snuggled herself there to wait.

It wasn't long before she heard the steady plodding of horses on Fleece Downe Road, saw the blinking orange lights from the lamps of a dozen riders.

It was Gabriel's company. Even from the other side of the green, she recognized their uniforms. They rode in a group until they reached her side of the green, then broke apart, all but a few remaining there while the rest trickled into hiding in the woods.

Vanessa snuggled a bit lower in the rocks where she could sit undetected and watch the antics of this famous company. She spotted Gabriel at once, he and another man dismounting beside the barn. Four other officers rode to a place not thirty feet from her hidden perch. These four seemed to be in high spirits as they hid their mounts in the woods, then settled around the base of an old oak to drink and enjoy the spectacle to come. Thanks to a cooperating wind, she could hear their lively conversation quite well.

Francis Stone sprawled his long legs across the ground and casually lit a taper. He elbowed the man next to him. "Out with your flask, Benny. We could all use a nip."

Benny. She'd seen this soldier before, a giant of a man with thick shocks of black hair and a broad fleshy face that was cupped in the stubble of a poorly shaved beard. He reached a hand under his waistcoat and pulled out a long leather sack. "Here," he said, tossing it at Francis, "but one gil is all you get, beggar!"

"Phewee! Will you look at him go!" The man beside Francis sat up and pushed away the brim of an enormous straw hat as he grinned at the sparring men on the green. "Gabe's getting better every year. I can't wait to see him tear up the Colonel!"

"He's gonna turn that redcoat into one long strip'a ribbon, ain't he, Francis?" Benny looked smug, as if personally responsible for Gabriel's prowess with the rapier. "Did you know he was the best tournament fencer in France?" he asked but no one answered him. Vanessa got the impression they'd all heard this a hundred times before. "No one could beat Gabe!"

Francis finally spoke up. "No one could beat him because he left France before anyone tried, Benny."

"Good thing," another straw-hatted soldier quipped. "If he hadn't left, they would've cut off his head!"

"That's not funny, Stevie," Benny growled. "And why are you shining up your rifle? Gabe says Will gets to pick off the second tonight."

Vanessa suddenly realized who these straw-hatted soldiers were. Will and Steve MacLeod, a pair of sharpshooting brothers who had quite a reputation in Pennsylvania. They were former members of Daniel Morgan's Rifle Corps from the Virginia colony, which explained their lazy accents.

She gave them a long and interested look, found them to be much too young and fair to fight in a man's war with their reputed skill. They were short, slender and sinewy, their narrow faces seeming boyish and pale compared to those of their rugged companions. But their undistinguished looks didn't fool her. These Virginia-bred men were dead shots with a Pennsylvania rifle, a gun rumored to be accurate at one hundred and fifty yards. With this particular weapon in their hands, the MacLeods could outshoot any British issue Brown Bess.

"I know what Gabe said," Steve said resentfully, "but just in case Will misses I'll be ready to shoot."

"Hell! I ain't missed a shot since I joined the army."

Will held up his rifle and smiled proudly at the four gold stars on the barrel, the mark of an expert rifleman.

"Braggart!" Steve grumbled. "My fourth star is on the way, you know. When it gits here, we'll be even up!"

"Ha!" Will gave his brother a playful sneer while filling his mouth with a healthy draught of rum. He swallowed it, shuddered hard, then grinned as he spoke, "Even? You gotta make Captain first. Then we'll be even."

"I might just git a new rank with my fourth star, Will! Ever think of that? Hell, I'm gonna ask Gabe right now." Steve jumped off the ground and hollered across the green, "Hey Gabe! Will I be a captain when that star gits here?"

Gabriel turned, his concentration broken by the unexpected shout. He didn't see the lunge of his partner until the blade was slicing clean through the sleeve of his tunic.

Vanessa gasped, watched Gabriel leap away just in time to spare an injury to his arm.

The four soldiers jerked to their feet, instantly alarmed.

"Look what you did!" Benny spat, grabbing Steve by the collar and giving him a mighty shake.

"Ow!"

"Dumb kid!"

Gabriel slammed his rapier into its sheath, spun on his heels and hurled a fist toward his rambunctious soldiers. He stalked forward, headed straight at them.

"Uh-oh . . . here he comes," Benny whispered nervously, hurriedly hiding his rum flask while glaring at Steve. "He's gonna whoop you good, Stevie!"

"Oh shut up, Benny! I was just clowning around."

"You alright, Gabe?" Francis asked, always the physician.

Gabriel didn't answer, coming to a halt in front of Steve and giving him a long and disapproving stare that instantly cowed the young soldier. Vanessa watched Steve's straw hat bend toward the ground in humble apology. Gabriel sighed at him, his chest heaving under his billowing white blouse.

All the playfulness seemed to drain out of the men under the tree until their poses were suddenly stiff with repentance. It was warming to see their obvious respect for Gabriel, how everyone seemed to fidget and squirm while encased in his momentary wrath, as if anger was not often displayed toward them and they weren't sure how to act when it was.

Gabriel waited until they were sufficiently subdued, then took a kerchief out of his torn sleeve to wipe the sweat off his brow. "What's on your mind, soldier?" He was still out of breath when he spoke.

"Nothing, Gabe," Steve mumbled at the ground.

"He was drinking and you know Stevie can't handle his rum," Benny tattled.

Steve's head snapped up. "You gotta mouth bigger than a rat's tail, Benny!"

"He wants to know if he'll get a Captain's rank along with that fourth star," Will spoke up.

Gabriel looked at the two brothers and sighed. "Shall I stop what I'm doing and petition Congress at this very moment?"

"Of course not, sir." Steve looked at the ground sheepishly but this time the top of his head received a resounding whop from his Commander. It sent his straw hat twirling into the dirt at his feet. The young man never moved, his head still bent in compliance as he said quite sincerely, "I'm real sorry, Gabe."

"You oughta be!" Benny added.

"Oh shut up!" Steve snapped.

Gabriel ignored them, let out another sigh as he leaned his tall frame against the same oak. "I could use a drink myself," he muttered.

Benny leaped to offer his flask, stepped on Will's toe and made the man yelp in pain.

"You clumsy ox!"

"I humbly beg your pardon," Benny huffed, eagerly

handing his flask to Gabriel. "That's what you get for being underfoot, you lazy squirrel!"

Gabriel didn't seem at all fazed by their bickering, which gave Vanessa the impression that this behavior was commonplace. Gabriel rested his head against the tree, closed his eyes and sucked a long draft from the flask.

Meanwhile, Francis opened his torn sleeve and checked to be sure his arm was uninjured. "You get any sleep tonight?"

"No. I was thinking about that letter from Moylan."

"What letter?" all three soldiers asked at the same time.

"Moylan wants me to report to Morrisville in three weeks."

"What for?" they asked as if any business of Gabriel's was business of theirs.

Gabriel shook his head at them and said dryly, "Probably to give me a lecture about the proper behavior of a regulation field Commander." He moved away from the tree and handed Benny the flask, then ran his hands through his hair, unbinding it and shaking it loose. It was long and thick, falling to his shoulders in glorious disarray. "He's mad because I break ranks so often to spy on the enemy. I'm supposed to let everyone else do that and remain in charge."

"That man is so dumb I bet he gits lost in his own home," Benny said. Steve let out a snort of laughter at the sentry's appalling irreverence.

Gabriel grinned at Benny and added, "He also wants to probe me about the Archangel. It seems Moylan has a new theory that he's been jabbering around headquarters, probably in search of a higher commission. He thinks because my name is Gabriel, like a biblical Archangel, I must be him!"

"You jest!" Francis gasped, astonished. "He can't be serious!"

"He's perfectly serious!" Gabriel exclaimed, his eyes twinkling with laughter.

"What a fool!" Benny exclaimed. "If I said something so stupid, I'd be ashamed to show my face for the rest of my life. So what're you gonna tell him, Gabe?"

"I'm not going to tell him anything. Just ask him if he thinks every man named Lucifer is the devil!"

They all burst into a fit of hilarity. Vanessa clamped a hand over her mouth and laughed along with them.

Benny shook himself off the tree, stuffed his shirt into his britches and chortled, "No wonder those she-rabbit Generals can't find the 'Angel. They can't find their way in the dark let alone catch the likes of that spy!"

"Some army this is," Steve said dryly.

"This ain't an army," Will announced throatily. "It's a revolution!"

"HUZZAH!" Gabriel shouted, whirling on his heels and thrusting his fist into the air. His battle cry sounded from everyone just then, the noise of their sudden valor filling the still night air with a momentary serenade of patriotic spirit.

Vanessa snuggled into the rocks and watched the Lieutenant Colonel stroll back to the green and resume his practice, his spirits as high and vibrant as the blade he sparred with the red-headed Quartermaster, Lauren Stuart. The weapon slashed through the night air with great cunning and speed, its finely pierced steel hilt glowing in the yellow light of a nearby lantern. It was a colichemarde blade, long and slender, the guard designed in the shape of a Maltese cross. It was the weapon of a champion competitor, she noticed, one with enough honor to sport a sword knot tied with silver threads.

Gabriel. What a complex and sophisticated man he was; yet at the same time so friendly and approachable. It made her observe him with an interest she didn't normally allow herself. What maid could not be affected by the sight of this young champion on the green? He looked so tall and powerful out there, twisting and pivoting and lunging at his partner, his unbound hair scattered around his face, his blouse billowing in the wind. Those tight regulation riding britches he wore left little to the imagination, every ripple and bulge proclaiming the endowments of man in all its virile glory. He was a beautifully constructed man and looking at him now only reminded her of how much was hidden under his stark white clothes, how warm and rugged was his tan flesh, what it felt like to hold him in her arms.

She blushed in the dark, appalled that she was even thinking about him like this. But how could she help it? She'd lain with him, knew him while he was naked and exposed, saw the man hidden in the freedom-fighter whose land chose to make him a hero. In spite of herself, she found him worthy of something she gave to no man.

Respect.

But she didn't want to feel it, struggled to push it away, wanting to dismiss the admiration that was growing inside her for this fearless Commander who was so obviously revered by the men he led to war. He had their complete devotion and she could clearly see why he earned it. There was nothing pompous about him. His personality was vibrant and genuine enough to make him very much a part of the rank and file who trailed his every step. They loved him, this gallant and elegant man, this master sleuth with the Bourbon tongue whose heart belonged to a New World.

As far as she permitted herself to measure men, he was on the high side of the scale. But not at all trustworthy. Oh no. This honor she gave no man.

The sudden call of a goldfinch brought the lazy hecklers under the oak to their feet, all of them darting into the woods to their assigned places. Barely a twig crackled as the huge Sergeant disappeared into the foliage. Will and Steve MacLeod slid under the bushes, the tips of their rifles aimed directly at the green beneath the natural camouflage. The Quartermaster sheathed his rapier, shook Gabriel's hand and took his place beside the rotted barn door where he would serve as his second.

A new kind of energy filled the air.

Tension.

Swanson was on his way.

A dull gray light was just beginning to seep into the night sky as the Colonel, alone with his second, rode onto the green. Gabriel greeted the man properly and listened to the bird calls coming from the woods. She guessed his scouts were telling him the area was secure, that Swanson was indeed alone.

Suspecting nothing, the British Colonel flexed and sported his blade for a few minutes of practice. He showed some amount of precision with the blade, Vanessa noticed, but his movements were slow and cautious compared to Gabriel's quick and confident skill.

Finally, the two men approached each other in the middle of the sloping green. Despite the dim and misty light, both were highly visible in their dress whites. The Colonel's second issued a short prayer, then requested the duelers to shake hands before opening the fight. They did so, quickly and expediently, then lifted their blades into the sky and stepped apart.

Gabriel made the first move, his rapier whistling downward with a flick of his wrist. The Colonel jumped backward and met the thrust. She heard metal blades clank and ping and rattle, then halt as the men drew apart. Again, Gabriel attacked first, springing forward into a deep and graceful lunge. Swanson was forced to whirl away and defend himself. Gabriel struck again and again, faster and faster, circling the Colonel in a way that caused the man to turn around and around.

"This is it!" Will hissed from the dark.

"No," she heard Francis counter. "Gabe's just playing with him."

Sure enough, Gabriel slowed and allowed Swanson his first opportunity to take the offensive. The Colonel showed some strength and slashed his blade every which way in search of a vulnerable position from his adversary. He found none even though Gabriel was forced to move farther and farther away to avoid being cut. The only evidence of his defensive skill was how he seemed to know Swanson's movements in advance. His rapier was always positioned properly when the next blow struck.

From this distance, she could see that both men were now panting. Swanson was tiring, but Gabriel moved with the poise of a panther, his long body stretched, his movements quick and smooth as he allowed Swanson to lead him into a wide and circling dance.

"Now!" she heard Francis announce, obviously speaking with authority on Gabriel's fencing strategies. No sooner did the word leave his lips than she saw Gabriel's conduct take a dramatic turn to the offensive.

His blade was suddenly flying at the Colonel with a lightning speed. Metal blurred, Swanson grunted, Gabriel forced his strength until she could see the sweat gleaming on his skin.

Swanson backed farther away, but Gabriel showed him no mercy as he pursued him, his blade cutting through the air at every possible angle. Up. Down. Under. Across.

Swanson was clearly startled now, realizing he was sparring blades with a true champion. He faltered, fell back. Gabriel came at him with unmasked aggression, thrusting his rapier again and again until Swanson was slowly driven to his knees. Gabriel's attack was too overwhelming, too fast, too perfect in form and execution.

And then it happened, so quickly Vanessa almost didn't see it. One slice of Gabriel's blade and the front of Swanson's blouse tore open. He gasped, started to double over but not before Gabriel seized an opportunity to cut him again. This time it was across the chest, just enough to sting the Colonel but not enough to seriously injure him.

Swanson dropped his blade.

"The lady is mine!" Gabriel shouted.

"Indeed she is," Swanson panted, holding his chest as he looked up at Gabriel. "You have won the duel. Do you choose to finish it?"

Vanessa held her breath. It was custom for Englishmen to sport honor to the death. Gabriel stood upright, looked at the fallen Colonel for a long moment, as if deliberating whether to spare his life. But then he laughed, wickedly, tossing his head back and hurling the evil sound of it into the night. Once again he looked down at Swanson, the point of his rapier coming to rest right between the Colonel's eyes. This time when he spoke, he was no longer the British Lieutenant Graves but the Continental master spy, Gabriel St. Claire.

"I concede nothing to you, *l'ennemi,*" he announced. Swanson fell back on his heels, stared up at Gabriel in a moment of speechless shock. "Allow me to introduce myself," Gabriel taunted his paralyzed prey. "My name is St. Claire . . . Gabriel St. Claire. You've heard of me?"

"Imposter!" Swanson exploded. He turned to his second and screamed, "Kill him!"

The second leaped out of the shadows of the barn, a loaded flintlock spinning out of his belt, taking direct aim at Gabriel's chest.

Vanessa gasped, sprang to her knees, staring at the place where the MacLeods lay hidden in the woods.

Shoot! Shoot! her mind screamed

"Will!" Francis cried. "For God's sake, will you—"

A gun exploded, sending a huge tongue of flame spitting out of the foliage. Swanson's second came to a sudden halt, and stood there staring at Gabriel with his pistol still clenched in his hand. Slowly, like the melting of a block of ice, the man slumped to the ground.

"Phewee!" Will howled in delight just as Benny came crashing out of the woods. "I got him!"

Gabriel moved over the stricken Colonel, his long legs spread, the tip of his rapier poking into the man's throat.

"Start talking, Englishman. What are your orders for Philadelphia?"

"I'll die before I tell you anything!" Swanson declared. But Gabriel would tolerate no resistance. He let the blade slice down the front of Swanson's chest, brought it to a rest against his belly.

"You'll die anyway," he breathed in a deadly whisper, "But if you want an easy death, you'll talk. If not, I'll lay out your guts, man."

"No!"

Gabriel's blade whipped downward, across Swanson's groin. The man screamed and Vanessa clenched her eyes tight.

"Talk!"

"To the Delaware . . . we're to wait for General Howe and his brother, the Admiral . . . come up from the Chesapeake—"

"An amphibious attack on Philadelphia?"

"Yes!"

"When?"

"In June they think . . . but the Admiral is having problems . . . in the Indies . . . might not get here in time."

"How many men are coming here to meet Howe?"

"A few thousand . . . we're the first of them."

Gabriel had heard enough. Before the Colonel knew what happened, his throat was cut wide open. He died painlessly, with his honor intact.

Gabriel leaped away from the dead man and walked toward his second. Vanessa watched a half-dozen men pour out of the woods. "Bury them!" Gabriel commanded and she watched a few men volunteer for the duty, dragging away the bodies of Swanson and his second to some place where they could be secretly buried.

No one would know what had happened here, that Swanson gave away a strategic British plan, that his sparring partner was a rebel spy.

Vanessa realized she'd been holding her breath. A long sigh escaped her lips. Dazed by what she'd seen, she suddenly regretted coming here.

She got up, her legs trembling as she started down the rocks. One bare foot found the ground just as something hard and cold poked into the base of her spine.

"Hold it right there, miss."

She froze.

"Come away from there," a Yankee voice hissed from the dark behind her.

"Please . . . " she whimpered, her face pressed against the rock face. "I'm a Whig—"

"Don't matter to me who you are, lady, just that you've been spying on us for the last hour or so. Gonna have to come along with me now."

"Where?"

"To the Lieutenant Colonel! Now why don't you let go of those rocks real nice and easy."

She obeyed, both feet on the ground before she could bring herself to turn around and see the man hidden in the woods directly behind her.

A Continental cavalryman used his free hand to tip his hat at her, issue a lazy smile and nod toward the green.

"Go on."

How the devil did he manage to get this close to her without her hearing him?

These men were good, damned good, despite their non-regulation behavior.

The sentry's muzzle gave her back a little prod and she moved forward at once, clenching her shawl and looking directly ahead as she approached the men on the green.

* * *

Gabriel sat against the barn wall, his field desk in his lap, hurriedly scribbling down the information Swanson had just revealed. He signed the note, folded it, handed it to Benny. "Send this to Moylan, but don't use a military messenger. Find a civilian who won't know how to interpret this if he reads it."

Benny stuffed the note into his pocket. "Where we going now, Gabe?"

"Home . . . for a three week rest. I asked for six weeks so we'd at least get three."

"Good thinking, Gabe."

"Thank you, Benny. I'm always honored to have your approval. Now go back to camp and see it dismantled. Dismiss everyone and tell them to prepare to muster at my home three weeks from tomorrow and—"

He stopped short, his concentration completely broken by the pair of figures who came around the corner of the barn.

Vanessa.

She was walking ahead of an armed sentry, clad in little more than a night shift with a shawl over her shoulders. Her eyes were pinned to the ground, her expression sullen as the sentry prodded her to a halt before him. She didn't look at him, just stood very still and stared at the ground under his boots.

"She saw the whole thing, Gabe. I've been covering her for the last hour. She was setting over there . . . on those rocks."

Every soldier on the green came to a standstill, stared at the raven-haired beauty with complete captivation. Few of them knew who she really was, the woman who had made this mission possible. At the moment, she was nothing more than a shapely young maid whose scanty apparel presented a rather luscious feast for their eyes.

"Very good, soldier," Gabriel awarded the sentry, then added sharply, "Get that gun out of her back."

"Yessir!" The sentry stepped away at once, surprised at his Commander's curt tone of voice.

"I thought I told you not to come here," he said to Vanessa's bent head. She didn't answer him, just scowled at the ground. "Very well. Why don't you sit over here and wait a minute while I finish my business?"

She obeyed, walked a considerable distance away from him, then slid to the ground and sulked against the barn wall.

Gabriel finished issuing orders to Benny about the dismantling of camp, the dismissing of the men, how they should be prepared to return to New York in three weeks. Until then, they were free to enjoy their Philadclphia homes. Only when his duty was sufficiently accomplished did he return his attention to Vanessa Davis.

"Why did you come here?"

"I couldn't sleep," was all she said.

"Why not have a cup of hot milk then, eh?"

"Because I was worried about the duel, if you must know," she snapped, as if it was his fault that she'd gotten caught.

"In that case, I can't be angry. You obviously care for me."

"You're overimpressed with yourself!" she contradicted him, even though her bottom lip was trembling. Gabriel could see she was more embarrassed than angry, and probably distraught after witnessing Swanson's death.

He softened his voice considerably, "Perhaps I am but I'm glad you let me see you again after your rather solemn adieu earlier tonight."

She felt like a complete fool. "May I please go home?"

"Of course," he said brightly, "when you'll agree to come to my home instead of *his*."

In one abrupt motion, she rose from the ground and

headed around the barn. "I refuse to argue about this any more, Gabriel!" she cried, completely oblivious to their enchanted audience. "I refuse to marry you."

"Marry you," Benny repeated, looking at Gabriel as if his head had just fallen off.

"Mind your own business," Gabriel snarled. He launched himself after her. "Vanessa!" She didn't respond, just continued to stomp toward the woods, her voluptuous figure bouncing and swaying in a way he couldn't help but notice. The sight of her bare feet told him she wasn't wearing anything under her loose-fitting shift. His blood warmed at the thought of the glorious prize she hid under that dress, every white velvet curve of hers that seemed burned into his memory.

"*Zut femme*," he cursed her under his breath, the way she could make him want her even while he was watching her walk away. "Damn you! You can't live the rest of your life like this . . . forsaking all men because of one!"

"What I do with my life is my business."

"Yo-hoh!" his men bellowed at her remark. "That's telling him."

Gabriel spun around, glared at them with unchecked fury. "Get the hell out of here!" Of course they didn't obey, too enthralled with the scene to turn away.

He ignored them, stalked the woman up to the woods' edge where she finally whirled around to confront him. With both hands planted firmly on her shapely hips, she said smoothly, "I've told you before that I'm not interested in marriage . . . to you or anyone else. And after the way you played with me tonight, I certainly cannot consider—oh!" He snatched her into his arms so quickly it drew a gasp of fright from her throat. "Gabriel! Unhand me!"

He didn't, just lowered his face until it was only inches away from her own, close enough for her to see straight into his eyes. How animated he looked just then, so fierce and determined, his mysterious eyes turning dark and hot with aroused emotion. "I'm tired of these accusations of yours, woman . . . especially when you're just as guilty as I—"

"What?" she fumed, tried to push away but his arm only tightened around her waist, drew her close enough to make her aware of his every manly inch.

The contact had an instant effect on both of them, a stillness falling over them as their eyes began to roam all over each other, as if in search of the meaning behind this strange attraction they had for each other. It made no sense yet it was relentlessly apparent the moment they touched. She suddenly hated it, hated him, hated herself for ever allowing a man to touch her where he did.

"Is this a game too," he asked, his voice thick and deep in his throat. "Are you playing your Tory game now, Vanessa Davis?"

"I hate you," she breathed, but it wasn't anger she conveyed, it was passion.

And he heard it.

His face loomed closer, until she could taste the breath of his words. "What your lips say and what they do are two different things, my beauty." He brushed his lips across hers just enough to make her remember the way he had kissed her in the garden tonight, so full of passion and fury.

Arousal bloomed within her, made her feel suddenly warm.

"Give me your answer this way, my beauty . . . no more words."

He nibbled at her mouth in a slow and tantalizing manipulation that sent a tremble of pleasure through her stiff body. She tried to fight it but it was impossible. Not with this man whose touch could so easily awaken her, this dauntless soldier with a stallion's body and the heart of a champion. The touch of him was like some grand fascination with another world, his masculine passion so mighty yet so breathtakingly tender. What he made her feel was simply irresistible, his gentle fires too capable of consuming those places left smarting by the cruel hand of another man.

Gabriel's pulse soared at the feel of her cold lips turning suddenly warm, how her tense body turned limp in his arms, molded against him while her mouth began to move back-and-forth against his own. She was conquered, and it drew a great surge of ego out of the center of his manhood, made him feel more male than he had with any woman.

This was the essence of his attraction to her, he realized, how she claimed to hate him while her hands groped for more. Breaking through her walls of resistance was a moment of sheer victory for a man, was surely the impulse that drove him to risk rejection for another taste of the reckless passion he knew her to be capable of. He felt it now and returned it fully, knowing the moment wouldn't last, hurriedly filled her with the heat of it until she finally remembered herself and jerked away.

She stumbled backward, violet eyes glaring at him in denial and the darkness of passion while her thick black curls swirled around her in a wild dance. With the winds of dawn adhering the scanty dress to her womanly form, an undraped shawl revealing every breathless heave of her swollen breasts, Gabriel couldn't take his eyes off her. In that moment, she was the most magnificent creature he'd ever seen.

And he wanted her, fiercely, powerfully, in a way he had never wanted any woman until he met this violet-eyed temptress.

"You belong to me," he told her in a harsh whisper, "and I will have you as my own, Vanessa Davis."

"Never!" she cried, her voice winded and hot with the desire she despised. "I never want to see you again."

She disappeared then, into the woods, a long white shadow flashing through the dark timber like an angel trapped between heaven and hell, not knowing how to get out.

He went after her and this time, when he caught her, he would never let her go again.

Vanessa was halfway across the field before she saw him, a lone figure standing in the middle of the backyard. Her feet slid to a halt.

Fred. What was he doing awake? He never rose before mid-morning on Sunday, especially not after a drinking bout the night before.

Panic sent a rush of frantic ideas spinning through her head. Run and hide. Go back into the woods. Don't let him see you out here.

It was too late. Fred looked toward her, one hand shielding his eyes from the sun rising in the sky behind her. An ugly look flashed across his bloated face.

"Vanessa! Get over here!" he barked. He snatched up a wooden hoe, angrily arched it over his head. "Hurry up, girlie!"

Real fear gripped her, made her stand frozen in the middle of the field in a moment of sheer terror. Dear God! He'd kill her for this, use that hoe on her the same way he'd once used a rake on Danny.

Run! her brain screamed. Facing him now was just too dangerous.

She spun around, about to launch herself back into the woods when a new sound made her stop in her tracks.

Crackling twigs, snapping brush.

Gabriel.

He was coming after her!

Indecision momentarily paralyzed her, then turned into the energy of terror, a strange vigor that made her eyes dart across the landscape in search of some safe haven from these dual threats.

The Morris farm! She could reach it through the higher fields. They'd be outside choring. They'd hear. They'd help.

Her feet whipped into motion, tore through the mud and weedy underbrush as she headed for the front of the house.

"Vanessa! Don't you dare run!" Her father croaked, his voice choked with rage. "Get over here and take what you deserve!"

She leaped onto the lawn, saw Fred careen around the side of the house and take flight after her. She ran faster, harder, her legs pumping against the damp ground until the muscles were smarting. Her eyes remained pinned to the hedgerow ahead, the separation between their land and the Morris'. Vivid yellow forsythia blossoms flashed in the sun as she leaped over them and landed in the adjoining field.

Her bare feet slid in the mud, tangled in a patch of thorns that scratched open the skin on her ankles before she could get free. With a whimper of pain and exertion, she forced herself to keep running even though her legs were weakening. Fred was too close for her to allow even the slightest stumble. If she fell, he'd be upon her in an instant.

The whole world seemed to whirl around her as she flew at a breakneck speed, the blue sky, brown earth, tall red cylinders of the Morris silos in the distance. She could hear Fred's ragged breathing behind her, his voice hissing with venom as he cursed her. The sound of him only fueled her flight, made her realize how much he must have had to drink already today if he could run this fast. Yes, his belly was full of whiskey. It was the only thing that put life into this evil, sickly man.

The mere thought made her cry out in panic and desperation, a lonely pathetic sound that rattled in her ears like the distant tolling of a funeral bell.

"Oh God! Help me!" she wailed as her aching legs finally began to give way. She'd never reach the silos. She could feel herself stumbling, the wild beat of her heart like thunder in her ears.

Fred's hand brushed against her back.

She screamed, spooking a flock of crows out of the field and sending them blasting into the sky in a flight that mirrored the frenzy of her own.

His fingers snagged her dress, a grunt of fury sounding from his mouth as he closed his fist around the fabric.

She screamed again, turned around just in time to see the blurring streak of the hoe as it came whistling downward, disappearing for an instant before the wooden rod slammed into her back.

It struck with a force so cruel her eyes were stunned wide, and she was only vaguely aware of the way her whole body reeled forward, her feet temporarily airborne.

She hit the ground hard, on her face, her cheek sliding a few feet in the mud and brush.

Fred was on top of her, straddling her, his hands suddenly full of her hair. "How dare you bed your men and leave your father alone to fend for himself!" He yanked her head up, drew it back so far she thought her neck would snap. "You were out whoring, weren't you? Do you sleep with the enemy too? Tell me! Do you sleep with the rebels?"

"No . . . no . . . " she was gasping, hearing bits of her own hair being torn out at the roots. "I j-just took . . . a walk . . . "

"Lying whore!" he shouted, shoving her head back down and holding it against the ground. Mud filled her nose, her mouth, every breath drawing in another gulp of gravel and dirt. She started choking, gagging, her airways slowly closing until nothing could get in but mud.

She couldn't breathe. There was no air, just dirt.

She panicked, jerked and struggled wildly, desperately

tried to get her face out of the dirt and into the air. But he was too strong, too enraged, angrier than he'd been in a long, long time.

Spots of color splashed behind her closed lids. The lack of air began to weaken her flailing limbs.

"I urge you to seek help from your relatives, Vanessa," the Millbridge physician whispered from her memory. *"You can't stay alone with him . . . he's killing himself . . . and he'll kill you along with him . . . "*

Consciousness began to leave her, her body feeling strangely limp and cold as it lay sandwiched between her father and the earth.

She was dying.

There was nothing left to do but pray, seek the face of God, ask His forgiveness for whatever she'd done to deserve this. To be killed by her own father, smothered in the dirt by the same man who gave her life.

Help me. Help me.

"Bastard!"

Chaos rent the quiet above her, a mighty wind gushing across her back as the man atop her was suddenly, savagely ripped away. He hit the ground in front of her with a force so violent she could feel the ground shake when he struck.

A pair of hands encircled her head, lifted it ever so gently and turned her face into the sun. She wheezed at the air, groped for it, realized from somewhere underneath the haze in her brain that someone was saving her. A sharp cuff landed square between her shoulder blades, just hard enough to jolt loose a mouthful of mud.

"Breathe!" a voice begged from somewhere close behind her. "For God's sake, breathe!"

There was no mistaking that voice, the accent, the breathless slew of French cascading down her muddy cheek in a feverish bath of words she couldn't understand.

Gabriel.

She gagged, clawed at his hands, holding them with all her might as she sucked in the air, once, twice. It slid down her throat, past the mud and gravel, made her lungs fill until they felt heavy and swollen in her breast. Harder and harder she breathed, clinging to his hands as she gasped at the sky, drinking it until she could feel her whole body blooming with life.

He turned her over and she watched his face materialize above her as if he was moving out of a deep, dense fog.

She blinked, cleared the mist from her vision until she could see the dark blue color of his eyes behind a bushy veil of fallen hair. It flashed in the sunlight, vibrant and copper. The ruddy shade of his skin was like burnished bronze against the stark whiteness of his blouse. All the colors of life came back to her then, embodied in the figure of this giant of a man who was suddenly, wonderfully familiar.

"Gabriel," she whispered in a voice too small for the huge rush of relief that sped through her limp body. It felt so tremendously good to be alive just then she couldn't bear it, actually clenched her eyes against the most tremendous rush of joy she had ever felt in her life.

"I'm here, *chérie* . . . just lie still." He brought a cloth to her face, the white linen glaring in the sunlight as he wiped and dabbed at the mud on her skin.

Tears gathered quickly, distorted the image of this mud-stained soldier who, by the grace of God, managed to be near enough to save her life.

Had Gabriel not appeared when he did, Vanessa had no doubt Fred would have killed her.

As if he read her mind just then, she watched a sad expression flow over his face, a look that somehow mirrored the sudden crush of sorrow this horrible reality brought into her soul.

Years of torment and grief and abuse weren't enough

punishment for Vanessa. Fred thought she deserved worse. To die, be killed, like a worn out family pet.

Tears oozed from her eyes, the pain in her heart bitter enough to pierce the numbing shock of this morning's episode, of what had nearly happened to her out here in the middle of the Morris' field.

She started to cry, softly at first, her hands fisting around the fabric of Gabriel's blouse as he gently lifted her out of the mud and started carrying her home. What a gentle cradle were his mighty arms, so strong and sure when she felt so broken within them. The feel of him made her cry harder, until she was sobbing against his shirt, her fingers clawing for a hold of anything that might spare her from dropping into the deep black pool of agony hidden in her shattered spirit.

Gabriel's fury couldn't stand beside the powerful pity that welled in his heart as he carried her through the house, the empty walls echoing the sound of her heart-wrenching sobs. What a strange affection she drew out of his heart just then, a sudden and overwhelming desire to open up his soul and hide her inside himself where no one could ever hurt her again.

Gone was the cold-hearted woman who walked the streets of Millbridge. In his arms he held the little girl who found her brother dead in the barn. She was the beautiful young woman who couldn't bloom beneath the hand of a violent man, a bud too tender for such a brutal grip. Fred Davis had nearly destroyed her, he realized, and heard this devastating truth in every sorry chord that played from her hidden, broken heart.

No, he hadn't a thought for the man left unconscious in the field. His whole attention focused on carrying this victimized young woman away from what he hoped would be her last scene of violence.

Her bedroom was neat, tidy, like she was. Her scent clung to the air, caught in the soft wind that blew through the pale blue dimity curtains on the window. He laid her down on the bed and fetched the pail of water sitting on the stoop of a small stone hearth, a clean towel carefully folded beside it.

Exhaustion was finally quieting her until she lay sniffling beneath the careful cleansing of her mud-caked face. She was watching him now, as closely as he was watching her, their gazes speaking what their lips dared not say.

"You should change your dress before we leave," he suggested lightly, as if this sensible suggestion might bring a bit of sanity back into this insane spectacle of life.

She nodded, took a deep breath, slowly rose on her elbows to look out the window. "What about father—?"

"Leave him there. By the time he regains consciousness, we'll be away."

"What did you do to him?"

"I don't remember," he said, looked down at his swollen knuckles and honestly couldn't recall. He shook his head in bewilderment, realizing how completely frantic he had actually been out there, blind to everything but saving this woman's life. It reminded him of what had happened when Michael died. One minute he was holding his bloodied twin, the next he was slashing the life out of Louis Montagne, killing a neighbor he'd known since childhood. Images flashed before his eyes, the colors of that moment forever burned in his brain. The bright white flash of a rapier's edge, stark golden sunlight, kelly-green grass, pools of dark red blood, the glassy blue horror in Louis' eyes.

He shook himself, suddenly disturbed, looked at Vanessa and defended, "I had to hit him hard enough to get him off you . . . keep him off you so I could revive you. He was suffocating you."

Her eyes clenched shut, as if she couldn't bear to remember those sickening moments. Gabriel could see her whole body tremble as she struggled against a new onslaught of tears. It would be a long time before Vanessa would be able to talk about this, to tell him if what he saw this morning was indicative of her childhood here on the farm. Until then, he could only assume the worst.

"Never mind . . . we don't have to talk about it." He leaned over her, gently pressed her back down on the bed. "It's over now. He'll never touch you again . . . not so long as I'm alive. My home is a quiet and peaceful place where you can finally live a normal life."

She looked like she wanted to argue, started to sit up again, then stopped. For a long, suspended moment, she just hung there staring at him, her eyes like violet flowers floating in a sea of sad and desperate tears as she searched for some argument to wield in the face of his proposition.

But there was none. Not now. Not after this.

She lay down again, her expression a bit frightened when she regarded him now. "I have an aunt in Erie," she began.

"Yes, I know. A Miss Elizabeth Gatling . . . who formerly resided on Eleventh Avenue but is now in the care of the Sisters of the Immaculate Heart due to the fact that she's eighty years old and completely blind."

Vanessa's eyes widened in surprise. "How do you know that?"

"I checked."

"Oh . . . "

"I also know you have no other relatives because both of your parents were only children . . . your Aunt Elizabeth being your grandmother's youngest sister."

In other words, she had no where else to go. Not even the Bordens were an option because that would keep her in Millbridge, too near her father's reach.

A strange feeling of numbness coursed over her just then, the kind a person might feel when suddenly finding themselves at the most critical juncture of their life.

"Don't be afraid," he said, his voice deep and low and elegant, almost capable of soothing her as he calmly explained, "We're not the first people who hardly know one another yet find ourselves marrying for honor's sake. Romance may not bring us to the altar, but our reasons are just as good."

Her eyes were following every movement of his lips, wide and staring in a kind of appalled rapture. "B-but . . . why would you do something like this to your life?"

"Because it's the right thing to do. I've told you this from the very start. A man of honor does not run around dishonoring young ladies."

"But it was an accident! I was pretending to be—"

"I know what you were pretending!" he said, put up his hand to halt her argument and reiterated, "but the fact of the matter is that you were a chaste maid and now you are not! Marrying you is the right thing to do and I've learned not to fear any consequence when doing what is right. Nothing bad can come of good. The right thing may sometimes be the hard thing, and it might make a man shudder in his boots, but if he shows some courage and goes through with it, a good end will be his. This I believe. This I have learned. This is the way it will be."

He got up, took the quilt off the foot of her bed and undraped it on the floor.

"What are you doing?"

"Packing for you, *mademoiselle.*"

"But I . . . I just don't know if I can . . . do this!"

"Neither do I," he said, stood up and looked directly at her when he announced, "You will carry the name of the man whose mark you wear. I will have it no other way."

"You are incredibly bull-headed!"

"The war did this to me . . . it made me tougher than I used to be. Now then, just lie still while I get your things together."

He opened her clothes chest, reached both arms inside and clumsily drew everything out at one time. The lot of it was dropped in a heap in the middle of the blanket. Next, he drew out the drawers and dumped the contents onto the pile.

"Gabriel—"

"My house mistress will straighten all this for you."

"That's not what I was going to say."

"Say whatever you want then."

It wouldn't make a difference, she knew, no word had yet been invented that would change this man's mind. With a long and rattling sigh, she sank back on the bed and finally acknowledged defeat.

"Very well. You win. I'll marry you but for reasons of convenience only. We will *not* be husband and wife."

He stopped collecting all the toiletries from her vanity and turned around, his arms full of perfume bottles, brushes, combs, ribbons. Such feminine things in the arms of so masculine a man looked almost funny, although she couldn't quite summon a laugh at such a momentous time.

Especially not when she watched that handsome mouth spread into a broad smile.

"*Très bien, mademoiselle,*" was all he said, not agreeing or disagreeing with her conditions. For some reason, she had the impression it didn't matter to him that she had just refused his bed; it was as if he knew something she didn't.

Curiously, she watched him lay all her bottles and paraphernalia in the pile, snatch the slippers out from under her bed, and proceed to tie together the corners of what became a giant bulky bundle.

He stood up, turned to her again and presented her with a very familiar dress.

It was the pink brocade dinner gown she had worn the night they met.

He remembered.

It touched a soft spot in her heart but she refused to show it in the gaze that caught his from across the room.

"Will you wear this for me today?" She didn't say anything, just nodded her head. "*Merci* . . . I will be pleased with this wedding dress."

Vanessa could barely concentrate on the next few hours of her life. Badly shaken, bruised and trembling, she participated in the events of her marriage as if they were happening to someone else.

For obvious reasons, Gabriel chose not to seek Isaac Borden, a Tory minister, and rode to the outskirts of town where James Winslow tended a small congregation of Whigs. The moment he announced his name, the Preacher and his wife forgot their waiting congregation while conducting the marriage ceremony of the honorable Lieutenant Colonel Gabriel St. Claire.

Their attention embarrassed her, made her feel so false and unworthy, especially when she was sitting in a stuffed chair with her face full of bruises and her back aching from the hoe. She kept her voice low, repeated her vows in somber tones as if muttering well-rehearsed prayers. Because there was no time to buy her a proper ring, Gabriel removed the signet ring from his right hand. He slid it on her finger, the size so big she had to hold it in place. Preacher Winslow blessed it as if it was suddenly sacred.

She was relieved to get outside, into the quiet calm of Sunday morning as if that might somehow redeem her from her wrenching anxiety.

Gabriel untethered her mount and tied the reins to his own saddle horn. "You'll ride with me."

"I prefer my own mount."

"I want to ride faster than your injury will permit."

"Don't be ridiculous. I can ride just as . . . oh!" She was suddenly swept off the ground, her feet spinning in mid-air for a moment before she landed squarely in his saddle. He ignored her startled gasp, moved back to give her more room and see her comfortably wedged between the spread of his thighs.

"That's better," was all he said, giving his mount a nudge.

The town was nearly deserted at this early hour; everyone was at Sunday worship. The few people on the street paid little heed to the young couple who rode slowly down the street. Vanessa looked inside Joshua's shop and silently said good-bye. She wouldn't be there on Monday, with Spearmint and Thyme and Basil.

They turned out of the village and across the Poquessing, slowly headed up the sharp incline of Orchard Road. Gabriel urged his stallion into a smooth trot, then settled into the ride. He gave her enough room to stretch her legs, to cradle her injured spine against him.

She wanted to resist but she was too tired, too spent, so she finally laid her head on his chest and found comfort in the circle of strong arms that wrapped around her. There was no boldness in his embrace, just a quiet and steady support.

Within minutes, her eyes were closing, her fingers absently twirling the bulky signet ring, her nostrils inhaling the cool spring winds dancing along the Poquessing and the musky scent of the soldier behind her. The aroma of honeysuckle and wild lilac was like a sweet balm on her tattered nerves as her drained spirit sank into the heavy weariness of her bruised body.

Within minutes, she was sound asleep.

They'd been riding for nearly two hours when Gabriel blinked up at the cloudless blue sky, yawned broadly, and decided to find a cool spot in the woods where they could rest for a while. He wanted seclusion from the frequent travelers on this road that began in Philadelphia and dead-ended in Kingston, New York.

They'd already passed several people, mostly lone riders and a few farmers with oxcarts who did little more than nod as they rode by. One family from Germantown stopped him to ask if he knew anything about the British being camped near Millbridge, if it was safe to go there, or if the invasion was about to begin. The young parents seemed so anxious, no doubt tormented by months of invasion rumors that made everyone nervous in these parts. The four children in the back of the wagon weren't at all concerned as they howled over the antics of a crate full of newborn puppies.

Once he convinced them it was safe, Gabriel tapped the brim of his hat at the man's wife and took his leave. As usual, he had no idea if he'd just spoken to a Whig or a Tory, if the family wanted independence or scorned the rebellion. Such was the case in America these days. Everyone had something to hide.

Gabriel steered his horse off the road, let it pick its way through the woodland border and into the deeper woods. As only a thirsty horse could do, it found water within minutes, stopped on the bank of a small creek and drank steadily.

Vanessa finally stirred, opened her eyes and looked around as if trying to remember where she was. She tried to sit up but an unexpected pinch of pain from the welt on her back brought a sharp gasp from her lips.

"Oh!" she groaned. "It hurts . . . "

"Just stay still." He immediately brought the horse around and dismounted, carefully drew her down and carried her to a stand of timber. He settled her against the gnarled old roots, genuinely concerned when he reached under her cloak and felt the swollen knot on her spine.

"I should have killed that bastard when I had the chance," he cursed under his breath. "If I ever see him again, there will be no mercy in my hand."

"Please . . . " she whimpered, not wanting to hear it and feeling her cheeks flame at the thought of what this valiant Continental hero had seen this morning.

She suddenly wished he wouldn't kneel so close, touch her so tenderly, speak so vehemently. The memory of that humiliating spectacle in the Morris field made her sick. A wave of revulsion shuddered through her. While Gabriel helped ease her aching back against the rigid bark of the tree, she was too ashamed to even meet his eyes.

"I'll have my surgeon check this in the morning."

"It's not serious," she said quickly. "It's nothing—"

"Don't tell me it's nothing! You flew off the ground when he hit you!"

"Oh stop it!" She was on the verge of tears again, but struggled to hide them because this was her way. Vanessa was always trying to appear calm and normal, like everyone else.

"Please let me help you." He touched her shoulder but she instantly shrank away, looking as though she wanted to hide in the grass rather than accept his comfort. "Surely you know by now that I'm not like him . . . I'll never hurt you . . . don't you understand? Your father is not like other men . . . he's abnormal and—"

"I don't want to hear any more!" She cried, her voice shrill, piercing. She covered her ears and burst into tears.

Helpless, he just sat there watching her weep until he finally accepted defeat and moved away. It would be a long time before this woman learned to trust him. A very long time.

He lay down on the grass, the sound of her sobs making him feel oddly tired and drained. He felt so powerless, so inept, so strangely confused where this woman was concerned. Just thinking about it made him weary, vulnerable to the exhaustion of the last sleepless night, to the cool damp shade of the creekside. He started to fall asleep, flat on his belly, his face in the moist green grass, the coolness of the earth slowly infiltrating his worn body.

His mind started to float randomly, from thought to thought, no connection between any, just a blissful wandering through the corridors of a tired brain.

Swanson. Philadelphia. Going home. Married.

Vanessa watched him nestle into sleep cautiously, as though she were watching a hearty bear relinquish itself to the inevitability of hibernation.

"Surely you know by now that I'm not like him . . . " his voice taunted from her memory.

No, she didn't know that. How could she? Men never gave to her, they just took away. Why would this one be any different?

She watched him as if in search of the hidden evil in his motives but instead saw his serious expression lose its strength, softening into the innocence of repose. Soft breezes played in the dense auburn mass of his hair, the locks tumbling and fluttering across a proud brow.

It was strange how serenity stole all the mightiness from him, from the sharply carved muscles of his powerful physique as he relaxed, long and lazy, against the earth. A broad back moved ever so slightly with the docile rhythm of his breathing, the contours of his torso tapering into narrow hips that hugged the ground. His thick thighs were slightly spread, powerful legs that were so capable in motion now content to do nothing.

Her eyes fluttered, slowly closed around the image of this sleeping hero whose name was now her own.

Dusk was already enlivening the sky with a mellow shade of amber when Gabriel shivered awake. The temperature dropped quickly at night in Pennsylvania in mid-spring, as if winter was still defying its own death by snatching whatever time it had left.

The woods were filled with a strange orange glow as he stumbled through the task of saddling his horse. Gabriel was still half-asleep, but his stomach roared for food, reminding him of the friendly taverns in Germantown that were only a few miles away. The thought of a good meal shot some energy through his groggy disposition.

Vanessa was lying at the base of the tree, curled in a ball, snuggled inside the woolen cocoon of her cloak. A slight tap on the shoulder brought her awake. They mounted, found the road, headed for the distant lights of the village with a brisk, hasty pace. Neither of them spoke but a few words to each other as they charged toward some relief from the empty bite in their stomachs.

The village of Germantown hugged the edges of the road. Most of the buildings bore the elaborately carved gingerbread trims peculiar to Rhine River homes in Germany, with bright painted shutters and porches. Old style Germanic script graced the signs labeling the various town merchants or declaring the denominations of the various churches and clerical homes.

Whenever he came to this quaint town, Gabriel was reminded of Europe, of the individual character of its villages. Each one seemed to have its own distinctive face. Germantown's expression was always gay and interesting, a face that never stopped smiling.

They reined in beside the Brechthaus, a tavern owned by a friend who wouldn't deny a Patriot some relief, even if it was the Sabbath.

Vanessa watched Gabriel hop to the ground, snatch a

few coins from his saddlebag and enter the building through a side door. He reappeared only minutes later, one hand toting a bottle, the other a foot-long loaf wrapped in cheesecloth. Both articles were handed up to her and the tantalizing scent of cheese and sourdough made her mouth instantly water. Gabriel slid into the saddle behind her and opened the bottle while she quickly unwrapped the freshly baked streusel. It was still warm.

They ate hungrily, sharing the bottle and the food until a glorious sensation of fullness returned. A sweet white wine eased her spirit and for the first time since they had embarked on the Swanson mission last night, Vanessa began to relax. Even the ache in her battered spine felt better.

"My!" she sighed with delight, "I never tasted anything so delicious."

Gabriel chuckled, glanced over the top of her head at the road and welcomed the feel of her tense body finally slackening in his arms. After such a long and harrowing day, it was a relief to share something that had gone right. Even if it was just dinner. "I used to visit the Rhine often while I was schooling in northern France and never lost my taste for its rich food."

Vanessa glanced back at him, this stranger who was now her husband. She realized she knew little about him, apart from his military occupation. "How long have you been here?"

"A decade."

"Do you miss France?"

He was quiet a moment, as if he had to think about his answer. "I suppose not . . . there was nothing left for me there . . . but I would like to see my fencing master again."

"He taught you well," she commented generously. "Your prowess with the rapier is quite obvious. No wonder you wanted to choose the weapon."

"Yes, my preference has always been for the blade

instead of the gun. Pity I have to war with it instead of sporting it. Fencing is too genteel a sport for the continent. It enjoys little popularity here."

"Perhaps you could go back one day—"

"Absolutely not," he interrupted, then laughed shortly. "You might as well know you married an exiled Frenchman. I can never return unless I want to face execution for my crime."

"What crime?"

"Murder."

She stiffened, looked up at him in alarm. "Are you serious?"

"Quite. But don't look so horrified. I don't enjoy killing in the least bit . . . not in war . . . and not when I killed that man on the front lawn of my parents' house."

"But why?"

"Because he killed my twin brother." A shadow passed over his face just then, stealing the lightness from his expression and leaving it veiled in darkness. He didn't want to talk about this, she could tell; he seemed to force himself to speak. "To kill a man's brother is bad enough, but to steal his twin is a worse crime. There's no replacement for someone who was at your side from the moment of conception. For this, Louis Montagne deserved to die and my only regret is the scandal it caused my family."

"Were they exiled too?"

"No, but I was only seventeen at the time so of course they came with me. My father was forced to leave vineyards that had been in the St. Claire family for three hundred years. Our cousins now control the land."

"But surely he can return now . . . a decade later."

Gabriel shook his head, a smile finally breaking through the tension on his face. "I doubt he'll ever go back permanently, just visits there once a year. He's as taken with this country as I am."

Prompted by her questions, Gabriel's memory returned

to that first landing upon the crowded piers of Philadelphia. How clearly he could recall his first sight of Dock Street even though, at the time, he was still shrouded in a blinding, numbing grief for Michael. He remembered the noisy menagerie on that busy street beside the pier, the thriving shops and warehouses whose doors opened right on the banks of the Delaware. The crowds were peppered with straight-faced Quaker ladies, ragamuffin dock workers, handsomely dressed gentlemen, everyone speaking at one another in every foreign language imaginable. Dutch, German, French, Swedish.

It was the epitome of an immigration port, the largest in the New World, and something about that classification made him feel oddly welcome. No one really belonged here, which was why everyone did. For the first time since the death of his twin, he started to feel alive again.

"My parents bought one hundred acres of land in Valley Forge and left the city within a fortnight, but I stayed behind. In France, it is a custom among noblemen to never again share a home with a child who scandalized the family name, and I insisted upon this tradition, much to my parents' protest. After all, I was their only surviving child. But I wanted to study the law and the city was the best possible place for such work so they agreed to it. I rented a room above a bakery just a block from Fairmount Park, placed an ad in search of an apprentice position and within a few days, was hired by Esquire Blaire, the father of my friend and second-in-command, Robert Blaire."

Months of rigorous study passed and thoughts of France and Michael began to drift into the background. Through Robert he met new friends, Francis Stone and Lauren Stuart, a host of lovely young ladies, bar rooms filled with ambitious young men who accepted anyone who could hold his liquor and his political ground. Philadelphia did not discriminate. If you lived within her boundaries, ethnic backgrounds were no longer as significant as whatever pulse your life added to hers.

Vanessa instantly warmed to his story, to the promise hidden in the tale of a grief-stricken young immigrant who managed to rebuild a life shattered by violence. Would she have the same opportunity? As they entered the city limits, she looked around at this tidy colony that nestled so civilly between the mighty Delaware and the roaring Schuykill Rivers.

There was power here, money and prominence and political muscle. Here lived the Biddles, the Franklins, the Rittenhouses. Inside the stately brick buildings sat Congress, the meeting place of the New World's greatest political, military, and philosophical minds. Jefferson strode these cobbled streets. John Adams frequented the famous City Tavern on Second Street and declared it the most genteel in America. Washington received his commission in City Hall and became the first Commander in Chief of the Continental Army. Dr. Franklin's home was nearby, as plain and unassuming as he was, merely a roof to cover the brilliant ambassador-scientist who startled the world every time he spoke.

"The city isn't normally this quiet," Gabriel said, noting a surprising amount of boarded shops around him, no doubt the result of rampant invasion rumors. "So many more have gone since I was here last December when the first invasion scare sent most of the Whigs running for their lives."

"Hmm," Vanessa hummed in thought, "which means only the Tories are left?"

Gabriel saw her facade brighten with interest. He laughed, tried to sound stern when he admonished her, "Still hunting Tories, eh? Beware. This town is a whit more dangerous than Millbridge."

"But think of the information we could get!"

"If there's any information to be gotten, I'll do it.

Besides, there are plenty of Whigs left to do the dirty work—many who refused to be bullied out of their own homes—like most of the residents of my neighborhood."

"They've stayed?"

"Yes. They won't start worrying until I leave. Apparently, they trust my judgment. Ah . . . here we are," Gabriel said and nodded his head at the avenue they turned upon.

Seventh Street was a narrow cobbled lane sandwiched between two long rows of townhouses and three-story tenements of red brick. The architecture was Federal, with a plain but simple elegance that immediately impressed the eye. Each dwelling had a small porch out front, a brass lantern, and a stoop with four steps leading up from the street. The woodwork was colorfully painted, each family presenting its own favorite shade on the lovely louvered shutters and porch eaves. Most of the second- and third-story panes sported window boxes, also brightly painted, some already blooming with spring flowers.

Gabriel pointed at number twelve, the residence located in the dead center of the block, its woodwork painted in a distinguished shade of deep red burgundy.

She smiled in spite of the flutter of apprehension that scampered up her spine. This was her new home and it was quite charming, more welcoming than she'd imagined, bathed in the subtle light of street lamps and the glimmering reflection of the moon on the wet cobbles. It looked so friendly just then, a warm yellow light glowing behind the drawn drapes in a first floor window.

Gabriel turned off the street and rode into a tiny arched alleyway that ran alongside his house. The dark tunnel brought them into a surprisingly large rectangular backyard, perimeters marked by a short brick wall. Above it, Vanessa could see clear down the block in either direction, into every backyard. They all had the same garden plots as number twelve, nestling here and there along the walls, in plain view of broad back porches where residents could sit and watch their blooms.

She liked this place. In fact, the coziness of it inspired a feeling that seemed very much like pleasure as her new husband guided them through the starlit yard. They reached the wooden carriage house at the far end of the yard; it was nestled alongside the rear gate in the brick wall.

Gabriel launched a boot into the carriage house door. It rattled open at the same time his steed let out a loud whinny.

"We're home, Fleet," Gabriel said with a chuckle, giving the horse's flanks an affectionate rub. "It's been a long time, eh boy?"

The horse knew its way inside, trotted past a smartly canopied landau and pranced into the next stall. He walked around in a wide circle, sniffing the hay, nudging the gate, familiarizing himself with the scents of home. Gabriel allowed him to settle before he dismounted and lit the lantern hanging from a nearby post. The small hut-like interior filled with a pale golden light, bringing into view a large pile of accessories pertinent to a soldier of the field. Obviously, his men had brought his belongings here earlier in the day.

"You will like the house," Gabriel said simply and tried not to derive any false hope from the unusual lustre on Vanessa's face just then. This cold and sometimes distant lady was not an easy woman to impress. He felt somewhat victorious as he witnessed her obvious pleasure.

"Yes," she said as if just remembering he was there, "It's a fine house . . . the way I suppose a lawyer's should look."

"You were expecting a soldier's tent?"

She laughed then, looked away shyly when he reached up to aid her dismount. Careful not to jostle her bruised spine, he took a firm hold of her waist and let her grip his shoulders as he swung her out of the saddle.

"I'd like to hear laughter from you more often," he said and his apparent sincerity caught her attention as her feet landed softly upon the earth floor. "If anything displeases you here, tell me at once."

"Of course," she said quickly, wondering why he continued to hold her. Feeling awkward, she dropped her hands from his shoulder and stood very still in the faint light, silently questioning his mood and her own sudden awareness of how close they were standing. "I don't want to be a burden to you, Gabriel," she announced, hoping it might interrupt whatever was happening between them just then.

It didn't. The sincerity in his voice, the warmth of his nearby body, the softness in his mysterious dark eyes, all combined into that strange compelling feeling he seemed infinitely capable of arousing in her.

"I don't want you to worry about me," she said in a last attempt to repel him but her voice couldn't carry the intention. No, it sounded too soft, vaguely sultry, more winded than she really felt.

"I will worry about you . . . and me . . . about how this marriage could be a mistake."

"Are you having doubts so soon?"

"Of course. I've had them all along."

"You didn't have to marry me."

"Let's not cover the same ground over and over again," he said quietly, trying not to notice how beautiful she looked just then, with her face turned up into the yellow light where her ivory skin was bathed in its amber glow.

He couldn't take his eyes off her, off the nervous tremble in her full pink mouth, the plush velvet texture of lips he had a sudden, compelling urge to taste. "I've already stated myself on this subject," he said, his voice falling lower and deeper until it sounded almost hoarse. "I took what did not belong to me."

He let the sentence hang, which made her strangely aware of what did belong to him now that they were bound.

For the first time since their union, they looked at one another as man and wife. They were no longer the Lieutenant Colonel and the Tory hunter named Lavender. No, at this moment in their lives, they were just a man and a woman, bound in vows neither could accept nor deny. And somewhere in the middle of these two extremes they found themselves trapped, swimming in the huge space between what their minds could accept and what their bodies could not deny.

Desire.

It was always there, like a beast lying in wait for the right opportunity to seize them.

Like now, when he drew closer, reached for her, caressed her cheek so lightly, so reverently, as if she was almost too beautiful to touch. Subtly, he wove his power over her, reached into those secret places where she knew only pain and humiliation and rejection. It would always be like this, she realized with a sudden sinking sensation. When Gabriel looked at her like this, touched her so tenderly, she felt instantly exalted, as though no woman on earth was as desirable as she was at this moment.

His hand swept down her spine in a careful caress, drew her against him. She didn't resist and he seemed to know she wouldn't. Through the padding of his clothing, her body was strangely able to realize every masculine inch of him, as if his virility was too strong to be smothered by anything. A primitive sensation of pleasure warmed through her, made her want to run from the feeling but she couldn't. It was more good than bad.

"I want you to be at peace here," he was whispering, his throat thickening at just the feel of her hands moving up his forearms . . . "to be happy in my home." Why was it that any time this woman reached for him, Gabriel readied to receive her like some rutting stud panting for a choice mare. He wasn't too sure he liked what she did to him. It disturbed him in those places where he was the most a man.

"But I don't think I've ever been happy," she blurted breathlessly, her words startling herself more than him. "There's always been something wrong with my life." *Why was she saying this?*

"Not here . . . not any more . . . we'll have peace between us."

Impossible! she wanted to argue. How could they have peace with this contrary excitement forever between them, this precocious heat that could rise like a monster any time they touched. Even now, as he tilted her face up into his, she couldn't stop him, couldn't refuse the tender rapture inspired by the tiniest brush of his lips across her own. His mouth was too warm, too inviting. She couldn't stop herself from drawing him down, pressing for more, urging him into a kiss that was as luscious as it was shocking.

A sudden flash of light invaded the stable. "Gabe?"

They leaped apart, appalled by what had just happened and shocked to see the man standing in the doorway. He held a lantern aloft, just enough light to illuminate a tall slender figure. As he strode into the stable, his youthful face peeled into an excited grin when he caught sight of Gabriel. He immediately hung his lantern and rushed across the stable, his blond hair falling into a pair of blue eyes that shone with total gladness.

Gabriel was caught in the man's embrace, his back slapped and his head cuffed by this exuberant young stranger who split the tension in the air with a resounding howl of welcome.

"Lord! But you're a fine sight, Gabe. I barely recognize you!"

"It's been a long time, Jonnie . . . too long."

"Eighteen months!"

They stood apart, laughing and eyeing each other from head to foot. "You look fit, Jon—"

"And you've got enough new muscle on you to fight the war yourself. Heard you saw some mean combat this time."

"Yes, hard fighting it was for awhile—more to come I hear. But let's forget it, eh? I'm home."

"How long?"

"Three weeks."

"Ain't enough time. Why, the whole neighborhood was celebrating today when your men came by and said you were headed home at last. But they've all gone to bed in a stupor. What took you so long?"

"I had personal business in Millbridge—"

"Gabriel!"

Vanessa jumped at the sudden shriek of a woman who flew through the carriage house door as if driven by the force of a storm wind. She leaped straight at Gabriel, airborne for the last few feet before he caught her in his outstretched arms. He spun her around, a happy grin on his face as he listened to her squeals of delight. For such a wisp of a girl, she was capable of a mighty noise. Even after Gabriel set her down, she continued to babble happily at the sight of him. She was so petite that the top of her head barely reached his breast. It was touching the way she looked at him, through tears of joy that made her saucer-like eyes turn into warm brown puddles, as rich in color as the chestnut shade of her thick, curly hair.

"How I missed you . . . worried about you . . . read all your letters over and over until the next one came!" She hugged him tight, sniffled against his shirt, "If only this war would end! We want you home, Gabe—"

"Hear! hear!" Jonnie agreed and for a moment, the three of them shared a reunion that Vanessa couldn't interrupt. Their close friendship was too obvious and despite her earlier chagrin with him, she knew such a brave soldier deserved every bit of this triumphant return home.

It was Jonnie who finally noticed her standing in the shadows, his eyes catching hold of her tall figure and widening ever so slightly. "Have you brought a guest?"

"Ah yes," Gabriel said, turned around and reached his hand into the shadows enveloping his bride. "Come . . . "

Vanessa gave him her hand, let herself be drawn into the light where Jonnie made no attempt to hide his first impression of the glamorous young beauty who materialized before him. He looked startled, clumsily brushed off his hands and accepted the one Vanessa handed him. "Vanessa, this is Jonnie Meeks and his wife, Martina. They keep the house for me."

Jonnie gave the back of her hand a pluck and hurried upright so he could look at her again.

Martina stepped in front of him, wiped her eyes, and asked sweetly, "We're happy to have you with us. Will you be staying long?"

Gabriel slid his hand around Vanessa's waist, gave it a little squeeze as if imploring her to play along before he glibly informed them, "She'll be staying until death do us part, Martina."

The young girl looked up sharply, blinked once, then looked at Gabriel as if he'd just gone mad. Jonnie's mouth dropped open, his eyes wide as he breathed, "What did you just say?"

"This is my wife, Jon. I married her this morning in Millbridge."

The two of them just stood there, too stunned for words. Vanessa felt awkward in the silence, but Gabriel seemed unfazed. He let out a short laugh of amusement as he looked from face to face.

"I don't think I've ever seen you two so quiet."

"Well . . . I . . . er . . . this is . . . " Jon stammered, finally looked at his wife who finished pertly, "The most wonderful news we've ever heard!" From behind Martina, Jonnie gaped, "But you said you'd never marry, Gabe!"

"I changed my mind," he said, obviously pleased with himself for shocking his two companions. "Now then, will you stop gawking and lead the way to my threshold? I've a bride to carry across it."

She was promptly lifted off her feet, landing squarely in his arms, "Gabriel . . . "

He gave her a playful wink and proceeded out of the carriage house with great ceremony. She couldn't help but laugh at his antics.

"You're the most impossible man—"

"Yes, but you never could resist me."

She gave him a warning glance through the darkness, not wanting to embarrass him in front of his friends, although she certainly had a prime opportunity.

"Oh! Isn't it wonderful, Jon!" Martina chirped with a gay little clap of her hands. "Newlyweds! Imagine that!"

"Have we any champagne, Tina?"

"Of course, Jon! Let's go on ahead and fetch it! Just think of how excited everyone will be when they hear the news!"

"Humph!" Jon snorted at his wife's retreating back, "Philadelphia will be riddled with broken hearts in the morning!"

"Sarah will be positively distraught . . . and what of Rebecca! Oh! She'll faint at the news . . . you know how she adores Gabriel . . . and then there's poor sweet Mathilda . . . "

Vanessa scowled at her husband when the Meeks disappeared through the back door. "Poor sweet Mathilda?"

"I'm encouraged by your jealousy—"

"Rogue!"

He threw back his head and laughed in that merry way of his, with his whole self caught up in his humor. She had to fight the smile that tried to form on her face as he stepped across the threshold and carried her into her new home.

It was a man's home, Spartan but tastefully furnished. Every room they passed through had papered walls in elegant but simple patterns, each embraced by thick wooden chair rails. A variety of woven rugs were scattered across highly polished plank floors. Every window was dressed in long, sweeping draperies in subdued shades of gold or burgundy or dark blue and matched the patterns in the upholstered chairs and divans.

The back entrance led through Gabriel's basement offices and into a narrow stairwell that took them into a small but tidy kitchen. The room was dominated by a brick hearth big enough to walk into. There were four ovens in the bricks, she noticed, the mantle strung with kettles, skillets, wooden ladles and blackened metal firedogs. Just ahead of the kitchen was the dining room where a tall hutch filled with expensive bone china reflected itself in the high sheen of a long rectangular table made of cherry wood. A dozen chairs were arranged around it, their seats covered in a pattern of burgundy and cream. It was a room meant for entertaining, she saw, with servers full of silver and butlers flashing crystal everywhere, the dark red decor matching the adjacent parlor.

This room conveyed a taste of Europe in its imported tapestry rugs, the velvet upholsteries in dark blue and burgundy, the expensive paintings that graced the walls and the collection of candle stands and figurines on every highly polished table. A giant plate glass window bigger than any Vanessa had ever seen overlooked Seventh Street. It was a beautiful room.

Another flight of stairs led to the third story and the family sleeping chambers. Vanessa started feeling tense again, especially when Martina pushed open the door to Gabriel's chamber and stood aside to let him pass. The girl had the bliss of romance on her face as Gabriel carried her inside. Martina shared a secretive wink with her husband that she thought Vanessa didn't catch.

The door shut behind them.

Gabriel set her down in the middle of the room and let her stand there alone while she stiffly looked around the chamber. It was large, apparently occupying the entire rear width of the house with a pair of tall windows that overlooked the backyard gardens. The furniture and woodwork were carved of oak, a lustrous golden wood against which the dark blue velvet curtains and blood-red rug looked bright despite their subdued hues. It was a handsome room, very much a man's, but it wasn't the decor that held her attention.

It was the bed, a huge four-poster canopied affair that seemed to dominate the entire room. It made her nervous just looking at it, even more anxious when she watched the Meeks carry her bundle in here and drop it inside the door.

Surely he didn't expect her to sleep with him at night.

Too afraid to ask, she feigned great concentration on the Meeks who fluttered in and out, depositing baggage, delivering a lovely silver service of champagne with a pair of crystal goblets. They had mischief in their eyes when they finally bid good night and closed the door for the last time.

Out of the corner of her eye, she watched Gabriel remove his cloak, open the tie of his blouse and let the neck fall open. "Make yourself at home," he coaxed from across the room. "You needn't stand there in your cloak all night."

She removed her wrap, walked a wide circle around him and hung it on the peg next to his. He motioned at his closet which she found much too full for her own belongings. She was about to plead for separate quarters when she turned to find him standing directly behind her.

She jumped, attempting to glide past. He caught her arm, gently but firmly holding her in place.

"What are you so skittish about, madam?"

Before she lost her nerve completely, she blurted, "Under the circumstances, I can't imagine why we should share a chamber. I would prefer my own room."

He didn't say anything. She looked up, watched the way his face fell just before he turned away. It gave her the impression she'd just said something very unkind.

Vanessa watched him cross the room, pick up a glass of champagne and stand before the fire. His tall frame temporarily blotted out the light, leaving the room in shadows that were oddly oppressive, especially when shrouded in the heavy silence that greeted her request.

"Shall I take that as a refusal?" she asked quietly.

He said nothing, just looked at her and nodded his head.

She stiffened, unaware of how her haughty pose pronounced the svelte young curves of her body beneath the thin fabric of her pale pink gown. Desire quickened his blood, tightened his loins, made him suddenly realize how much he yearned for another taste of the splendors that lay beneath that gown, a delicacy he had known only once before. It took every ounce of manly control to look away from her stiff expression.

"I will ask little of you, Vanessa, except that you spare my honor as a man and at least pretend to be a willing bride in the face of my friends and family. Please don't embarrass me. This is all I ask."

She opened her mouth to argue, then quickly silenced herself. It was a genuine plea from a genuine man, she realized, and one who had not only spared her own honor, but her life as well. The very least she could do was agree.

"Very well," she said through gritted teeth, able to agree but unable to be a good sport about it yet. Anger sent her flouncing across the room to the fireside divan. She threw herself on it and snatched up a glass. Above the rim, she glared hatefully at her new husband. The man at the fire chuckled, his eyes sparkling in amusement at her fiery spirit.

"This arrangement is not at all amusing to me, Gabriel!"

"Forgive me," he said and forced the smirk off his face before he took a seat beside her. He sat back, draped his arms across the back of the settee and casually crossed his legs. "My humor isn't directed solely at you . . . but at myself as well. This is hardly the kind of marriage I ever imagined for myself in those scant few occasions when I even thought about it."

"Why don't we just get this annulled?"

He completely ignored her suggestion. "A Tory hunter and a spy," he philosophized. "Neither seems suited for marriage . . . let alone to each other. People like us don't belong in intimate relationships."

"What do you mean?" she asked, her eye straying across every tightly muscled inch of the reclining man beside her until she caught herself and looked away.

"Our skill is in discovering the secrets of others, not revealing our own."

Gabriel's attention shifted from the fire to the lovely speculation on the face of his bride. He let her see his appreciative gaze because it always stifled her, seemed to set her off guard.

She looked away. "Don't worry. This marriage will never get that intimate anyway."

He chuckled softly, looked at her as if she'd just said something charmingly naive. "If it makes you feel better to think this way, go ahead."

"I don't understand."

"I'll explain it the next time you allow yourself to be willing—"

Her eyes widened, appalled at what he'd just said. "You are overimpressed with yourself if you think—"

"You want me as much I want you . . . " he boldly interrupted.

"That was not what I was going to say."

"Any other statement would be a lie and you know it."

Her temper flared again, brought her upright on the divan. She had no idea how striking the pose was. Her injured spine was cradled against a cushion, and she was unaware of the way her body thrust out at him as if to taunt him with what could ease the ache she had inspired in the carriage house.

But he was a man of his word. He would not touch her until she allowed it. To spare himself any further torture, he tossed down the last of his drink and abandoned the settee. She cast him a livid glare as he walked toward the bed and began removing his shirt.

"What are you doing?"

"Undressing for bed. For the sake of your modesty, I'll wear a nightshirt—if I can find one."

He started hunting through his clothes chest, then the closet, finally found a nightshirt that looked as though it had never been worn. It was tossed onto the bed while he bent over and pulled off his boots, then stood upright to unhitch the stays of his britches.

Vanessa clenched her eyes shut and didn't open them again until she heard him climb into bed.

"You can open your eyes now . . . I'm covered." he said, chuckling in amusement.

She hurried across the room, grabbed her bundle and hid herself behind the closet door while draping in bedclothes. A moment later, she emerged in a fleecy gown that left everything to the imagination, buttoned to the neck, the hem dragging on the floor. With the painstaking movements of a woman approaching a den of napping lions, she carefully climbed into bed, then huddled herself on the very edge of the feather bed. When he rolled onto his stomach, she nearly fell off the edge.

"Vanessa . . . this bed is big enough for both of us."

"I hardly find it so!"

Gabriel's deep sigh turned into a broad yawn. The feather bed shifted as he snuffed the bedside lamp and brought the room into darkness. Vanessa clung to her small space in his bed, so acutely aware of him she could almost count every time he took a breath. It was a tense, awkward silence, one that soon left her joints stiff from the lack of ease. The welt on her back began to ache. She should rub the spot but didn't dare move. Not when he was lying so close, listening to her as intently as she was listening to him.

Finally, when he could stand no more, he let out a sleepy growl and sat up. "I can see you won't rest until I get out of this bed."

She didn't answer.

"Very well . . . I'll sleep on the divan." He got out of bed.

Vanessa rolled over, watched his tall silhouette pad across the floor to the small divan by the fire. He tossed down his pillow, took a moment to stoke the fire to keep himself warm and made an honest attempt to fit himself on the divan. His legs were too long, his shoulders too broad, and no matter what angle he tried, he simply couldn't fit.

He finally gave up, issued a disgusted curse in his native tongue and ended up on the floor beside the fire. With nothing but the thin hearth rug under him and a lone pillow, he stretched out on his stomach.

Within minutes, she heard him sigh to himself and drift off to sleep.

She relaxed, resettled on the bed and finally found some comfort. Despite her unnerved disposition, sleep came swiftly.

It was some time during the middle of the night when the fire in the hearth dwindled and sent the temperature dropping that Vanessa was stirred by her own shivering. Still half-asleep, she gathered the coverlet close and checked to see where Gabriel was.

On the floor, sound asleep, both arms tucked under his pillow to keep them warm while the rest of him shivered under his thin nightshirt.

Guilt stabbed at her drowsy heart. For the sake of her own rest, she'd banished this soldier from his bed, made him sleep on the floor his first night home in eighteen months.

The thought pricked her conscience. It just wasn't right that he should lie there shivering while she stole the comforts of his warm bed. Feeling selfish, she reached for the coverlet that lay folded across the foot of the bed.

Gabriel heard the quiet tread of her feet across the floor, peeked open an eye to see what she was about. But he saw nothing in the dark, only heard her pass around the other side of him and stop in front of the fire. A moment later, the swish of a bellows sounded in the stillness as she stoked the flame, then added a piece of kindling from the nearby pile. Curious, he wondered why she didn't move for what seemed like a long time. Finally he turned around and saw what she was doing.

Warming a blanket.

He resettled, glad to see her making herself at home and waited for her to carry her coverlet back to bed.

A moment later, something warm and soft was falling over him, the hem of it carefully drawn down until his bare feet were completely covered.

Gabriel was so stunned at this unexpected gesture, he just lay there listening to her move around him, then sigh to herself as she stood up and started back to bed.

He rose on his elbows, watched her tall slender form disappear into the shadows around the bed.

"Vanessa," he whispered, watched her figure stop short when she heard him and realized he was awake.

She just stood there, not knowing what to say, like a child caught doing something wrong. "You were shivering," was all she offered.

Gabriel could see the tension in her movements as she slowly climbed back into bed and lay very still in the darkness, knowing she was aware of his every movement beside the crackling fire.

Fear. He sensed it in the room just then as if a whiff of foul air had gusted through the window sash. She was afraid of him and no woman on earth had more reason to fear men. But he could feel some other emotion rippling through the fear, a soft undercurrent that seemed to be flowing against the tide.

Respect.

There was goodwill in this gesture of hers, he knew, and as he laid his head back down, he was content to accept this tiny step forward from the troubled young woman who was now his wife.

"Thank you," he whispered into the darkness.

She didn't answer.

9

The noise was what woke her, the rattle of carriage wheels against a cobbled street instead of a creaking barn door, the yelp of children in the place of chickens in a henhouse. Vanessa sat up, realized the banging sound was the back door of a house as unfamiliar as this city and this room and this man's bed. She felt a pang of longing just then, for the serenity of a country dawn, the lumps in her old feather bed, the way her lace curtains fluttered on breezes full of the earthy scent of plowed fields.

Only the sunlight was the same, the way it bathed everything in the pale ochre hues of morning. Her sleepy eyes took in the room in all its simple elegance, the heavy wood furnishings and velvet drapes. Then she noticed the lumpy pile of shadows on the floor beside the hearth.

It was a crumpled blanket. A man's nightshirt was partially draped over the red satin arm of the fireside settee, the hem trailing on the floor.

Gabriel.

She was immediately aware of his voice coming from

somewhere in the backyard. She tossed aside the coverlet and got out of bed. She went to the window, parted the drapes and looked down into a lovely green square of grass where vivid blooms flashed from a half-dozen garden plots in the bright morning sun.

Gabriel was there, dressed in black britches and an ankle-length robe of dark blue velvet. It was loosely tied around his hips, the lapels gaping around a chestful of auburn hair. Casually leaning on the squat brick wall, he was busy arguing with the man next door. This neighbor was short and round-faced, an older man who hadn't a lock of hair on his gleaming pate. There was a woman at his side, of about the same age and height, her white hair neatly tied beneath a black lace cap. She coyly fluttered her lashes at Gabriel and beamed over a wicker basket full of golden brown croissants.

"I asked you three times for one of your croissants and you refused," the older man complained bitterly. "Este asks and you give her a whole basket full! You drive me to drinking, Frenchie!"

Gabriel flashed the woman a charming smile and explained, "I gave Este the croissants because she never calls me Frenchie. Besides," he snatched up her hand and smoothed it as if it were made of the finest silk, "I cannot resist her gentle beauty." He put her hand down then, crossed his arms over his bulging chest and snarled at the man, "And she's not a deserting *kraut* like you, Harvey!"

"I did *not* desert the army! I came home to get something to eat!" Harvey snapped, his face flustering until even his bald head turned red. "They thought I was too old anyway!"

The back door slammed. Lauren Stuart sauntered into view, toting a cup of coffee in one hand and a large parchment scroll in the other. He yawned, seeming unperturbed by the squabbling at the fence and swatted Gabriel's arm with the papers.

"Did you see these court-martial cases? The Department of War wants us to review them for validity." He stopped long enough to take a sip of coffee and grin at Harvey. "You know he hates it when you call him Frenchie."

"He calls me a *kraut*!"

"I don't think we should handle these," Gabriel was saying as he flipped through the parchments. "This is a conflict of interest. We're not only Whigs but soldiers besides. There are plenty of neutral lawyers in this city to serve the War Department. And never mind Harvey. One day I'll sue him for libel!"

"I dare you!" Harvey boomed. "You're as French as I'm German!"

"I'm an American," Gabriel said with equal gusto. "And a citizen besides."

"So am I!" Harvey said. Este just looked at him, sighed, then shook her head and disappeared into her own yard with her precious basket of bread.

Harvey angrily hitched his britches, stomped to a patch of pepper plants and started furiously weeding it.

"Now that you and Harvey have re-established your peculiar friendship," Lauren chuckled, "it's beginning to feel like home around here."

Vanessa finally realized that Gabriel and Harvey weren't at all serious in their unfriendly treatment of one another.

Her husband started across the yard, still reading the papers. He looked up just in time to see a pair of red-headed boys tumble over the wall on the other side of the yard.

"If it isn't the Sullivan twins!" he exclaimed with exaggerated surprise as the boys rushed around in an excited frenzy.

"Welcome home, Uncle Gabe!" "How many redcoats did you kill?" "Were the battles bloody?" "Are we winning yet?" The boys bombarded him with questions, each of them tugging on his robe in a fight for his attention. "When are we old enough to join the army?"

"You're both old enough to become honorary members of my company." Gabriel bent over and gave each head a playful tussle. "What does honorary mean?" one twin asked while the other chirped, "Can we have guns like yours then?"

"No guns yet, boys . . . in time perhaps."

"Boys!" A woman called after them. "Give the man a whit o' peace his first morning back!"

Vanessa watched a tall, stockily built young woman stand up from where she was working behind the wall, giving her children a reprimanding eye that hustled them back into their own yard. She didn't seem bothered by the rambunctious gang of youngsters who ran through the yard behind her. Her vivid green eyes were firmly planted on Gabriel, instantly filling with tears as she watched him approach.

"Could it be the fighting man back for a mid-year leave," she asked, her voice rich with a Gaelic accent. She pushed back her starched white bonnet and immediately fell into the arms that opened for her across the fence. She hugged him for a long and somber moment. "God love you, Gabe," she sniffled, wiping at her eyes, "I keep the Lord busy with prayers for you."

"No wonder I lead such a charmed life," Gabriel said warmly, soothing the woman's sturdy cheek with a gentle brush of his hand, "The most beautiful mother in all Philadelphia keeps me safe—the lovely Dierdre Sullivan!"

"You've a smooth tongue, Yankee!" She giggled at his flattery with girlish delight.

A tall sinewy young man came up behind Dierdre, his sleeves rolled back over a pair of sun-browned arms. He had a quiet, almost vacant expression until he caught Gabriel's eye. A wide smile filled his bony face, pride and pleasure brimming in his eyes as he welcomed home the city's hero.

"You did a fine job this campaign, Gabe," Patrick Sullivan praised, putting aside his wooden rake and clasping Gabriel's hand between both of his own. "Washington owes Trenton to your boys! Finest group of fighting men in our Army, you are!"

"That kind of flattery is why you have so many children, Patrick!" Gabriel laughed. "How many more babes did you give her since I've been gone?"

"Just one," Patrick said, as if this was an improvement in his record.

"Gabe! Lauren!" They were interrupted by a shout from Martina through the kitchen window. "Mr. Reed's man is here. Can you go to dinner with the Reeds and the Blaires on the tenth?"

Gabriel gave her a quick nod. Lauren did the same, then shrugged at Gabriel, "We're not going to get much accomplished in three weeks, Gabe," he said, referring to their legal practice.

"I'll be lucky to get through the mail by then! Maybe Jon should send it along more often next campaign so I don't have to come home to a foot-high pile of paper and—"

He stopped short as a clatter of horses drew up to the rear gate, a pair of smartly dressed Continental soldiers dismounting in the alley.

"Oh no!" Lauren cried with a comical look of horror, "It's the army!" He made a dash for the back door and informed anyone who was listening, "I'm not here! Better yet, tell them I'm deceased—for the next three weeks!"

Gabriel smirked, straddled the flagstone path as if to guard the privacy of his leave and told the approaching sentries, "The Quartermaster is dead."

The soldiers completely ignored his antics. "Sir!" they saluted, handed him a package wrapped in plain brown cloth. "A message from Morrisville."

"Hmm," Gabriel hummed, took the package. "At ease."

He unwrapped it, withdrew a set of decorated epaulets and a long chord of golden braid.

"General Washington sends this in reward for your work, Colonel," the soldiers said and gave the traditional first salute to a newly promoted officer. "And he sends his gratitude for your message from Millbridge."

Vanessa smiled. No one deserved a promotion more than Gabriel.

Gabriel looked pleased as he read the note accompanying the new accoutrements to his uniform, his smile unassuming until he reached a point mid-way through the letter.

The smile suddenly vanished, his whole face turning so rigid that she could see the muscle working in his jaw. Very abruptly, his head snapped up, his voice crisp and cold as he commanded the sentries, "You are dismissed." With a sharp glance at the back door he barked, "Lauren! Get out here!"

"Will there be a message for the General, sir?" the soldiers inquired.

Gabriel looked at them so sharply, the braids and epaulets clenched tightly in his fist, that Vanessa had the instant impression he was about to give them back. He was clearly outraged about something and no one in the yard could miss it.

After a tense and bristling pause, he leaned toward the soldiers, his teeth still clenched. "My pride remains in the service of liberty. May God and the people prevail."

"Huzzah!" the soldiers awarded as they issued a snapping salute. "Will you be needing anything else, sir?"

"Yes," Gabriel said, still fighting with himself against what she could sense was a far less honorable retort, "three weeks of uninterrupted leave. Now get out of here."

"Yes, sir!"

Intrigued, she watched Lauren come out of hiding,

snatch the note from his hand and start reading it as Gabriel led him to the seclusion of the back porch. It was directly under the bedroom window. She could hear every word.

"This is impossible! There was no one else on the green that night! Our sentries were everywhere!" Lauren gasped in astonishment. "The Archangel could not have been there!"

Archangel? Real interest made Vanessa lift the sash another inch, lean closer to the pane so she could hear better.

"He was there, Lauren. He had to be. How else could he have informed Washington of Swanson's orders?"

"Maybe he learned them some other way—"

"No. They were the same orders I sent from the green that night."

"But I saw you write the dispatch and hand it to Benny with my own eyes! No one read it, not even I! It must have been intercepted between Millbridge and Morrisville."

"It was sent through civilian channels, Lauren. If the Archangel intercepted it, then he must sit and wait to intercept every rider on every road between here and the Kingdom of God. He was there . . . on the green . . . watching the duel from some hidden place we could not discern."

Vanessa's eyes widened in excitement. Could it be true that while she sat watching the duel with Swanson, the Archangel himself was near? Had he actually seen her sitting there on the rocks?

"I swear to you the area was completely secure!" Lauren said vehemently. He simply could not accept what he was hearing.

"Not secure enough," Gabriel said, his voice finally reflecting the defeat he was obviously feeling inside. Vanessa felt a sudden pang of pity for him. What a cruel injustice that this mysterious Archangel should steal

Gabriel's glory, robbing him of the credit he so richly deserved. It had been Gabriel's courage, Gabriel's blade, Gabriel's own life at risk on the green that night, not the Archangel's.

"Gabe . . . " Lauren said, "you don't deserve this."

"Nor these braids," Gabriel remarked stonily. "These promotions are meaningless. They're nothing but a bribe to keep me content while I lead their master spy to glory."

"Don't say that—"

"Why not? It's true, isn't it? You can't deny it! There's only one reason we're sent to the war's most critical theaters—because the Archangel follows us wherever we go."

Vanessa couldn't believe what she was hearing. The Archangel following the First Squadron?

"I don't want to hear this," Lauren said in disgust.

"Well, you better hear it," Gabriel commanded in an ominous whisper, "because I'm tired of risking my company's life for this cowardly spy who can't lift a hand to help us . . . just steal off with the information we nearly die to get."

"Gabe, please . . . I've never heard you talk like this."

"Because I have never been this close to resigning."

Vanessa's excitement vanished. She had a strong compulsion to run downstairs, to plead with this valiant soldier against abandoning the Cause. Maybe it was true the Archangel followed Gabriel's company, but Washington was not a witless man. He knew a good soldier when he saw one.

But she didn't move, just stood there gripping the window ledge, her heart filling with genuine compassion when she heard Lauren say, "I beg you not to leave us, Gabe. Please. We're nothing without you. You're the heart and soul of this company . . . and wherever your boots walk, your men will follow. Is this what you want . . . to cost the Cause so much?"

Vanessa's throat was tight in the ensuing silence, Lauren's heart-wrenching testimony summoning emotions she wasn't sure she wanted to feel for this man who was now her husband.

Gabriel left the porch and came into view again, shoving the handsome braids into the pocket of his robe.

She let out her breath in a long sigh, imagining that Lauren must have just done the same. Then she turned away from the window where she could no longer see Gabriel, no longer feel the sharp tug in her heart at the sight of those mighty shoulders sagging in defeat.

He shouldn't be allowed to affect her like this, Vanessa scolded herself as she tried to set her mind on getting dressed for the day. The only dress she could find in her bundle of clothes that wasn't too wrinkled was a plain white cotton dress. The choice seemed oddly befitting of this first day in a new life, fresh and untainted, like this home and the new status of her name.

Yesterday she was a bitter and battered daughter. Today she was a Colonel's wife.

She dressed quietly, still alert to the sounds of life in this amiable bachelor's home. There was laughter here, shouts of welcome and friendly banter. No one stalked these halls in menace, barked at her to hurry up and fetch breakfast, condemned her for laziness before the sun had even risen, presented her with an agenda of lonely chores that she would hasten to in a daily effort to avoid confrontation. The mere sound of this home was uplifting, ringing inside her head like the call of a strange new songbird. Normal life happened here, healthy and simple and real.

She was eventually drawn to the window again, and stood there brushing her hair and watching the way his officers began to trickle into the yard. Robert Blaire arrived with his lovely young wife. Francis Stone looked half-asleep as he dismounted in the alley. As if in support of Lauren's poignant remarks a few minutes ago, she noticed how everyone seemed so drawn to Gabriel, this dynamic man who strode into her life and turned it upside down.

What manner of man was he who could crush her best defenses with a mere brush of his hand through her hair? Who was this man who caused her bitter heart to warm at the sight of him shivering in the middle of the night? Why should she stand at the window and feel pity for this scorned soldier, pity mixed with the guilt at having driven him out of his own bed on his first night home in eighteen months?

Apprehension wrapped around her inner calm. She didn't like the look of the woman reflected in the sunny windowpane. Fear etched itself into the graceful lines of the face everyone thought was so beautiful. But it could never be pretty to a girl who was hated by her own father.

Until Gabriel came along. The way his touch made her feel was too exquisite, irresistible to such a shattered spirit. In the carriage house last night, the press of his desire was like the brand of a hot iron that put a new mark on beaten flesh and broken hearts. The way he wanted her was a kind of thrill she found both exciting and utterly terrifying.

Yes, the power this man had over her was the only menace in her life now and he suddenly loomed in her mind like an enormous new threat. He could kill her in that dark and dirty place where she had learned how to live, a place ruled by hate and rage and fear.

She turned from the window and headed out of the room, her footsteps hard and exacting upon these strange new floors. Somehow, she must find a way to survive this marriage, to keep Gabriel away, not let him shake her in the only place where she had strength no matter how ugly that place was. It was all she had and she was determined to keep it, not to let him get so close again.

* * *

"I want you to be the first to know," Robert Blaire announced, looking at Gabriel and actually smiling. Gaiety looked odd on such a sober face. Gabriel studied him more closely.

Polly Blaire was blushing, her soft chestnut locks flowing around the delicate oval face that tilted toward the ground. She was the most demure woman he had ever known, so feminine and shy in her pink-and-white striped gown and matching bonnet.

"Let me guess," Gabriel breathed, snatching up her hand and giving it a kiss despite her timidity. "You're expecting."

"Oh my dear!" Polly gasped and her cheeks burst into flames.

Robert threw back his head and roared with delight. "Not yet, but I'm working on it!"

"Robert!" Polly was appalled, whipped out a fan and began beating it back and forth before her scalded cheeks. A pair of round green eyes glanced at her husband in genuine reproof. But this was the most chagrin she could muster; her spirit was too tender to convey real anger.

"Here . . . look at this." Robert handed Gabriel a folded note.

It was a message from Morrisville much like the one he had just received. Robert's smile returned when Gabriel read the note, his eyebrow raised in happy surprise.

"Congratulations, Lieutenant Colonel," Gabriel awarded, shaking the hand of his faithful second-in-command. With a sly grin, he challenged, "I suppose you think you don't have to salute me anymore, eh?"

"Well, we're equal in rank now and—"

"The hell you are!" Lauren blurted, grabbing a braid out of Gabriel's pocket and flashing it at Robert. "Salute your Colonel, sir!"

Robert did so at once, his hand snapping into a genuinely glad salute. Gabriel could see Robert was proud of their promotions and was about to utter his congratulations when his eye fell upon something in the yard that immediately silenced him.

A woman moved through the back door, stood in the shadows of the porch and watched the boisterous group in the yard as if determining how to approach so many strangers at one time. But it wasn't her discomfiture that stole everyone's attention, it was her almost startling beauty.

She was young but her tall figure lent her a stately air in spite of her youth. The slender curves of her body were draped in a delicate white dress that danced around her slippered feet with every turn of the wind. Jet black hair shone with a blue lustre, unbound except for the white ribbon around her crown, the curling ebony mass cascading down to her waist like a gleaming satin shawl. Sultry eyes, large and thickly lashed, made her innocent glance seem almost glamorous.

Everyone's attention was caught. She was momentarily unable to do anything but issue a nervous little smile, which might have looked timid on any other face but appeared coolly sophisticated when framed by such beauty. Her presence beguiled everyone in the yard; they stood so still and quiet, one would have thought they were suddenly frozen in the cold depths of winter.

"Good Lord, Gabriel," Robert breathed, "who is she?"

"The Davis woman," Francis answered before Gabriel could. "You know, the woman we used in the Swanson mission."

It was completely uncharacteristic of Gabriel to have a woman in his house, especially one who had obviously spent the night here. No, this was not his way. Gabriel was a very private man and a discreet gentleman, careful to tend his needs elsewhere or otherwise engage himself in the proper rituals of courtship.

They were all bemused, looked toward Gabriel for some explanation as to what was going on between him and this beautiful young compatriot.

But Gabriel didn't seem to notice their silent inquiries, just shrugged his shoulders at them and said something everyone heard quite clearly but were strangely unable to comprehend. He started across the yard and they all stood there mutely staring at his back.

"What did he just say?" Lauren asked Francis.

"His wife? Is that what he said?" Francis asked Robert.

"I think he just said that . . . yes." Robert replied soberly even though he was staring at Gabriel's back as if it were the face of God.

Gabriel didn't hear them as he slid into the shadows of the porch, didn't see the way their jaws gaped after him.

He leaned toward Vanessa, within the proximity of her fresh floral scent and took up her hand as if it were more delicate than a rose petal. He bowed low, kissed the soft white skin and murmured, "Do you always rise so radiantly?"

She looked away when he stood up, as if he might not see the glimmer of pleasure his compliment brought. But he did see it, caught her chin in that familiar way of his and gave her face a very thorough review. "How do you feel?"

"Fine," she remarked in a small voice that stopped in her throat when their eyes met.

A memory of last night flashed between them, the man who shivered in the dark and the woman who brought him warmth. The unspoken implications of her gesture made her feel oddly exposed.

"Your friends are staring at us," she said, hoping to change the subject.

"What?"

"Your friends . . . "

"Oh." He finally looked away, glanced over his shoulder at their dumbstruck poses and issued a derisive snort. "Perhaps I was a bit too blunt, eh?"

She couldn't help but laugh at the comment even though one look at the yard made her feel like the most conspicuous creature on earth. "Stunning is a better word."

He grinned, his penetrating gaze turning bright and friendly. "I should get married more often if it'll shut them up so well."

"Gabriel!" she scolded and he laughed in that throaty way of his. She almost didn't notice the deft way his arm slid around her waist. A moment later, she was pressed against him, close enough to feel both the strength and the warmth in his powerful physique. She stiffened at once, tried to ward off the intimacy creeping back into his gaze and the deeper tone of his voice.

"I'll get to them in a moment but first, tell me how your back fares today?"

"It's fine . . . really."

"Tell me the truth." His hand was already searching for thc welt. It was badly swollen, the feel of it making him grimace and growl something in French that she suspected was quite foul. "Francis!" he barked over his shoulder. "Go home and fetch your bag."

"No, really, Gabriel."

Once again he caught her chin, made her look at him and see how suddenly stern and serious he was. "I will not be dissuaded from pampering you, Vanessa, whether you like it or not. Get used to it because I intend to make it a custom."

She would have pushed him away just then, refusing his care, but they had made an agreement last night and she couldn't bring herself to fight with him in public. "Very well," she breathed, putting up a hand that accidentally landed against his naked breast. The feel of his solid muscle was an instant reminder of how much of a man she knew him to be, which she had learned in a barn, in a shocking encounter neither of them could ever forget.

He was aware of the sudden stillness in the hand on his breast, the fleeting glimpse of anxiety in her eyes. The reaction bothered him just then, making him realize how his touch disturbed her, how hard she tried to resist it. Gabriel felt a flash of hurt, remorse at the knowledge that his want of her could only bring her pain.

"Come and meet your new friends" was all he said, striding off the porch and leaving her nothing to do but follow him out into the sun-drenched lawn.

"Yes, you heard me right!" he said to his stricken companions as he reached back and snatched her hand, his voice full of merry mischief. "Meet my new bride."

His words were like a cork being popped out of a bottle. Celebration burst around them in a rush of infectious excitement. Gabriel enjoyed the sight of her being drawn from one person to the next, her hand kissed as often as his back was slapped in praise of his magnificent choice.

"My Lady . . . " Lauren breathed over her hand, holding it a bit too long for Gabriel's approval. He snatched it away and handed it to Robert.

"I'm stunned," the newly promoted Lieutenant Colonel admitted. "Absolutely shocked."

"Isn't this marvelous?" Polly gasped, radiant with pleasure as she gave Vanessa a brief but heartfelt embrace.

"Poor thing," Harvey Broomall said, dropped his pepper plant and brushed the dirt off his hands before clumsily reaching for Vanessa. "Such a lovely *fraulein* to be caught in the fangs of this Bourbon snake!"

"She's absolutely beautiful," Este Broomall decided, still holding her basket of bread when she hugged Vanessa.

"Oh Patrick! The very saints be praised to have found a mate for him at last!" Dierdre Sullivan cried as she flounced over the wall with more energy than her children. "God love you, lass!"

"I can see why he kept you so well hidden," Patrick Sullivan boldly flattered in his thick Irish brogue. "But no corner of earth could be dark enough to hide such radiance—"

"Never mind charming her the way you charm me, Patrick!" Dierdre scolded in the best of humor, then shooed him away. "Go on and tell the neighbors! Let our work rest a day! The Lord's smiling on us this morn, He is! He's brought Gabriel home safe and him with a bride no less! Go on . . . hurry . . . and may everyone bring their pantry's best!"

Within an hour, the newlyweds of Seventh Street were hosting their first party as word spread and neighbors came to pay their respects to the hero and his bride.

The merry rush of people overwhelmed her at first, so many kisses and embraces and exuberant welcomes, as if she were some kind of celebrity. It felt awkward to be the center of attention, showered with praise and affection. This was not like anything she had experienced before. They'd had few guests on the farm in Millbridge, and the excitement of entertaining friends was entirely new to her.

Gabriel could hardly take his eyes off her as he watched this new side of her emerge. She was kind and attentive to everyone who approached her, so genuinely gracious she won instant approval from everyone. To be so remarkably beautiful, yet so completely unpretentious were qualities that impressed them all. Only he knew the source of such profound humility, the kind one learned beneath a heavy and hurting hand. Yes, there was a reason for the gratitude in her gestures, the thanks of the undeserving in her comments.

Gabriel was touched with compassion for her. Of course she'd feel undeserving. This woman had been crushed by the hand of her own father, denied the most basic form of trust in a human life. That of parent and child.

It was the only sorry note in this gay day. By the end of it, she was flitting around like a lovely butterfly, bantering here, serving there, happily accepting a dozen invitations to tea and dinner and trips to market. She seemed almost dazed by it all, by this exciting new life, this world where her only anxiety would be a choice of dress for the day. Her cheeks were flushed, her eyes sparkling and animated, her whole complexion seeming to shine with radiance.

The sight of her was captivating to him, making him seek her out the moment he bolted the doors after the last guest.

She was in the kitchen with Martina, both of them giggling like schoolgirls as they whispered about a few of the neighbors. He didn't announce himself, just leaned against the door frame and lit a taper, content to smoke it and admire this dazzlingly complicated young woman of his. While thinking herself unobserved, Vanessa bent over the warming kettles on the fire and presented him with an exceptional view of her rump. He enjoyed it immensely until Martina saw him and gave him away with a naughty giggle.

Vanessa stood up, hurriedly straightened her gown and blew a lock of hair out of her eyes. "Was that the last of them?"

He nodded and she wondered at the thoughts behind the tender amusement on his face, how boldly yet how warmly he admired her from across the room. But he gave no explanation for his mood, just dragged on his taper and let the smoke rise before him like the gossamer flutter of a drape on a window. He looked the part of a master spy just then, cloaked in his mysterious mood and the shadowy kitchen doorway, his secretive eyes watching her through a haze of smoke. His dark crimson blouse and snug-fitting black britches seemed appropriate attire.

"I saved a tray for you, Gabriel," Martina piped up. She received a look from him that calmly but pointedly communicated his need for a private moment with his wife. "Yes . . . well . . . it's on the top shelf of the pie keeper," she said airily, then promptly vanished through the dining room door.

Vanessa wiped her hands on her apron and went for the tray.

"I'll fetch it," he said and finally eased off the door frame. "You should do as Francis advised and stop lifting these heavy trays." He took out the tray and set it aside solely to prevent her from doing it.

"He's being overcautious—"

"And obedient to his employer."

She looked up at him, a silent question in her eyes.

He came upon her then, seeming unusually tall in such a tiny room as he urged her to turn around.

"What are you doing—"

"Taking this off," he said. He untied her apron and tossed it aside. "That's better." She was turned around and met with a dashing smile. "You are the mistress of my house, Madame St. Claire, not my housekeeper. Let Martina do the work."

"But what will I do with myself?"

"From the sounds of it, your schedule is quite full."

She blushed as if ashamed to have been caught having fun today and making so many wonderful plans.

He found her modesty quite fetching. "You were a smashing success today."

"I was?" she asked shyly, her eyes fixed on the floor, her fingers nervously twirling the signet ring on her left hand.

"Indeed. And I was delighted at your . . . er . . . performance with me. I'm grateful for it, Vanessa. Not only did you spare my pride but you left everyone with the impression that we're quite smitten. That was most generous of you." Was it just a performance? he seemed to be asking in the silence following the comment.

She swallowed hard, didn't want to admit aloud that touching him affectionately had been unnervingly easy today. "I've always been a good actress."

"Yes," he agreed. "Only the best can fool me."

He moved away then and she had the feeling his softer mood had just been destroyed. Perhaps she shouldn't have said something so harsh. After all, he was a man, his pride was as vulnerable as any other man's.

She decided to busy herself with undraping his tray rather than say anything else offensive. He reached around and stopped her fidgeting hands.

"It doesn't matter," he whispered, his voice deep and thoughtful as he smoothed her hands in his own, as if to work out the nervousness that made them shake. "You honored me and so I'll honor you by insisting you follow doctor's orders for a night of good rest after a long soak in a hot bath."

This instantly cheered her. The mere prospect delighted her. "I would like that!"

"Would you now?"

She giggled at his teasing tone, unable to resist his playful side, then let out a whoop of surprise to suddenly find herself swept up in his arms.

"Don't . . . put me down."

"Martina! Fetch some hot water to my chamber and see my lady bathed, will you?"

Martina smiled blissfully as they passed her in the hall. "At once, Gabe."

"But the dishes!" Vanessa fussed.

"Just throw them away and we'll buy new ones in the morning!" Gabriel quipped, a true bachelor. Both women laughed as he pompously carried her upstairs.

She was ceremoniously placed on the center of his bed. "And don't try helping with the buckets," he warned, wagging his finger at her. She laughed, swatted it away. "Because Tina is about to get the same instructions about your care that Francis received earlier."

"Which are?"

"None of your business." He showed himself to the door, issued her a charming smile, then promptly disappeared.

Vanessa was like a woman caught in a whirlwind, spinning into a new life full of exciting activities and wonderful friends with the sudden prestige affixed to her as the wife of Colonel Gabriel St. Claire. There were dinner parties to attend or hostess, mid-day teas with neighborhood ladies, extravagant shopping trips financed by her generous husband, long and intimate conversations with her new best friend, Polly Blaire. She sometimes felt like an old rag doll that someone had chosen to dress like a queen, once discarded and now sought as if she had unknowingly become special.

Letters to Malinda Borden and Joshua Stone were filled with new people, new places, new things to do. By the time Gabriel's leave was drawing to a close, Philadelphia began to feel like home, from the constant spin of carriage wheels down Seventh Street to the never-ending talk of invasion, to Harvey Broomall's frequent greeting over the backyard fence, "Hey, Frenchie!"

She loved it here. Who wouldn't? Had she known

married life could so elevate her standard of living, she might have tried this a long time ago.

It was Gabriel's doing. He spoiled her beyond reason. Her every need was instantly fulfilled despite her protests. There was a new vanity in their bedchamber that he promptly filled with every kind of notion, perfume, mirror, brush, hair ribbon, aigrette and pin he could find. She had a chest of drawers filled with the most lavish under things a lady could want. Gowns of every pattern and color filled the closet with bonnets and slippers to match. She could wear a different nightdress every night for a month.

He was impossibly big-hearted and after just a few short weeks in his company, she knew this was a truly genuine man. The passage of days showed many sides of him: anger, anxiety, gaiety, repose; but there did not seem to be even a breath of violence in his nature. He was always the perfect gentleman, forever concerned by her slightest displeasure. Because their sleeping arrangement made her uncomfortable, he never came into the chamber until after she was asleep and was gone before she woke. The only evidence that he'd slept there was the warmth his body sometimes left in the feather bed beside her. In every possible way, he substituted tenderness where her life had only known pain.

As far as she could tell, Gabriel St. Claire had only two dark spots on the dynamic sheen of his personality. One concerned his twin brother, Michael. Unless Gabriel mentioned it first, the circumstances surrounding Michael's death were never spoken about. It was a sacred subject. Somewhere beneath all those magnanimous layers of his character, Gabriel hid a grief so profound that it made Martina's eyes tear just to mention it.

Vanessa learned this soon after becoming a member of his home when a search for a lost piece of silver found her and Martina in the attic. Propped against a wall in a corner was a giant portrait of two young boys, about the age of twelve, with thick shocks of auburn hair and deep blue eyes. They were beautifully dressed in matching velvet suits, standing alongside a gilded chair behind which a vista of the vineyards was painted. No matter how discerning was her eye, the boys were so identical Vanessa couldn't tell one from the other.

"It's uncanny," she remarked to Martina. "They're the image of one another!"

"Gabriel claims he's the one on the left," Martina said.

Vanessa studied this boy, momentarily enchanted by the youthfulness of the face she knew only as a man's. "But why has he discarded this painting?"

Martina looked furtively at the attic door, as if afraid someone might catch her speaking about this. Her voice softened as she explained, "He can't bear to look at it, is why. His parents gave it to him as a gift, but it upset him so terribly we immediately took it down and brought it up here." Something sad and secretive flashed through her eyes as she regarded the portrait for a long moment.

"Gabriel claims he doesn't need a painted likeness of his brother. Whenever he wants to see his twin, he just looks in the mirror." Martina shivered just then, as if spooked by this concept. "He's never gotten over it and I don't think he ever will. He blames himself, you see, because of the game they always played."

"Game?"

"They traded places."

"What do you mean?"

"You know . . . pretended one was the other." She glanced nervously at the door just then, giving Vanessa the impression she was revealing a closely guarded secret. "They were playing their game with Collette, a woman Gabriel was betrothed to marry. That's how Michael got killed. Why else do you think Gabriel has such a penchant for honor?"

"I don't understand."

"Michael loved her, not Gabriel . . . so they did what they always did . . . traded places."

"Do you mean . . ."

Martina nodded briskly, put a finger to her lips and whispered quickly, "But Michael bedded the girl and she conceived. That's how they got caught!" Martina rushed to the attic door, looked down the ladder to be certain no one was standing below. "Collette's father was outraged," she continued, "in a drunken fit the day he came to the St. Claire estate to confront Gabriel, whom he thought was the culprit. But in those last moments of his life, Michael told the truth, not by words, but by jumping in front of Gabriel when the gun went off."

"How awful," was all Vanessa could say. She felt like a person who had just stumbled into a tomb not meant to be disturbed. She could only shake her head at these tragic circumstances. "But this game of theirs . . . it sounds so . . . so impossible!"

"You wouldn't think so if you saw Gabriel mimic Michael. He can mimic his twin down to the tiniest nuances. To this day, Gabriel can show you Michael any time you want to see him . . . down to the little hitch in his walk! It's chilling! Absolutely terrifying! Jon and I watched him one night and were speechless afterward. It's the most uncanny mimicry I've ever seen."

They were both sniffling when they left the attic, the lost silver forgotten beside this tragic misfortune that would forever haunt the heart of the master of this house.

The other dark spot on Gabriel's soul was a newer one. It concerned her father. She would never forget the moment when Gabriel summoned her into the parlor for a private word, something he'd never done before. He was sitting in his favorite chair, the only one big enough to cradle his brawny figure. He had a letter in his hand, ever so slowly tapping it against his thigh with a look of perfect calm on his face.

"Why have you written this?" he asked her, his voice very soft as he lifted the unsent note to her sire.

She gulped, suddenly feeling like a disobedient schoolgirl, ashamed of having caused her happy benefactor any displeasure. Although his expression was very still and relaxed, his gaze was cool and penetrating as he waited for her answer.

"I . . . er . . . " she stammered, "felt compelled to inquire as to his welfare . . . to tell him where I am and—"

"I've already told him this. He is aware of your marriage to me."

She was surprised to hear this.

"He's also aware that if I ever catch him within the confines of this city, he'll die in his footsteps."

The deadly tone of his voice sent a chill racing up her spine. She said nothing, just stood there staring at him in a kind of dumbstruck stupor. It wasn't the threat he made as much as the unexpected passion behind the words.

"I can't stop your hand, Vanessa, but I implore you to cease any form of communication with him."

"But he's my father . . . " she gasped.

Gabriel's eyes turned the color of a night so dark she swore only hell could exist under such an ominous sky. Never before had she seen such a menacing look on his face, nor heard the serpent-like hiss in his voice when he said, "He is not a father because he is not a man. He is an *animal!*"

Her feet went cold, as if they were frozen to the floor. Only a witless fool could overlook the seriousness of the warning he launched across the room just then.

"If you leave me with no other recourse, I'll get rid of him just to keep you from having any further connection with him." He didn't say how he'd be rid of her father, which only made his plans sound more menacing. "Does this convince you of how powerful my feelings are on this particular subject, or should I explain what it does to a man to watch his woman being smothered to death in a farmer's field?"

"Stop it . . . "

He bit his tongue, silenced himself with the most supreme effort. "Very well. Enough said. Now what will you have me do with this letter?"

She fetched it from him at once, as if it were precious, then looked at the face of it, at her careful and exact penmanship, and suddenly saw the farce of it all. This was not a real letter, the kind a newly married daughter would write to her former home, full of endearments and reassurances about how well she was faring, meant to brighten the heart of a parent who cared.

Not her parent.

Something inside her cracked just then, the place where she still yearned for her father's love, for some brighter day when he might finally put down the whip and pick up the little girl who never stopped trying to win his heart.

It would never be. She knew it now like never before and the realization tore through her heart like a cold, cruel blade.

She burst into tears, right there in front of him, buried her face in the letter as if it might lend her some reprieve from this humiliating outburst.

He reached for her in an instant, let her crumple to the floor between his spread thighs, those mighty muscles like a pillow of stone unable to absorb the sudden flood of tears. "What is it? Why are you crying? Tell me so I can help you . . . "

"It'll never be . . . a real letter . . . " she remembered choking aloud, caring not the least bit what she divulged. What did it matter? She was already a shattered mess. How much worse could he think of her anyway?

"Is that what you want . . . to write a real letter to a real father?"

"Yes!"

"Then save it. Put it away somewhere . . . so it might remind you of how honorable you remain in the face of his complete disgrace."

The name of Fred Davis was never again mentioned in the house, nor was the incident about the letter. It was forgotten, dismissed, swallowed in too many days of too many happier pursuits.

She was a woman living a delightful dream, her spirit soaring like a trapped melody set suddenly free, creating lilting music she hardly knew herself capable of. Never before had she known such compelling feelings of hope and promise. For the first time in her life, tomorrow was something to look forward to. Such a lighthearted bliss was unknown to one so heavily burdened by life's misfortunes and she rarely knew a moment of disquiet until the day her husband left for Morrisville.

Gabriel answered his summons to duty and left the city along with his energetic inner circle of officer-friends. The house in the middle of Seventh Street fell conspicuously quiet, subdued, as if some of the life had been drained out of it. Gabriel's leave was almost over. The war would soon reclaim him and she would be left alone here, in this new life, for an indefinite period of time.

Forever, if his life was lost.

This thought did not inspire good feelings in her. In fact, it bloomed into outright anxiety for every day he was gone. What if he was killed? What would become of her? And what about the invasion, now imminent and causing large sections of the city to be abandoned in the wake of fleeing Whigs? Into whose care would she be placed during such a dangerous time?

Ever so gradually, Vanessa began to feel unsettled again, afraid, the way she had felt while living with her father on the farm, always expecting disaster around the next corner. Even more disturbing was how precious this home in Philadelphia had become in so short a time.

The only way to quiet her brain was by doing mechanical tasks. On his first day gone, she dusted and polished every leather-bound volume in his library. On the second, she busied herself with shining every piece of silver in the house. On the third, she went to market with Polly where they shared their private woes while pretending to care about their household purchases. The men were due home today, by mid-afternoon, and they were both settled on the porch swing by precisely three o'clock.

Lauren was the first to appear, trotting up to the back gate and tethering his mount in the alley. Vanessa immediately noticed the lack of energy in his gait as he came up the walk. He gave a brisk greeting, found a seat on the opposite swing and swiped off his hat. "Gabe's furious."

"Why?" she and Polly both asked at the same time.

"Moylan!" Lauren breathed, rolled his eyes at the sky and said with a disgusted sigh, "Last I saw of Gabe he was nose to nose with Moylan . . . mad enough to pump him full of lead."

"Oh dear," Polly sighed, abruptly fanning herself and giving Vanessa a secret frown. "Is Robert in the same poor state?"

"We all are!" Lauren exclaimed with his usual exuberance. "Congress allowed Washington to reorganize his mounted troops into what will eventually become a new branch of the army, a military intelligence unit that he plans to call the Secret Service. Our name is now the Fourth Continental Light Dragoon with a new headquarters Commander who is entirely intimidated by Gabriel's reputation. Colonels Moylan and St. Claire do not get along, which is a dangerous animosity between a headquarters and combat Commander."

Stephen Moylan, although a devoted Patriot, was also

extremely political, Lauren explained. He had a showy thirst for power. It was no secret Washington planned to form a new army intelligence department within the year and ambitious officers were already sparring for the top commands. Lauren felt certain Benjamin Tallmadge would head the new department, a man of considerable expertise in military espionage and a highly regarded personal friend of Gabriel's. Tallmadge had a sterling reputation in the management of reconnaissance companies and had been very successful in keeping these shadowy units acting in unison.

Much to Moylan's distress, there was no doubt as to the man Tallmadge wanted as his counterpart in the field, the combat reconnaissance officer who was steadily rewriting the handbook on effective intelligence tactics.

Gabriel St. Claire was more than qualified for the post.

Vanessa was glad for this recognition because no one deserved it more than Gabriel, especially in light of what she'd overheard her first morning in Philadelphia. His connection to the Archangel was obviously a well-kept but thorny secret, and she hoped Tallmadge's regard would help soothe those places where he ached for personal acknowledgment.

But the more Lauren talked, the more skeptical she became. "Moylan's trying to crush him under a load of new procedures that won't do us any good except add to my paperwork duties. He's doing this to control the number of Gabe's victories in the field . . . make him look bad . . . slow him down. Worse, he's saddled our Company with twenty-eight new recruits who don't know the difference between a bayonet and a shoehorn!"

Benny Cooke thundered into the yard just then, leaping the wall and letting his horse charge up to the back porch without the slightest regard for the torn turf he left in his wake. Gabriel's belongings were dumped on the stoop, his personal equipment rolling to a halt against the back door.

Benny yanked on his hat brim in a kind of clumsy courtesy to the ladies and spluttered at Lauren, "You better git his lawyer papers packed up like he said because he's in a real bad way. And he told me to tell you not to worry the missus about this assignment."

One look at the concern on Vanessa's face told Benny he was already too late.

"He's gonna slit yer throat, Lauren!"

"For what? I didn't say anything!"

"If I were you, I'd git my tail outa sight before he gits here and finds out you worried her!" Benny warned in the over-inflated tone he used whenever he was on Gabriel's private business. "This ain't a day to be aggravating him. No sir! Last I seen, he was about to skewer that blockhead Moylan with his bayonet! Bunch a good-for-nothin' she-rabbits, those blamed officers . . . er . . . pardon me ladies. Now go on and fetch those papers, then get outa here lickety-split! Go on! Git!"

Despite his lowly rank, Benny had a way of imposing obedience in officers twice his rank. When he barked, they moved. Like Lauren, who turned to the bossy Sergeant. "You're just sore because Gabe put you in charge of those half-naked, half-dead recruits," he said spitefully even though he was already hurrying into the house.

"Gabe said to tell you he'll be home in a while . . . he's going to the Blue Dolphin to cool off first." With that, Benny reared his horse and galloped through the yard leaving a second trail of muddy pits in the lawn before he leaped into the alley and thundered away.

Robert arrived next, abruptly collected his wife and rode off without once forcing a smile onto the black mask of his face. Dinner was a quiet affair; Vanessa and Tina were left alone with their mounting anxieties when Jonnie chose to join Gabriel at the Blue Dolphin instead. Hours passed with no sign of either man. They stitched, ran to the window every time a rider came down the street, made several attempts to talk about something else but finally gave up to sit in silence until bedtime.

Vanessa was abed with a book when a pair of riders clattered through the cobbled alley and came to a halt beside the carriage house. Doors opened and slammed shut. From the basement, she heard Gabriel speak to Jonnie in short, crisp syllables. The thud of his heavy boots against the stairs told her his anger had not been completely consumed in the potent Fish House Punch so famously served at the Blue Dolphin.

Vanessa rose, draped her scanty summer gown in a flowing gold silk robe with the intention of searching him out. Much to her surprise, he had the same idea, knocked once on the door to announce himself and came into the chamber.

"I saw the light," he said simply and shut the door behind him.

What a magnificent sight he was in his Colonel's regalia, both shoulders dripping with golden braid, the breast of his dark blue waistcoat glinting with medals of valor. His weapons of war were handsomely polished yet deadly, like the ornate sword sheath that swayed against his leg when he walked.

It was rare for him to come to their chamber when she was still awake, but she refused to be concerned about that now. He was a soldier whose cause she shared, one in need of good companionship, not a skittish female.

He went straight to his bureau, barely a break in his stride or a glance in her direction as he snatched off his black leather gauntlets and tossed them aside. The waistcoat came off next, its crimson lapels and gleaming epaulets flashing in the shadows as it landed across the bed. It was only then that he took notice of the spun gold vision standing beside their candlelit butler.

He leaned on the bureau, his tired eyes scanning her every elegantly dressed inch. Although she looked worried, there was a streak of blue light dancing magnificently down the length of her pitch black hair. "The mere sight of you eases me, my beauty," he sighed as he snapped open the buckle of his saber and took it off while crossing the room.

"Did it go so badly in Morrisville?" she asked sweetly, not wanting to let on how much Lauren had told her. She poured him a drink, watched him settle into his favorite chair and motion for her to join him on the ottoman at his feet.

He wanted to talk.

A sense of things ominous settled over her as she took the seat.

For a long moment, his attention remained pinned to the fluid in his goblet, his dark brow creased with concern. Long legs were spread open, elbows balanced on his knees, the pose reflecting more worry than she had ever seen in him before. It made her own fears grow with a shuddering poignancy.

Finally, he looked up, his dark gaze taking in the soft amethyst lustre of her eyes. "If I obey Moylan, the lot of us will end up in the Continental Cemetery. I'm going to do this my way and risk insubordination."

She swallowed the anxiety rising in her throat. "You know what's best for your company, Gabriel. I know you won't jeopardize your men because of Moylan."

"Of course not," he said quickly, as if the decision had just now been made in his mind. "I intend to accomplish this mission and get us a victory in New York. It's imperative we prevail during this campaign because the French are seriously considering aligning themselves with us. The only thing holding them back is our lack of military accomplishment."

"Can you do it?"

"I think so."

"When do you leave?"

"Tomorrow morning."

She was startled, looked at him and breathed, "Tomorrow?"

Although he could hardly believe his eyes, there was no mistaking the disappointment on her face just then. The distasteful residue of the last three days vanished. He leaned forward, cupped a soft cheek in his hand and asked, "Have you become so attached to me, madam?"

Her eyes dropped in embarrassment. "You have been more than kind . . . and I'll miss your conversation."

"And I yours . . . "

For the first time in weeks, he allowed himself to notice the perfection of her beauty, the exact arch of her brow, the subtle slope of her nose, the way her tempting pink mouth curled up at the edges. The sight of her brought a quickening in his loins. He was torturing himself but it didn't matter tonight. To be lost inside this titillating woman was exactly what he needed.

"Will you be gone long?" she asked, not wanting to feel so breathless and nervous while under his close scrutiny.

"Until the winter."

"Oh," she said lamely, turned her face out of his hand and decided to fetch a cup of bourbon. The drink might help maintain her courage. "By then, the British will have invaded the city."

"You'll be safely away long before then," he said confidently.

She returned to the ottoman, tried to mask her concern in a casual glance at the fluid in her cup. "Where will you send me?"

"If I'm successful in New York, my field headquarters will be far enough behind enemy lines to permit family visitation. Washington allows this . . . although I hear he may do away with the habit next campaign . . . unless Martha talks him out of it. You and Polly will be brought to us in New York as soon as safety permits."

Vanessa hadn't thought of this option and was delighted with it. She'd never been to New York. The prospect was appealing enough to bring a smile to her anxious face. "I'll be praying for your success."

He chuckled, sat back in his chair and relaxed into the seat cushion. The sprawled pose seemed to pronounce every masculine angle of his body. Her glance strayed over him, from his wide shoulders to his narrow hips, to the place where his virility strained against the seams of his stark white britches. It seemed hard to believe that such a vital man could possibly fall into the black jaws of death.

"But if this doesn't go as I plan," he was saying, "you'll be sent to Valley Forge and reside with my parents. They've been in France all summer, but they'll return in early August. A letter announcing you already awaits them."

"Oh." She secretly worried about meeting his family because of the unusual circumstances of their marriage. "Will they be surprised to hear of our marriage?"

"Astonished, I'm sure."

"Have you told them the truth about it?"

He didn't answer, just looked at her and shook his head.

"I'd rather go to New York—"

"And I'd rather see you in Valley Forge because I'm afraid you'll plunge your lovely fingers into my war business in New York."

"I wouldn't think of it!" she said, then scowled at his devious laugh.

"You're an enchanting liar, my beauty."

"Gabriel . . . "

"Alright then, no arguments on my last night home," he said, giving her a playful wink. She didn't think it was funny, the double meaning in his joke, that he could die and this would indeed be his last night with her.

Her heart felt suddenly heavy in her breast. Like Martina,

she wished this war was over, that they could be rid of the dark cloud of its menace, the subtle threat of death that always seemed to be hanging over them.

"Have it your way, Gabriel," she said and kept her voice light only by force of will. "I've been an obedient wife thus far and I'll not ruin my reputation by fighting with you before you go off to battle."

He chuckled but there wasn't as much humor in it, as if her reminder of where he was headed tomorrow struck a morbid note somewhere in his spirit. "No . . . you wouldn't want to do that, would you?" He leaned forward, caught her chin between his fingers and lifted her face to where she could see the sudden seriousness in his eyes. "While I'm gone, promise me you'll not venture to Millbridge . . . or try to contact your father."

"No . . . I won't."

"And do as Jonnie says, eh? He's been told how to care for you in my absence and I want you to heed him the way you heed me. In the event of disaster, he'll know what to do."

"Disaster? Don't say such things . . . "

"I'm not trying to frighten you . . . just reassure you that your future is certain."

"I don't want to talk about it," she said, pushing his hand away. She wanted to run from the lump of fear that jammed into her throat. But he wouldn't have it, put his glass down and this time reached for her with both hands. Gently but firmly, he framed her face in those mighty palms of his and watched the confusion of emotion that played in her eyes like a frantic melody. His closeness only made her feel worse, reminded her of how much she denied him in the face of his constant kindness. It made her feel wicked and cruel, completely ungrateful toward this dynamic man who somehow managed to turn her violent life into a fairy tale. If he died, she would carry the guilt of her poor behavior for the rest of her life.

As if she hadn't enough to regret already.

"We must talk about it, *chérie,*" he said quietly, his vision calm and penetrating as it wandered across every line of her face. "This is why I came to you tonight . . . to tell you not to fear if the worst should happen."

She winced, then said in a whisper, "Nothing bad will happen, Gabriel. You're the best . . . you can't fail."

She meant it. In spite of her best defenses, Gabriel St. Claire managed to rise into those superior ranks of the few men Vanessa could ever bring herself to respect. Noblemen like William Penn, statesmen like John Jay, brave military men like Washington, all men who lived and fought for a higher cause. This young and valiant Colonel stood easily among those prominent figures, a man of honor, courage, strength, commitment. Yet tonight he loomed even greater. Here he sat, on the eve of a battle he would wage for everyone else's freedom after having surrendered his own to an insignificant farm girl.

For honor's sake.

Gabriel was taking the glass from her trembling hand, lifting her off the ottoman and onto his lap where his strong and capable arms could envelop her in a comfort she hardly deserved. "Come now . . . it's important for me to tell you these things . . . so I might go without the burden of it on my mind."

She felt so frail and vulnerable just then, shaking in terror at the thought his shelter might be stolen away.

"You have nothing to fear . . . it's all been arranged for you. This will be your house and your possessions . . . enough money to finance the rest of your life in complete comfort."

She felt so guilty just then it made her shudder. Gabriel mistook the sensation and tightened his arms around her as if wanting to calm a frightened child.

"I don't deserve this . . . " she muttered into his blouse.

"I think you do."

"What you've already given me is enough . . . I've been so happy here—"

"I know you have," he said softly as his fingers stroked through her long and silky locks. "And I'm delighted to see it . . . to watch you blossom in a good and healthy way. So let's not be morbid together tonight, eh? A soldier's wife should be brave and confident . . . as he must be."

She looked at him then, those great lavender eyes rising into the candlelight like a pair of glittering moons. She looked so beautiful just then, her skin bathed in the soft golden light, her expression so innocent and imploring. He would remember this view of her, recall her beauty to comfort himself while caught in the ugly talons of war. "You're right . . . I'm acting childish . . . shouldn't send you away with such a pitiful memory of me."

"No, you shouldn't," he agreed, still reveling in her beauty, in an unspoken desire to carry a far different remembrance of her into battle. To be with her tonight, reap her richest blessings, sip from this sweetest nectar only known to him once before, would be the finest farewell she could render.

He couldn't hide such compelling thoughts, keep the darkness of desire from his eyes, the long-suppressed yearning that crept across every stoic angle of his face. She saw it, her whole body falling still on his lap.

He wanted her tonight and no man on earth deserved to have his way more than this one.

A raw and naked fear prickled up her spine at the idea of submitting to a man. But this one was different. He'd always been different, from the very start. He made her feel things, want things, she shouldn't dare to consider.

Like now, when she realized her will to deny him was lost, buried under layers of guilt, remorse, regret. As if seeing herself from some distant place, she watched her own hand rise to his face, wildly trembling fingers touching his face ever so lightly.

It was her permission.

And he saw it.

"Vanessa," he whispered in utter disbelief, blinked down at her as if seeing someone else, some total stranger. "Don't play with me . . . "

"I'm not . . . " she whispered as boldly as her courage would allow.

A rush of words fled his lips just then, deep and fierce and fluent, but she didn't understand. He'd spoken in French. With a shake of his head, he corrected himself, lifted her in his arms and brought her face within a scant inch of his own as he breathed, "Is this what you want . . . to ease me?"

She swallowed hard, a virginal gesture of timidity that seemed in direct contradiction to the sensual feelings in her body. Confused and afraid, she just nodded her head and said, "Be gentle with me."

These scant words of permission drew out the hunger he had been repressing for so long, his touch sudden and impassioned as he showered her face with a rush of caresses. The taste of her, feel of her, thrilled him, immediately launched him into a place too far away from where he could remember the perils he would face tomorrow. None of that mattered now, not in the face of this unexpected benevolence of hers. Like a man sinking into a deep pit of temporary madness, he slid his mouth over hers and kissed her with a passion so fierce, so genuine, it sent flames of heat into every hidden crevice of her body.

She gasped, startled at her own reaction, at how brilliantly his spark ignited the flames of her own desire. Like that night in the barn, her mind rebelled furiously while her body responded and somewhere between those shocking extremes she was left to melt in the belly of the sweetest fire. Gabriel's passion consumed her until she felt utterly stripped of will, unable to do anything but submit to what he wanted, to the delicious way that he took possession of everything.

It all began to run together, as if it was some kind of semiconscious state of half-sleep and half-awareness, the fury of their physical attraction seeming to envelop the world in a misty, sensual fog.

They were on the bed, his body sliding over hers, pinning her down and ravishing her everywhere he touched. Pleasure rose from places so deeply hidden she never knew they existed, only knew this man had a way of finding them and exposing them and worshipping them with his hands and his lips and his body until she felt totally and utterly loved.

Once again, she was at the mercy of a man but not through the fury of his fists. Oh no. This man commanded her through her own pleasure, drew out of her the most spectacular physical sensations she'd ever experienced. And all the while, her hands were unable to keep away from the glory of him, from his fallen hair to the tight lines of his face and the mighty sculpture of muscle in his every curve. She could not keep away from him, from the fire he stoked in her body, the way he made her world consist of nothing but a swirling vision of sensual delights.

She was lost in him now, only vaguely aware of how frantically they were undressing each other. The barest whisper of timidity was all she felt just before her nakedness and his met and entwined, her shyness immediately swallowed by the pure pleasure that rippled through them in that moment.

It was instinct that opened her body to him, allowed him to finally claim his skittish bride. She could hear the breath catch in his throat as they joined, wholly and completely, so close she could feel every tremble in his body, every thud of his heart. How gentle and adoring he turned just then, his furious kiss now deliciously soft, his panted words rushing through her mind like a hot August wind.

"You are my paradise . . . but always so far away."

She twisted under him, whimpering against the sudden ache his fullness made her feel. But it wasn't pain. It was a strange throbbing pressure that grew with each slow and gentle pulse of his hips against hers. Every motion of his made it grow larger and larger until her blood began to race through her veins. In a moment of genuine fear, she gripped him tight, held him still.

"I'm frightened!"

"Don't be . . . not now . . . you deserve this . . . to burn from love, not hate."

Is that what this was? Love? Could any man desire a woman this much and not love her?

He kept moving, every stroke of his making her body feel more and more full. Too full. She could hardly breathe, think, reason. What was happening to her? Why did she feel so out of control, so confused in this blinding rush of physical sensations that were far beyond any she had ever imagined.

She panicked, pushed against him with both hands. "Stop!"

"Vanessa, please—"

"I want you to stop!" She twisted, tried to get away from him but he caught her hands, held them down, his grip firm and heavy.

"I can't, for God's sake . . . it's too late."

Panic wrenched a cry from her lips as she felt some strange inner limit being suddenly, horrifyingly crossed. Her whole body seemed to lift under him, pin itself to the cause of this exquisite pain, this unbearable intensity of sensation that made her shudder so violently she thought her very flesh would split. For the longest moment she could do nothing but hang there in his arms, staring at him in a kind of awestruck wonder, unable to understand what was happening to her.

She had never seen such an expression on a man's face

as the one that loomed above her now. It was pure rapture, so poignant and rich with satisfaction she felt as if she could see the movement of his very soul in the dark sapphire glint of his eyes. They saw all of her in that moment, the wild confusion and the rampaging lust, the unholy wickedness of it and the sacred delight. There she was, caught between heaven and hell, and he was enjoying it.

Fiend!

She should have known better than to trust a man, especially this one whose weapons were the cruelest of all. He would turn her against herself! Yes! It was the same war as before, with her father, just a whole new tactic. As the fires within her finally ebbed, her senses returned with a furious clarity. If he wasn't holding her hands just then, she would have slit his throat.

But then his face dropped away, fell against her neck, all his motion freezing into a moment of utter stillness just before she felt the same rattling shudder course through his body the way it had just rushed through her own. His arms folded around her, held her very tight, very close, until he finally fell still again.

She didn't dare move, just lay there listening as they gasped for air as if they'd just run from one side of the city to the other. She could not remember a moment in her life when she felt so completely disgusted with herself, so totally ashamed for having let this happen. Like a sacrificial lamb she'd come to him, offered herself in payment of her debts to him, then let him take such a sordid advantage of her.

"You took advantage of me!" she blurted angrily.

"What?" His head snapped up, a tumble of hair falling around his face, framing its sweaty contours in a wild rush. "Are you angry at me?" Auburn brows slid together above the rigid line of his nose. He didn't understand, which only made her feel more confused. "Tell me—"

"You had no right to do that!"

"But you gave me permission," he began in defense of himself until a look of sudden understanding made him fall quiet, his gaze momentarily softening. "Oh . . . well I . . . er . . . wanted to waken you. Perhaps I shouldn't have—"

"No you should not have!"

He moved away then, slowly and carefully, realizing the acute delicacy of the moment. "Forgive me," was all he said, watching her closely.

She looked away, struggled to catch her breath, to gather the wits that were quickly unraveling from somewhere inside her stricken spirit. Tears rushed into her eyes, but she didn't want them to flow, to let him see how suddenly bewildered she was to realize the truth of what happened on this bed to the battered girl who had just become the Colonel's woman.

He had showed her the miracle of ecstasy. He wasn't trying to hurt her at all!

What was wrong with her? How could she possibly manage to twist an act of love into a rite of torment?

A sob flew out of her throat with such force it choked her, made her cover her face in shame and confusion as she fell onto the coverlet. She wept like a gushing stream, the whole bed quivering under her as she spilled her blackest grief into the pure white sheets of her marriage bed.

Gabriel was there, stretching out beside her, a protective arm falling across her trembling back. "It's alright . . . you have every right to hate me . . . I shouldn't have done that . . . you're too tender yet."

His apologies only made her feel worse. It wasn't his fault at all. Even in the peak of a man's ecstasy, he had been completely gentle. What unraveled her wits was her own response to him and her absurd inability to accept it. "Oh! Why don't you just leave me be!"

She wanted her mother, Danny, anyone but this sorcerer of goodness who deserved exactly what she was too damaged to give.

Love.

Gabriel obeyed her wishes, moved away, to his own side of the bed, feeling too clumsy and inept to bring comfort to this fragile creature at such a delicate moment in her life. He just lay there, alone, listening to her broken sobs, wondering how such a blissful union could possibly end like this.

He finally snuffed the lamp. There was nothing he could do but let her cry herself to sleep. For a long time he lay there in the dark as her fitful tears slowly dwindled into a soft, sad lullaby. What a sorry farewell this was. Even worse was his last wakeful thought.

This marriage was a disaster.

The first light of day came too quickly. Vanessa was only half-awake when she heard the sound of her husband's voice speaking to Jonnie just outside the door of their chamber.

"Let her sleep . . . and don't let her out of your sight, Jon . . . stay near her."

"I will, Gabe . . . now stop worrying about her. She'll be fine! Just concentrate on staying alive up there."

Gabriel was leaving.

She shook herself awake, remembered last night and felt a hot blush rush over her skin. A private ache announced itself as she reached for her robe, stark evidence of a marriage now completely consummated. She scrambled into her robe and rushed to the window.

The entire company was assembled in the narrow street, seventy-five mounted soldiers standing two rows deep. Bathed in the stillness of a damp summer morning, they stood at proud attention before an already large collection of neighbors who crowded the walks. How glorious they looked in their dignified blue wool coats, underlying red jerkins swathed in black leather carbine belts that had the same polished sheen as their knee-high boots.

Gabriel mounted his steed near the front of the company, beneath the quietly rustling banners of his flagmen, his voice deep and harsh as he barked the last order to come to arms. Weapons snapped upright, a column of deadly bayonets rising into the mellow morning mist. He trotted down the length of his ranks in final inspection of their readiness.

He didn't see her standing at the window until he returned to the head of the company, the color of her golden robe catching his attention. He looked up, his dark eyes bright with a kind of worried surprise to find her standing there.

He made no gesture, nor did she. They just stood very still and looked at each other for a long, sad moment.

Then he jerked the reins and turned away, spurred his horse and headed up the street with his company following proudly behind.

He never once looked back.

11

Dierdre Sullivan circled the bush in the backyard with Vanessa moving in the opposite direction. A five-year-old child was wedged into the innermost branches, only her face visible through the branches. Tiny Erin Sullivan was hiding in there. She'd been missing for two hours. Her eyes grew big and round with fear as she watched her mother approach, too young to realize Dierdre was too relieved to thrash her.

"Please Erin . . . your Pa's packed and ready to go . . . come on out, love." Dierdre pleaded at the tiny tear-streaked face in the bush. "You'll make plenty of new friends in Reading. You'll see! And we'll be safe from the limeys . . . won't that be nice? They can't get us in Reading!"

Admiral Howe's fleet had been spotted in American waters three days ago. He was fifty miles south of the city, headed in their direction. Because of what she had heard from Swanson on the green two months ago, Vanessa knew the invasion was about to begin, the pieces of the amphibious attack finally falling together just as the

Colonel had predicted. Although the threat was still distant, Philadelphia's fate seemed sealed.

And in response, the entire city became a crisscrossing exodus of people, the streets jammed with overloaded wagons, wailing children, spooked horses. Everyone was running for their lives, clogging every avenue leading out of the city, many roads impassable because of the commotion. Even now, the noise on Seventh Street made Vanessa want to cover her ears, every rattle and bang and shout seeming to scratch at her raw nerves.

"Erin!" Vanessa shouted above the noise, "Reading has so many stables full of horses you can ride! Think of it! Ponies! You can ride your own pony!"

The idea didn't move the girl. She simply refused to leave her home.

Distraught to the point of tears, Dierdre finally hurled herself at the bush, tackling both limb and child until she had the girl safely in her arms.

"Oh thank God!"

"Go, Dierdre . . . hurry!"

Dierdre started across the wall to her own yard, then stopped. She turned around, looked at Vanessa with an expression of desperate longing.

"I can't just leave you here, Vanessa—"

"Don't be ridiculous. You have to go! Gabriel would want it that way."

"What's Jon going to do?"

"We don't know yet."

Vanessa didn't realize she was wringing her hands again, her stomach souring and her mood sinking into a festering pool of anxiety that had been growing daily these last few weeks.

There was still no word from Gabriel. Nothing. She hadn't heard from him since he left five weeks ago. They had no idea where he was, how his mission had fared, if he was still alive. Even though none spoke of it aloud, they were all fearing the worst, especially now that the invasion was near and most of the houses on the block were boarded and empty. After today, they would be the only family left on Seventh Street.

Dierdre wouldn't budge off the wall, her eyes glittering with tears. "Come with us . . . please!"

"We made a plan last night," she said, hoping to spur Dierdre onward. She could not carry the additional burden of endangering Dierdre's whole family for the sake of the stranded St. Claire household. "We'll go to Princeton if we don't hear from him by week's end. Please, Dierdre, you must go . . . for the children's sake. We'll be fine—"

"Yes, but Gabe . . . " Dierdre stopped, made the sign of the cross, bit back the morbid words she didn't have to voice. They were heard with the profound clarity only known to spirits who bore the same weighty cross. Vanessa was moved, rushed to the wall and embraced both mother and child.

"God bless your journey and keep you safe, Dierdre."

"Amen," the woman whispered, slid off the wall and disappeared into her boarded home.

Vanessa felt very alone, standing in the middle of a yard that was usually so busy with activity, neighbors calling to one another as they tended their gardens or relaxed on their porches at sunset. It was too still, too quiet, and the silence only enhanced her inner feelings of guilt and alienation. They hung over her heart like a dark cloud since the morning she watched her husband ride away, so honorable and beloved by everyone except the broken woman he took to wife.

No man deserved what she did to him the night before he left, least of all such a good-hearted champion. Although she had told no one about that sorry and shameful episode, Vanessa was torn between needing to hear he was safe and knowing she couldn't stay in this marriage. She had to leave him, couldn't ruin his life with her twisted hates and misguided rages. He deserved better, a woman who could give him love and affection, not send him off to war with a memory of fitful weeping and the sting of unfounded accusations. Every time she thought of his last night home, she hated herself all the more.

She started toward the porch, worried that it could be her fault he hadn't written. Maybe he'd reached the same conclusions she had, that this marriage was already a failure, with little hope that the damage of her childhood could ever be rebuilt into something normal and healthy and real. Maybe he just didn't want to tell her now, with an invasion coming, that he couldn't go on with their union. It would be just like him to put himself aside and think of her best welfare first, wanting to see her somewhere safe and comfortable before he broke the news.

She reached for the latch on the back door, just about to release it when the bolt snapped upward and Martina exploded out of the house.

"Vanessa!" she shrieked, plowing headlong into her and grasping her in such a frantic embrace that it made Vanessa stumble backward. They fell against the porch rail, Martina clinging and crying and clutching a note in her hand.

"Tina! What is it?"

"A note! It's come! It's from him! I know his writing! He's safe!"

"Give it to me!" Vanessa had to struggle to get the note out of her flailing hand, her doleful heart suddenly illuminated with frantic hope. "Let go of it, Tina!"

The girl collapsed against her, sobbing, but Vanessa no longer cared. The mere sight of that familiar handwriting stole every trace of wind from her lungs.

He was alive. Despite the odds against him, he had survived!

She broke the seal, unfolded it, his message bringing tears of utter relief to her eyes.

"Vanessa . . . forgive me this delay. The battle waged longer than expected. We have a victory, but the fight cost us many good soldiers. My camp is built and secured. It's safe for you to come here now. Tell Jon to do as I instructed and see you, Tina, and Polly safely enroute to Kingston Headquarters. My adjutant will meet you there and escort you to my location. Bring sturdy clothes because we are woodland bound. Forgive what humble quartering I offer but it's the best I can do."

She felt momentarily faint, managed to get herself to the swing and sit for a moment to catch her breath.

They were saved. Despite her own plans to leave this man, she could not deny a strange feeling of redemption to find nothing in the note even remotely suggesting a divorce.

"Vanessa? Are you alright?" Tina was at her feet, clasped her trembling hand and looked up at her, her olive cheeks gleaming with water and a silent plea. "You look pale."

"It's . . . nothing . . . I'm just . . . well . . . relieved to hear he's safe."

"Thank God! Once again, He's spared our dear Gabriel."

Vanessa blinked, cleared her mind, looked directly at Martina and said, "We've no time for vapors. We're to tell Jon to make us ready for the trip to New York. Come, we've packing to do and I'll be damned if we leave one stitch of aid or comfort for the enemy!"

It was near midnight when the heat of late July forced Gabriel to stop and soak himself in a stream before arriving in camp. Hours in the saddle left him sore, his throat hoarse from barking at soldiers, his spirit weary from trying to rally men who were already embittered by defeat. And the campaign of 1777 had hardly begun.

As he did so often in his darker moments, he thought of Vanessa, of those cool orchid eyes, the softness of her skin, what he felt in her arms the night before he left. He could escape into these inviting memories if he chose them carefully enough, forgot the mental anxiety of his strained marriage, the deeper wounds of how his love-making had made her weep.

The farrier was asleep in the dark beside his hut. Gabriel didn't wake him, just tethered his mount nearby and hoped the soldier would wake long enough to refresh the horse before the dawn brought another hard day in the saddle.

He went into his hut, a small one-room building they managed to fashion out of raw timber. It had no floor, just dirt, the same earth they used to fill in the cracks between the log walls and mix with straw for the roof. It was primitive but his army sappers were fine engineers who had even built him a stone hearth on the wall beside his maps. He'd eventually use it if it ever got cold enough. For now, it was even too hot to cook inside. He ate with the rest of the troops on the ground beside the central cooking fire.

It was dark inside but he knew his way to the tinder-box beside the hearth, then to the wooden table he used as a desk where he kept his regulation-issue army lantern. He struck a flint, lit the lamp, brought to light a strange addition to his piles of paperwork.

A lady's bonnet.

He stood upright, looked around, saw the three leather satchels sitting on the floor beside his chair.

"Vanessa?"

He saw her then, a long slender figure lying across his cot, hidden in the deep shadows of the six-foot walls.

Every ragged edge in his demeanor disappeared upon sight of her. He went straight to the cot, knelt beside it, watched her stir awake like a man gazing upon a strange and mystical phenomenon.

Pale lavender eyes opened, sparkled awake, a slim white hand brushing aside a magnificent tumble of pitch-black curls that spilled across his pillow in playful disarray. She looked so beautiful, so soft, so alien to this primitive place. A new gown of mauve silk cuddled every long and elegant curve of her body, dainty tufts of rose-colored lace brushing against her chin.

"Hello, Gabriel," she whispered sleepily.

He forgot himself then, so glad to see her that he scooped her off the cot and ceremoniously carried her to the chair at his desk. He ignored the way she stiffened at his touch, the flash of suspicion in her eyes when he sat her down and stood back to look at her in unbridled relief.

"You look marvelous," he said hoarsely.

She blinked up at him, took a long look at his condition and gasped, "Gabriel . . . what's happened to you?"

He'd lost weight, his eyes were ringed with circles of fatigue. Masses of auburn hair fell to his shoulders, long and untethered and obviously not cut since he left Philadelphia. Life had been hard on him since she saw him last, but somehow he managed to wear it well.

His skin was ruggedly tanned, gleaming like rich brown syrup against the light fawn shade of a buckskin blouse. It was open at the throat, the ties dangling on his breast, a muscular chest covered in auburn hair presenting itself to her wandering gaze. He wore britches of the same earthy fabric; they were tight, displaying his masculine form. Despite his poor condition, Vanessa thought he looked like some young and virile woodland beast, his weapons of war shoved into a thick brown leather belt that slumped low on his narrow hips, the buckle resting just above the swell of his loins.

Desire quickened in her womanhood. She looked away, embarrassed by the way her body remembered the splendor of their last intimate embrace.

Her blush easily communicated her thoughts, made the

memory of that shocking encounter rise in the air between them. She became very aware of how still he was standing beside her, of how warm his gaze felt as he shared her recollection. She didn't need to look up to see the heat in his eyes. She could feel it, sense it, almost taste it.

He cleared his throat. "Would you like a drink?"

"Yes," she said too quickly, inwardly hoping he'd cross the room and stay over there until she recovered herself. Strange, but she was aware of his every footfall, each step required to cross the tiny cabin and come back.

Seven.

She noticed he set the mug on the table rather than handing it to her, as if the slightest contact between them might make them say aloud what they were both thinking.

The ecstasy. It was burned into their memories like some brilliant flash of light in the midst of the blindest bargain ever struck between a man and woman.

She sat poised on the edge of her seat, waited for him to say something about it but he didn't. He just drew another chair to the table. He bent into it with a slight intake of breath that made her look up just in time to see him wince.

"Gabriel? What's wrong?"

"Nothing," he said quickly although his teeth were clenched and his hand gripped the table edge in a moment of genuine pain.

She was instantly alarmed. "You're hurt!"

"Just some broken ribs—"

"Dear God—"

"Never mind," he growled, waving a hand to dismiss her worry, but she only saw more cause to be anxious. His palms were full of blisters, evidence of how hard he was sporting his blade these days.

She wanted to fuss over him but knew better. He was too manly to tolerate a fretful woman. "Has it been so bad?"

"War is hell," he said, his voice deep and raw. He soothed it with a gulp of bourbon. Recovering himself, he looked at her from across the table and flashed her a dauntless grin. "But don't worry, *chérie.* Nothing's changed. We're still losing."

His dry humor made her laugh, but the sound quickly died in her throat when he explained.

Since claiming this territory, Moylan's Horse had nothing but bad news to report to General Schuyler. John Burgoyne had a large and powerful army who marched behind the protective screen of an exceptional mounted reconnaissance company commanded by St. Luc. England sent her best, her most flamboyant General, a well-equipped army, arrogant young soldiers. The Continentals made two puny attempts to harass them but one look at such a formidable army sent half the rebels running back home. Worse, Burgoyne struck a deal with local natives, the Mohawks, whose random scalping expeditions left this picturesque valley littered with the gruesome remains of Continental soldiers trying to desert.

American morale plummeted.

No one had much hope these days, especially not after the stunning defeat suffered by the rebels at Fort Ticonderoga. This was Burgoyne's first strategic move, and he did it with great style. With his flashy army in tow, wagons of artillery and triumphant pipers announcing his advance, the notorious "Gentleman Johnny" marched straight through the gates of the Fort and found it deserted. The Americans fled the night before. Not a single shot was fired.

"The least they could have given us was the honor of a good fight," Gabriel grumbled. "Washington was so outraged by this news, he demanded the resignation of Philip Schuyler and appointed a new General, Horatio Gates. As if we're not in enough disarray, now no one is in charge while we wait for Schuyler to leave and Gates to arrive."

"Lord have pity on us," Vanessa prayed, certain only the Almighty could save them from such bleak circumstances.

"But enough war talk . . . " Gabriel said, dismissing the subject with a toss of his head. "Tell me how the city fares . . . if our friends are safely away."

Vanessa leaped into the change of subject with great energy, her inner nervousness emerging as she babbled about everything he could possibly want to know. She told him about the besieged city, their neighbors, the chaos, her trip to Kingston and how Martina chose to stay with a relative there which would keep her closer to where Jonnie had remained behind in Princeton.

He listened intently, his eyes focused on her face, alert to every nuance of emotion that passed over it. As he sat back in his chair, mighty arms crossed over his chest, there was a kind of enchanted quiet about the way he watched her. He made her hurry on to tell him more about her days without him because it seemed to be pleasing him, calming him.

"Even though so many shops are closing because of the invasion, new ones are opening . . . owned by Loyalists of course . . . hungry for the coin they'll gather when the British invade. Polly and I found a delightful new dress shop one afternoon on the far side of Dock Street. The seamstress has her windows decorated with dolls dressed in all the latest fashions from Europe. It's really quite clever! A lady simply goes inside, selects the doll wearing the dress she wants, and the seamstress makes it from whatever fabric the lady wants! I've never seen anything like it! Polly had a fabulous gown made. I just love it!"

"You've changed." Gabriel remarked quietly.

"What?"

"I've never seen you like this before."

"Like what?" The way he was looking at her made her feel suddenly self-conscious, strange, like she might have a smudge of dirt on her face. "What do you mean?"

"You're happy, aren't you?"

Happy? Now she really felt awkward. She looked down at her hands and watched her fingers nervously weave themselves together. "Well . . . I . . . it's all been very . . . er . . . different."

"Different," he repeated to himself, as if testing the feel of the word in his mouth. One of his hands reached across the table, settled over her knotted pair.

She tried to draw her hands away but he wouldn't allow it. Not now. He wanted only to restore her stolen radiance, savor just a few more minutes of observing this startling transformation in his haunted bride. He'd never seen her so animated and alive, smiling and laughing as she rarely did when he first met her. Could a scant two months away from her brutal father have rendered such a remarkable change?

"Look at me," he coaxed, gave her fisted hands a friendly squeeze. From behind a dark net of lashes her pastel eyes rose like a pair of wild orchids caught blooming in the dark. She looked at him then, timid and afraid and so sweetly vulnerable, the way she always did when he touched her. "No matter what trouble lies between us, I daresay this marriage is agreeing with you."

Her eyes dropped immediately, as if the mere mention of their marital state forced her to remember the way they sealed those vows the night before he left. "Yes, but I hardly deserve it, and you know it."

He let her hand go, sat back again. "Let me be the judge of what you deserve . . . not you. You only know what your father taught you to deserve."

She didn't say anything, only shifted in her chair and looked around the floor, as if she was considering something else to do. "Let's not bring him into this—"

"It's not a matter of bringing him into this . . . it's a matter of getting him out of it."

Now she acted on her instincts, got up and started

fussing over her bags. "Where should I put these things?"

"Beside my bed . . . where they belong."

She paused in mid-stride, just about to ask what he meant by the comment, then checked herself. She was too afraid he'd explain it. Instead, she ignored him and placed her satchels beside the only cot in the room.

The tension came back between them. From behind, she heard him sigh, his mug thump against the table as he finished another sip of bourbon. She could feel his eyes upon her as he murmured, "I'll have another bed brought in."

"That would be kind of you."

"Yes, I suppose it would," he remarked dully.

Guilt stabbed at her conscience. "Gabriel, I—"

"Never mind," he said and shook his head at his cup. "I don't like us to be upset with each other. The way we parted company in Philadelphia wears heavily on my mind."

"And mine," she admitted, sighing as she looked down at the floor.

"But I'll not make the same mistake again and damage your . . . er . . . innocence . . . with my aggressions. I meant you no harm, Nessy."

The mere utterance of that nickname made her spin around, stare at him in complete surprise. Only one other person ever addressed her like that. Her mother.

"Why did you call me that?"

"What . . . Nessy?"

"Yes! My mother used to call me that. No one else, just her!"

"I know."

"But how?"

"Come. Sit with me a moment longer. There's something else I want to talk with you about."

She knew just by the tone of his voice that whatever he wanted to talk about was serious. As she sat down, she watched him shift backward in his chair and stare pensively at his cup, as if trying to collect his thoughts.

The cabin fell still, silent, just the two of them sitting in the dim circle of light surrounding his desk. She felt very alone with him just then, in this tiny woodland hut that would somehow become a home. It was a pitiful replacement for the one she had left behind, but there was an air of comfort here. It was, after all, her only refuge from the invasion looming over Philadelphia. While she waited for him to speak, she let herself be surrounded by the place, smell the burnt lantern oil in the air, the wet ink and damp parchment on his desk, the ripe bourbon in their cups.

"I went to Erie on my way up here, Vanessa."

She looked up, met his eyes across the desk. They watched her with a kind of calm deliberateness that instantly conveyed something important to her. "Erie?" She didn't understand what this could mean, just shook her head and asked, "Whatever for?"

He seemed to brace himself for a moment, as if wary about how to say what was on his mind. He reached across the desk and very lightly covered her hands with one of his own. All the while, he held fast to her inquiring gaze, spoke in a whisper so soft she almost didn't hear him.

"That's where your mother is."

She blinked, startled by what he just said. "Mother? What are you talking about?"

"Your mother is in Erie. That's how I knew your nickname."

She stared at him in a kind of petrified enchantment, certain she'd heard him right but completely unable to accept it.

"Gabriel, my mother's dead."

"No, she's not."

"I know what happened to my own mother," she scoffed.

"Do you? Have you ever questioned what happened to her when they took her from your house?"

"No! Why should I? She was dead when they carried her out! I saw her. She was lifeless."

"She was drugged," he quietly informed her. He saw the impact of his announcement finally strike her. She fell very still and mute, staring at him as if seeing something supernatural.

He went on much more slowly now, aware by the shocked expression on her face that he was scratching at a deeply disturbing aspect of her life. "I never believed she was dead, mostly because there was no evidence of it. I found it strange that a resident of Millbridge wasn't buried anywhere in her hometown . . . that she would be carried off somewhere else. The only logical place was Erie because of your relative there. But I found her in none of those cemeteries. That's when I realized she was probably still alive. So I made a few inquiries . . . started to check around . . . and eventually found her."

"Why?" she suddenly blurted, the suspicion in her eyes turning cold and chill. He was instantly taken aback.

"Why what?" he softly urged. He could almost feel the hostility rising within her. Bemused, he couldn't fathom what was making her so suddenly angry. "What's wrong? Why are you angry?" Lord! But she was unpredictable. Would he ever understand her?

"If what you say is true, she would have contacted me! You're lying!" she accused, grabbed the edge of the table and wrenched herself out of her chair. She snapped upright, fixed him with an icy glare and hissed, "My mother would never have allowed me to believe her dead if she wasn't!"

This conversation was veering off in the wrong direction.

"She didn't know you were told that, Vanessa," he defended, wondering if her unfounded anger was just a mask for her hysteria. "Besides, she's being kept with the insane. Letter-writing is not one of their privileges."

"Insane?" This silenced Vanessa for a moment. In that instant, she looked suddenly small to him, helpless and unable to protect herself against what was, in reality, her father's cruelest and most despicable abuse.

"But Francis isn't so sure she's insane. He saw her and—"

"Saw her . . . " The words left her and took every ounce of rage with them. She seemed to deflate against the side of the desk, holding it as tightly as she gripped his every word.

"Yes, he saw her. Apparently, she suffered a nervous fit the day Danny died. Your father had her committed and told you she was dead so you'd stay with him and take care of him. It's the only motive I can find for why he would have told you this."

It struck her then, somewhere in the middle of her shock and shame. Gabriel was telling the truth. Her mother was alive!

A sensation of utter rapture wrapped around her spirit then. But something still held her back, something very dark and ugly.

It was the realization of her father's treachery.

How could anyone be so inhuman as to tell such an unspeakable lie to his own child?

She started backing away from the table, slowly, her eyes turning glassy, her skin draining of all color. Whatever intangible device had held her together all these years began to unravel from somewhere inside that was so deep, so black, she was certain her very soul was crumbling. One part of her spirit soared to a height she had never experienced before, a state of total joy that could almost swallow the black sin of her father. Both emotions clashed, her deep love for her mother and the grim outrage caused by her father's hideous deceit. Dazed, confused, she fell against the far wall and felt her legs give way under her.

She hit the ground, both knees slamming hard into the dirt floor.

Gabriel rushed over to her, genuine alarm turning the lines of his face stark and rigid. She just stared at him, this man who was part of a species that should degrade and torment women, hands that should hurt now extending to her a gift more priceless than any she'd ever received.

Her mother.

He gave her her mother back.

In this single spinning moment, she could not find the words to explain how precious this gesture was, yet how frightening for her to realize this beautiful gift was wrought by the hand of a man.

No. She could not accept this. Not from him. Not from a man. It was a trick. He was hiding his own motives somewhere inside this exquisite gift and she would not be fooled!

And so she did the only thing that felt natural, what she had been doing all her life.

She ran.

Vanessa shot out of his arms, ran to the door, and fell against it. Her hands were trembling so hard she could only fumble at the crude jute latch, trying to get it open so she could run, escape, get away from him.

But where would she go? She was out in the middle of the woods somewhere, in the belly of a war!

"Vanessa . . . please . . . "

The mere touch of his hand on her shoulder made her jump in panic, whirling around to watch him like a cornered animal confronted by its attacker. With only her eyes she communicated the blackest rage she could muster, a furious warning to stay back, stay away.

"Leave me alone . . . get away from me!"

For the first time since their marriage, she didn't want this glorious new life. No, in her madness, she wanted only the strength and security of her rock-hard heart. Hatred and rage were her only methods of survival. If she accepted any more of his kindness, she would surely die.

Gabriel didn't know what to do just then as he saw that she was completely hysterical. "Forgive me for being so blunt. I should have realized what a shock this would be."

"Why? Why did you do this?"

"Because I care about you . . . want to restore your life—"

"You don't really expect me to believe that, do you?"

He just looked at her, utterly confused. "What are you talking about?"

"You think I don't see through your kindness? Well, I do! You're trying to trick me."

The woman was obviously shocked out of her senses. "No," he whispered gently, soothingly. "This is not a trick. I swear to you. Now come away from the door and lie down . . . you've suffered a great shock . . . "

The moment she saw his hand reach in her direction, Vanessa responded in the only way she knew how.

She hit him, hard, sliced her hand across his cheek with enough force to send him staggering backward. He recovered himself, reached for the sting on his cheek and stared at her in complete astonishment.

Silence fell over them, harsh and heavy. There was only the sound of their ragged breathing.

"What's wrong with you?" he finally demanded, his voice harsh and raw. "Why are you doing this to me?"

The question brought a pinch of pain to her face, made her momentarily clench her eyes shut against a new stream of tears. "Because I'm sick . . . ruined . . . can't you see that?" She looked at him, very directly, as if trying to prove her words with the cold fear in her eyes. "I can never love you . . . never love any man. Hate is all I know. And all your kindness will ever do is make me distrust you more!"

He stood there, momentarily pinned beneath the doom in her words, absorbing them. They registered on his face in a look of the most intense hurt she had ever seen there.

But then the look disappeared, his feelings quickly masked beneath a hard, grim expression. He didn't say anything, just walked to the door, threw it open and slammed it shut behind him.

12

The Blue Dolphin was nearly deserted, like most of Philadelphia. A sweaty barmaid delivered the two men a bowl of punch and two mugs, and nervously wiped at a few empty tables on her way back to the bar. She seemed more concerned with the noise seeping through the tavern windows: coaches clattering, voices raised in shouts to hurry, move along, get out because the British were coming in.

The men waited for their contact. More than an hour passed. The heady blend of dark rum and cognac punch made the wait seem much shorter, more bearable. They drank quietly, absently watching the only other occupant of the room. An old man, as weathered and yellow as the mammoth whale jaw that decorated the wall above him. His gnarled hand fingered the tail of the creature as he gulped down a tankard of ale and belched loudly.

"Ain't seen your likes in this town before," the old man called from across the room. "This here's a Whig tavern, you know. Won't find much company here anymore.

Whigs're all gone. Yup. No more meetings in this part of Pennsy."

"We're meeting a friend," one of the men called back.

"Sure he ain't moved out yet, are you?" The old man squinted at them suspiciously.

"No, he's still here."

"A Whig, is he?"

The question wasn't friendly. The men looked between themselves, then one of them shrugged and said, "He never said—"

"Damned liar, you are," the old man growled, then grinned evilly when the two men looked at him in surprise. He shot a spray of spittle through the hole of a missing tooth. "Patriots are the only men with guts enough to tell who they are in this underhanded war. If your friend don't say which side he's on, then he sleeps with the enemy."

Both men decided to ignore him. They ladled more punch into their mugs, watched the shadowy doorway until it finally produced the tall, cloaked figure of a man.

"Thought you went to Princeton, Jonnie," the old man said.

"Came back to see my friends," Jonnie Meeks told him and nodded toward the men at the far table. "Where you holing yourself up these days, old crow?"

"Staying in my own house! Humph! I ain't leaving on account of no weak-spined foreign fellas! Hell with them! I'm gonna stay long enough to watch them git whooped!"

"Suit yourself," Jonnie muttered, slid into the empty chair at their table and said, "Let me see your papers first, then we'll talk."

The information was shown. Jonnie looked at the signature and glanced up, surprise arching his bushy blond brows. "So what do you want to know?"

13

Vanessa awoke to a sinking sensation of shame just to remember her behavior with Gabriel last night. She sat up in the middle of his rickety cot, rubbed at her tear-swollen eyes and looked for some evidence that he might have slept here last night. There was none. She felt doubly ashamed, not only for having acted so poorly with him but for having denied this tired and wounded soldier his own bed.

An apology was in order, she grudgingly admitted to herself. It wasn't his fault the news about her mother came as such a shock. Nor was it his doing that she was so emotionally crippled by her past. No, he didn't deserve her violent outbursts, neither the episode in Philadelphia nor her cruel rebuff last night. What Gabriel deserved was his freedom from this disastrous marriage, and as she climbed out of bed she was determined to tell him so.

She dressed quickly, used his shaving mirror to dress her hair for the day. Anxiety knotted her stomach as she mentally searched for words that would bring this sorry arrangement to an end.

Nothing sounded right. Especially not when she looked back over the last few months of her life and realized how good they were. He denied her nothing. Anything her heart desired he laid at her feet.

Even her mother.

Just the thought of her mother brought a cool bath of delight to her dry and arid spirit. These should be the happiest moments of her life.

So why weren't they? What was wrong with her?

Gabriel knocked once at the door, waited for her permission, then strolled into the cabin with an entourage of officers in his wake. He barely nodded in her direction as his men gathered around the highly detailed military map of the region that hung on the wall beside the fire well.

A winded and muddy scout stabbed a finger at the map. "There—that's where I saw them marching. They were headed in that direction."

"Away from the Fort?" Intrigued, Gabriel watched the scout nod confidently.

"Yessir. I seen Burgoyne with my own eyes. He's on the march alright."

"How many men did he leave behind in the Fort?" Lauren interrogated.

"About a third of his army, I'd say."

"So he's got his baggage with him?" Francis asked.

"Some of it."

"How much baggage?" Gabriel wanted to know.

The scout shrugged, "Don't know that, sir."

Over his shoulder, Gabriel tossed an order at Will MacLeod. "Get a scouting party together. Send it to Ticonderoga and find out the state of Burgoyne's provisions. How much did he take with him and how much did he leave behind."

"With pleasure, sir," Will said with a grin, tipping his straw hat at Vanessa on his way out.

Benny Cooke collided with the Captain in the doorway. "Sorry, Will—"

"I almost swallowed my tongue, you clumsy lump!"

"Aw! Quit your whining. Hey Gabe, look at this." Benny handed the Colonel a folded note. "From Schuyler. He said the Archangel just told him Burgoyne left Ti . . . "

Gabriel looked as if someone had just stabbed him in the back. He grabbed the note, looked at it, then viciously crumpled it in his fist. He clenched his teeth so hard the taper in his mouth was cut in half and dropped to the floor.

"Damnit!" Robert Blaire snapped, stomping on the taper with such venom the walls shook. "He's back!"

Frustrated glances ricocheted between Gabriel, Lauren, Benny, and Francis but none said a word aloud. They wouldn't. Only a few men knew about Gabriel's "ghost."

Gabriel pitched the crumpled note into the fire well, still struggling for composure when he snapped at Lauren, "Inform Schuyler that I'm sending a dozen scouts after Burgoyne to make his march more difficult. Get the men together and tell them to fell trees, dam creeks, make swamps of dry land—do anything they want—just make his passage rough."

"Sure, Gabe," Lauren said, still sulking as he drifted out of the cabin.

"Why doesn't Schuyler give orders to harass the enemy, eh?" Robert asked no one in particular. "What's he doing up there anyway? He's not even attempting to confront Burgoyne!"

"Because we haven't a chance against them in the field," Gabriel said with a long sigh. He looked tired, drained, as if he hadn't slept much the night before. Vanessa looked away, besieged by guilt. "We need to wear him down first . . . exhaust his men . . . spend his food and ammunition. Harassment is about the only thing we can do right now."

"But that ain't our fault!" Benny jumped up from the cot to point out. "It's them nit-wit officers they send us . . . like this new General Gates. Why, I hear Congress thinks he's nothing but an old granny. Yup! That's what they call him, Granny Gates!"

"Is that so?" Gabriel turned on Benny. "If you don't stay off those rum wagons I'm going to get you assigned as the personal sentry of Granny Gates."

Benny paused in his boots, dumbstruck with horror.

"That's right, Benny. I mean it this time. If you don't get those damn recruits in order I'm shipping you to the Granny." Francis had to turn away to hide his smile. Even Vanessa had to shield the amusement on her face. No one could strike fear into the crude heart of Benny Cooke like his Commander. "I'm tired of being woken up every night to the sounds of them wasting my ammunition on the damn crickets!"

"But the noise spooks them!" Benny cried, desperate for some defense against the Colonel's wrath. "They're too dumb to know better!"

"MAKE MEN OUT OF THEM!" Gabriel shouted, and they all jumped in their skin.

"They're awful dumb, Gabe," Benny muttered, shaking his head sadly. "I mean it. They were all born without a brain. I swear it. Look in their ears sometime, Gabe. There ain't nothing in their heads but bone—"

"Put something in there, Benny, like the fear of God—otherwise known as the Colonel's wrath."

"Yessir. I'm doing my best, Gabe."

"Nonsense. There's not a man in this army who's doing his best, which is why we're losing."

"Makes sense," Benny agreed solemnly. Francis choked into his hand and even Gabriel seemed to be fighting back laughter.

"Move out and get it done."

The room slowly vacated after the disgruntled Sergeant. Gabriel lingered only long enough to secure his saddle and toss it outside, the signal to the farrier that he was ready to mount and ride.

Vanessa suddenly realized her moment with Gabriel was at hand. She stood up, desperately trying to summon her nerve. "Gabriel? I know you're busy but—"

"I'm never too busy for you, madam," he said curtly, his voice conspicuously lacking its usual flattering tone. For a moment, he faced the door, his back to her, then slowly turned around. Their eyes met across the room and she was momentarily struck by the coldness in his gaze. "What is it?"

She looked away, quelled by his chilling regard. "I . . . uh . . . well . . . it's about last night—"

"What about it?"

"I'm sorry," she blurted suddenly, wanting to be out with it, then stood there wringing her hands and trying to remember what else she planned to say.

He paused at the door, long enough to make her look up at him. Their eyes met. His gaze was so deep and penetrating she felt as if her very soul was pricked. Disturbed, she looked down at her feet, realizing she had forgotten her rehearsed speech and wishing he'd just berate her and get it over with.

"I wonder what you're sorry about," he finally asked, "Hurting me?"

"Yes," she said quickly, forcing herself to look up so he could see her sincerity. "You're too good a man for me. If you want to be out of this marriage, I'll cooperate."

There. She had said it.

But he didn't respond, nor did his expression change to reveal how he felt about her proposition. Stranded in his silent stare, she looked down at her slippers again.

"I'm not ready to do that," he said, thought a moment, then added, "yet."

He left the doorway, crossed the room in two long strides, stopped only when he was close enough for her to catch his scent, the warmth in his body. The tips of his boots were only a few inches from her slippers.

"Your apology is unnecessary, Vanessa. I'm sure your reaction to the news of your mother was quite natural—as honest as your reaction to the ecstasy you found in our marriage bed."

She stiffened.

He ignored it and went on. "No . . . I'm not going to leave you yet because the truth is, I still want you—"

"I don't know why," she interrupted.

"Neither do I," he said and looked at her very directly, very boldly, until she was caught in that penetrating stare of his.

"Just because my life is ruined is no reason to ruin yours. I think we should just part ways, Gabriel."

"No."

Why was he being so stubborn? "This is ridiculous!" she cried, thoroughly frustrated with him now. "If you don't let us end things peacefully, I'll—"

"You'll what?" he asked, took a step closer, until his body made contact with hers.

"I'll leave you," she threatened, trying to step away. But his hands were suddenly encircling her arms, tightening, holding her as firmly as he could without causing her pain.

"Don't you dare try to leave me," he warned and she was struck by the sudden fierceness in him, by how possessively he spoke. This wasn't like him, and she had the feeling she had just pricked some deeply hidden and sensitive place in his masculinity, the place where a man defended his claim to a woman.

"There's no place on earth you can run from me, Vanessa Davis. I'll find you."

She made a vain attempt to get loose, but it was a mistake. He only drew her closer, his mighty arms enveloping her until her body and his met in places too intimate for such a dark moment.

"Put the idea out of your mind," he demanded, his voice thickening, his eyes darkening as a new kind of passion leaped into his anger. "You belong to me . . . only me."

"How can you say that?" she railed even though she already knew the answer. It was rising between them now like the reckless spark beneath a pile of ripe kindling. "How can you even want me?"

"I don't know," he said sharply and she could feel his hand in her hair, turning her head up. "It makes no more sense to me than it does to you." He bent until his lips were but a hair's breadth from her own.

"Don't . . . " she gasped, tried to turn her face away but he wouldn't allow it. His hand cupped the back of her head, forced her to look into his eyes and see the precocious passion that always managed to bloom whenever they came this close.

"But this is the only reason I have left," he whispered, "the way I want you and the way you want me. For this, we've never needed a reason, have we?" His lips brushed against her own, ever so lightly, too lightly for the powerful reaction that surged through her.

She swallowed hard, struggled against the heady sensations and her own growing desire to touch him, taste him, uncloak the master spy, and discover the deeply passionate man he hid under all those magnanimous layers.

"Answer me," he commanded softly, his lips finding hers, lingering just long enough to melt her and make his point perfectly clear. "Tell me you can walk away from this."

"I can't," she moaned, reached for him with her hands while every other part of her wanted to run away. She felt so torn, confused, unable to understand the power this man could wield over her. "But it frightens me—"

"Of course it does. Everything about this confuses you, doesn't it?"

"Yes!" she cried, looking up at him as if he might explain it all.

But he didn't, just paused while his eyes momentarily searched her face. Some of the fire went out of him then, his expression softening as he gently drew her hands from around his neck. "You're every bit a lady, Vanessa, but you have no conception of how to treat a gentleman."

This stung, especially because she wasn't sure why he had said it, to compliment or insult her. She pulled her hands free, stepped away. "What do you mean?" she demanded.

"A gentleman would never hurt a lady, is what. And that's what you're waiting for, isn't it? For me to hurt you, beat you, punish you for my own weaknesses. Isn't that the kind of man you want?"

"No!"

"Damnit! It is!" he insisted. But he was quick to regain himself, lowering his voice. "You want me to be someone I'm not. Well, I can't. I have never—in my twenty-seven years of life—lifted a hand against a woman or child and I have no intention of starting now just to please you!"

"Why you—" Infuriated, she raised her arm, intent on slapping his face for such a crude comment, but he instantly caught her arm, held it firm and fast.

"And don't you ever raise a hand to me again, young lady. I'll not stand for that behavior in *my* family. *My* house is a peaceful place. There is no violence. That's not how we settle our disputes. We *talk* . . . like civilized human beings!"

Vanessa just stared at him, too dumbfounded by his righteous fury to concentrate on her own anger. She had never seen him like this before and stood there feeling totally unnerved.

He let her arm go then, whipped around and stalked back to the door. "If there's nothing else . . . " he remarked coldly, tossing the comment over his shoulder.

"There is," she said before she even knew she was speaking. She had to stop him, didn't want him to leave things like this. Some tiny shred of dignity forbade her from acting so poorly in the face of this distinguished man. Especially not one so obviously hurt by the ill treatment she wielded in the face of his constant kindness.

He paused, and the room was suddenly heavy with silence. He did not turn around, just stood there and waited.

Vanessa swallowed hard, tears of pain filling her eyes as she stared at his broad back and forced herself to whisper aloud, "Thank you . . . for mother . . . "

He turned around to look at her but in that moment, she was too ashamed to meet his eyes. She knew she was a complete disappointment to him, just another source of dismay to add to the load he already carried in this world at war, his life surrounded by the troubled and misguided.

"Don't do that," he said quietly, "look at me."

She did so, her wet eyes round and brilliant, full of a request for mercy that her lips couldn't voice. In that single gaze, he suddenly saw every complicated and conflicting emotion that formed the woman who stood before him. She could be as hateful as she was compassionate, but on her face he saw the pain of being torn in life, and her deeply hidden and distorted wish to find some love in her cold and tormented world. No wonder she looked so helpless to him now, as she stood on the receiving end of a gift that touched her in the dead center of where she raged.

She didn't flinch when he came upon her, that familiar and powerful compassion of his returning to his eyes. All the anger and the passion was gone, replaced by a warm sympathy, the gentle mark of how much she had just moved him with this first utterance of gratitude.

He reached, traced the magnificent curves of her soft chin as if trying to communicate the comfort he wanted so much to bring her. "Be at peace with me," he finally said, "because I can't fight you and this war at the same time."

She agreed with a nod of her head.

"Très bien . . . "

He walked away, straight through the cabin door and into the morning sun, leaving her to stand there watching from the shadows.

In the following weeks, Vanessa wasn't sure if it was the war or a change of mind that kept Gabriel so distant from her. He wasn't cold, just impassive. They were rarely alone and when they were, their talk was friendly and about the war, not themselves. He didn't mention her mother again, nor did she, even though she yearned to learn more about his investigation. She didn't dare ask him, especially not when he seemed so intent upon keeping a discreet distance from his marriage. Nor could she press him when he was so busy and harried by the war.

Moylan's Horse never rested. They worked twenty-four hours a day. Although she saw only the eighty men who comprised Gabriel's main company, his command included five separate surveillance units totaling three hundred soldiers. It was their duty to protect the main army encamped only fifteen miles northwest of their location in the lower Catskills, to watch the enemy and to report their doings to headquarters.

This was where Gabriel's brilliance as a military spy far surpassed anything she'd ever seen him do in Millbridge. The flamboyant Englishman, John Burgoyne, had no idea that his every movement was meticulously recorded on Gabriel's huge map of the Mohawk Valley. Colonel

St. Claire had a knack for placing scouts throughout a theater. Nothing moved that he didn't see. And when it came to stalking the enemy, Gabriel was relentless. He did anything for information, including impersonating British officers, posing as local citizens, even stealing enemy mail. All the while, he conducted ruthless harassments of Burgoyne's army, night-time raids, daylight ambushes, spooking off the horses, setting wagons of provisions on fire. By mid-August, John Burgoyne was quite lost in the Mohawk forests and his food supplies were dwindling fast.

Vanessa tried not to notice their doings even though her cabin was the nucleus of the Northern Department's intelligence unit. It was impossible not to overhear their activity, and she was of course intrigued by their operation, their ideas and tactics.

But she minded her husband, dutifully mending for the soldiers with Polly, taking only occasional excursions to picnic in a favorite woodland spot or ride through the countryside. It was entirely safe in their location and she was free to travel about the area. They often visited a large encampment of citizens who were displaced by the war, their homes stolen by the enemy. It was common for these people to trail after the army in order to find protection, perhaps food and lodging if needed. Most lived out of wagons and tents that contained all of their earthly possessions. Visits here were usually enjoyable. There was always music played on fiddles and drums to which the ladies could dance while the men clapped and watched. For the soldiers, there were poker and dice games, riding and gunning contests. The encampment was one of the few places they could all go to find a temporary hiatus from the war.

But after three weeks in the hectic environment of a military camp, Vanessa awoke one morning with a compelling urge for solitude. A stroll through the surrounding hills would be a perfect way to start the day.

She took up her bonnet, snatched a basket off the hearth floor and went to the desk where Gabriel was already busy reading over the last night's information. He barely looked up when she approached.

"Do you need something?" he asked.

"I'd like to collect some wildflower seeds for the garden."

"Do we have a garden?" he asked dully, then yawned at whatever he was reading.

"Gabriel, I'm talking about our garden in Philadelphia."

"Ah yes . . . Philadelphia." He looked up then, his great eyes weary until they focused on her face and became more alert. "While I was with Gates yesterday, word arrived that the British have invaded the city." She caught her breath, stared at him in instant alarm. "Washington is doing his best to defend it, but it's expected to fall to Howe." Sorrow flashed between them, deep and genuine, but then he quickly looked away. "Forgive me if I've ruined your morning."

She just stared at the top of his bent head, so very sorry for him and the city he held so beloved. "I feel very badly about this," she said.

"Don't say anything on your way out. I've not told the men yet."

"So much for picking seeds. I suppose I should abandon my plan—"

"Absolutely not. Go. It will cheer you."

She did so, with a heavy heart, leaving her husband alone and without the consolation he didn't seem to want from her anyway. It was only the beautiful August morning that managed to revive her spirits. The greenery was vibrant today, tipped by the golden light of dawn, broad beams of it penetrating the dense forest on either side of the trail. Pine needles crunched under her slippered feet, a wide variety of flora blooming across the earth floor in giant puddles of color.

She started collecting flowers, her basket filling with

fleabane, black-eyed Susans, daylilies, and bushes of wild horse nettle. Late summer varieties were still in full bloom. The spent blossoms produced a heap of seeds that she greedily added to her basket. Maybe one day they would form a lovely wildflower patch in the backyard of their Philadelphia home.

If the British didn't destroy it first.

Vanessa was squatting over a bud full of wild orchid seeds when a movement on the path ahead caught her eye. Fearing an animal, she fell still and watched the thin shadow moving along the edge of the path.

Finally, she looked squarely at the path and was instantly startled at the sight of a young girl standing there. When they saw each other, both women stopped short and just stared at one another for a moment.

The girl was a pathetic figure, thin and gaunt beneath a dirty cotton shift that looked as though it might have once been a pretty day dress. Now it was dirty and torn at the waist, the hem ragged and fraying. She wore her brown hair in a pair of misshapen braids that looked as though they hadn't been washed in a year. Her big brown eyes stared at Vanessa in frightened uncertainty.

Pity wrenched her heart, made her rise slowly so as not to scare the girl away. With a friendly smile, Vanessa said, "Hello, young lady. Are you lost?"

The girl shook her head briskly, began wringing her hands in her dress. "I'm looking for a bite," was all she said.

"Oh! Then you've come to the right place," Vanessa said cheerfully. "We've plenty of food. Come! Don't be afraid. I'll take you to camp and—"

"I ain't going down thar!" the girl blurted, her big eyes turning wide and fretful. "The Whig women already beat me off once, they did. They won't share even a crumb!"

Whig women? "Are you from a Tory camp?"

The girl didn't answer right away, just rolled her lips between her teeth, looked at Vanessa with the keen sight of a hunted animal before slowly nodding her head. "We're camped over yonder . . . a half day's journey northa here."

Vanessa's mind absorbed these details, churned them for a moment, then found herself pressing for more information. "But I thought John Burgoyne sent food to your camp."

"He does but we're only getting one cart a week of late!" the girl explained, as if she had to defend her hunger. "Barely enough for the babes, let alone the mothers!"

"Oh dear," Vanessa consoled, still thinking about how to use this chance encounter for the Rebels' best advantage.

Gabriel's scouts were constantly seeking information about Burgoyne's food supply, not so much the quantity but the logistics of how it was distributed. Only with that information could they calculate how long they might keep Burgoyne marching before he ran out of food.

"But I thought Burgoyne was so generous."

"Used to be!" the girl admitted. "But not lately. Last three weeks we ain't seen much . . . just a cart full . . . bread, rice, vinegar . . . that's all he sends."

"Hmmm," Vanessa said, looking between the girl and the camp and feigning a secretive whisper. "I'm only with the rebels because my husband changed his loyalties a few months back but I've been yearning for word of my kin—"

"Where they from?"

"Albany."

"Got lotsa Tories in camp from thar, ma'am!" The girl finally rushed forward, her eyes bright with relief. "What'd be their names?"

"Sullivan," Vanessa contrived, not entirely sure where her thoughts were leading her. "In fact, I think they might be inside the Tory camp, but I've not the slightest idea how to find it."

"I can tell you! I come from thar!" the girl excitedly offered. "There's a valley 'bout thirty miles north and the Tories are living in it. St. Leger gave us some scouts to guard us, but we ain't seen him nor Burgoyne for a month! Some say he's gone fer good!"

"Really? You mean it might be safe to travel there?"

"Sure! I just did it! Ain't hardly seen a face since I left there a week ago."

"No Indians?"

"No. St. Leger keeps them in line, he does. We hear the Mohawks are restless but none of us see any. Not a one." The girl spoke hurriedly now, over-anxious to be helpful because Vanessa could see she was desperate for food. "Sullivan, eh? There might be some folks by that name in camp."

The girl was probably lying, Vanessa knew. But it didn't matter. A plan was finally beginning to jell in her mind. She pointed to the base of a massive oak and directed, "Sit there and wait for me. I'll bring you some food if you promise to tell mc thc way to your camp."

The girl nodded, flew to the base of the tree and sat down.

"But I can't take you, ma'am. I ain't going back. I'm headed to Kingston. Lotsa Tories in Kingston . . . army ain't scared them off yet."

"Alright, I can find my way without you," Vanessa agreed. "Now stay here and I'll be back in a moment with a sack of food, alright?"

The girl agreed, the tip of her tongue already licking her lips.

Vanessa ran most of the way to camp, stopped just long enough to catch her breath before she made her way to the batmen at the commissary wagon. As usual, they filled her request without question. The Colonel's wife was never made to wait or want for anything. A loaf of bread and a sack of salt pork was promptly presented to her. She thanked the batmen and skipped back to the trail.

The young girl began eating at once, stuffing fists full of bread in her mouth and giving Vanessa directions to the camp between swallows.

Oh, how she hoped Gabriel would allow her to go, spend a day or so in the Tory camp and get firsthand information about the enemy's food. Why hadn't she thought of this before? It would be far easier to sneak a woman into a Tory camp than to redress a soldier and infiltrate the military!

Her feet danced across a little knoll in the woodland path, slid down the incline, then ground to a sudden halt.

Gabriel was standing in the middle of the path, arms akimbo and legs braced. He didn't utter a word, just gave her a very thorough look and waited for her explanation.

Vanessa tried not to look as startled as she was. He must have seen her with the batmen. She collected herself, puffed at a stray lock of hair and blurted, "I just found a starving Tory girl, and she gave me directions to her camp in exchange for a sack of food and—"

"No."

"No what?"

"You're not going there."

How did he know that? "But I've not told you my plan!" she insisted, giving him a lovely pout that was full of feigned dismay. He hated to displease her. And she knew it. "You've been trying to discover Burgoyne's food supply for weeks now. The Tories will know because they're fed by him! Think of how much safer it will be for me to sneak into a Tory camp than to risk one of your soldiers. It's much safer for everyone, Gabriel!"

"I knew you were going to do this," he said gruffly, "collect all this war information in that cunning little mind of yours, then decide to play Tory hunter again. This is a war, Vanessa. We're not spooking cattle on a country farm."

She was offended by his remark, or at least pretended to be. Her lovely shoulders shrugged indignantly, lavender eyes sparkling gloriously in the morning sun as she demurred, "I don't claim to be as sophisticated as you, Colonel, but my efforts are just as honorable!"

"Is that so?"

Coy now, she let her provocative eyes meet his in a way they hadn't in weeks. "Why must you be so stubborn, husband? I promise not to linger there. I'll go in, get whatever information I can, then leave within a day. If you'll feel better about it, allow your men to cover me."

Gabriel sighed, directed his eyes at the heavens and growled, "Why do you set your heart on such dangerous activity? Aren't you content to fool with your hair or gossip or do whatever it is ladies like to do to amuse themselves?"

She laughed softly, amused by his masculinity, and leaned close enough for him to feel the warmth of her breasts against his arm. Her eyes found his again, deliberate and seductive, the way she had once gazed at him from the opposite end of a Tory dinner table. And like then, her gaze found its way straight into his manhood. "I have long desired my freedom, Colonel. That makes me as good a soldier as any."

By mid-morning, the plan was formalized although Gabriel had severe misgivings about it. Knowing of her expert assistance in the Swanson mission, his officers were swayed in favor of her plan. They did not overlook Gabriel's chief concern, however. A woman sporting the looks of his wife should not be allowed to wander the unpredictable theater of this man's war.

She dressed in a dirty, over-large shift that was donated by a buxom Whig woman, then subjected herself to Gabriel's expertise in costuming. Around and around she was turned while his blade fringed a hem, frayed a thread. He tugged at her braids, pulled some tendrils loose, complained that the sheen of her hair didn't suit a starved person. He powdered her tresses lightly enough to dull the lustre, then whitened the healthy peach color of her cheeks in an effort to produce a gaunt appearance.

When he was finally satisfied, he dismissed the officers and sat her down at his desk. On the back of a relay slip, he carefully sketched the formation in which she would ride, in the center of a ring of snipers spaced at three-hundred-yard intervals. If she got into any trouble, she would not have far to run, in any direction, to find help.

She was anxious to go, her fingers tapping on the table, her eager gaze sliding into the grips of her husband's dark and worried eyes. It seemed like a year since they'd looked at each other so directly.

"I'm sure I'll be fine, Gabriel."

"One is never sure of anything in war. Your travel will be long, hot, and tedious. I'll see you equipped with a British canteen and some food in case you can't get any in the camp." He reached down, drew his own dagger from his boot and slid it across the table. "Put this on your person somewhere. And don't be afraid to use it if you must."

A bit of her eagerness slipped away. As if to reassure herself, she rehearsed the plan aloud. "When I get inside the camp, I'll screen myself into the crowd, then wait until mealtime. If possible, I'll try to glean information from the commissary officer, but if it isn't safe, I'll come back later and try again."

"Good. And remember, you have but one night in camp. Whether you learn anything or not, I want you out of there at dawn. My men will escort you to within a quarter mile of the camp, then wait there for you in the morning. St. Leger is guarding those people, and he has several hundred Mohawk Indians in his employ. If they get restless, which they've been doing a lot lately, you'll be removed from camp by the man I've assigned to that duty."

Will MacLeod. His best marksman. Gabriel wasn't taking any chances.

She nodded, declared herself ready and headed for the door. But her husband wasn't finished yet, she realized. She was startled by how quickly he came up behind her and slid his arm around her waist.

"One moment," he said, moved against her until her head felt the unyielding hardness of his chest. Absently, his fingers reached for her hair, dabbing at it here and there as if to put the final touches on a fine piece of art. When he spoke again, his voice was throaty, husky, the way it always got when they touched. "I suppose you plan to employ your best devices to get this information, eh?"

She didn't say anything, just looked up at him and saw that telltale glint in his eyes, one she hadn't seen from him in a long time. Desire.

It turned the shade of his eyes darker, so blue they were almost black, like a storm creeping across a night sky. The sight of it held her fast, like it always did, arresting her in those inner places where a woman felt the most female.

"What do you mean?" she asked, surprised at how small her voice sounded in the quiet cabin.

"I mean you'll seduce a man to get what you want . . . like you did to me."

His eyes roamed across her face, slowly, warmly, made her feel so completely aware of him she could count each thump of his heart beneath her head. Instinct made her want to draw away but she could never quite summon the strength when he was this near, when the scent of him, feel of him, sight of him, overpowered her. This was a side of him no red-blooded woman could resist.

She just hung there against him, disarmed, fascinated,

her senses completely captured. She could not resist the bold caress of his hand across her flat belly. It moved slowly, in a leisurely manner, feeling every inch of her slenderness beneath the baggy shift. Possession flowed from that touch of his, from his eyes as they watched every reaction on her face.

Now that he had her complete attention, he leaned close, whispered against her temple, "No matter how capricious is this marriage of ours, you still belong to me, Vanessa . . . perhaps not in mind, but clearly in body."

The comment startled her, made her stiffen in a way he couldn't tolerate. No, he wanted his message heard, brought her close enough to remind her of how much of himself she had once known. Her breath sighed loosely, turned short and deep, but she did not repel him. She couldn't. Not when he smoothed his hand across the forbidden reaches of a body he hungered for no matter how foolish was the desire. It was a weakness of his, something he must learn to detest but now wasn't the time. He wanted her to know it, that he would one day take what belonged to him. Her lavender eyes watched him, afraid yet strangely curious, wary yet vaguely willing, provoking a touch she might or might not scorn.

"I don't understand you, Gabriel," she said in a trembling whisper, remembering the last time he looked at her like this. The night of the Swanson mission, just after he proved that a ruse wasn't necessarily a ruse with a man like him.

"Oh yes you do," he reminded softly. "You understand me very well, Vanessa . . . well enough to know why I won't tolerate another man touching you the way I have. You do what you must . . . just remember what I told you."

He released her, suddenly, went to the door and opened it.

"I'll be waiting for you at the meeting place at dawn."

She blinked at him, as if to shake off a daze. "You don't have to come, Gabriel—"

"I'll be there. *Bonne chance, madame.*"

He walked away, his gait powerful and determined, his head not once turning back.

14

Vanessa slid from the saddle, worn and sore, leaned against an ant-ridden stump and looked at the Tory camp sprawled below. It was much larger than she expected, nestled across a deep valley that looked more like a groove in the Catskill foothills.

All kinds of paraphernalia littered the wooded site: wagons, carts, tents, cattle, whatever these refugees deemed sacred enough to tote out here into this temporary shelter.

She was glad to finally find it, despite its being behind enemy lines. The thirty-mile ride had been exhausting. Baked by the sun, her rump full of saddle sores, sweaty skin itching from the dust of a dry forest floor, Vanessa could only think of finding a refreshing stream, then getting on with her duty.

She sprinkled her face and chest with the dregs in her canteen. The water was warm and rusty-smelling. After an extended moment, she pushed herself off the stump and limped afoot the rest of the way into camp.

Five hundred aimless wanderers made quite a racket. Children yelped in play, women cackled in humor and reprimand, pots banged, dogs barked, canvas tent flaps snapped in the light winds of dusk. No one seemed to notice her as she moved through the camp, followed a makeshift path carved by hundreds of wagon ruts. Her over-heated and disheveled appearance made her blend easily into the crowd. When she could hardly walk another step, she finally turned to the first person she saw and asked for water.

"Is there a stream nearby? I've just come and I don't know my way about."

A heavy-set young woman looked up from the shade of her tent, her hand absently stroking the sleeping baby in her lap. "Sure is, lass. But it's a walk from here. Come sit for a spell 'til the sun goes down. Too hot for walking now."

Vanessa accepted the invitation. The ground felt so cool and soft it made her sigh.

"Where you come from?" the woman asked, her rotund figure shifting clumsily to allow Vanessa more room. The woman's hair was stuffed into a dirty cotton mobcap, a hastily drawn string causing the ruffles to bunch unevenly around her face. She had fat cheeks, bulging and sunburned, and a set of badly discolored teeth. But there was cheer in her dull gray eyes, a lazy contentment as she enjoyed the shade and her baby.

"I'm from Albany," Vanessa fabricated. "Things aren't much better there so I came back."

"It ain't going to get better, miss," the woman said quietly, "not 'til Johnny stops his blamed marching and gits on with the war. M'name's Maggie by the way."

Vanessa introduced herself as Sullivan, the same name she concocted earlier just in case the young Tory girl decided to come back. She and Maggie chatted a few minutes, until a drum roll from somewhere in the middle of camp drew a commotion of people onto the path. Curious, she noticed it was mostly men in the crowd, each one toting wooden food trays that many used to bat their way forward in the throng.

"Look at them fighting!" Maggie shook her head. "That's why the ladies won't go near them food wagons anymore. The way the men fuss'n shove . . . for just a few morsels! It gits wild at feeding time!"

A few minutes later, men began to return with food on their trays, muscling their way against the crowd to return to their makeshift homes. One man picked his way toward Maggie, handed her a tray and gruffly introduced himself to Vanessa as Jack Kirby. He didn't seem to care that Vanessa had nothing to eat. With her stomach growling noisily, she watched the couple devour a small ration of food, a slice of salt pork, a gil of rice dressed in vinegar. She didn't dare withdraw her sack of food, which was carefully hidden in her garters. The food was too wholesome to eat around these unsatisfied people. There would be time to eat later, she consoled herself, secretly grateful for her husband's foresight.

"No bread again!" Maggie complained as she fingered a spot of rice into the baby's mouth. "It's getting worse, Jackie! Can't feed the babe if I can't feed myself!"

"You'll live a year on what you already got, cow," Jack grumbled, tossed aside his empty tray and stood up. His eyes ran over Vanessa's reclining figure. "What's your name, wench?"

"Her name's Vanessa," Maggie answered. "Leave her be. She's just keeping me company for a spell."

Jack shrugged, a disinterested look on his face as he strolled away. Maggie finished feeding the baby, then finally rose and led Vanessa out of camp to a small woodland stream. While she plopped herself onto the banks and proceeded to wash and diaper her child, Vanessa waded into the stream, hoisted her skirts and slowly lowered herself into the cool water. She sighed and groaned at the same time.

"Albany, eh," Maggie casually conversed. "Shame what them rebels did to that perty Anglican Church, ain't it? Burnt it to the ground! Evil bunch, them Whigs, the way they're carrying on, hating England and her mighty church, making the whole land suffer! Shame it is!"

"I wish it was over," Vanessa agreed and tried to sound sincere.

"It won't be if Johnny don't quit that blamed marching of his! Keeps changing his mind, he does, out there in the middle of nowhere, thinking he'll find an easier place to march on Gates. Won't happen. Not up here in the likes of Mohawk country. Blamed Continentals are holed up in the middle of swampland. We keep telling Johnny he's gotta sit still and wait for 'em to come out but he don't listen. Nope. Just keeps marching around and around, getting himself mired in the swamps. That's why the food's running out! Can't cart wagons through swampland!"

Maggie continued to babble about the war, camp life, babies, long after they reached the tent and settled in the same shady spot alongside the canvas walls. At some point during the conversation, Vanessa finished a slow descent to the ground, nuzzled her face against the cool grass and fell asleep.

It was dark when she awoke. There was no sign of Maggie or the daylight crowds. She had no idea what time it was, noticed the Kirbys' tent flap was closed and quiet, like the rest of camp.

She rose, affected a calm meandering along the dark path until it eventually brought her to the commissary wagons in the middle of the community.

A small group of soldiers had collected there, most lying on blankets under the wagons, a few tossing dice beside a small cooking fire. She didn't recognize their uniforms, dark green waistcoats with buff lapels and britches. It was only their belted carbines that told her these were mounted troops, most likely a detachment from St. Leger's cavalry company.

Just for effect, she stopped within sight of them, yawned and stretched languidly until one of the batmen issued a low whistle in her direction. She feigned a timid smile and watched one man boldly come to his feet while his friends heckled him on. "You looking for someone, doxy?" He came close enough for her to see the eager sparkle in his eyes.

"No one in particular," she demurred with a shy glance at the ground, then furrowed her brow in an expression of innocent trouble. "I can't sleep, is all. My stomach's growling . . ."

Disappointment flashed across the man's face, as if he was instantly irritated to discover she was just another beggar in the night. He sighed, walked away with a disgusted roll of his eyes.

She flew after him, pretended rising hysteria by clutching his arm and whining, "Surely you can spare one piece of bread! I'm with child! I can't keep from getting sick when my stomach's empty!"

"I got m'orders, miss. One loaf of bread per family every two days—"

"But I've not had any bread in a week!"

"They all say that!" he grumbled, trying to shake off her grip but she held him fast. He turned around, confronting her with a nasty scowl. "It'll do you no good to beg. This is all we have! Word came today Johnny's not sending anymore carts. He's only got a few weeks of food left for his army! Do you understand that? We're running out of food!"

"What!" she wailed in panic. "No more carts?"

"Shut that dame up before she riots the place!" a soldier shouted from the fire.

"Look, lassie," the soldier said, pulled her against the wagon and whispered, "the army's organizing a food raid in Bennington next week. There'll be more then. All you have to do is live on a bit less for a week."

"Are you sure?" she asked, as if unwilling to believe him.

"I'm sure, alright. We've been told to sit tight with what we got because they're planning a big raid over there. Be more than enough for us all when they get back. You don't think Johnny's going to let his army get weak, do you? Ha! We're the best in the world! We don't panic over a few low rations. Here," he said, looked around, then thrust a hand into his pocket and withdrew a fistful of raisins. "Take these but don't tell anyone I gave them, alright?"

"Oh! Thank you! Thank you!" she whispered fiercely, gave his arm a grateful squeeze.

"Pretty little wench, ain't she," a soldier commented as she ran back to the path, stuffing the raisins in her mouth like a good starving Tory. In the dark, no one could see her triumphant grin as her brain absorbed every word of his loose talk.

Back at the Kirby tent, she settled on the raw earth, withdrew her sack of edibles and quietly ate them until she was full. Contentment drew her back to the ground where she could enjoy a heady feeling of victory. It seemed to soften the uneven clods of dirt beneath her bones, make all the hardships of this day quickly disappear. Gabriel would be delighted at what she had learned in here tonight. Burgoyne planned to raid Bennington for food! His supplies were critically short!

Vanessa smiled to herself, laid her head on her arm and thought about that far-away Johnny Burgoyne, wondered if he knew a mere woman would betray his secrets tonight.

* * *

"We've got trouble in Skenesboro, Gabe," Robert Blaire announced on his way into the Colonel's hut. The Commander looked up from the last of the day's military paperwork and noticed the grim expression on Robert's face. More bad news, Gabriel thought as he sat back and prepared to hear the worst.

"A young girl was just murdered outside her home in Skenesboro . . . her name was Jane McCrea . . . the fiancee of a Tory Lieutenant. I hear the entire town is in an uproar over it."

His first thought was that Skenesboro was only about three miles north of the Tory camp Vanessa was in. "Was she caught in a skirmish?"

Steve MacLeod sauntered through the open door of the hut, his boyish face drawn tight and hard as he waited for Robert to answer the question.

"Gabe," Robert began, grimaced at Steve and announced, "the girl was scalped. I think St. Leger's Mohawks have finally broken away from him. They've gone out of control."

Both men watched the weary disinterest in Gabriel's eyes turn into a crisp, keen vision. This placed Vanessa in real danger. In order to leave the camp and reach his men, she would have to travel a quarter mile alone.

He got up, headed straight for the door. "Let's get her out of there," he commanded, grabbed his saddle and heaved it out into the night. A sharp whistle brought the farrier scurrying. "Get my mount." Standing half in and half out of the night, he started muttering under his breath, "The one night I let her out of my sight . . . those restless Mohawks decide to spook."

Why did everything with Vanessa go wrong?

Gabriel's black stallion was brought to the stoop, the farrier hastily tossing the saddle over its back. The soldier was still buckling the girdle straps when the Colonel leaped atop it, all the while muttering under his breath,

"Damn woman . . . forever seducing me away from my better judgment. Steve! Let's go!" To Robert he called, "Take command until I get back."

Steve hustled out the door, straight into the cloud of dust kicked up by the sudden bolt of Gabriel's steed. He choked, barked for a horse, watched his Commander ride off into the enveloping darkness, nothing but the thunder of hooves to tell him what direction to follow.

Gabriel and Steve rode hard, stopping only to water their horses and hear the details of the McCrea murder as the news hummed through the advanced outposts of Moylan's Horse. The closer they got to Skenesboro, the more grisly the tale became. Young Jane was shot in the back, then dragged into the woods to be scalped while her terrified aunt looked on.

"Don't like the feel of this place," Steve whispered as they picked their way toward the hillside overlooking the Tory camp. The woods were so dark they could barely see one another's faces. "It's too still out here."

Gabriel noticed Steve was chewing hard on a mouthful of tobacco, a sign of rising tension in this otherwise tranquil southern son. Other than the racket of crickets, theirs was the only sound in the woods on this windless night. Gabriel looked around for some sign of the riflemen sent to guard his wife but there was none. They fell quiet, let their horses feel the way forward until they reached the place where the land began to slope downward.

"Here," Gabriel said, dismounted and tethered his horse to keep it still. "When the sun rises, we'll be able to see the entrance."

A turkey gobble sounded from very close by. They both stopped, looked up.

"That's our boys," Steve announced. "They're in the damn trees! Must be something wrong . . . "

Gabriel issued a soft birdcall into the night, listened to it echo back at him from only fifty feet away. He followed it, let the hidden sniper draw him to the base of a mammoth old oak. Although he couldn't see in the dark, he whispered up at the branches. "What's the trouble, soldier?"

"Indians . . . "

The hair on the back of his neck stood up. "Where?"

"They're all over the place, Gabe! Look yonder . . . on the other side of the clearing . . . you'll see their fires . . . been watching them all night!"

"Is someone getting her out of there?"

"We can't get near it, Gabe . . . "

"I don't want her coming out of there alone!"

"We got the best sniper right there beside the path, Gabe. She'll make it . . . "

He was already moving through the dark, back to where he left Steve on the hillside. He climbed a tree and looked out across the dark clearing.

He saw the campfires at once, tiny specks of orange in the blinding blackness.

"Damnit!" This was his worst fear. Just the thought of her coming out of the camp alone in the morning, directly beside those campfires, made the hair on his arms stand up. "I've got to get in there—"

"No, Gabe . . . wait."

He was already moving down the hill, Steve cursing and sliding after him.

A crow screeched from somewhere close by, a signal from another sniper that instantly halted their advance. It was a warning. They shot behind the nearest tree, squatted low, their carbines cocking in perfect synchrony.

Frozen in place, they huddled for what seemed like a long time, waiting, watching, listening.

Nothing happened.

"I don't believe this!" The words tumbled off his lips

like the sudden gust of a fierce wind. He started to get up but Steve grabbed his arm and jerked it hard.

"No . . . we've gotta stay here . . . there's no telling how many of them are down there—"

"I don't care. My wife's in there and I'm getting her out!" There was no stopping him, no strength that could withstand the brutal power in the arm wrenching out of his grasp. Steve had no choice but to follow, to cover him, to creep along behind his dark figure as it leaped and darted through the foliage.

Another birdcall screamed through the air. They hit the dirt again, face down and rigid, lay there and waited with every nerve in their bodies ready to spring at the slightest movement.

None came.

Gradually, they got up again but stayed huddled against the gnarled roots of a half-dead evergreen. They were both breathing hard, ragged, their eyes darting around until one of them finally noticed the sun starting to rise. Faint slivers of light began to creep through the black sky above them.

"Let's wait . . . a few more minutes . . . let the light come . . . " Gabriel commanded and Steve breathed a sigh of relief.

They waited, the minutes ticking by, each one making the Colonel more and more restless. He fidgeted constantly, taking his field glass in and out of his belt, resetting his hat four different ways, checking the load in his carbine over and over again.

"Gabe, will you *please* sit still!" Steve finally snapped at him.

Gabriel just growled at him, stood up and poised his glass on the entrance to the camp. His figure fell very still as the glass moved between the campfire and the half-hidden path between the Tory tents and the hillside they were perching on.

He saw her then, just a glimpse of her black hair and faded yellow dress before she moved behind a screen of trees.

"There she is . . . " he announced, "right on time."

The screech of a blue jay rent the air. It shrieked once, twice, loud and rakish.

"To hell with it," Gabriel cursed the signal and the danger it announced. "I'm going after her—"

"Gabe!" Steve shot to his feet, leaped into the same frantic downward motion as Gabriel.

The Colonel issued a new birdcall into the air, the scream of a crow that told his hidden snipers it was time to load. Although they couldn't hear them, they both sensed the cocking of carbines in the still morning air.

Vanessa was in no hurry, Gabriel could see through his glass, probably heard the birdcalls but didn't suspect they were unnatural. He focused his glass on where she walked a few hundred feet below him, moving calmly with a metal canteen swinging at her side. Like some earthy woodland nymph she looked, clothed in that loose shift, her feet bare, black braids bobbing on her breasts.

A crow screamed back at him, made the hair on the back of his neck tickle upright. He raised his field glass again, stopped moving just long enough to whirl the lens across the edge of the timber that surrounded the clearing she was now crossing. Human silhouettes blurred between the trunks of the trees. The crow screamed again, then once more.

Danger. Danger.

His heart began to pound, the hand around the glass fisting into a tight squeeze. He watched the forms in the woods slowly materialize through the trees until they moved into the soft new light of day.

Mohawks. The sight of their gleaming red skin brought him to a sudden halt. There were four of them, moving quickly, their bodies slightly hunched as they stalked the unsuspecting woman in the middle of the field.

He could hardly believe this was actually happening, that any man could possibly be this unlucky. Even worse was to stand here and watch this scenario unfold into such a horrifying reality.

As if to taunt him further, his glass slid across her figure, saw her face turned up at the sky, so sleepy and lazy and unaware of the danger that was creeping up on her from behind. Just to look at her serenity while those barepated savages stalked her made the blood in his veins swell with a kind of raw and terrible energy.

The glass dropped out of his hand, his legs tensing with a sudden influx of wild strength. He started to run, faster, harder, speeding downward through a blurring rush of trees and brush and woodland mist. They were too close and he was too far. He could just barely hear Steve crashing after him, desperately trying to keep up with him as he leaped and twisted and slid around anything in his path.

He was close enough to see without his glass, to notice how the Indians focused their eyes upon her back, seemed riveted to that moment when she finally heard some sound of theirs and turned around.

Time faded into the pounding rhythm of his own frenzied heartbeat, the sound of his short ragged breaths. His vision sharpened until he could see the entire picture of this moment and every tiny detail within it. Red skin flashing with body oil in the newly risen sun, the abrupt motion of a savage finally lunging across the final gap of space between them and her.

A tomahawk whipped upward, the metal edge glinting as vibrantly as the gay-colored feathers on its handle, the wooden grip hidden by the hard-knuckled fist of the Indian's hand. Vanessa spun around, her skirt fanning outward in a whirl of yellow. She saw them, screamed.

The canteen shot out of her grip, flew across the sky just as a gun exploded in front of Gabriel's face.

It was his own carbine. He was in the clearing, on his belly in the grass.

Vanessa screamed again, looked toward the flash from his muzzle, then at the blood that splashed up her arm from the Indian he just shot. She recoiled, her face twisted in sudden horror, her arms flying up before her face as another tomahawk rose in the air above her.

Gabriel's gun was spent. He grabbed for a ball, powder, realized he couldn't load fast enough and used the only other weapon he had.

His own voice.

"Fire!"

Snipers opened up from everywhere, sent bright orange blasts of fire spitting through the dense green cover of trees that surrounded the green. Plumes of smoke frothed into the field, billowed around the Indians who were suddenly darting off in every direction.

Great clouds of spent powder swept through the clearing. He momentarily lost sight of her, kept watching the spot where she was until her form slowly reappeared.

She was teetering, falling forward. Her knees finally hit the ground and she bent forward to present a sight that stole all sanity from his brain.

She had an axe in her back.

Dear God! They'd killed her.

"NO!"

His spirit recoiled with a pain that sliced through his brain like a stunning blow. He no longer knew who he was, what he was doing, where he was, just that he was on his feet and running straight into this deranged moment. Steve screamed something at him but he couldn't hear what he said, only felt the cloth of his legging tear as he whipped his leg out from the sniper's frantic grasp.

Enemy soldiers started pouring out of the woods and

the air split with rifle fire. A new flood of smoke poured across the field, covered the place where he hit the ground and started crawling toward the now prostrate figure of his wife. His fingers clawed at the ground, heaving him forward, his belly banging and thudding into clumps of rock and knotted weed. Pungent powder formed a thick haze over his head, the deafening sounds of violence roaring in his ears even though he felt strangely distant from it all, as if it was coming from some other world.

Only once before did he ever feel this queer displacement between world and self.

It was the moment he watched Michael die.

Gabriel reached her, his fingers sliding over her outflung hands.

"*Vive . . . vive . . .* " he heard himself begging over and over again. Live! Live! "Nessy . . . please . . . "

Movement. Her fingers. They were moving, twitching under the envelope of his hands, then suddenly groping for a hold. Her head lifted from the grass, orchid eyes spinning upward with a roll of pain and horror until they found his face and widened in frantic recognition. "Oh my God . . . Gabriel . . . "

A new feeling surged through his body, the most powerful and magnificent sensation he had ever felt.

She was alive.

The ax was behind her shoulder, not fatal, just bad enough to make her blood seep down the fabric of her shift in long feathery dribbles.

Vanessa felt herself being pulled forward until the top of her head collided with his. They both had their faces in the dirt, nothing but their fingers free to communicate this first moment of cognizance between them. Long brown fingers entwined with trembling white, caught and held so tight she could only lie there and absorb the feel of him in a rush of desperate relief. From somewhere inside the raging fury in her brain, she saw herself in this exact scenario only a few months ago, in a field alongside her father's house. With her face in the mud, and it was this same pair of hands that lifted her back into life.

"Gabriel . . . "

"Just hold on . . . as tight as you can . . . "

She obeyed, tightened her grip, which brought a hot flash of pain from her back and sent it shooting clear up her arm. She cried out, but he couldn't hear her under the gunfire, just continued to inch backward and drag her with him. The agony made her sob aloud, pant and whimper for mercy, but she wouldn't let go of her mighty hold on his hands. The pain didn't matter. Not now. Not here in this field full of thunder and smoke and the wild shouts of men clashing in war and hate. It was utter bedlam, the air split with the steady staccato rhythm of gunfire, burnt powder stinging down her throat with every breath.

By the time his boots inched into the woods, they were both choking on the acrid smoke, their eyes stinging, their throats parched. Only when the trees sheltered them from the haze of violence did Gabriel roll over, snatch her against him and get to his feet.

He started running up the hill, his boots digging into the earth, scattering dirt and leaves and fragrant pine needles. Stray bullets whistled and pinged through the woods around them as he scaled the hillside with an incredible speed, demanding the fullest strength from every muscle in his body as he clutched her in his arms and hurtled toward his tethered mount.

She started drifting in and out of consciousness, awake only enough to keep her grip on two fistfuls of his linen shirt. It seemed like only a split second between when he ripped the tether loose and they were atop the mount, speeding recklessly through the woods, away from the unearthly din in the field.

There was a new flash of pain in her back, then something cold and wet splashing over her face. She choked back into reality, opened her eyes just in time to see the hatchet whirling away into the woods.

"Help . . . hurts . . . oh God . . . " she heard herself babbling, grabbing at him against the wild bouncing motion of their frantic flight. She watched his face loom over her, his eyes intense and piercing from behind the auburn density of his billowing hair. In that single glance of his Vanessa saw the reality of what had just happened, of how narrowly they had both escaped death.

She couldn't look away. Their gazes were glued as tightly as her body against the solid mass of his heaving breast. How differently she saw him now, this towering champion of peace and good will, this brilliant and brutal soldier who somehow managed to redeem her. Once again he ran straight into the jaws of death for her, making the life of this beaten woman suddenly, overwhelmingly, valuable.

She reached for him, by instinct alone, a shock of pain and blood coursing down her back as she cradled his face in her dirty hands.

"Gabriel . . . "

He dropped the reins. The horse reared. Gabriel clutched her and issued some deep guttural moan through his parted and panting lips.

The reaction was mindless, the way their lips suddenly, savagely joined. The boiling terror in her gut slowly released, pouring the warmth of life through her body, and then into his. Up the front of his chest she could feel herself climbing, as if trying to get inside him, her eyes closed and her ears shut against anything but the feel of his mighty hands fisting in her hair, the breathless sound of his sighs beneath her wild kiss. They just hung there in the saddle of his wandering steed, groping, moaning into one another, the muffled sounds of two spirits soaring in a sudden and breathtaking relief to find one another so unbelievably alive.

They snapped apart in the same moment, dazed by the intensity of it, yet too stunned by the morning's events to wonder why or what they were doing. With her face pressed deeply into his sweaty blouse, she touched her bruised lips with a wildly shaking hand and finally burst into tears.

"It's alright, Nessy . . . we're safe . . . it's all over . . . "

He was riding again, hard and fast, barely noticing the route as mile after mile fell behind them. She was bleeding hard, weakening fast, lying limp and spent against him by the time he thundered into the confines of his camp.

One sight of them brought a shout of alarm through the camp. Soldiers stopped their drills, dropped their weapons, ran toward him. Francis came speeding through the crowd at Gabriel's hut, took one look at Vanessa's blood-soaked back and ran for his bag.

Gabriel went inside his hut and kicked the door shut. He laid her face-down on his cot and cringed at the gory sight of her wound. He rose to fetch something, anything that might stem the bleeding.

"Don't leave!" she nearly screamed the minute his weight lifted off the cot.

"I'm here . . . " he said, his whisper so close she could feel the breath of his words rustling through her hair.

"Come closer . . . " she begged, waited until she could feel his long hard body sliding alongside her, partially covering her like a warm blanket on a cold winter night. She was shaking so hard her teeth chattered. "L-listen to me . . . you've got to do something . . . "

"About what?"

"Johnny has no more food . . . "

"What?"

She could feel him stiffen in attention. "There won't be any more wagons for the Tories. Those people are half-starved already . . . " She stopped as a wave of pain rattled through her, making her clench her eyes and gasp through her teeth, "The commissary told me that Burgoyne plans to raid Bennington . . . "

"New Hampshire?"

"Yes! He's sending a large group there next week . . . to raid for food. You've got to do something, Gabriel!" she insisted, her voice rising into an almost hysterical pitch.

"Be still! Please . . . let me handle this."

A food raid to Bennington. He couldn't spare the men for a counterattack but Gates could, Gates and the Captain of the New Hampshire militia, John Stark. Gabriel swung a leg off the bed, attempted to get up, but once again she cried out to him.

"Don't leave me! I don't want to die . . . "

"I won't let you die . . . I swear it . . . "

"I need you, Gabriel . . . "

Silence fell over him, his whole body seeming to pause at the sound of her words. A soft moan of his whispered against the side of her face, "I know . . . "

Gabriel appeared in the doorway of his hut, dazed and disheveled, his left sleeve splattered with blood. The sight of him instantly quieted everyone, stopped their arguments about what happened, who did it, what was going on. Few of them had ever seen their fearless Commander look as shaken as he did at this moment.

"Gabe?" Francis took hold of his arm, searched for the injury there. "What happened . . . where are you hurt?"

Gabriel looked down at himself, at his wife's blood. "It's Vanessa . . . " he said quietly, focused on the Surgeon's dull blue eyes. "She took an ax in the back . . . "

Polly Blaire nearly swooned. "No!" she cried, rushed forward, her face drained of all color by the time she reached Gabriel. "Is she alright?"

"I think so," he told Polly, gently moving out of her clutches as he said to Francis, "Go to her." He looked around, found Benny, brought the sentry alongside him and started to issue orders as they walked.

"Tell Gates that Burgoyne is in more serious trouble than we thought. He has no food for his camp followers and plans to raid Bennington to get more. Suggest he notify the New Hampshire militia to give the enemy the welcome they deserve."

Gabriel walked away and everyone followed him. They were asking him questions but he couldn't answer just then. He kept seeing a vision of her falling forward in the field, the decorated wooden handle of the ax imbedded in her soft flesh.

They meant to kill her, snuff out her life.

Anger. It started to swell through his dazed body until he felt warm and stiff all over. Just the idea of what those savages nearly did to his wife made him sick with rage. Even worse was the rising of his own guilt for letting her go there in the first place.

"Here Gabe . . . drink this." Benny was falling into step beside him, handing him a flask of rum.

Gabriel grabbed the sack, tilted his head back into the sun and gulped it down until that golden orb started to float around and around in the sky.

The flask emptied. He hurled it away, heard it slap into the wall of a hut. The sound was like an invisible key turning in the lock of a door he knew he shouldn't open.

But he couldn't help it.

Rage exploded in a sudden, violent burst of strength that found his arms wrapping around the belly of a barrel of rainwater, hoisting it up, flinging it into the air. The crowd of soldiers scrambled for cover as the toe of his boot ripped through a stack of muskets and sent the guns scattering across the dirt. A water trough was wrenched from the ground and sent to the same fate as the rain barrel.

"Cursed Mohawks!" he bellowed aloud, his English breaking apart until he spoke entirely in French. "Can't I do anything right with her? One time! Just one time I let her out of my sight and once again she nearly dies! Damnit! Will no one let her live?"

First her father, now the Indians. Who would be next? And why her? Why Vanessa Davis? What was it about this innocent lamb that all the forces of evil felt so compelled to destroy?

Gabriel wrapped his fists around a tethering post, yanked on it furiously. It finally broke loose. The splintered bits of it were hurled at an oncoming soldier.

Steve MacLeod. He was back from the skirmish.

Steve popped out of his saddle and flew straight into the body of his furious Commander, slammed him against the wall of a hut.

"Damn you, Gabe! The next time you run into a field full of Brunswickers I'm not covering you!" Steve barked into his face, his eyes dazed with the same delirium Gabriel felt inside. Combat. It had a way of doing this to men. Especially hard, mean combat like the skirmish they had just engaged in. Steve pushed his mighty shoulders against the wall and hollered, "Not one of us got cut down . . . we got out of there alive even though you ran right off with her . . . never even looked back—"

"She's my wife!" Gabriel thundered in defense of his conduct. With one swing of his forearm, Steve's hold was broken, the young soldier sent staggering backward.

Steve fell against the wall of the next hut, banging his head hard enough to momentarily stun him. "Phewee! That was one helluva skirmish, Gabe."

They both looked at each other, suddenly cognizant of what they were doing, then burst into a fit of hilarity that had them both careening against the wall of the hut. They roared until the sounds of their laughter seemed to fill the entire camp, from one end to the other.

A large group of stunned soldiers stood around them and watched in wide-eyed disbelief, having never seen these two hardened soldiers act this way.

"St. Claire? Which one of you is Colonel St. Claire?"

An unfamiliar Continental regular was moving through the crowd, looking at everyone as if they'd all gone daft.

"I've a message from Horatio Gates . . . can you show me to the Colonel?"

Benny Cooke lumbered over to the hapless soldier, sighed in acute irritation at this regulation interruption. "Can't you see we're in the middle of something here, soldier? Give me that damned note."

"I can't, sir! I'm told to deliver it straight into the hands of Colonel St. Claire."

"Suit yourself," Benny growled, pointed at Gabriel. "That's him . . . the one with the bloody arm."

"Colonel?" The soldier didn't see any indication of rank on the appointed man. He saw only a mud-stained and disheveled giant who was perched against the wall of a hut, using his blood-stained sleeve to wipe away tears of laughter.

He was still chuckling when he looked at the Continental sentry. "State your business, boy."

"Colonel St. Claire?"

"Yes! Yes!" He popped off the wall of the hut, crossed the distance between them in three strides of his long, muscular legs. Only when he was nose to nose with the sentry did he say in his deep, rugged voice, "Where's your salute, soldier?"

"Sir!" The young man snapped to attention, barely aware of how quickly the Colonel snatched the note out of his fisted hand. "I'm honored to meet you, sir."

"Oh? Why is that?" Gabriel was already breaking open the seal of the note.

"But sir! You're quite famous!"

"Quit blubbering over him," Benny commanded, steering the soldier away. "What you got, Gabe?"

Gabriel read the relay twice, he was so shocked at the news. The fifteen-hundred-man army of Colonel Barry St.

Leger was in retreat, having been abandoned by his large contingent of hired Mohawks. Without the natives as guides, he'd lost track of Burgoyne in the New York wilderness and finally ordered his half-starved and frightened men to retreat toward Albany.

Gabriel handed the note to Benny, looked at Steve and said, "Those Mohawks were part of St. Leger's army."

"What?"

Benny hurled the note into the sky and bawled, "HUZZAH! ST. LEGER IS IN RETREAT!"

Gabriel watched his men let out a roar of triumph, their fists thrusting into the sky, grins of victory covering their faces. Despite his own discomfort, he wouldn't steal this from them. He spread his arms and declared the day devoted to celebration. A part of Burgoyne's army had just fallen. They deserved the day off.

Although it took a while, he rose to the occasion himself, joined in the camp's merriment as they lavished themselves on roasted beef, barrels of ale, whatever else suited their fancy.

It was a well-earned respite from too many depressing defeats, and in his usual generous manner, Gabriel decided not to care what they did with this victorious moment, regulation or not.

"Didn't Gates once serve the British?" Lauren Stuart asked, his head full of red hair firmly planted against the rough bark wall of a hut.

"I believe so," Gabriel said absently, swallowing another gulp of rum as he continued to watch the door to his hut. "I think I'll fetch my bourbon—"

"Gabe, leave Francis alone in there. She's in good hands." Lauren grabbed his arm, yanked him back down to the ground.

"What's taking him so long?"

"Phewee!" Steve whistled through his teeth. "That woman's got a hold on you, man!"

"What?" Gabriel threw back his head and scoffed at the sky. "Listen to him, will you? The one who writes his woman so many letters we need an extra packhorse to send the mail—"

"Go to hell, Gabe!"

"I think you two had a bit too much combat today," Robert opined intelligently. "You'll both feel better in the morning."

"I don't like the idea of an ex-limey being in charge." Benny was still grumbling about Gates. "Humph! Figures they'd replace a she-rabbit with a pig-nut."

Gabriel looked at the Sergeant curiously. "What the devil is a pig-nut?"

"That's a nut with a skin so tough, ya' need a sledgehammer to crack it open. Once you do, there ain't nothing in it!"

Gabriel roared with laughter, delighted by the analogy. He lifted his cup, just about to toast his clever Sergeant when the door of his hut opened and Francis stepped outside.

The Surgeon found him in the crowd, squatted before the Colonel and reassured him, "It was a deep enough wound that I had to stitch it." Gabriel winced. "But she's alright."

"Poor lass," Benny offered clumsily. "Did it hurt?"

Francis ignored him. "She's resting now. I gave her something to help her sleep for awhile. It'll be sore when she wakes . . . her arm a bit stiff for a week or so but I expect she'll recover completely."

"My thanks to you, Francis."

Francis accepted his gratitude with a nod. "She was lucky to have you so near, Gabe. That was quick thinking to get her back here so fast. The blood loss might have cost you the child."

Gabriel's hand paused in the process of handing the flask to Francis. He fell very still, stared at the Surgeon with a suddenly blank look on his face.

"I didn't know she was with child, Gabe," Lauren commented and grinned in congratulations.

"Hey! Let's drink to the Colonel's babe!" Benny suggested as if they needed another excuse to drink. "Go fill my flask, Will."

"Fill it yourself, *Sergeant!* I'm a Captain. I don't take orders from you."

"You're always bragging about being a Captain, Will. You're getting big-headed," Steve told his brother with the utmost seriousness.

"What child?" Gabriel asked, but no one heard him.

"So what's all the ruckus about out here, eh?" Francis wanted to know.

"St. Leger's in retreat," Robert explained just as Gabriel leaped off the wall and headed toward his cabin.

Francis tried to waylay him. "She's sleeping now, Gabe . . . it might be better if you didn't disturb her."

It was dark inside his hut, the shutters drawn against the daylight. Polly was sitting at the table, her lap full of stitching, a lone candle lit to aid her vision. She looked up when Gabriel entered, gave him a soft and comforting smile.

"She's sleeping, Gabriel."

Vanessa was on his cot in the far corner, near the fire well, a warm blanket covering her figure. She was lying on her stomach, only the lumpy bulge of bandages behind her left shoulder betraying the near fatal injury that had her abed in the middle of this harrowing day. It wasn't until he came closer that he saw her eyes were open.

"Ness . . . " was all he said, watched a slim white arm come out from under the blanket, reach for him. He took her hand at once, came to his knees beside the bed and looked at her thoroughly, as if in search of some evidence of the child he now knew her to be carrying.

She tried to smile at the tender kiss he awarded her hand, but her teeth were clenched. "Francis said I'll be fine . . . " she reassured, but her voice was weaker than he'd ever heard it before.

His earlier concern doubled now because it was not just for her but the child too. "Don't speak . . . save your strength," he said, leaned over her, smoothed the hair away from her cheeks and whispered for only her ears to hear, "Everything will be alright. I'll take care of you . . . and the child."

His mention of the baby brought a flutter of nervousness through her. It was still so new to her, the whole idea of being a mother, of having the life of this man imbedded within her body. It made their precarious marriage seem so much more permanent.

Her eyelids felt unusually heavy when she looked at him, at the worry and concern etched upon his face. Guilt raked through her heart just to see his anxiety, realize how trapped he was now in a relationship with a woman who could only deny him.

"I can't bear the unfairness of it," she said and closed her eyes against the sight of him. Maybe Francis was wrong about her symptoms. Maybe it was something else.

No. She hadn't bled since Gabriel left for New York.

"What's unfair?" he asked while his powerful hand toyed with her hair.

"What I'm doing to your life. I'm ruining it, Gabriel . . . "

He sighed at her, the movement of his hand pausing for a moment. "You're not responsible for the choices I've made with my life, Vanessa. I'm a grown man. I make my own decisions. No matter what problems we have, I will not leave you. Do you hear me? Nothing will make me leave you now—"

Leave? Had he been thinking of leaving her? She almost didn't want to know but felt compelled to ask him. After all, she owed him her life and if the situation called for it, she would be willing to return his own. "Have you considered leaving?"

"Yes," he admitted without hesitation, "more than once." She flinched, swallowed hard, tried not to feel so disturbed at what he was telling her. "But there's no point in discussing it now."

"No point?" She tried to lift her head but the motion sent a jab of pain stinging across her back, fierce enough to rip a cry of agony from her lips.

"Mon Dieu!" Gabriel rasped, eased her back down and held her there. "No more of this talk—"

"But I can't do this to you!" she cried, her eyes filling with tears from both the sting in her back and the emotion rising in her throat. "Please . . . we can come to some agreement about the baby—"

"Stop! I'll agree to nothing but what is right."

"You and your godforsaken righteousness!" she cursed, clenched her eyes. "You deserve so much better than this!"

"What I deserve and what I want have always been two different matters with you, woman. Now be still!"

"What do you see in me?" she wailed aloud. "For God's sake, my own father wanted me dead! How can you ruin your life over someone like me—"

"Stop it! I won't listen to such talk from you!" She was getting hysterical and it was his fault. Once again, he felt like a fumbling fool with her and it made him angry, frustrated. "I risked my life for you today, woman! Why don't you base your opinion on that instead of what your father thought, eh?"

"Because I don't know how!" she choked, a throat full of sobs suddenly spilling loose. Her misery resounded in the room like a cloudburst, bringing Gabriel onto the cot where he could use his own body to stifle her.

"Hush now . . . please . . . I beg you."

He draped himself over her, his long hard body resting alongside her. She could do nothing more but cling to him and weep, holding onto him with all her might just like she'd done this morning in a field full of bullets.

And in another field, not so very long ago, when these very hands snatched her back from the death she thought she deserved.

She realized it then, somewhere in the middle of the raging turmoil in her heart.

It wasn't just Gabriel she clung to now, it was herself. It was life. It was the woman he found so valuable he would twice risk his own life to spare.

Who was she?

It was a long time later when she finally wept herself to sleep, her fists slowly unraveling from the blouse she clung to. Gabriel untangled himself from her, swung his legs off the side of the cot and just sat there staring at the floor between his boots. He never felt so overwhelmed by life as he did at this moment. The only thing that was clear to him right now was that he wanted the child and he wanted his wife, no matter how misguided those desires seemed to be.

The creak of leather boots made him look up.

Francis was there, leaning on the edge of his desk. One look at his face told Gabriel he'd heard everything. There was a flood of question in the Surgeon's glance, bewilderment and a silent entreaty to discuss what was normally a man's private business.

Gabriel came to the desk, pulled back a chair and motioned Francis into it. He sat across from him, Polly's abandoned stitching piled on the tabletop between them.

It took a long while to tell the tale but Francis was patient, never once interrupting him. Gabriel divulged it all, from the moment he met Vanessa at the Borden dinner party to how narrowly she escaped death on the morning of their marriage. Francis was clearly moved by what he was hearing, by the tragedies of this young woman's life, by how twisted and complicated her relationship with Gabriel really was.

When he was finished, Gabriel sat back in his chair,

crossed his arms over his chest and looked at the astounded Surgeon sitting across from him.

"It sounds worse than it is, Francis. We've had a few good moments between us."

"Gabriel," Francis began, then stopped to run his hands through his hair. He sighed once, shook his head at the top of the desk as if frustrated by an attempt to collect his thoughts. "What I don't understand is why you felt so compelled to marry her under these conditions. Surely a man of your considerable wealth could have made some other arrangement."

"The only arrangement I could tolerate was this one. Her honor was stolen—"

"For God's sake, Gabriel, many a woman loses her honor by accident in this day . . . especially in the chaos of war! I hardly think you needed to go so far."

"I've gone further than this," Gabriel said, "far enough to see my brother murdered."

"But that was ten years ago—"

"I know *precisely* how long ago it was, Francis," he said, his voice sounding much sharper than he intended. Francis stopped short and just looked at him. He saw the anger in his Commander's eyes, bitterness and pain.

"Gabriel, I know this is a sensitive subject with you, but it frightens me how acutely you still grieve for Michael after all this time. You must try to get over it."

Gabriel shot out of his chair, propelled by that tell-tale sting he felt any time someone scratched at this raw and aching wound in his spirit. "Get over it? You can't understand the way of twins, otherwise you wouldn't ask this of me. Twins aren't like other brothers. They're closer somehow . . . more combined. Michael was as much me as I am. Can you understand that?" He turned around, faced Francis from across the room. "Well?"

"No."

"Then don't tell me what to get over—"

"Gabe, you can't live the rest of your life like this . . . always suffering inside."

Francis was right and this unnerved him, made him want to kick something, but he was too afraid of waking Vanessa. Instead, he leaned over the fire and brutally stabbed at the wood with an iron poker. "You can't help me. I'll always be like this . . . always see his face when I look in a mirror . . . hear his voice whenever I speak." He stopped, tossed aside the poker with a deep-throated growl. "Enough of this. Leave me be where Michael is concerned."

"That's not a good idea any more, Gabe. You've got a wife now . . . a baby on the way. They deserve all of you, Gabriel. You're too fair a man to argue with that."

Gabriel heard him, Francis knew, because he seemed to quiet for a moment. His gaze shifted to his sleeping wife, his eyes lingering upon her for a long moment. "I believe I gave her all of me, Francis. That's why she's with child."

He went to the door, pulled it open, looked back at Francis as if he would say something more but changed his mind. Instead, he just stepped outside, then quietly shut the door behind him.

16

The two men arrived at the Hoffman House in Kingston, paid for their beds and followed the maid upstairs. The stairwell was so narrow they could barely fit themselves and their belongings through the tiny tunnel as it wound toward the second floor. When they emerged, they found themselves in a giant room with sloped ceilings and a lone window at the far end, which had obviously once been an attic in the old fieldstone house. Two rows of straw mattresses were tidily arranged across the room and the maid pointed at a pair of them, dropped linens and a blanket on each, then left.

A public sleeping place was all they could find in a town full of adjutants to Washington's Northern Department. This was Continental territory and they would no doubt be sleeping alongside many men here on war business just like they were. One glance around the loft told them ten men were already staying here, their mattresses heaped with satchels, clothing, spare boots, riding accessories.

They arranged their own belongings on the assigned beds, then went downstairs to the taproom. There was little else to do but sit and wait for their contact to appear, which could be days from now. Until then, they would drink, wander through Kingston, try to decide the best way to make St. Claire talk once they were led to his camp in the northern woods.

It wouldn't be easy. Neither man was excited about the prospect of dealing with this notorious young Colonel, a man known to be the finest Continental spy on the continent.

Weeks ago, at the Blue Dolphin, Jonnie Meeks told them everything he knew about Gabriel, including his history in France. This aspect of the St. Claire enigma was the most fascinating: not the death of his twin brother, but the strange circumstances surrounding their lives.

Gabriel and Michael St. Claire were identical twins, supposedly a mirror-image of one another. So alike were they in physical appearance, their own parents could easily mistake one for the other, and the twins were known to take advantage of this situation. The trading of identities was like a game to them because they could mimic one another so faultlessly. They were rarely caught at it.

Until that last fateful afternoon of Michael's young life.

They were caught trading places with the woman Gabriel was betrothed to marry, and it was the last time they would ever play their game. Michael bedded the girl and she conceived. Her father was so outraged he came to the St. Claire estate on that fateful afternoon with every intention of punishing the man he thought was Gabriel. Much to their parents horror, the last moment of Michael's life was when he threw himself in front of Gabriel, revealing the game, then dying for it in the arms of his twin. Gabriel immediately drew his sword and cut down Michael's killer on the front lawn, in broad daylight. A field full of workers saw it all.

Murder was punished by guillotine in France. The St. Claire family had already lost one son, and realized their only hope of sparing the other was to flee the country. Michael St. Claire's body was interred the same evening of his death by the family's faithful servants, a lonely burial the survivors still grieved about. They never saw him buried.

This was where the tale turned chilling.

Meeks claimed Francis Stone once told him that facial bullet wounds were only fatal half the time. Perhaps this was why Gabriel always spoke about his twin in queerly living terms, as if in some deep place in his heart, he hid a hope that Michael might not have died after all. "Michael does this," he would sometimes say, or "Michael always says . . . " But these comments were rare, Meeks claimed, rare enough to be, perhaps, a slip of the tongue.

"I tell you," Meeks said at the end of their meeting in the Dolphin, "Gabriel can imitate Michael so well even the look in his eye changes . . . as if that dead twin is standing right in front of you. My wife claims the hair on her arms stands up whenever he does that . . . downright unnatural it is. No wonder he's so good at what he does. The man was born and raised in the practice of imitation."

"What are you driving at, Meeks?"

"That Michael is still alive . . . that *he* might be the Archangel. I swear to you, no two men on earth are more capable of managing such a ruse. I daresay, those two could fool their own parents if they wanted to. They can certainly fool the lot of us!"

"But why would they do such a cruel thing to their parents . . . let them believe a son is dead when all along he's been alive?"

At this, Meeks could only shrug. "I agree that Gabriel would never do that to his parents, which leads me to believe his parents might know more than we think." He pushed back his chair and got up. "But that's for you to figure out . . . that and why this anonymous spy always seems to be wherever Gabriel is." Meeks grabbed the back of his chair, leaned forward, and whispered something that made the blood in their veins run suddenly cold. "I've always found it strange that he chooses to call himself the Archangel. Funny, but in the Bible, the two archangels mentioned most are Gabriel and Michael."

With that, Meeks slapped a hat on his head and walked out of the Tavern.

Vanessa was recovering beautifully, Gabriel noticed as he sat across from her at the desk and tried to concentrate on reading his mail. Her hair was loose, the way he liked it, partially obscuring her face as she read one of the several letters she had just received from her friends. A yellow cotton shift left her arms bare, the skin glowing soft and white in the early morning sunlight that poured in through the shutters. Every now and again she'd look up, the radiant light of a thousand amethysts glimmering in her violet eyes as she related some news from a letter.

"Dierdre's with child again!" she announced, the edges of her lips curling up into a winsome smile. There was a bit of shyness there as she considered her own delicate condition and dropped her eyes demurely. "Wouldn't it be grand if our children were the same ages."

"Knowing Patrick, no matter how many children we have, he'll be sure to produce a playmate for them all."

She giggled, something blissful passing over her face

just then, a kind of quiet pleasure that he suddenly wanted to indulge himself in.

But he didn't. Although she was softening toward him, especially where their child was concerned, he knew how quickly her bliss could be shattered by the wrong amount of male aggression at the wrong time. Instead, he went back to his own mail, secretly clenching his teeth against a wave of want that would only frighten her.

"Ah! Here's a letter from Tina!" she said gaily, tore it open and read a few lines. "What a marvelous idea! She wants Polly and me to meet her in Kingston for shopping! Can I go?"

"Of course you can," he said at once. Denying her was not his habit and she knew it. "And I'll expect you to buy things for yourself—"

"I can't think of anything I need!"

He could think of many things he needed, especially when he looked at this violet-eyed beauty with her soft white skin and her ripe young body. He looked away.

"I won't allow you to go until you've created of list of things you intend to buy."

"Gabriel! Don't be a tease."

"Then buy something for the child."

He glanced up long enough to watch a look of enlightenment dance across her face.

"Yes . . . I never thought of that." She looked positively blissful for a moment, then regained herself to say, "I suppose we should start preparing—"

"I'll leave that business to you . . . I haven't the slightest idea what babies require."

In spite of herself, there was a moment of soft regard for him that he savored for as long as it lasted. "I'll take care of things then," she offered quietly, responsibly, then hurled her complete attention at smoothing the wrinkles out of Martina's letter.

He decided to concentrate on his own mail, flipped

through the pile of letters again and selected one with a penmanship he didn't recognize. A glance at the signature revealed the writer's identity and Gabriel was instantly intrigued.

George Chaffe. This old whaler was as much a part of the Blue Dolphin pub in Philadelphia as the stools at the bar. Gabriel didn't even know Chaffe could write, let alone that he would get a letter from the man.

Interested, he read through the scrawled and childish script, gleaned a message he wasn't sure he read correctly. He started over, read it again, and this time understood every word.

Nearly a month ago, Chaffe had overheard a meeting between Jonnie Meeks and two unidentified men who presented papers supposedly signed by George Washington. They asked questions about the Archangel, his affiliation with Gabriel St. Claire. Although Jonnie knew never to reveal the link between the two spies, under any circumstance, Chaffe clearly overheard him doing so at this clandestine meeting. In addition, Jonnie gave the two men information regarding the location of Gabriel's intelligence headquarters in New York.

Stunned, Gabriel sat back in his chair, stared at the ceiling and mentally searched for some explanation as to why Jonnie would so blatantly violate his trust. There must be some other reason why Jonnie would tell two strangers such a closely-guarded Continental secret, while endangering Gabriel by disclosing the location of his field headquarters.

The only explanation he could find was that the men presented legitimate papers. They must have been issued from a very high-ranking General. Who? Washington? Gates? Green? And why would they be searching so seriously for the Archangel?

Gabriel got out of his chair, started pacing before the fire well. It didn't make sense that the Continentals would be this driven to discover the Archangel's identity. What did they care who he was so long as they got his information?

No. It wasn't the Continentals. It was the other side. The British had far more reason to be tracking down the Archangel. This spy was a constant and serious threat to their every activity in major theaters of the war.

So they presented phony papers to Jonnie and he was duped by them.

Impossible! Jonnie Meeks was too experienced, too seasoned in underground war activities to be fooled by forged papers.

The man was bought.

"Damnit!" He hissed, stung by the mere thought.

"Gabriel? What's wrong—"

"You'll excuse me, madam," he snarled on his way out the door.

Lauren Stuart didn't believe what he read. "Gabe, Jon wouldn't do this to us—"

"How do we know what Jon would do, eh?"

Lauren just looked at him, stupefied at the mere idea of being betrayed by such a close friend as Jonnie Meeks. For the right price, Jon could tell the British enough about Gabriel and the Archangel to pose a serious threat to his life. A British General would put a high price on Jon's information, perhaps enough to seduce away his loyalties.

Lauren sat in the dirt against the wall of a hut and looked momentarily crushed by the news. "After all you did for Jon and Tina . . . bringing them into your home . . . offering them employment when they'd lost everything."

Gabriel didn't want to be reminded of those early days but the memories were already flooding his mind, reminders of a ten-year friendship that he valued as much as his friendships with Robert and Francis and Lauren.

Jonnie Meeks was born and raised in Pennsylvania, a

true native son, a typical New World man. Perhaps this was why Gabriel was so fascinated by him, spent so many hours drinking with him in the Blue Dolphin. They each had an equal dose of a dry and witty humor that kept everyone laughing inside that busy Philadelphia taproom. Long before Gabriel mastered the English language and became a city hero, he and Jonnie Meeks were a familiar association about town.

Then Jonnie lost his job at the docks. Newly married, his relatives and Martina's living in distant and rural areas of the colony, they decided to stay in the city and try to find work. Weeks passed without an opportunity. Their funds dwindled. They became desperate. When Gabriel was made aware of the situation by a mutual friend, he didn't hesitate to offer the young couple the opportunity they needed.

The Meeks moved into his newly purchased townhouse on Seventh Street, Martina to tend the house, Jon to help him with the extensive renovations Gabriel planned for the interior. Although the arrangement was supposed to be temporary, before long, they'd become like a family.

And then there was war.

Gabriel could still remember how hard Martina cried when he volunteered for service. She clung to him like a sister would, then wrote him daily, told him how dull it was for Jon to go alone to the Dolphin. Gabriel remembered how sad he felt when he read this, during those first few weeks away, when he realized how much he missed the happy home he shared with Jon and Martina Meeks.

"I'm sorry, Gabe."

He looked up, into the sad eyes of Lauren Stuart, and could do little more than shake his head in complete despair.

"We better check with Moylan . . . " Gabriel sighed, stood up and swatted irritably at the dust on his britches, "find out if someone on our side is conducting an investigation."

Lauren nodded without much enthusiasm. "We better secure the area, Gabe. There's no telling where those men are by now."

The warning made Gabriel look back toward his cabin, where his pregnant wife sat contentedly reading her mail. Just the thought of anything happening to her and to the baby was so awful he immediately pushed it out of his mind. "I want those men found . . . whoever they are . . . wherever they are."

"We'll do our best, Gabe—"

"No, you'll get it done."

Vanessa stood before Gabriel's shaving mirror, a palm-sized looking glass hardly big enough for a woman to try on hats. But she managed anyway, and decided to wear a wide-brimmed felt for the day's shopping trip to Kingston. She and Polly had looked forward to this day for weeks now. It would be delightful to escape the camp and the recent surge of activity brought on by an escalating war.

Gabriel groaned in his sleep, tried to roll over, but his carbine was in the way. Fully armed and dressed, he lay sprawled on his back, one arm and one leg dangling over the edge of the cot. He was driving himself to the point of exhaustion every night and she didn't want to think of how late it was when he finally came here. Once again, he had found his bed by collapsing into it.

Just then the bugler's trumpet pierced the still morning air. Gabriel's hand twitched, the tired lines of his face crinkling into a frown. He groaned once, cursed in his native tongue and slung an arm over his eyes as if it would blot out the noise of the bugle.

Vanessa immediately put a pan of water on the fire to

boil for his tea. Since coming to New York she learned that Gabriel was not the most amiable sort in the morning. He did not like being woken up. The tea would help.

"Zut!" he snarled at the continued piping of the bugler, finally sat up and looked around the dimly lit cabin. Her lantern made him squint. "I can't bear his racket . . . close the shutters, Ness."

"They are closed, Gabriel," she said lightly, put a palm full of tea leaves in a cup and poured water over them. "Your tea is almost ready."

"I don't want tea," he growled like he always did. "I want to sleep."

"Of course you do," she soothed, brought him the cup and stood over him with it. Sleepy eyes floated up the front of her, wearily noticed her purple velvet day dress, lingered a moment on the place where the snug-fitting bodice revealed the white curves of her bosom.

He groaned again, swiped a hand across the stubble on his chin and looked away as if he couldn't bear the sight of her. Their forced abstinence was wearing on him, making her feel like she was just another ache to add to his collection. She put the cup on the floor and walked away.

The bugler launched into another round of reveille.

"Oh for the love of God—" Gabriel shot off the cot, stalked to the window and threw open the shutter. "ENOUGH!" he barked into the dawn, bringing a muffled snort of laughter from whoever was outside.

The Colonel was awake.

"Gabriel, come drink your tea."

He growled irritably, withdrew from the window and went to the water basin.

Vanessa grimaced at the weary pose he affected, leaning over the bowl, tossing handfuls of water on his face to force himself awake. She brought him a towel, heard him sigh as he closed his eyes and mopped his face.

"You're nearing exhaustion, Gabriel. Why can't you take a day of rest—"

"Because this war is about to start . . . finally." His voice was deep and gravelly with the remnants of too little sleep. He tossed the towel away and went for his tea, spewing war information all the while. "Our Captain John Brown is about to reach Fort Ticonderoga and will attempt to retake it. Burgoyne is so desperate for food and provisions he's had to send for General Clinton in Albany. We're doing everything in our power to circumvent their communications. I swear we catch a half-dozen enemy scouts a night . . . " He swallowed the entire cup of tea in one gulp, handed it to her for more. "The British are scared now. They thought they'd have an easier go of it. I tell you, the murder of Jane McCrea is what started this . . . has brought a rash of enlistments to our side. Gates is nearly eleven thousand strong."

She was impressed by this news, her smile wide with hopeful cheer. Again, Gabriel's eyes floated over her, slow and appreciative just before he turned away. She watched him tug a strongbox out from under his cot, unlock it and start counting out coin.

"What are you doing?"

"Getting you some money for shopping."

"But you've already given me money!"

He ignored her, counted out a large sum of coin and slid it into the lace purse she always hung beside the door.

"Buy me some tobacco while you're there, eh?"

"Of course I will! But I really don't need—"

"Vanessa!" he growled in warning, leaned against the door and crossed his arms over his chest. A reprimanding expression slowly filled up his face. "There is only so much denial a man can take from a woman. You press me sorely when you do this . . . argue against my only satisfaction . . . which is spoiling you. Stop. I've no patience for it anymore. You will take this to Kingston and buy whatever catches your fancy so I might have the pleasure of knowing I made you happy in some way."

She just stared at him, surprised by this unexpected diatribe of his. With an indignant huff she stomped back to the mirror and feigned great attention to her coiffure.

After a long moment, while he was busy changing his shirt for the day, she seized an opportunity to remind him, "I've given you other choices, Gabriel."

"I don't wish to discuss them."

Tension rose in the air between them, the way it always did when Vanessa brought up the subject of releasing Gabriel from this obligatory marriage. He absolutely refused to consider it, to even talk about it.

"I can't bear to see you unhappy, Gabriel."

He had his back to her, thick brown muscle temporarily rippling in all of its powerful beauty before once again hiding itself beneath a fresh white shirt. "I wish you'd stop saying that—"

"But it's true!"

"Then do something to make me happy. Otherwise, why mention it?"

She could tell by the weary tone of his voice that his patience was thinner than usual. He was tired, she told herself, tired and overwhelmed with the war.

With a sigh of resignation, she took up her cloak and purse, prepared to fetch Polly and get on their way to Kingston.

"Very well. I suppose I could buy a few yards of fabric to fashion a new chemise."

"Have mercy on me by not including me in a discussion of your undergarments—"

"Oh!" she fumed at him, flinging herself into her cloak. "Your tea is on the table. Is there anything else you want before I leave?"

"Yes, the surrender of two of my most formidable adversaries. Burgoyne and you."

* * *

It was early afternoon when Moylan's messenger rode into camp, winded and dirty after a long ride from New Jersey. He handed Gabriel a sealed note and took his leave to refresh himself.

The dread he dismissed weeks ago came flooding back as he carried the note into his cabin and shut the door. For a long moment, he sat with it in his hand before he broke the seal with his thumbnail.

Washington knew nothing about a mission to find the Archangel, Moylan wrote. If there were two soldiers claiming to be acting under the authority of the Commander in Chief, they were lying. Their papers were obviously forged.

" . . . The General is greatly distressed that the British have learned of the connection between you and the Archangel. This severely compromises our intelligence capabilities and places you under direct threat by the enemy. He has ordered the immediate arrest of Jonathan Meeks and suggested you be temporarily removed from the field in order to foil these enemy plans, a suggestion I was forced to appeal in light of General Gates's preparations to finally confront Burgoyne on the battlefield. You will be of critical importance to Gates now and my recommendation to leave you in the theater was approved by Washington.

"However, your camp is to be placed on alert, with the strictest security being enforced, particularly to your own personal safety. I am urging you to remain at post, to cease the covert activity you so relish . . . "

Gabriel tossed down the note, in no mood for another lecture from Moylan. He left the hut, followed a private path into the woods and settled himself on the banks of a stream.

Jonnie had sold him to the British.

The mere thought made him shake his head in disbelief. This was the hardest part of the rebellion to endure, the rampant treason that occurred because so many people couldn't decide which side to join. Loyalties shifted like the wind. Worse, with the currency problem on the Continent, anyone could be bought with a handful of worthwhile specie. Betrayal was better than starvation.

A hand settled on his shoulder, startled away his thoughts. Gabriel looked up into the unusually sad eyes of Robert Blaire. The letter from Moylan was clutched in his hand.

"I'm sorry, Gabe . . . " was all he could say.

"Why would Jonnie turn on us?"

Robert was completely bewildered, just shook his head at the sky and muttered, "God only knows . . . but they must have paid him well."

"I just can't accept this, Robert. There has to be some other explanation."

"Yes, but what? Jonnie knew never to disclose the connection between you and the Archangel . . . no matter who was inquiring. And he was too experienced in the rebel underground to mistake a forged signature."

Gabriel didn't say anything, just stared at the ground between his sprawled legs in a kind of numb acceptance.

"We better get this camp secured, Gabe," Robert suggested while morosely kicking at a lump of moss. "And take the rest Moylan suggests. You've been prowling enemy lines every night. Meeks knows where we are . . . which means those spies are out there somewhere."

Gabriel got off the ground and started walking back toward camp with Robert alongside. They were both absorbed in their own thoughts, silent and gloomy as they moved out of the woods and into the hastily-cleared area of their camp.

"What should we do about our wives?" Robert asked.

"I'm surprised Moylan didn't demand we send them home."

"What home?" Gabriel scoffed. "I don't want my wife in an occupied city."

"Nor I."

They fell silent again, strode past the commissary wagons where Gabriel immediately noticed one was missing.

"Where's the fifth wagon?"

"The women took it. It was empty."

"What did they want with the wagon? I thought they were riding into Kingston."

"No. Martina asked them to bring a wagon. Apparently, Jonnie sent her money enough to purchase some kegs for the—"

Robert stopped in mid-sentence, looked at Gabriel and breathed, "Dear God!"

Gabriel didn't hesitate for an instant, suddenly barked out a command for a small contingent of men to saddle themselves. "Damn! How could we be so stupid?" he snapped as he rushed toward his cabin and his own saddle. "By now that wagon is loaded heavy enough to leave tracks into this camp—"

"Martina, too?"

"Why not?" Gabriel growled, his face chiseled with a dark and ugly pain. He was outraged at how completely he'd been betrayed by people from within his own home. "She's his wife, isn't she? Of course she's in on his schemes. Let's go . . . "

The bunting looked so tiny in her hands, the neckline barely large enough to encircle her wrist.

"Isn't it precious," Polly cooed. "And look . . . here's the bonnet to match it."

Vanessa looked at the little white hood, its soft satin ribbons and the carefully detailed embroidery on the sides. Holding it in her hands just then made her realize that seven months from now there would be a child in it, a little replica of Gabriel and herself.

"It would be perfect for the christening, wouldn't it," Martina was asking, her big brown eyes looking so warm and soft as she considered the occasion.

Vanessa just nodded, once again feeling very overwhelmed and mystified by it all. Shopping for the child made it all seem so real. A baby. Hers and his. Conceived in the only moment of ecstasy this union had ever known.

"We better be going," she said, laid the bunting and the hat on the counter with her other selections. "We've a long ride ahead of us . . . and Gabriel wants us back before dark." She nodded at the proprietor who immediately began to parcel her purchases.

"He just dotes on her now," Polly was saying to Martina. "Why, he told the entire camp that if anyone sees his wife lifting anything heavier than a fork and does not come to her aid, he would declare the man's hands useless and cut them off."

Vanessa had never heard this before, looked at Polly and gasped, "He didn't!"

"I heard him myself!"

"Oh! That man!"

They all giggled and even Vanessa found herself grinning at his antics. Despite their disturbing relationship, he'd been on her mind in unusually tender ways today.

As a father.

No man on earth could be more opposite from her brutal sire than Gabriel St. Claire. This was suddenly, overwhelmingly important to her. No thought of the child came to her without an anxious feeling about her own miserable qualifications as a parent. But of Gabriel she had no doubt. He was genuine, righteous, even-tempered, so completely gentle despite his enormous physical strength. Even more important, his parents were normal, from what she'd heard, and had given their mischievous twin sons a loving and happy family life until tragedy sent them fleeing to America.

Yes, he was better suited to be a parent than she.

The three of them climbed into the lumbering old commissary wagon and started toward the Hoffman House, their last stop of the day. As they drove down the main avenue of town, they made plans for another shopping trip.

"If we're still here," Vanessa advised. "It seems an engagement between Burgoyne and Gates is imminent now. Gabriel thinks we might have to break camp and travel a bit farther north to where the confrontation will take place. Once we break camp, it may be too far from Kingston."

"But how far away are you now?" Martina wanted to know.

"A few hours' ride," Polly said. "We'll write you when we know more."

"My goodness! I didn't realize you'd come from so far today," Martina commented.

Vanessa just shrugged, not sure herself exactly where the camp was except that it was in a valley north of here. "Ah! Here we are."

They were behind the Hoffman House, and Martina rushed inside to collect the six kegs of ale she'd purchased earlier. It took several men to load the huge barrels into the wagon.

"Won't Sergeant Cooke be thrilled?" Polly asked with a naughty chuckle.

"Oh dear, but this wagon is heavy now," Vanessa said and had to struggle to maneuver the team around in the drive with such an over-laden wagon in tow. The horses whinnied bitterly but obeyed, finally tugged the wagon forward and brought it lurching down the drive. They were nearly in the street when Vanessa checked their parcels to be sure they weren't being crushed by the heavy kegs.

Just then, the front door of the Hoffman House swung open and a pair of men stepped out on the porch. They looked directly at their wagon, then hurriedly found their mounts among the many horses tethered in front of the Inn.

Vanessa turned into the street, the wooden wheels hammering loudly against the cobbles as they headed north to where Martina's relatives lived on the outskirts of the city.

Once again, she turned around, glanced over her shoulder and was immediately alarmed at what she saw.

The two men were following, slowly, at a distance.

"What's wrong, Vanessa?" Polly asked and turned around to see what had Vanessa so interested. "Do you know them?"

"I don't." Vanessa pulled back on the reins, brought the team to a halt.

"What are you doing," Martina asked in a tone of voice that sounded sharp in Vanessa's ears. But when she looked at the young girl beside her, Martina just laughed in that high-strung, nervous way of hers. "I really should be back. My aunt is probably waiting—"

"She can wait a bit longer," Vanessa said, responding to a very uneasy feeling inside herself. "I want those men to pass us by . . . "

They did so within a few minutes, casually tipping their hats at the ladies as they sauntered by.

"There! You see? They're just passersby!" Martina chirped.

Vanessa didn't say anything, just watched the men until they rounded a bend in the road up ahead and disappeared. "I didn't like the looks of them—"

"Come along, Vanessa!" Martina scoffed, then added

with a wink, "You've done a bit too much spying for your own good. Now really . . . I must be home."

They drove onward, Polly and Martina gaily chattering about the day's purchases while Vanessa wrestled with an inner feeling of uneasiness. Around every bend she expected to see those two riders, but they seemed to have disappeared. There was no sign of them and she began to think Martina was right. She'd spent too much time Tory-hunting and living with a spy.

She finally relaxed, started to enjoy the scenery along this country road, the first signs of autumn sprinkling the vista with bright flashes of color. The trees were beginning to turn from green to gold, leaves just barely tipped in orange and red. The barest hint of autumn was nipping in the mid-September air and the prospects of an Indian summer began to seem wistful. It would be an early winter, she knew; she could see the signs she'd learned while growing up on a farm.

Oak Lane loomed up ahead and Vanessa struggled to turn the team against the straining weight of the wagon. She finally managed to make the sharp right turn, and was just about to urge the team forward when a gasp from Polly brought her head upright.

"Dear God!"

There were six Continental soldiers only twenty feet ahead of them, spaced at regular intervals until they were stretched completely across the road.

All six men sat rigid in their saddles, staring straight at them.

They were cavalrymen, Vanessa recognized. Gabriel's men. Something was wrong. Very wrong.

Martina came to the same realization, seemed to freeze on the seat beside her. Her face slowly drained of color when Vanessa looked at her.

"Tina? Do you know anything about this?"

"No . . ."

The wagon rumbled to a halt. One soldier finally broke ranks, rode alongside the wagon and inspected the contents. He stopped beside the front seat and said, "Martina Meeks?"

"Yes?"

"You'll have to come with me."

"What? But why?"

"Just come along, ma'am."

Martina didn't move, sat paralyzed in fear.

Vanessa looked at the guard. "Did my husband send you?"

He didn't answer, just nodded his head toward the road. She looked up the narrow dirt lane, startled to see the figure poised on a distant knoll, so tall and erect in the saddle of a huge black stallion.

Gabriel. He was up there, alone, watching them.

"What the devil . . . " She dropped the reins, leaped out of the wagon and started running toward him. "Gabriel?"

There was a crash in the woods beside her. She cried out, whirled around, watched Benny Cooke emerge from the thick foliage to prevent her further advance on the road. "Just be still 'til we git this situation secure—"

"What situation? What are you talking about?"

Her distress made Gabriel spur his mount. The horse danced restlessly a moment before the Colonel's heels brought it loping forward. He trotted up to her, his dark gray cloak billowing around him like so many storm clouds as he reached down and easily scooped her off the ground. She was swung into the saddle and settled between his thighs, a rigid arm clamping around her and holding her in place as he trotted forward.

There was no expression on his face, nor did he give her the slightest glance, his attention wholly focused on Martina Meeks. Bewildered, she just sat there staring up at him, clenched against a body that felt so solid and tight with tension he seemed carved out of marble.

"Gabriel!" Martina cried when she saw him, tried to scramble out of the wagon, then found herself blocked by two soldiers. Undaunted, she leaned between them, her hat tumbling down her back, "I can explain this! Jonnie said you wouldn't let them near your camp . . . but Washington's men must talk to you—"

"They're not Washington's men," Gabriel said in a crisp, clear monotone. Martina was silent then, looking at him in confusion. "The men Jonnie contacted at the Dolphin are British agents."

"What?" Her huge brown eyes looked suddenly desperate when she searched his face. "What are you talking about?"

"He was bought, Tina—"

"No!" she cried, tried to push away the soldiers who stood between her and Gabriel. They wouldn't move. "But that can't be true! Jonnie wouldn't do such a thing to you!"

It was obvious Martina didn't know the truth. Jonnie had duped her too. Betrayal had no heart, Gabriel thought. It was a cold, cruel beast.

He came forward then, reached down and slid a hand under Martina's quivering chin. He lifted her stricken face and said quietly, "Just go with them and be calm. You won't be hurt, just kept under surveillance until the action here is done."

"Taken where?" She was starting to cry now, hysteria bringing a rash of color up the sides of her neck. "I don't want to go, Gabriel . . . help me."

Vanessa could almost see the way he struggled against her plea, his want to help her torn by his duty to country. He urged his mount backward, moved away and nodded at Benny Cooke to secure the wagon.

"My things . . . " she said to Gabriel when he spurred his mount.

He didn't say anything, just let her point out which parcels she wanted and silently tied them to the back of his saddle. Vanessa and Polly exchanged a silent stare just before she was led off by a soldier to join her husband in the woods.

"Gabriel?" Martina cried out to him. "Don't leave me here . . ."

Gabriel began to ride away, kept his eyes pinned to the road, refusing to look back while Martina's cries assailed their ears.

Vanessa cringed, frightened tears filling her eyes as she watched the soldiers swarm over the wagon and carry Martina away.

They rode in silence for a short distance, until Gabriel turned off the road and began to pick his way through the woods. This was not the usual path to camp, but he seemed to know his way. All the while, she waited for his chiseled expression to soften, then finally asked for an explanation.

He gave her one, his words short and clipped, revealing as much personal hurt as anger at being so betrayed by Jonnie. Vanessa never once interrupted him, let him finish, then lay back in his arms to consider everything he'd said.

"Of all people, Jonnie was the last person I thought capable of such treachery," she admitted sadly, genuinely sorry for Gabriel and the hurt he must be feeling at this moment. She felt a bit betrayed herself. "How did you find out about this?" she asked and wished he'd look at her.

But he didn't, just continued to stare at the woods ahead of them and said, "An old friend at the Dolphin wrote me about seeing Jon with a pair of strangers one night . . . overheard Jon talking about me . . . telling them things a man wouldn't want strangers to know."

He wasn't telling her everything. She could sense it. "What things?"

"About me and my brother."

"But why? What bearing has this on anything?"

"None. Just forget about it."

"It's about the Archangel, isn't it?"

Gabriel stiffened, drew up his reins and stared down at her in honest surprise. "Why would you think that?"

She might as well tell him what she knew, seeing no point in continuing to hide this knowledge from her husband. "Because you're connected to him." She went on to tell him what she had overheard the night of the Swanson mission, about Moylan's theory regarding Gabriel's biblical name, then what he and Lauren talked about on the porch the day he was promoted to Colonel.

Gabriel was amazed at her listening abilities and seemed almost impressed when he suddenly spurred his mount back into motion.

"I'll assume you never mentioned this to anyone . . . like Malinda or Dierdre or whoever else you write to."

The mere question offended her. She puffed at a lock of hair, blew it out of her face and snapped, "You're crushing my hat."

He chuckled at her temper, a merry amusement finally sparkling through the sorrow in his dark eyes. "I'll buy you another one."

She was about to hurl a quip at him when she suddenly remembered the two riders who were following them. With great energy, she leaped in his lap, took hold of his breast straps and blurted, "I think we were followed today . . . by two men . . . they were dressed as civilians, but I was immediately suspicious of them."

His expression turned serious despite the reaction she sensed from their close posture. "Where?"

"On the main road out of town! I stopped the wagon, in fact, wanting them to pass us by."

"Good thinking, *chérie,*" he awarded, a gloved hand sliding up her back to give her shoulder a thankful squeeze. He turned around then, looked over his shoulder and barked, "One of you get back to Benny and tell him to scout the main road."

It was the first time Vanessa realized they were being followed by armed scouts. One of them drew alongside, listened to her explanation about the riders she'd seen, then rode away. The other remained in place, spurred his mount forward at the same time Gabriel did.

He saw her perplexity, shrugged and said, "Get used to it. My back will be guarded everywhere now."

"Are you in so much danger?"

"Never mind that. I'm too tired to think about it right now."

They were both chilled by the time they reached camp, immediately sought the hearth in their cabin and stoked a roaring fire. Vanessa spread a blanket across the dirt floor and sat close to the warmth while unwrapping the day's purchases.

Gabriel's shadow loomed over her for a moment before he decided to join her in the fire's glow. He sat down, propped himself against the wall where he savored a long, leisurely stretch. It ended in a windy yawn.

"You're exhausted, Gabriel."

He grinned sleepily, motioned at the parcels in her lap and asked, "Are they bags of tobacco?"

"Yes! Yes!" She handed him two bulging sacks of fresh tobacco, both of his favorite flavors.

Clearly delighted, he opened the sacks, inhaled deeply and sighed in utter satisfaction. "How did you know what I like?"

"I checked."

A dark auburn brow rose in surprise. "Have you become so interested in my pleasures?"

"Don't be a tease . . . "

"I'm encouraged by your attention," he continued, playful now as he stretched out his legs, comfortably crossed them. "What else did you buy?"

She decided to ignore his antics, opened her parcels and displayed an assortment of garments that had a strangely quieting effect on him. Diapers, tiny cotton shirts, bolts of felt for the making of baby buntings, and several large balls of knitting yarn.

Despite the day's sorry end, Vanessa managed to rekindle the happy excitement she had felt earlier in the day while shopping for the baby. Before long she was spilling her plans for its wardrobe. "I'll use the wool to make boots and blankets for him . . . er . . . her . . . and the felt will be perfect for nightshirts. It will be born in the spring so we won't need woolen things for a while yet. We can get them next summer . . . and look! Isn't this darling? Polly found it." She held up the white dimity bunting, finally noticed her husband's strange mood as he sat so quietly watching her. A bit of the energy ran out of her voice. "I thought it would be perfect for the christening . . . " She stopped then. "Gabriel?"

He didn't say anything, just reached down and plucked up the tiny hat. It suddenly looked so small and white and pure when held by such a huge hand, its delicate cloth starkly contrasting with Gabriel's deeply tanned skin.

She sat back on her haunches, watched him study the item for a long moment, turning it this way and that in his hand as if trying to comprehend the little creature who would soon wear it.

Perhaps she should have been more sensitive when showing him these things, Vanessa thought to herself. Gabriel was, after all, a man who expected to remain a bachelor until their gross indiscretion had destroyed those plans.

Ever so carefully, he laid the hat down on top of her little pile. He leaned against the wall again, his pose seeming a bit heavier than before. Their eyes met, his anxious, hers curious.

"What's wrong, Gabriel?"

"Nothing . . . I . . . er—" He stopped, just waved a hand through the air as if to dismiss himself. Vanessa was really intrigued now, having never seen this perpetual smooth-talker so obviously bereft of words.

"It's a bit overwhelming, isn't it?"

He just nodded, stared at her but made no move toward her.

"I think you'll make a fine father," she said.

He blinked as if this new title caught him by surprise. "After all, you come from such a good strong family. You're far more fit to be a parent than I—" She stopped herself from saying anymore.

But it was already too late. Gabriel's gaze turned from his own thoughts to the one she left unfinished in the air between them.

"Look at me."

She didn't, tried to shrug away the subject and started to refold the baby's things.

"Vanessa . . . "

"Never mind. These are my own thoughts . . . I shouldn't have said it. Why don't you . . . oh!"

She was suddenly tumbling across his lap, once distant blue eyes staring down into her face with complete clarity. "When will you stop doing this to yourself?"

"Doing what?"

"Belittling yourself," he said, their closeness affecting him until his voice dropped into that deep rumbling pool of passion he hid somewhere inside himself. "How can I convince you that you have a worth despite what your *father* thinks?"

His thighs felt so warm beneath her, so thick with strength. "Please . . . "

He sighed, swept a hand up the side of her face and pressed it against his breast. "You must listen to me, Vanessa . . . now more than ever. I want my child to have the mother I chose for it."

"You didn't choose me . . . it was an accident."

"*Mon Dieu,* but you're stubborn!" He blew out a sigh of utter frustration, then growled against the top of her head, "The way I made love to you in Philadelphia was not an accident."

He needn't say more. The sentence finished itself in the rise of sensual tension between them.

She didn't dare lift her head to look at him. "I don't understand you, Gabriel. You could have any woman you want—"

"Yes, but I want you—

"Why?" she cried, exasperated with him. "How can you sink yourself so much further into this union . . . insisting we remain married for the child's sake when you know damn well it's a farce! We're not husband and wife! You're a saint who chose to rescue a sinner and I—"

She was suddenly sprawled across the blanket, pinned beneath the powerful body of her husband. Two hands slid up the side of her face until they formed a dark frame around her startled expression.

"No . . . we're not saint and sinner. More like the exiled and the abused. That's how I see it and that's how you'll see it, Vanessa Davis." The tone of his voice was low and raw, as fierce as the desire that blazed in his eyes just then, turned them dark and hard and penetrating. "If you were truly incapable of caring, this wouldn't happen between us . . . " He stopped, letting her recognize the arousal rising steadily between them. "Nor would you want something better for me."

She didn't say anything, once again outwitted by his clearer logic, his overpowering presence, the way he made her want him.

"Has it ever occurred to you that wanting something better for me is just another way of caring about me?"

She just looked at him.

"Well?"

"No . . . " she breathed, "it hasn't. And I'm not sure it's true—"

"You hate me then, is that what you're saying . . . "

"No! I don't hate you!

"Then what?"

"I don't know!" she cried, confused and upset by all the conflicting emotions he made her feel. "I've never known how I feel—"

"Yes, you do." He moved over her, completely, until she was totally covered in his warm, hard body. Excitement flashed between them like a bright flare in a dark sky, made her want to repel him, refuse him, resist surrendering to this total command he could take whenever he wielded that exquisite touch of his. But he was too overpowering as a man, too capable of inspiring the woman in her, the woman he created with his own hands and was now so completely capable of controlling.

Pleasure roared through her body, swift and shocking, made her shiver under him in a way that drew a sigh of satisfaction from his lips. "Yes . . . listen to me this way if you can't hear my words just yet." He leaned down, leisurely bathed her throat in a warm trickle of kisses. She shuddered, appalled by how delightful he felt.

Her response excited him, made him savor how beautiful she looked just then, so frightened yet so aroused, those full sensuous lips parted in want yet trembling in fear. The contrariness of her, how staunchly she resisted him yet how deliciously she could submit, brought a surge of heat into his loins.

"I want you," he whispered fiercely, "more than I dare tell you."

"You frighten me!"

"No . . . don't be afraid because these hands will never . . . ever . . . hurt you. I will use them to adore you . . . to prove to you that in my eyes, you will always be my Madonna . . . my dark Madonna."

He kissed her then, long and hard and hungry, until she belonged to him again in those deep inner places where this man wove his mighty magic. But then he stopped and it seemed almost deliberate the way he slid off her just then, when she was completely at his mercy.

His mouth was still reddened by her passion when he looked down at her and made his point with brilliant clarity. "This child was no accident."

With that he got up, tossed on his cloak and left the cabin.

Sweat beaded on the brow of the agent as he lifted his head from the decayed leaf bed and looked around. It was nearly impossible to discern a direction in the black woods. Only the barest trace of starlight filtered through the trees around them, dusting the forest floor in beams of silver.

"Where the hell are we?" he asked the man huddled behind him.

"I don't know!" his companion whispered. "We needed that wagon to lead us—"

"Well, we don't have the wagon anymore," the other agent snapped, "but we're close enough to find our own way. His camp must be around here somewhere. This place is swarming with his scouts."

Just as he said it, something moved in the distance, once again forcing them to lay low against the soggy ground. A lone horseman picked his way through the trees, a loaded carbine drawn across his chest, his head constantly turning as he perused the surroundings. They dared not breathe into the easily scattered leaves, tried to lie as still as possible without causing the fallen foliage to crackle and give them away.

Finally, the guard moved out of hearing range. "These aren't typical scouts, man. These men are alert, well fed, well armed. This is a top-notch field operation I'd say."

"Humph! Not only must we try to penetrate St. Claire's headquarters, we've got to do it while they're under top security."

Again, something moved to the right of them, so close they both dropped their heads and lay frozen against the ground. Only their eyes followed the movement of a dark shadow as it slipped between the trees. The figure was on foot, cloaked but not in uniform. He seemed to be trailing the horseman who had passed a few minutes ago, moving through the timber with a peculiar silence. Slowly, ever so quietly, he eventually melted into the darkness and disappeared.

"Who the hell was that?"

"I don't know but whoever he was, he didn't want to be seen by that scout."

"Hold on a minute!" The agent lifted his head, stared hard at his companion for a long moment before he said, "The Archangel trails St. Claire, right?" He didn't wait for an answer. "What if that was him?"

"What if it was just another enemy scout," his companion countered.

"No enemy scout in his right mind would be this far behind British lines . . . especially not with St. Claire's scouts on full alert."

"You're right. So what are we lying here for? Let's follow him!"

Gabriel followed the dark shape in the woods, watched it flit between the night-blackened tree trunks. It was so quiet he could hear his own heartbeat drumming in his ears. Excitement coursed through him. This was the closest he'd ever come to trailing this shadowy figure, this unnamed spy who haunted his every field operation.

Finally, after all this time, he'd catch the Archangel. With meticulous care, Gabriel moved forward, choosing his every step to be sure his feet fell on solid ground and not the crackling leaf bed. His eyes were pinned to the figure ahead of him, watched it descend a slope in the land and veer right. It passed through a beam of moonlight, temporarily illuminating its black cloak. For just an instant, Gabriel caught sight of the figure's hair, dark and auburn, just touching the collar of his cloak.

Gabriel froze, his every sense keening to the suddenly familiar height and build of the man. He was tall, broad shouldered, long-legged. Every time he took a step, his figure gave a slight jerk, a halting gait that was too familiar. Gabriel could mimic that walk in his sleep.

Michael. Michael.

His heart skipped into a wild beat as he moved faster toward the shadow ahead of him, studying it every time it passed through a shaft of starlight. High cheekbones, thick hair that curled on its own, deep set eyes that seemed burrowed under his brow.

It was him! It had to be him! Michael was alive!

Exhilaration made his feet stumble for a moment, slide off the edge of a flattened rock. A few twigs split with a loud cracking sound. The figure whipped around, piercing blue eyes finding Gabriel and widening in instant recognition.

"Gabriel! I knew you'd find me sooner or later—"

"Michael! I can't believe you're alive—"

"Yes, my beloved brother . . . I'm alive alright . . . and I've been one step behind you everywhere for the last few years."

"It's you, isn't it? You're the Archangel!"

"Yes . . . "

They just stared at each other, their faces so identical it was like looking in a mirror. Some strange moaning sound escaped Gabriel's throat as ten years of grief spilled out into the night.

Tears filled Michael's eyes, his arms opening to receive the brother who was already rushing toward him.

A gunshot rang out.

Gabriel jumped, whirled around, saw the flaming muzzle through the dark foliage and instinctively spread his arms wide to protect Michael.

"Get down! Michael—" The words stopped in his throat.

Michael just stared at him, the smile frozen on his face as a trickle of blood seeped down the side of his face.

"NO!" Gabriel screamed, reached for him just as his brother's figure crumbled at the knees. He fell to the ground and Gabriel fell with him. "No . . . Michael! Michael!"

Vanessa snapped awake, sat up so fast her blanket slid to the floor. She looked across the dark cabin, saw Gabriel sitting up in bed. Naked to the waist, he was drenched in sweat, his soaked skin gleaming in the vague light.

Instantly alarmed, she slid out of bed, rushed across the room and fell to her knees beside his cot. "Gabriel?" He was not fully awake, stared sightlessly into the dark, a horrible expression of pain on his face. Frightened for him, she took his hand, squeezed it to let him know he was awake and that someone was near.

He didn't respond at first, just sat there in stunned silence, breathing fast and hard, the dazed expression on his face making his eyes glitter in the faint light.

"Come awake, Gabriel . . . it's just a dream . . . "

He heard her, turned his head and looked down at her. *"Michel . . . "*

"No . . . it's me . . . Vanessa."

He blinked, still disoriented, shook his head just hard enough to send trails of sweat dribbling down his neck, into the dense auburn hair that covered his chest. "I saw him . . . "

"Hush!" she whispered, squeezed his hand again and felt tears of pity rush into her eyes. "It was just a dream."

How he suffered for this long-lost brother of his, rarely allowing anyone near that place where he hid his memories of a beloved twin. He looked so alone in his grief just now, trembling hard against a pain that seemed big enough to swallow this magnanimous man.

It frightened her, made her want to do something she'd never done for him before.

Hold him.

Gabriel closed his eyes, shrank down on the cot and tried not to see the way Michael's face looked when death arrived. He would never forget how beautifully serene and quiet his brother had seemed in the moment his life left his body.

The memory was so painful it made him shudder all the way down to his soul. "God have mercy on me," he moaned into the thick veil of raven hair falling around him.

Just to feel his trembling sent a slice of pain through her heart. She slid her fingers into his sweaty hair, suddenly wanted to reach into this private place of his where he suffered so terribly for Michael, yet always so alone and silent.

Her body slid against his own, soft and warm and supple beneath her dimity nightdress. Her hair fell around him, filled the air around his head with the sweet, fresh scent of her.

She was in bed with him.

From somewhere inside his cold remorse a flame flickered into life.

His eyes popped open, instantly aware.

"Are you awake now?"

"Yes . . . "

"You cried out in your sleep," she whispered.

"I saw him so clearly," Gabriel told her, not really knowing why except that she had lost a brother, too. Maybe she would understand. "His face . . . his voice . . . his walk . . . " Michael's face appeared in his mind the way it had in the dream, so full of color and vitality. For a moment, it obscured the soft compassion on the face above him.

"How you must have loved him," she was saying, her words so gentle and soothing in his ears, " . . . like I loved Danny. But his life was hell . . . I was glad to see the angels take him away . . . to heaven . . . where he belonged."

He looked up at her as if trying to see how she managed to reconcile herself to Danny's loss. "I can't let him go . . . "

"You must, Gabriel . . . it was his destiny to die young. But not yours. Our Lord had another plan for you . . . that you should be a freedom fighter. Look what your life has done for us all . . . how much further is the cause of liberty because of your efforts."

He looked at her strangely, having never heard such praise from her lips before. It stirred him, made him wrap his arms around her slender form and savor the perfection of her beautifully tapered back. How magnificent she looked with a face full of compassion, not a shred of her usual coldness toward him. Instead, he caught a glimpse of that tender and loving person inside her, the one who lay trapped in her own kind of painful remorse.

It was a dark spell she wove around him now, sad and sorry but compelling just the same. He let her weave it, too weak with grief to resist the soft press of her lips against his brow, the tender trail of caresses she brought sliding down the side of his face.

Rapture bloomed between them, slowly and quietly, his pain turning to pleasure as she comforted him with the same devices she once used to manipulate young Tory men. Ah yes! Vanessa Davis knew how to make a man sigh, how to touch him in places that made him quiver. But hate was not her motive tonight. For the first time ever, she touched a man because she wanted to soothe him, not hurt him, just bring him peace.

It worked. The man beneath her began to arouse, slowly, languidly, a lazy flame of desire lapping into life between them. It inspired her, the way he reveled in her touch, as if hers was some sweet internal medicine that could bathe his wounded spirit with a warm and glowing relief. It spread across his face until the furrows of agony were gone from his brow, tight lines of pain loosened in pleasure. She tasted his sighs, let her mouth travel down the front of his throat until she felt his body shudder in surrender.

He belonged to her now in ways that only a woman could capture a man, even this mighty warrior. Seeking hands traveled the round curves of his muscled breast, slid along every curve and indentation. Thick shocks of auburn hair felt soft beneath her kisses, thinning as she traveled downward to where his body tapered into the narrow tautness of his torso. How beautifully he was sculptured, so tight and hard, yet his flesh was so exquisitely warm. She savored him for both his masculine beauty and his righteous but broken heart, how tender he could be yet how brutally strong, how fiercely he aroused her yet how gentle was his touch.

"I need you . . . " he moaned, clutched her close, "the way you love me . . . when you let yourself . . . "

She adored the sound of him, his deep hard breathing, the way his body writhed on the rickety cot that was barely sturdy enough to support them both. But it held, long enough for her to savor the flat expanse of his belly, hold those narrow hips of his in her hands until she felt them twist in the last shreds of his control.

He was suddenly reaching for her in the dark, pulling her up and over him until he could find her lips and kiss her with an abandon so wild and reckless it sent a bolt of fire through her veins. She gasped, shivered at the feel of his hands smoothing across her buttocks, molding her hips to his until she felt every inch of his swollen desire.

"Gabriel . . . " she gasped.

"Enough . . . I must have you . . . " He rolled over, trapped her beneath his muscle and might until the reins of control were suddenly and completely his. "Give me your permission," he groaned, his hungry mouth blazing a fiery path up the side of her neck. She clenched him tight, his hair and hers tumbling together on the pillow like two storming currents rushing into one. "Say you want me . . . tell me this is what you want . . . say it!"

She couldn't think, breathe, answer him in any way other than to clasp him in her arms and mold herself against the source of this exquisite pleasure. The way he adored her, so frantically, so wildly, made her head spin in every direction. She was barely aware of her nightdress wrenching open, only that his big strong hands were sliding inside, covering her naked breasts in such a fiercely tender way it made her cry out his name.

"Gabriel . . . Gabriel!"

Something banged against the side of the hut, so loud and harsh it instantly brought her husband's head up. His whole body froze, turned rigid as he cocked his head to the wall and listened intently.

It came again, this time a scraping sound as if whatever hit the wall was now sliding along it. The sound moved across the front of the hut, toward the door.

Gabriel shot off the cot so fast he drew a frightened cry from her lips. She sat up, clutching her bodice, watched him rush across the room and disappear into the shadows by the door. Dazed, breathless, dizzy, she just sat there staring at the place where he'd disappeared.

"Gabriel?"

"Get under the bed—"

"What?"

"NOW!"

She flung herself off the edge of the cot, hit the floor and rolled under it. From behind the dangling blanket, she looked out and saw Gabriel beside the door, flattened against the wall, a loaded carbine in his hands. He was still panting, out of breath, but there was no more passion on his face. In its place was an acute, animal-like alertness as his eyes pinned to the door.

The latch jingled from the outside.

Real fear seized her, drew her face down to the floor.

The agents. They were still on the loose. Could one of them have crept into camp tonight?

Gabriel reached for the bolt on the door and ever so carefully slid it open. Why was he unlocking the door?

"Gabriel . . . don't . . . "

He didn't say anything, just motioned for her to be silent.

The door began to creak open and she put a hand over her mouth to keep from screaming. Gabriel tensed against the wall behind the door, the metal edge of his bayonet gleaming in the thin light.

The dark shape of a man materialized in the open door. With the light behind him, his face was too shaded to recognize.

Gabriel moved so fast she saw only a shadowy blur of motion overtake the figure, the sharp intake of someone's breath just before the intruder thumped against the wall.

Silence. The movement stopped. Vanessa saw the door swing shut just as Gabriel released the man and stepped away.

"Will?"

"You could've killed me, Gabe!"

"What the devil are you doing sneaking into my cabin in the middle of the night?" Will slumped forward, his head dropping into his hands. "Have you lost your . . . Will? What's wrong?"

Will didn't answer, just made some strange choking sound that ended in a kind of garbled sob.

Vanessa was stunned to realize he was crying, this tough-skinned Virginia rifleman, covering his face to spare his pride when a deep sob moaned out of his throat.

"Here . . . sit down," Gabriel was saying, urged the man away from the wall. Will followed sluggishly, came to the desk where Gabriel lit a lantern and pulled back a chair. Will fell into it, his face wincing with the strain of trying to stop what seemed to be an overpowering grief.

"Drink this . . . " Gabriel said, handed him a cup of water. She watched the soldier toss it down his throat, choke, spit, then shake himself hard.

"Steve's dead . . . "

Vanessa froze on the floor, stared at Will in a moment of disbelief.

"I was scouting yonder ridge . . . about ten miles south of Gates. Our boys were coming back from Bennington. I hear Stark whooped Johnny's food raiders . . . killed six hundred British . . . took two hundred prisoners. The Continentals stole off with wagons full of ammo and supplies and . . . "

"You mean we routed them?" Gabriel's face split with a victorious grin, a smile that faded gradually as he watched Will double over in a new rush of grief.

"Steve ain't coming back, Gabe! No one knew how to tell me. I was riding alongside our boys and they were looking every which way but at me. I knew it then . . . I just knew it . . . kept riding up and down the lines, looking for Steve . . . hoping he was just dallying somewhere . . . "

Gabriel's eyes closed in a moment of genuine sorrow for the loss of Steve MacLeod. He had been a compatriot and a good friend. Vanessa watched him straddle a chair, reach across the desk and take a firm hold of Will's forearms. "Steve was a genuine soldier . . . died the way all fighting men want to die . . . in the service of their country."

Will found no solace in Gabriel's words. His head fell to the desk where he wept in uncontrolled fits.

Vanessa finally slid out from the under the cot, hastily refastened her bodice as she got off the floor. Gabriel caught her gaze, let her see the acute longing he felt just then to have lost this rare moment with her for such a miserable reason. She sighed through lips that were still warm from his passion, the scent of him trailing around her as she fetched a bottle of bourbon and two mugs.

Will lifted his head off the table, choked at Gabriel, "How am I going to tell Mama? She said I've got to watch him. And what about his girl? You know he's got himself the finest looking lady in Norfolk . . . and she was fixing on marrying him when this . . . this bleeding war's over—"

"Easy, Will . . . " Gabriel began but Will was out of his mind with grief.

He lunged across the table, grabbed Gabriel's bare arms and cried, "He can't die and leave me here without him! He's my brother! You lost your brother. Tell me how, Gabe . . . how do I do this . . . "

Gabriel just blinked into the wild face in front of him, finally realized why Will sought his company at such a terrible moment in his life. Only Gabriel could understand what kind of agony filled a man when a close brother died.

The angry loneliness, the desperate disbelief, the stubborn incomprehension of life without one another.

Gabriel felt it all just then, in the wake of that stricken dream, and thought that Will could not have picked a worse time to ask him about Michael.

Vanessa's fingers danced across his shoulder just then, soft and light and soothing. He tilted his head back, looked up at the woman behind him, into the cool lavender depths of her strange eyes. She met his gaze squarely, allowed him to recapture some small element of the ecstasy she had soothed him with earlier. But she said nothing, just stared into that place in his soul that she had chosen to invade so intimately tonight.

He looked away, feeling oddly exposed.

"I don't know what to do, Gabe," Will pleaded, his wet face gleaming with desperation and anguish. "How do I live without my brother?"

"You don't," Gabriel said in a tone of voice so dull, so lifeless, it almost frightened her to hear it. Even Will was affected by the unfamiliar mask that seemed to slip over the Colonel's face just then, robbing it of all expression until it looked like stone. "You die with him, Will. The part of your life that included your brother is gone now. You'll see. Steve will take that part of you with him to the grave."

Will didn't move, just stared at Gabriel in a kind of terrified fascination.

A shudder coursed through her, made her attempt to break the morbid silence by pouring each man a mug of bourbon. Neither noticed her service; they just sat very still and stared at one another.

From across the table, she watched her husband's vision turn cold and hard and piercing, until he seemed completely engulfed in the pain of his own memories.

"Gabe?"

"What?"

"I feel so helpless . . . like I should do something to help him but he's already dead . . . there's nothing I can do."

"That will pass . . . " Will was momentarily heartened, eagerness making his eyes brighten until he looked almost normal again. “Helplessness is soon swallowed by vengeance. That’s the way it was with me. I knew Michael was dead because I was holding him, and I could feel the life leave his body. So I laid him on the grass and I picked up my sword and plunged it straight through the heart of his murderer . . . Louis Montagne.”

Vanessa just stood there as if her slippers were stuck to the floor. She had never heard Gabriel talk so gruesomely, nor had Will. The young rifleman just stared at his Commander as if he didn’t recognize him.

What he said next sent a furious shiver up her spine. “Avenge him . . . kill his enemies . . . find them and kill every last one . . . ”

Will sat frozen in the chill of his Commander’s deadly advice, his whole face filling with bloodlust. “Yes! That’s what I’ll do now . . . I’ll catch me a redcoat . . . tear out his guts with my bare hands! I’ll do it, Gabe! I swear!”

Vanessa couldn’t bear it, not Will’s maniacal grief nor Gabriel’s shocking testimony. She moved across the room, away from them, into the corner where the cot was in the shadows.

Only when she was alone, hidden from the men, did she let out her own frightened tears. They spilled loose, first for Steve, then for Gabriel whose unmasked grief had so moved her earlier tonight. The mere memory of their impassioned embrace made her tears turn to shivers of fear. Who was the woman who climbed into this bed only an hour ago and loved a grief-stricken man until he moaned with pleasure? Would she have given herself to him if Will hadn’t interrupted?

Yes. She would have let him take anything from her in those moments. Anything.

A chilling disbelief turned her tears cold as a rush of new fears raced through her mind. What was happening to her? Where was that battered girl from Millbridge who could stand like a marble sentinel against a man’s best romancing? No man could move her, touch her, reach her. She had been beaten until she turned tough, hard, impenetrable and in this way, she could be completely safe from any more pain.

Until Gabriel.

Never before did she realize what he was doing to that battered girl who lived inside her. He was killing her, slowly, tenderly, in a way that made her want the kind of death only this man could render.

The death of Steve MacLeod shocked the members of Moylan's Horse. On a day when the entire Northern Army was celebrating Burgoyne's smashing defeat at Bennington, Gabriel's camp was in mourning.

Will MacLeod sat beside the cooking fire all day, numbly staring at the flames. Benny drank himself into a stupor, unable to believe that "Stevie" was gone. Francis sulked in his cabin, imagined all the medical devices he might have employed to save Steve's life had he only been given the chance. Lauren and Robert rode the countryside, submerging their heavy hearts in the search for the two British infiltrators who were still at large.

Vanessa didn't know where Gabriel was. She hadn't seen him since he left the cabin last night with Will. He'd gone off to be alone, Benny had told her, and she suspected he knew exactly where Gabriel was but the Sergeant wasn't telling.

It was late in the day before anyone saw the Colonel again. As usual, he seemed to have just appeared out of nowhere, and was suddenly strolling through camp as if he'd been there all along. He was out of uniform, clad in a buckskin suit, his hair unbound and a day's growth on his chin. For just a few minutes he stepped inside the cabin to refresh himself, then reappeared with a newly shaved face and his hair once again bound behind his neck.

He called together his mournful camp to address their sorrow and pay a final tribute to the memory of Steve MacLeod.

He gave a short but inspiring address that ended when he hoisted a sleek Pennsylvania rifle over his head in a way that presented five gold stars to the company. There was no mistaking that fifth star. It sat above the four that Will MacLeod so justly earned.

It was Steve's fourth star, the one he'd awaited so anxiously but now would never see. Only a few weeks ago, Congress had responded to Gabriel's persistent requests for this medal that put a marksman into the most honorable and elite corps of shooters. Few had four stars on their barrels. Only the best.

As twenty-one guns fired in salute, Will took his newly decorated weapon, too moved by the Colonel's gesture to do anything more than bend his head and quietly weep.

Few people were near enough to hear what Gabriel said to the heartbroken soldier, but Vanessa caught every word. "Wield your weapon well, Captain . . . his honor is now and forever in your hands."

Above the weeping man's head, his eyes found hers, caught and held her gaze for a moment, just long enough for her to see the dark storms inside him.

Michael.

Gabriel was still full of grief from last night. The dream must have upset him more than she thought. He looked now just as he did in the wake of his dream, that raw and unhealed wound in his soul suddenly wide open to her view. She was just about to reach for him when he suddenly withdrew, looked away, retreated back into whatever lonely place he'd come from.

She didn't see him again until late in the night when he returned from his usual evening inspections. Stirred awake by the gust of wind let in by the open door, she watched him remove his cloak and gloves, then turn around and look directly at her.

"I didn't mean to wake you . . . "

"I wasn't asleep . . . the winds set this whole camp to rattling sometimes."

He smiled wearily, crossed the room and sat down on the edge of her cot.

What a weary pose he struck in the faint moonlight, streaks of silver illuminating the tired, sad face he bent as he stared at his muddy boots.

Vanessa wanted to reach out, smooth that broad muscled back that wasn't meant to slump the way it was now.

"What you did for Will today was beautiful," was all she said. "Steve's star was the finest gift you could have given him just then."

A brief nod was all she could draw out of him. "I had that star for a few weeks now . . . should have given it to him before he left for Bennington."

"Never mind," she said, giving his shoulder the barest brush of her hand, "your intentions were good." And then, as if in afterthought, she added, "As usual."

He didn't say anything, didn't turn around or move in the slightest way, just sat there staring at the floor until the cabin fell completely silent. He seemed to want the quiet, the peace, to sit there with her even though he seemed to be millions of miles away.

"Why did you come to me last night?"

The question startled her. She moved away and he seemed to expect that reaction, remained perfectly still on the edge of her cot and made no attempt to even look at her. He sensed her withdrawal, she knew, and was too tired to fight it.

"Why . . . I don't know . . . " she stammered, looked at the back of his head and said, "I just wanted to . . . to help you."

He nodded, fell silent again for a long, tense moment.

"You did," he finally whispered, his voice deep and low and thick in his throat when he added, "You took my breath away . . . "

His words trailed through the room like a thin chord of faraway music.

But then he rose, as if wanting to break the spell, to let it all end right there, on that final note. Bewildered at his mood, she watched him go to the desk, snuff the lantern, then quietly put himself to bed.

19

The two scouts sat within an amiable circle of Continentals and enjoyed the camaraderie around the fire in the middle of this wilderness post. It was small, relaxed, easily penetrated by a pair of men in civilian clothes who claimed to be looking to join Gates's army. The ruse worked without a problem. And so here they sat, in the pouring rain, imbibing a bit more than a gil of rum and shooting dice with the regulars.

"Uh-oh," one of the soldiers said, hopping off the ground. "Here comes the Captain." He started brushing off his britches to make it look like he hadn't been loafing.

The dice disappeared, a wineskin full of rum hidden under someone's coat. Everyone scattered, went about their business and left the two scouts sitting alone at the fire.

The unit's Commander, Captain John Moynihan, rode into the clearing. There was a man slung across the rump of his mount, obviously a captured scout. "You two—" he barked at the agents. "Keep an eye on this man." The captive was unceremoniously dumped to the ground. Moynihan strolled off, left the man bound in the dirt.

"What are we supposed to do now—"

"What he says . . . keep an eye on him."

They got up, sauntered over to the struggling man and stood mutely watching him try to get his hands free.

"Straighten up, I say!" they heard Moynihan yelp at the nearby contingent of soldiers. "I want you to look good if the Colonel comes tonight . . . they say he might."

Both agents looked at each other in surprised delight. Wouldn't it be grand if this lazy night would somehow manage to bring them the opportunity they'd been seeking for two weeks.

"Hey! I said watch that man, you two!"

Moynihan came back, gave the prisoner a swift kick in the ribs to stop him from further unwinding the ties at his wrist.

Thankfully, two other soldiers came around to assist the Captain in what was obviously a routine interrogation.

They fired questions at the scout, slapped him around a bit, tried to make him talk.

It didn't work.

The agents slid into the shadows and watched from a safe distance as the Continentals proceeded to strip the man.

"Found him climbing out of the Hudson," Moynihan was saying as he tossed away the man's drenched clothing. "Just the right direction if he's bringing word from Clinton."

One of the soldiers searched the prisoner's clothes while the other gave the man's body a thorough search to be sure he wasn't hiding anything.

They found nothing.

Stumped, Moynihan tried to pound the information out of him again, but the prisoner refused to talk.

"Oh hell!" Moynihan growled, gave the beaten captive one last kick in the ribs and said, "I give up. Hang the bloody devil. Then we'll be sure he's not carrying any information. Go on and take him away."

Moynihan stood up, wiped his hands on his britches, finally noticed the subdued posture of his two assistants.

"What the devil's wrong with you two, eh? Move, I said!"

"Er . . . Cap'n . . . we got company—"

"What?" They were staring at something behind Moynihan.

The Captain whirled around, startled to see the Colonel himself leaning against a nearby tree. He was watching the whole spectacle while casually smoking a taper between the rivers of rain streaming off the edge of his hat brim.

"Colonel, sir!"

The two agents looked at one another in barely suppressed excitement. After crawling around in the woods for so many days, creeping from post to post, here the Colonel stood like some giant gift just dropped from heaven.

The Colonel came away from the tree, awarded Moynihan a return salute, then gave his back an approving cuff.

"Good work, Captain."

"But he won't talk, Gabe—"

"Yes, he will."

"Sir?"

"Get me some brine water."

Soldiers began to collect in the clearing again, all eyes pinned to the Colonel. They were excited, eager to watch their famous Commander at work.

He walked a wide circle around the fallen prisoner, studying him with a cool, concentrated vision. "I think he's got something to tell me," he confided to the onlookers. "They say only the best spies refuse to talk."

The fallen prisoner didn't look so dazed anymore. He clearly recognized the Colonel, if not by sight, because of his obvious French accent. He struggled up on his elbows, gave the Colonel a vicious scowl.

"Bourbon pig!"

A soldier leaped for the prisoner's throat, but the Colonel easily waylaid the young man's enthusiasm with a curt command for silence. He drew back, glaring in hatred at the prisoner.

St. Claire was nonplused, stood over the furious captive and planted the toe of his boot firmly against his brow. Ever so slowly, he pushed the man back to the ground, until he was lying flat on his back.

"Relax! And let's try to be gentlemen about this, eh? I'd introduce myself but you apparently already know me. My name, by the way, isn't pronounced *Bourbon pig.* It's St. Claire . . . Gabriel St. Claire . . . you know, a fellow countrymen of your own honorable St. Leger. Ah! So you know St. Leger as well, eh?"

Excitement pulsed through the ranks. The Colonel was gleaning a surprising amount of information just by reading the man's reactions.

The Colonel motioned at Moynihan for the cup of saltwater.

"Have a drink, won't you?"

No one had any idea what the Colonel was about, which only made things more fascinating. Moynihan dutifully forced the brine water down the throat of the unwilling captive, then held his head back long enough to be sure he swallowed it.

"Bastard!" The Englishman spat, doubled forward and instantly began to heave at the ground.

"I've been called worse," the Colonel remarked, then added mischievously, "and certainly deserved it."

Everyone guffawed in delight, including the two scouts who were sitting in the shadows beneath a towering evergreen. The laughter drowned out the noise of the prisoner's distress as he relieved himself of the Colonel's hospitality.

Something metal clicked against the side of Moynihan's boot.

"Sir? Look at this—"

"Open it, Captain."

"What?"

"It's hollow. You'll see. I'll wager a lock of my wife's hair on it."

"Take him up on the wager, Tommy!" Benny Cooke came crashing out of the woods, obviously unable to stay quiet any longer. "Besides, his woman's got the most beautiful hair I've ever seen . . . as black as a raven's back. Ain't it, Gabe?"

"Open it, Captain."

Sure enough, the bullet snapped apart, a thin strip of paper rolled inside. In a slow, almost awestruck tone of voice, the Captain read aloud, "Nothing stands between us now but Horatio Gates. General Clinton."

The Colonel let out a shout of victory, took off his hat and sent it spinning into the night. "Let's go, Benny."

A moment later he was gone, vanishing into the dark woods with his sentry struggling to keep up.

Both agents rose, slid away from the soldiers gathered around Moynihan and the moaning prisoner. They were all chattering in amazement and wonder, commending themselves for what was obviously a stroke of enormous good fortune, happy to have found the Colonel here at so crucial a moment.

When they were beyond the range of the camp, they ran through the woods, desperate for their hidden mounts. Once found, they leaped into their saddles and roared off in the same direction as the Colonel.

* * *

Benny was a big man but quite capable in the saddle. It took a few minutes but he managed to overtake the racing Colonel and swing ahead of him where he belonged.

"Stay behind me, Gabe!"

"I'm right here . . . just hurry. We've got to get word to Gates tonight. Johnny will fight now that he thinks Clinton is coming. If we wage the battle before he gets here, we might win the day after all."

"Sure hope so . . . let's cross the creek."

Benny's mount leaped off the banks of the stream they were following, its hind legs splashing into the water, kicking up a spray of mud and gravel. Gabriel's steed caught the debris in its snout, whinnied in anger and threw up its front legs. He clutched his saddle horn with both hands to keep from being thrown off the back of his mount.

"Easy Fleet . . . " he soothed the horse, felt its front legs once again drop to the ground. "Good boy . . . " A jab of his heels brought it up the other side of the bank where it once again reared with a snort of agitation.

A mouthful of gravel wasn't enough to upset a warhorse.

There was something wrong. The horse sensed it, dropped its legs and took a nervous leap after Benny's mount.

"Ho!" the Sergeant barked from somewhere ahead of him on the path. "Who goes there?" Benny was suddenly swinging around, galloping full speed toward the Colonel. *"Gabe! Get down!"*

"What the devil—"

Shots rang out, a burst of flame temporarily brightening the woods around the charging sentry. Benny ducked low as grapeshot splattered through the foliage. He cursed, grabbed his right arm, his eyes pinned to Gabriel's figure as he cried, "Get off your mount, Gabe!"

Gabriel didn't question him, jerked his feet out of the stirrups.

"Hold up!" a strange voice barked from the woods. "We've got papers! St. Claire? Just stay where you are!"

A figure appeared on the road ahead. He and Benny saw it at the same time, their carbines lifting in perfect unison. They both fired, watched the figure jerk backward and land in the brush with a loud crash.

"We got him . . . " Benny whispered, still clutching his arm.

Gabriel slid back into his saddle but he couldn't ride. Benny's horse was blocking his way.

"Let's go, Benny—"

"No wait . . . I hear something . . . "

Another figure loomed out of the woods ahead, a dark silhouette flitting from tree to tree.

"Hold up, man, or I'll blow your head off!" Benny commanded, using the muzzle of his carbine to follow the moving shadow. "Stop moving, I say! You're behind American lines! We shoot to kill!"

"Damnit! Listen to me!" the voice shouted just as Benny fired in a last warning.

The shot was misunderstood, taken as a threat. The figure fired back and his aim was better than the first man's. The shot found Benny full in the chest, sent the sentry pitching backward until he nearly fell across Gabriel.

With the weight of the sentry pushing him sideways, Gabriel took up his carbine and aimed it straight at the advancing figure on the path.

He cocked his gun, the sound ripping through the still woods like the toll of a bell. Benny moaned something inaudible just as an explosion of bright orange light flashed around him. He wasn't sure whose gun it was, only felt something red-hot and piercing against the side of his head.

Gabriel must have lost consciousness for when he woke again, he found himself sprawled against the neck of his horse, its wiry hair in his face. Benny was lying across his saddle, face down, one of his feet still caught in the stirrup of his own mount.

They were moving forward now, directly toward the place from where the gunfire had come. If anyone was still out there, he had little chance of escaping alive.

Images of his life began to parade before his eyes but he fought them off. He wasn't ready to die. Not yet.

Only with some supreme effort of will did Gabriel manage to reach under his arm and pull out a powder horn. He drew up his carbine, loaded it, cocked the trigger. His mount responded to a slight tug on the reins and fell still.

For a long moment, he just lay against Benny's back, breathing hard into the sentry's dirty wool coat, listening to the woods around him.

Nothing. There was no sound. Just Benny's heartbeat hammering from somewhere deep inside his chest.

He started to move again in an effort to draw out his hidden enemies but none came. Instead, his horse moved around the place where a crumpled body lay across the path. Gabriel didn't know if this was the first gunman or the second, could hardly bring himself to think clearly through the haze of pain in his skull.

He just kept moving forward now, winding through the woods, letting his horse find its own way. There was nothing to do now but hope: that he'd make it back to camp alive, that Benny would live, that this night would not be his last.

It was nearly midnight when the winds rose, another autumn storm come to call on the towering but tired forests of the Mohawk Valley. Such was the nature of the season, so capricious, offering little more in warning than to send a sudden punch of wind spinning through the camp. Kettles rattled, shutters slammed, soldiers scrambled to protect whatever perishables lay about.

Vanessa looked up from a half-written letter to Malinda Borden and listened to the wind gasp through the coarse cabin walls. She set aside her quill, hardly able to concentrate on what was normally a relaxing project. Tonight she was too preoccupied with the present, with a compelling need to dwell upon a subject of increasing fascination to her lately.

Gabriel.

Where was he? What was he doing? Where might those two British agents be?

Rain sprang out of the sky and hit the roof with a noisy clatter. She rushed to secure the shutters but not before half the lamps were snuffed by the penetrating wind. Through a crack in the sash she watched a soldier chase his hat down the path, followed by another who ran while comically entangled in his own cloak. She clucked her tongue in reprimand at the foul weather and hastily built a fire to stave off the dampness.

Wind and water seized the valley while Vanessa sat on the floor before the fire, hugged her knees tight and cast her thoughtful mood into the flames. She wasn't tired, a restless spirit keeping her body tense. She wouldn't rest until he came home, out of the raging dangers of this night, safe from the many foes who stalked him.

With a cheek resting against her knees, she closed her eyes and found herself entertaining gentler thoughts of him.

Dancing in his arms on the front lawn of the Borden home. The long-legged sprawl he affected upon the settee in the parlor of their Philadelphia home. The way his fingers felt sliding through hers in a field full of gunfire and pain.

Every tiny detail of him absorbed her mind, the husky drawl of his speech, the dark intensity of his eyes, how incorrigible his grin looked on such a strong and sturdy face. So many poses of life she'd seen him in, laughing and playful, concerned and attentive, frightened and trembling, proud and powerful, deadly and fierce, tender and in love.

The last thought brought her upright. It had never occurred to her that Gabriel might be in love with her and she wondered about it now for the first time.

No. It couldn't be. Even in the heat of their ardor, he never mentioned love. Only desire. It made her wonder if lust and love were the same.

Confused, she grabbed the poker and used it to stab at the coals. Why was she thinking about this so much lately? He kept creeping into her mind like a ghost in an attic full of what should be forgotten. "I need you . . . the way you love me . . . when you let yourself . . . " " . . . I want you . . . more than I dare tell you."

She looked down at her hands, saw the way they were stroking the poker. Maybe she should be wondering about herself, if she was the one falling in love in spite of herself.

But then another memory whispered through her mind, words of his that she could never quite forget. *"Has it ever occurred to you that wanting something better for me is just another way of caring about me?"*

Unnerved, she put the poker away, hoped the activity might swallow the nervous feeling she had every time those particular words were recalled. They made too much sense, especially to the woman only he seemed capable of awakening, the one who didn't want to be beaten anymore. She was someone new in his arms, someone who had been trying to be born for a long time, perhaps since the day she met him. This woman wanted to entertain the idea that she might be capable of love one day, that her broken heart could mend until it was whole again.

Maybe. Just maybe.

A great thundering sound vibrated through the room, instantly dispelling her thoughts. She jumped up, startled by the noise, the sudden shout of men's voices from somewhere in camp.

Horses clattered, men's boots pounded at the ground, splashed into puddles of mud. Voices bellowed above the wild winds like dogs barking in frantic confusion.

She ran across the room, hardly aware that the hair on her arms was standing on end. She reached for a shutter, just about to unlatch it when the cabin door exploded open.

Gabriel slid inside, fell back against the door to slam it shut.

"Oh!" she gasped at him. "You frightened me!"

He didn't say anything, just stood there with his back against the door, his face hidden inside the drenched hood of his cloak. He was completely breathless, almost gasping for air.

Something felt very wrong to her just then. "Gabriel? You're drenched—"

She started toward him, that terrible inner feeling getting stronger when she noticed not the slightest reaction from him as she approached. It was as if he didn't know where he was.

He was frightening her now. Why didn't he move, say something? Why was he just standing there staring at the thin air.

"Gabriel . . . what's wrong?"

She stopped in front of him, looked up into a face that was strangely quiet, almost serene. Except for his eyes. They were wide and glassy and vague.

"Ness?" he finally asked, panting hard for a moment until he caught enough breath to say, "Is that you?"

He couldn't see. His eyes were wide open but they were completely blind. Time froze, chilled the very blood in her veins. "Yes . . . it's me . . . I'm right in front of you . . . can't you see?"

"Not well . . . I . . . it's . . . so dark . . . "

She brought a hand to her lips to stifle the terrified sound that wanted to come out. "Can you tell me what happened . . . "

"I got shot . . . "

She felt suddenly weak, faint, but somehow managed to take hold of his arm. "Come away from the door . . . and show me . . . "

"No." He brushed her hand off his arm, motioned her away from him. All the while, he kept his head firmly planted against the back of the door. At the thin air, he sighed, "Just stay back . . . where I can't hurt you . . . and take this . . . to Robert . . . " A piece of curled paper was held up in front of her. "Take it . . . "

She did. "And go . . . hurry . . . "

He let go of the door latch, immediately slumped to his knees.

"Gabriel!" she screamed, rushed around him, swept back his hood to give him air.

Blood. The right side of his head was soaked in it.

Shock made her heart momentarily race in her breast. She put a hand there, just stared at the place where the blood was still oozing. It was just above his right ear, but the wound was hidden beneath thick waves of wet auburn hair.

A soft moan escaped him as he bent forward, rested his brow on the floor. Both hands reached up to encircle his head.

Francis! She had to get Francis.

"Don't press on it," she cried, her hands trembling wildly as she tried to move his hands away. Huddled over him, she drew her arms tight around him, let her terrified tears rain into his hair as she held him with all her might. "I'll help you . . . let me help you . . . "

The strength ran out of him just then. She could feel it leave his body at the same time that a single breath of air floated through his lips. He went slack in her arms, his body dropping limply to the floor.

While the storm raged and the winds howled, she lay holding his bloody head in her lap and wailed for help, hoping someone, anyone, might hear.

20

It took four men to hold Benny down when he finally regained consciousness.

"GABE!" he shouted.

"Easy, Benny!" Francis soothed, "You've got a chest full of grapeshot."

"What . . . where . . . " The Sergeant's eyes rolled backward in his head. "Gabe . . . " he groaned weakly.

Francis sighed in relief when he plucked out the last piece of metal and realized Benny's muscle had spared his life. Not a single bit of lead managed to penetrate his chest deep enough to cause him any permanent injury.

"I gotta see Gabe . . . " Benny whined, tried to twist away from the arms holding him down. "He was moaning . . . I heard him . . . on the trail . . . I came around once . . . he was hurt . . . "

"What?" Francis looked at him sharply, then glanced over his shoulder in search of Gabriel. An uneasy feeling passed through him when he realized the Colonel wasn't there. He always disappeared when he was hurt, Francis knew; he would steal off and try to tend himself.

He looked at Benny just as the sentry let out his breath in a long sigh and fell unconscious again.

"I'm going to find Gabe," Francis announced, handing the other end of a long strip of cloth to Polly and motioning for her to continue wrapping Benny's chest. "I'll be right back."

Francis was already out the door, bending his head into the wind and trotting across camp to Gabriel's hut. There was a light on inside. He knocked once, opened the door, and went inside.

Vanessa was sitting on the floor just to the right of the door. Gabriel lay crumpled before her, legs and arms sprawled, his head buried in her lap. She was leaning over him, whispering to him, dabbing at his head with a piece of her own petticoat.

The door slammed behind Francis.

Vanessa jumped, looked up. She said his name but no sound came out of her lips. They were trembling too hard. She looked so pathetic in that moment, her cheeks gleaming with tears and smudges of Gabriel's blood, dazed and desperate, and so terribly afraid.

"Help him . . . " she said in a lifeless tone of voice that instantly warned Francis she might be in shock. "It's his head . . . "

Her announcement made something grim pass over his heart just then.

He instantly fell to his knees beside the Colonel, gently moving her hands away from his head. The wound was just above his right ear. It was deep, gory, bad enough to make Francis's insides shrink with dread. He dared not look at Vanessa for fear she'd see his reaction and become hysterical. Instead, he kept his attention focused on the wound he began to examine.

Gabriel's head was cut to the bone, a long thin gash extending halfway around the back of his head.

"I have to do something . . . " Vanessa said.

"What?" He looked up at her, saw that she was showing him a thin piece of torn paper. He took it, read it.

Clinton.

"Alright . . . I'll take care of it . . . " Francis almost didn't care about the war, could hardly think of anything except the pleading prayer racing through his mind as he began to probe for the bullet hole.

Please God, not Gabriel.

He couldn't find a hole.

He searched again, more deftly this time, using the tips of his fingers to hold back Gabriel's hair and scrutinize the cut in his scalp from one end to the other.

He could find no bullet wound.

For a moment, Francis was so grateful he bent his head in a moment of sheer thanksgiving.

"Is he dead?" Vanessa asked, her voice tiny and hoarse. Francis looked up at her in a moment of complete pity.

"No," he whispered, giving her shoulder a comforting squeeze. "I think he's going to be alright . . . "

Violet eyes welled in a new rush of tears. "Oh thank God!" she breathed against her blood-stained and shivering fingers. "Are you sure?"

Francis nodded, her emotion so poignant it momentarily roused his own until his throat felt choked. "There's no bullet wound . . . it just missed him . . . by the length of a hair and the grace of God . . . it missed him."

Her eyes shone with joy, glimmered at him like a pair of rain-drenched orchids. Dear God, but she was magnificent, he thought, so breathtakingly beautiful despite the dark tragedy of her life. In that moment it was completely obvious to Francis why Gabriel loved this woman so fiercely. She was the most fascinating creature he'd ever encountered.

"I'm going to lift his head now," he said to her, keeping his voice calm and quiet as he instructed, "and I want you to get me help to move him. Can you do that?"

"Anything," she whispered. "I'll do anything you say."

"Good. Easy now . . . "

She watched the Surgeon's hands ease around Gabriel's head, then slowly lift it out of the blood-soaked lap of her gown. For a moment, she couldn't make herself move, sat there staring at how helpless Gabriel looked in Francis' hands just then, his face so serene and quiet and unaware of what was happening to him. He looked like he was sound asleep.

If only that were true!

"Oh Gabriel! Gabriel!" she whimpered, unaware that she was talking out loud.

"Hush now . . . " Francis said, still speaking in that unnervingly calm voice, as if everything was perfectly alright. "This kind of injury can keep a man unconscious for days, but he'll come around . . . now please . . . go outside . . . get any soldier you see to help us move him."

"Yes . . . yes . . . " she babbled, leaped off the floor and ran for the door. Once outside, she found several soldiers milling around in the rain, talking about what had happened to Benny Cooke. Her call brought them all running, sent word spinning through camp that the Colonel had been shot.

A moment later the cabin was full of people, the atmosphere charged with a heightened energy as everyone rushed to help. Francis took charge, issuing orders in that crisp decisive way of his, sent people moving in every direction in their haste to do as he bid.

"Heat some water . . . warm those blankets . . . get those wet clothes off him . . . don't jostle him! Easy! You men . . . move the cot away from the wall so I can move around it . . . "

It took four men to carry the Colonel across the room, each step taken with painstaking care so as not to jostle his head and cause any more injury to his skull. And all the while Gabriel slept on, hanging in their arms without the slightest flinch of awareness.

Lauren seemed particularly disturbed by Gabriel's helplessness. "I always hated those jokes he made about getting shot," Lauren said, his normally jovial expression pinched with anxiety as he watched Francis ease the Colonel's head onto the pillow. "You know . . . so he could get some sleep . . . "

"Don't be morbid, Lauren," Francis quipped, stepping over the place where Vanessa knelt on the floor beside her husband. She clung to his limp hand as if afraid death would snatch him if she let go. It was foolish to hang on him like this, something his masculinity would never allow were he awake, but she didn't care. She was never so afraid of losing something in her entire life.

Francis inched around the head of the bed and ordered the Quartermaster, "Bring me that bucket . . . and some cloth. I need bandages . . . "

Vanessa watched Gabriel's face for any sign of cognizance as Francis went to work on his wound. It was cleaned, inspected for a third time, a few flecks of metal all that could be found of the lead ball that came so close to killing him.

"This is one lucky man . . . " Francis said over and over as he tended his Commander. "A hair's breadth is all that spared his life."

They all just stood around the cot, shaking their heads soberly, stricken by the thought of how close the Colonel had come to being killed tonight.

Lauren couldn't stand to think about it. "He always was lucky . . . except at dice. Lousiest dice player I ever met . . . "

A few men snorted a laugh, just to relieve their own tension. Vanessa found their humor appalling even though she secretly wished she could share it.

"Here . . . let me wipe your face," Polly said from behind her, easing a warm cloth against her cheek to wipe away the smears of blood. "You're trembling so . . . why don't you come away . . . sit with me by the fire—"

"No!" Vanessa said more vehemently than she intended. "I want to stay by him . . . I'm afraid for him . . . "

"Alright then, my dear," Polly soothed, brought a blanket to wrap around her shoulders and keep her warm where she sat on the cold floor.

Francis started dismissing men, tried to clear out the cabin and let the Colonel rest. Within a few minutes, only the officers remained, each of them finding a place to sit and wait for Gabriel to come around.

The cabin fell quiet, everyone drifting off to sleep, lulled by the drumming staccato of rain against the thatched roof of the hut. It was just as the first glimpse of morning light trickled through the closed shutters that Vanessa felt Gabriel's fingers move in her hand.

"Gabriel?"

Everyone bolted awake.

One eye opened, the other swollen shut from where his wound had grown thick and sore. But his gaze was clear. The sight of his awareness brought a powerful sense of relief to her ragged nerves.

He blinked once, as if trying to keep his eye open, but he lost the fight. It closed as a deep sigh made his chest rise and fall. "Why are you sitting on the floor like that? It's cold . . . "

She bit her lip against a rush of happy tears just to hear him fretting over her in his normal, wonderful way. "Oh Gabriel! Thank God!"

Francis leaned over him, his blonde hair sticking out in every direction; he'd slept with his head in his arms all night. "How do you feel?"

A lone eye once again opened, peered at the Surgeon. "You look like hell, Francis . . . "

"Well if that isn't the pot calling the kettle black!" Lauren said from behind her, his broad grin flashing at his groggy Commander. "You don't look so good yourself, *sir!*"

Beneath the tender press of her compress, Vanessa watched his brow furl in confusion. "What the hell's going on . . . where's Benny?"

"Is that all you two can talk about is each other?" Lauren joked. "He's fine. How do you feel?"

"It's just a headache," Gabriel scoffed not understanding what everyone was fussing about.

"Which is to be expected of a man who nearly had his head blown off," Lauren was saying.

Vanessa paled visibly.

"Lauren . . . you have a fabulous bedside manner," Francis remarked.

"Thank you, doctor."

Francis ignored the Quartermaster as he inspected the dark stain on the bandages that completely encircled the Colonel's head. With just his fingers, he tested it to see how fresh it was. The stain was dry. "Alleluia," he breathed. "It stopped bleeding . . . "

This slight movement was enough to make him grit his teeth in agony.

"Don't hurt him, Francis . . . " Vanessa said, leaning over her husband. "There now . . . what can I get you—"

"From you? A night of unending love," came his witty reply. They all guffawed with delight, including Vanessa who had to stop herself from hugging him just then. "From Francis . . . some water . . . "

The Surgeon grinned from ear to ear as he fetched the Colonel a mug of water. With Vanessa's aid, Gabriel weakly rose on his elbows and drank thirstily. Over the rim of the mug, he looked at the faces hovering above him, Lauren and Robert grinning down at him like a pair of smug schoolboys.

He finished the mug, lay back down. "Stop making a spectacle of me," he growled. "Besides, you've work to do. Clinton is coming—"

"Never mind," Francis said, "we've taken care of all that. Now stop fidgeting and lie still."

"Don't start mothering me, Francis. There's a war on . . . "

Francis rolled his eyes. Gabriel had the greatest respect for the medical profession until it came to being doctored himself. Then he despised it.

"Why don't you try to get more rest?" Vanessa whispered, smoothed his cheek in her hand and pressed a tender kiss there.

Her sweetness surprised him, made his eye pop open and gaze up at her in search of some explanation for her unexpected benevolence. Despite the audience, their gazes met and locked for a long, quiet moment, enough time for her to communicate the blissfulness in her heart just then.

He saw it and it pleased him. She could tell by the contentment with which he sighed and closed his eye again. "Come into bed and be off the floor . . . " His hand slid up the length of her arm in a silent invitation. "Rest with me . . . "

"But—"

"No . . . don't argue . . . " He was weakening fast, his voice trailing into a thin whisper. "Just lie with me . . . keep me warm . . . " She did so, ever so carefully, easing herself against his side and covering them both with his blanket. "*Merci* . . . " was all he whispered before letting out a long contented sigh and going back to sleep.

It rained throughout most of the day and Gabriel was able to sleep for long, uninterrupted hours. Vanessa kept a vigil near his bed, contentedly stitching a new bunting for the baby, then embroidering its tiny hem with an assortment of forest animals. Less than an hour after dinner the rains quit and the activity in the cabin increased immediately.

Relays began to arrive, bringing news that a seven-thousand man army under the command of General Gates had officially begun a five-mile march southward to meet the questionable forces of John Burgoyne. The two armies were expected to clash somewhere near Bemis Heights.

Gabriel awoke long enough to eat and be kept abreast of the activity by Robert Blaire who had assumed command of Moylan's Horse. "Gates panicked when he heard about your narrow escape yesterday, Gabe. He said you couldn't have picked a worse time to go out of action."

"I'm not out of action!" Gabriel rebuked vehemently.

"It's just a headache," Lauren reminded everyone with a mischievous grin.

"Gates is moving out rain or shine!" Robert continued with more excitement than Vanessa had ever seen in the man. A battle was finally going to be waged after months of delay. They were all looking forward to it. "Our scouts claim the countryside is swarming with soldiers . . . most of them Continentals . . . all hoping to get a shot at John Burgoyne while he's in so much trouble."

"What's Burgoyne's position?"

"He's three miles south of the Heights. He's got Fraser and Hamilton with him."

"Who do we have?" Gabriel wanted to know.

"Daniel Morgan just arrived from Virginia."

"Morgan." Gabriel was impressed at the support of this exceptionally skilled General. "Very good . . . who else?"

"Arnold and Greene."

"Excellent! And how can we help?"

"Our cavalry may be called to defend the eastern edge of Morgan's flank. I say we let Will MacLeod command.

He could use a good fight to take his mind off Steve and we'll need good snipers for the task."

"Good suggestion. What about those scouts we killed? Does Gates know anything about that?"

"He hasn't responded to the papers our men found on the bodies. There were two of them . . . both had orders that looked to be signed by Washington. An obvious fake. I expect Gates will contact the General just to be sure."

"He's wasting his time," Gabriel said wearily. "He should think of nothing now but the chance to conquer Burgoyne and bring us the greatest victory of the war. I tell you, I'd sell my home to mount up and ride to the Heights myself tonight."

Vanessa looked up from her stitching, her heart touched by the obvious longing in his voice. How unfair it was to see this great soldier confined to bed at such a crucial time.

It was the next day when word reached their camp that Horatio Gates had arrived at Bemis Heights. The famous American engineer, Thaddeus Kosciuskzko, designed fortifications that the Continentals were now feverishly digging in preparation for battle. Gabriel's own sappers joined in the effort but not a day's work was done before a new storm rolled over the countryside. Once again, the war came to a standstill.

Worse, the rains caught Gates's men barely in their tents and a sizable amount of black powder was soaked, further delaying the battle until their stores dried or a fresh supply was brought.

However frustrating were the delays, Gabriel was secretly glad for the extra healing time. A week after the ambush, the pain in his head was still so ruthless at times he could barely hold it up. His patience was wearing thin, his body restless for action. If not for the timely arrival of a sack of mail, Gabriel thought he'd go mad from boredom.

There were two letters from Martina begging him to

have some sense and free Jonnie, who had been arrested in Princeton and was now languishing in an army prison in Reading. Her words tore at his heart, only added another pain to his collection. He put those notes aside, reached for a letter that carried the careful script of the Millbridge Apothecary, Joshua Stone.

It was addressed to him, not Vanessa, which he thought was strange for the two corresponded regularly. He broke the seal, read the first few lines of the note and instantly realized why the letter was addressed to him.

Fred Davis was dead. He'd been found on the divan in the parlor by a neighbor who grew suspicious when he didn't see Fred draw water from the well for several days. James Morris told Joshua he had no idea how long Fred was dead or what killed him, just that he was stone cold and blue by the time his body was found.

Gabriel sighed dismally, watched his wife yawn herself awake on the cot across the room. She looked over at him, sleepy-eyed and tussled, stretched in a way that pronounced her finest assets against the dimity fabric of her sleeping gown.

"Good morning," she said sweetly and slid out of bed, her long legs silhouetted between the folds as she moved gracefully toward him.

Gabriel moaned against a new ache, one that stabbed at his loins. He looked away. "I wish you would wear your robe around here, Vanessa. Injured or not, I'm still a man . . ."

Vanessa rushed to cover herself with a modest robe, then daintily perched herself on the chair beside his bed. "Did you sleep well?"

"No. I was too busy to sleep."

"Busy? With what?"

"With deliberating the merits of the guillotine."

"Poor Gabriel," she soothed. Beneath the clean white cap of bandages on his head, his auburn hair curled wildly across his shoulders, perfectly matched to the hair on his bare chest. With the blanket drawn only to his waist, a magnificent physique exposed itself to her admiring eyes even though he was too frustrated to notice. Such a vital man was not suited to bed rest and she could tell by the stiff line of his jaw that Gabriel was losing patience with his slow recovery.

"I'll fix us tea," she said, went to the fire and set water to boil, then carefully measured tea leaves into a pair of mugs.

A moment later, she delivered his tea with a tender smile, her eyes soft and warm as she regarded him.

Something about her had changed since his brush with death. Her mood was much softer toward him, gentle and caring as she nursed him through the worst moments. She never left his side all week, proved herself to be a dedicated and devoted wife when the moment required it.

Vanessa could feel his eyes upon her as she sipped her tea and enjoyed the early morning quiet. This wasn't the first time she had felt her husband's close attention this week, as he noticed her changed attitude toward him. But he said nothing, kept his thoughts to himself.

For such a genuine and friendly man, he had an unnerving ability to keep things to himself, she mused. Like the broken heart he hid for a murdered brother.

But she said nothing, was secretly glad for his discretion because she didn't understand herself lately. If he asked, how could she answer him? Like the night of the ambush, her thoughts frequently pondered the possibilities of love between them, if it had grown in spite of themselves. Was he in love with her? Was she falling in love with him? Could this be the source of their intense physical desire, an attraction that had dogged them since the moment they'd laid eyes on each other from across a Tory dinner table? She could still hear his spoon hitting the edge of his Truffle dish.

A warm hand slid over hers, made her jump with a start. Ever so slowly, he unwound her fingers from the tight fist they had formed in her lap.

"Every time I see you looking so anxious it burdens me with guilt for bringing you here," he said quietly, curled her fingers through his own and caressed them softly in his hand. "Forgive me for neglecting to tell you how grateful I am for your help this week. For your sake, I hope your trials will be over soon."

"Trials? I wanted to come here, Gabriel. You know that."

"Yes, but I know how much more comfortable you could have been in Valley Forge with my parents. I was selfish to bring you here, where I could see you, know you were safe. I wanted to spare myself the worry."

He let go of her hand, looked up at the ceiling, studied the knots in the wood.

She abandoned her chair, perched on the edge of his cot. "Nonsense, Gabriel. Have I ever complained about your decision?"

He looked at her then, blue eyes haunted with intrigue as he gazed upon her. "You never complain about anything, Vanessa, not even when that savage sunk his ax in your back. Will you tell me you wanted that too?" He reached, cupped the shoulder that would forever bear the scar of that horrible encounter.

"I served my country," she told him very directly, "and I'm proud of it."

"You're as strong as you are beautiful," he whispered, longing to slide his fingers through her black satin hair but he didn't. He could no longer trust himself to be a gentleman with her. Since the night of his dream, the way she had touched him, his want of her was an almost constant ache. "Death seems to stalk you, Vanessa Davis. I hate to think of how close I came to losing you . . . twice now."

"Why did you save me?"

Her question surprised him. He looked at her strangely. "Why? Because I don't want you to die. Is that so odd?" She didn't say anything. "You should know by now that your safety, health, and happiness are cherished in your new life. With me, you'll never be so cruelly maligned." She stiffened at his reference to her past but he ignored it. "Never again will you be hurt . . . beaten with wooden objects . . . struck with hoes—"

"Stop!" she gasped, dropping her face in her hands in instant shame.

"I can't . . . not now. It's over, Ness. It's all over now."

She looked at him, bewildered.

"He's dead. Your father is dead."

"What?" The word barely escaped her throat, just a faint whisper born more of shock than understanding. "Father?"

Gabriel nodded, decided not to offer Joshua's letter for fear the sorry details would only upset her more. "I'm sorry . . . for your sake . . . not his."

For a long moment she just sat there staring at him, slowly absorbing the news until it finally made her head sink back into her hands. Ever so softly, she began to weep.

Gabriel turned away, frustrated by her reaction, unable to understand why any child so abused could possibly weep for the death of her abuser.

"How?" she finally choked. "How did he die?"

"No one knows, just that he was found on the divan—"

"Oh God!" she moaned, rose on unsteady legs and went to the fire well. In the flames she watched her memories form, the sight of him lying on that blue brocade couch with a jug of spirits beside his hand. He'd died there, in that very same spot.

Other images flickered in the flames, the sight of him at dinner when the family was still intact, those rare moments when he actually seemed to enjoy their company, their conversation. He could be so likable when he wasn't drunk, so normal and attentive like fathers were supposed to be.

She hadn't remembered this side of him for years. Had it been that long since she'd seen her father sober?

"Why do you weep for him?" Gabriel growled as if he couldn't bear another moment of her weeping.

"Why? Because he was my father!"

Gabriel just muttered something under his breath and looked away.

"It was the liquor!" she stated in her father's defense. "He didn't know what he was doing!"

"Don't defend him to me!" Gabriel snapped, his eyes momentarily flashing with anger. "No one forced his hand to take a cup. Bastard!"

She whirled on her husband then, furious at his lack of compassion. "I won't have you talk about him like that anymore . . . he's dead now . . . I want to remember him in peace—"

"Peace?" This brought him upright in bed, perched on his elbows as he remarked, "Yes, I suppose he does have peace, eh? After all, he's never had to pay for his sins. I pay his prices, don't I? While you stand and weep and make excuses for that bastard . . . I lie in an empty bed every night . . . unable to touch my own wife because of what he's done!"

She couldn't believe what she was hearing, just stared at him in a moment of complete astonishment. Never had she heard him talk like this, nor dare to reveal the true depths of his bitterness. Stunned, she stood there and watched him sink backward on the bed, looking almost as surprised as she was.

"I'm sorry," he muttered darkly. "I shouldn't have said that—"

"No, you shouldn't have. Now is hardly the time to berate me about your loins!"

This stung him, made his voice snap across the room like a cracking whip. "Damn you for that . . . " he said, looking away in complete disgust. She was obviously distraught, he told himself, otherwise she would never make such an unwarranted accusation in the face of his constant patience. "Let's drop this subject . . . " he commanded. "I refuse to discuss it with you when you're in this mood."

"What mood?" she demanded haughtily.

"The mood to make me look like Satan and your father an Angel of Mercy. It's twisted and it's wrong and I'm tired of being cheated because of your distorted logic!"

"Cheated? *You* feel cheated?" she gasped, "No one has been more cheated than I! How do you think I felt when you told me about my mother . . . when I realized how his lies caused me years of grief for a mother who's still alive?"

She slowly crossed the room, her insides hardening into rock as she whispered fiercely, "You're not the only one paying for his sins, Gabriel. Do you think I want to weep for him? Do you think I wanted to crave his love for so many years, like any child would, just to have him reject me and break my heart time and again?

"You don't know . . . can never understand . . . you with your perfect loving parents. Have you any idea what it's like to be beaten by the hands that are supposed to love you? Have you? What can you possibly know about being cheated?"

Gabriel never heard her talk like this, and just lay there staring at her, momentarily subdued by her cold remarks. Never had she spoken so poignantly about her past, dared to reveal so much of how she really felt inside.

She stood over him, violet eyes like shards of ice behind the black veil of her hair. She looked so tragic, as if her dark soul was gleaming in her eyes just then.

"I thought Danny's death would teach me a lesson, but it didn't . . . even under all that hate, I still hoped he'd change . . . be better . . . stop drinking . . . "

"Vanessa . . . " he began but she whirled away from his reach, whipped a kerchief from the sleeve of her robe and sought the dry heat of the fire.

"I don't need your pity, Gabriel," she snapped.

"No?"

The question made her turn around, a chilling look in her eyes. "What's that supposed to mean?"

"That I think you do need pity. And compassion. But most of all . . . mercy."

"You're patronizing me!" she spat, stood up, grabbed the poker from the hearth step. "I won't stand for it!"

"Go ahead . . . throw it . . . "

She stopped, looked up, saw the poker in the air above her head, her fist clenched around it, ready to hurl it across the room. Dear God! What was she doing?

All the anger drained out of her. She had the same feeling she'd had that night in Philadelphia when she rewarded her husband's love with this same kind of twisted cruelty. She was sick, she realized, and felt suddenly ill.

"Oh, my god . . . " She looked around herself, disoriented.

"If it makes you feel better to hurt me, then go ahead!"

"Oh! why don't you just leave me alone—"

"Because you're my wife, damnit! You have my child in you!"

She pitched the poker aside, listened to it hit the wall, then the floor, rattle to a halt under her bed. Frustrated beyond reason she blurted, "But I never wanted to be your wife! You insisted! And now you've made me pregnant. Well, you can have the child when it's born! I'll give it to you!"

"You don't know what you're saying!"

"I do! What kind of mother will I be anyway? Look!"

she cried, her face suddenly animated as she pointed at the poker under her bed. "I nearly hit you with it! Do you want your child left in such wicked hands as mine . . . "

He could stand no more, whipped away the blanket and swung his legs off the side of the cot. "I won't listen to you berate yourself like this . . . because of that bastard . . . nor will I let you go on destroying this marriage *in his name!*"

"Gabriel!" she cried, the sight of him struggling to stand up suddenly bringing her back to her senses. "Don't! You must lie still!"

He tried to stand, an expression of excruciating pain shooting across his face, fierce enough to rip a grunt of agony from his throat. He slumped backward, momentarily dazed by the savageness of the pain.

"Let me help you," she cried, dropped to her knees beside the bed and reached for him.

"No," he said, genuine anger making his voice brusque and hard. For the first time since she met him, Gabriel actually pushed her away. "Enough from you—"

"Gabriel . . . I—"

"Enough!" he thundered, rising up on both elbows and staring into her startled face, "You have pushed me too far . . . leave me be!" She fell back on her haunches, having never seen him so incensed. "Now go somewhere else to weep for him. I can't stand the sight of it—"

"Gabriel—"

"Just get out," he demanded, the furious pounding in his head making him gasp aloud in pain. "And send Francis in here . . . "

Gabriel could barely speak to her; their smallest communication was so strained it made Vanessa nervous just to be around him. Even worse was the rising tide of war as Gates and Burgoyne drew near and began to prepare for a long awaited battle. The tension rose until it was nerve-wracking and brittle, only enhanced by Gabriel's sudden orders to break camp. Moylan's Horse was to join the Continental Army and their tiny woodland village was slowly dismantled until all that remained was a small group of deserted huts.

Gabriel sent Robert to collect her the morning they left, told her to ride with Polly to the headquarters of Horatio Gates where she'd stay with the other army wives until the battle commenced.

The ride was long and hard, grueling at times when their wagon sank into pools of mud left by weeks of drenching rains. It seemed like an eternity before they reached a place called Freeman's Farm in a tiny town called Bemis Heights.

A red brick house was tucked into the background of the scenic farm, snuggled at the edge of the woods and looking like a palace from a fairy tale to the travel-weary wives of Moylan's Horse. After spending months in a woodland camp and this entire day bouncing around in the back of a rice wagon, the comforts of a real home made Vanessa and Polly misty-eyed with relief. They couldn't wait to get inside, have a real roof over their heads, the luxuries of a feather bed and a hot bath and upholstered chairs.

The overwhelming presence of soldiers didn't dampen their expectations. This was, after all, the main headquarters of the Continental army under General Horatio Gates and hundreds of soldiers' tents speckled the cleared acres of farmland as far as the eye could see. Nearly eleven thousand men camped here, with hundreds of artillery pieces, wagons full of powder and cartridges, the flags of many different battalions waving proudly in the mild winds.

The wagon stopped at the porch and they hurriedly smoothed their wrinkled skirts before being introduced to the officers. Few of the men paid much attention to the ladies as they gazed down field to where Gabriel assembled his company for a formal review. Judging by their keen interest and the amount of soldiers flocking to watch, her husband's notorious reputation preceded him here today.

A plump and elderly woman greeted them at the porch stoop, her snowy white hair neatly arranged into a starched lace cap. "Welcome, ladies!" she said, beaming, her eyes full of motherly warmth when she took Vanessa's hand. "Madame St. Claire. I'm honored to have you here."

Every head on the porch turned when her name was announced, as the officers looked at the violet-eyed beauty from Philadelphia and instantly came to their feet. They drew off their tri-cornered hats and awaited introductions.

Mrs. Freeman escorted her from officer to officer, so many famous men whose names thrilled her. Generals Nathaniel Greene, Daniel Morgan, and Horatio Gates himself.

General Gates was a man of short stature for such a big reputation, his stocky figure looking quite distinguished in a well-tailored uniform. Sagging of jowl, his white hair thin and wispy, he bent over Vanessa's hand and gave it a surprisingly gracious kiss.

"I trust your husband has fully recovered from his injury in the field," he inquired.

"He is completely restored," Vanessa assured, "and eager for a fight, I daresay."

This made the General laugh appreciatively, the other officers dutifully echoing his humor as Mrs. Freeman hurried Vanessa and Polly inside.

The house was overrun by the military, Vanessa quickly noticed. The dining room walls were pegged with maps, the table piled with scrolls of parchment and cups of ink. Mrs. Freeman apologized profusely for the clutter of military accoutrements littering the first floor of her tidy farmhouse. There were powder horns, soldiers' satchels, idle muskets and a pile of muddy boots and spatter dashes beside the front door. Although only the Generals slept here at night, during the day this house was the nucleus of activity for Gates's eleven-thousand man army.

Vanessa was given a small corner room on the first floor, a plainly decorated chamber that once served the family as a birthing room. A four-poster bed stood beside a window that overlooked the front yard and the porch where the officers sat. Vanessa was pleased with this chamber, let a soldier bring in her bags while Mrs. Freeman escorted Polly to another room upstairs.

She was momentarily free to bathe and rest after the long ride from camp. Her first impulse was to discard her damp and muddy gown, drape herself in a warm wool robe and stretch out across the soft feather bed.

She sighed blissfully, laid her head down and listened to the steady thump of drums and horses plodding across the lawn. Benny Cooke's voice bawled commands that drew the metallic hiss of drawn swords and the snapping rattle of carbines. Spectators cheered from the distance, their throaty cries wafting through the open window on the cool, wet breezes.

"Look at those men gawk!" she heard Gates exclaim. "Now they'll know what professional soldiers are supposed to look like in review, eh?"

"I think most of them came to catch a glimpse of St. Claire," another General responded. "Where is he?"

"With his flagmen over there . . . on the black horse . . . with the rest of his officers. Lord, has he drilled these men! They're almost better than yours, Daniel."

"Almost," General Morgan grumbled.

Hurried footsteps pounded across the porch.

"What is it, soldier?" Gates asked, clearly annoyed at the interruption.

"Urgent, sir. This was just brought by special courier."

"Oh? From where?"

"They didn't say, sir."

Vanessa listened as paper tore, momentarily rustling in the wind. A man's harsh exclamation broke the silence. "Take a look at this, Daniel."

Intrigued, Vanessa sat up, reached over the headboard to part the curtains just enough to see the men on the porch. She watched Daniel Morgan hand the paper back to the Commander. Gates snatched it, rolled it up into a tight ball in his hand while his eyes followed Gabriel's every move. She could see his fluffy white brows arch together in a frustrated expression.

"Who is this Archangel?" he asked no one in particular.

Morgan shook his head. "God knows . . . I thought it could be St. Claire but how can it, eh? Here's a note from the Archangel telling us Burgoyne is heading toward us from the northeast. St. Claire has been traveling toward us all day from the opposite direction!"

Gates responded by rigidly crossing his legs, growled in a voice so low Vanessa had to nearly lean out the window to hear him. "I've been in the military all my life and I've never seen anything so preposterous as this! Who the devil is this Archangel, eh? Why hasn't anyone seen him? Not a blessed man in the army has ever laid eyes on him! I'm sorry, Daniel, but I find this too hard to believe. This whole situation is absolutely absurd. He's got to be found! Do you hear me? I want that man found!"

"Let's talk to St. Claire later."

"Humph! I wager he'd be real interested in knowing about this note."

Both men fell quiet for a moment, stared at the Commander of Moylan's Horse with an intensity that she found suddenly disturbing.

"He must know something about the Archangel. If what we heard is true, that the Archangel trails St. Claire, then I find it hard to believe the Colonel knows nothing about him." This disclosure immediately alarmed her. No one was supposed to know the two men were connected, or at least that's what Gabriel had told her.

Gates stopped rubbing his chin for a moment, looked at Morgan and said sternly, "I wager St. Claire knows the man as well as he knows his own brother."

"Yes," Morgan agreed, looked at Gates with a long, hard stare. "But they say his brother is dead."

Gates blinked as if Morgan's comment somehow surprised him. But he said nothing, just turned away and stared into the distance with deep concentration.

"Madam?"

Vanessa jumped away from the window, hurried across the room to open the door. Mrs. Freeman brought in two pails of hot water, poured them into a barrel in preparation for a bath. Vanessa was glad when she hurried away, feeling a strong need to be alone with her thoughts.

She slid into the water, slowly scrubbing at her skin and wondering about the conversation on the porch. Why did they look at each other so strangely when Gabriel's brother was mentioned. Gates's startled reaction to Morgan's comment made her wonder if some private speculation of his had been tapped by that remark. But what? The only thought that came to mind was that someone, somewhere, was pondering the possibility that Michael was alive.

Good heavens! What an unnerving thought that was, especially in light of the fact that Gabriel and Michael were identical twins.

So many connections flew through her mind in that moment that Vanessa could hardly make sense of them. One twin could easily pose as the other, and they could travel together, share information.

No. It couldn't be. Gabriel's brother was dead, his whole family forced into exile over Michael's tragic murder. Whoever was spewing these theories was making wild and nonsensical assumptions, she decided, sinking deeper into the water and trying to shake away a feeling of being profoundly unsettled inside.

Although it could hardly be true, Vanessa was sure General Horatio Gates was pondering that exact possibility.

She was preoccupied all day by these thoughts, found it difficult to concentrate on dinner. Thankfully, she was excused early to bed in deference to her delicate condition. If her quiet mood was detected, it was attributed to pre-battle jitters and travel fatigue. She went to her room, immediately noticed the addition of Gabriel's bags in the room and realized he planned to stay with her.

A moment of relief washed over her, the hope that they might somehow mend the rift between them.

But then she realized another reason for his choice of beds. His pride. Like in Philadelphia, he'd stay with her for appearances sake, not their own. How would it look if the Colonel didn't sleep with his beautiful young wife?

She undressed, pulled on a white flannel gown and slid into bed. Mrs. Freeman had warmed the blanket but it didn't comfort her. As much as her weary body wanted sleep her mind was too restless, too anxious. She could manage little more than to doze fitfully until the sound of voices outside the door brought her fully awake.

"Beware of Horatio Gates, Gabriel. He's not a General's General. He's a politician's General. Every move he makes is to further his own political aims. More than just the war motivated him to summon you to Bemis Heights this dawn."

"What do you mean?"

"I mean he wants the Archangel, my friend, and you're the closest thing to him."

"How would you know that?"

"Come now, Gabriel. You don't think Washington's aides keep secrets, do you? Word's gotten out that the 'Angel trails you."

"So Gates brought me here to see for himself, eh?" Gabriel chuckled in derision.

"He's pricked because the Archangel favors Washington instead of him . . . sends every bit of intelligence information to the Commander in Chief instead of himself." This stranger's voice lowered then, a barely audible whisper as he said, "Those two spies you shot . . . the ones Meeks tried to lead here . . . were probably Gates's men."

Vanessa sat upright, stunned at this revelation.

Gabriel's voice was nonplused, however, very quiet and controlled when he said, "Which is why Washington denied signing their papers . . . because he didn't know about the investigation—"

"Exactly. I tell you, Gates has ulterior motives where you're concerned and I wouldn't take this chance tonight if I weren't damned sure about it."

"You've done me a good service, Benedict."

Benedict? Could he mean General Arnold? Vanessa heard he was expected at Freeman's Farm.

"I know another overlooked soldier when I see one. You're good, Gabriel, damned good at what you do. It's a shame this Archangel has to tarnish your list of accomplishments."

Vanessa was secretly glad to hear someone applaud Gabriel for his own merits, not the Archangel's.

"You don't look too worried, Gabriel."

"Why should I be? The more a spy knows, the less he has to fear."

Benedict Arnold laughed wickedly. "Very good then. I'll leave you to your wife. Watch your back, soldier."

The General's footsteps traveled down the hall as Gabriel lifted the latch and came into the room. Moonlight streamed through the window, illuminated the place where she sat in the middle of the bed, wide-eyed and watchful.

One look at her face told Gabriel she'd overheard everything in the hall just then.

"What's going on around here, Gabriel?"

"Nothing. You should be asleep. It's past midnight," he replied dully, fixing his attention on the whereabouts of his bags. With a clatter of sword and carbine and spatter dashes, he crossed the room in three long strides and squatted over his belongings. What a handsome sight he was in full military dress, a chestful of medals gleaming from the breast of his bright blue waistcoat, its white collar riding high and stiff around his sunburnt neck. The golden braids of his epaulets turned silver in the moonlight, sparkled at her from his shadowy corner.

She wanted to talk to him. This was the first opportunity she'd had in almost three weeks.

"Gabriel . . . Gates knows about you and the Archangel. I heard him today."

This got his attention. He glanced briefly at her from over his shoulder, then went back to rooting through his bags for something. She heard him chuckle under his breath, something vaguely sinister in the sound. "What did you hear?"

Vanessa told him everything, sparing no details. "Something about the way Gates looked at Morgan just wasn't right. I swear Gates thinks Michael is alive. I'm sure of it, Gabriel."

She stopped, aware that her husband didn't seem at all distressed by what she was telling him. Knowing Gabriel, he already knew this but she told him anyway, just in case. He listened quietly, without comment, seemed more interested in changing his clothes. While she spoke, she watched him discard his rebel regalia and drape himself in the crimson colors of the enemy.

He was obviously planning a bit of espionage tonight.

"Gabriel, this affair is becoming more serious by the moment. It's frightening me!"

Those words somehow managed to touch him. He stopped fiddling with the buttons on his jerkin, came to the bedside and looked down into her fearful eyes. He looked so big and capable just then, swathed in shadow while dressed in the pure white linens of war. The billowing white sleeves of his blouse looked elegant on such a finely sculpted body, the way they draped around his wrists and partially hid his hands. A white linen vest fit him snugly from shoulder to thigh, made his muscled torso look unusually slim beneath it, as slender as the narrow hips around which his saber was so comfortably snuggled.

"You have nothing to fear," he said simply, his dark eyes glinting down at her in the pale light. He saw the way she was looking at him just then, seemed to stiffen against it even though his own vision was drawn across the creamy curves of her upturned face. "I know what Gates wants from me . . . which is precisely why he can't tangle with me . . . not if he wants the Archangel."

"But aren't you concerned that this information has gotten out?" she asked, inching closer to the edge of the bed and looking up at him for some sign that he might be disturbed.

She saw nothing, just a warmer response to how close she was. Eyes the color of night slid down the length of her neck and found the place where the bodice of her gown was left open. The way he looked at her ample cleavage just then made her shiver.

He still wanted her.

Her flickering hopes began to rise from where they'd been languishing in some dismal place inside her.

But he moved away then, clearly unwilling to be distracted by her.

He went back into the shadows, returned to dressing.

"I always knew this would happen sooner or later, Vanessa."

"But you've got to do something!" she insisted. "For God's sake, Gabriel, this affair is getting serious now. Just when you think the 'Angel's gone away, he pops up again and everyone points their finger at you! Aren't you concerned about this? Now they're dragging your dead brother into it! Where are they getting these outlandish ideas? They're going to force this issue one day, Gabriel. What then?"

He sighed from his corner, the sound as weary as the squeak of cane weaving in the chair he found to sit on. She watched him set his elbows on his knees and lean forward, looking directly at her when he spoke.

"I want you to calm down and leave this affair to me. Stay out of it. It's too dangerous for you."

He could see the worry on her face, how it made her eyes turn big and round and plaintive. She wouldn't rest until he told her something, anything that proved his command of this intrepid affair.

"This nonsense about Michael is coming from Jonathan."

"What? Damn him!"

"Indeed," he agreed. "He knows too much about my past . . . in France . . . what Michael and I used to do with our identities."

"What do you mean?" she asked just as she remembered a discussion with Martina months ago, when some hint was given about a kind of "game" the St. Claire twins used to play. She fell silent, sat back on her haunches, waited for him to speak about a subject that she knew was difficult for him.

He seemed to be grappling with whether or not to tell her, ran his hands through his hair and stared at the floor for a long, thoughtful moment. A far-away look was in his eyes when he looked at her again. "It was just a game . . . a children's game . . . something we should have stopped doing when we became men but by then it was so easy . . . we were so good at it. We'd switch identities, assume each other's personalities. We could become the other as easily as we could be ourselves. I know it sounds absurd . . . " He shook his head, his voice dropping into a whisper when he admitted, "But twins can be that close . . . close enough to think like each other."

His chilling admission made her shiver again. The room fell very still and quiet. This strange capability he described made Vanessa feel strangely intimidated by him. She knew he was good, known as the Great Imposter to some, but now she understood how he'd acquired those skills.

In that moment, when she regarded her husband, she suddenly realized the power he had, how dangerously easy it was for him to sneak into anyone's life and discover their secrets. But what made him dangerous was not that he knew everyone else's secrets. It was because no one knew his.

Her voice emerged as little more than a trembling whisper when she asked, "But what has this to do with the Archangel?"

"I was hoping you wouldn't ask me that." He looked at her then, the distance in his eyes suddenly gone. In fact, his regard of her was bolder than it had been in weeks. "It's a long and twisted story, but I believe Jonnie Meeks is unsure if Michael is really dead and, for that matter, if he might be the Archangel."

She just stared at him, completely appalled.

He rose, came to the bedside and flicked a hand through the air as if dismissing the whole theory. "Enough of this talk now. I want you to lie down and rest. We'll be here a while . . . at least until a battle is waged and some outcome determined. Until then, you're to avail yourself of this warm house and capable women to look after you."

"You act as though I'm ill."

"You've been looking tired lately—"

"I'm just out of sorts—"

"About what? If something's bothering you, you know you can come to me."

"Humph!" she scoffed, surprised he'd even suggest this after how aloof he'd been these last few weeks. "You've hardly been approachable lately, husband!"

"Touché," he awarded with a nod of agreement, started to turn away, then thought better of it. He looked back at her, caught her gaze and quietly delivered, "I will always care about your welfare, Vanessa."

She rolled her eyes, her lips forming a scornful pout as she flounced backward on the bed and started heaping the blanket over herself. "You have a strange way of showing it," she grumbled.

Gabriel was surprised at her reaction, that she could possibly be disgruntled by his lack of attention. But she certainly was and it made him grin in spite of himself. "I think you're spoiled," he remarked, turning away so she couldn't see his amusement.

"What? You have your nerve saying that!" she replied and his grin broadened. "You've treated me like a leper since our . . . er . . . argument about father."

"I have my reasons," he said, sliding his arms into a British-issue waistcoat.

"Such as?"

"I'm tired of fighting, Vanessa."

"Fighting who? Me?" *What a silly question,* she thought.

"No. I'm tired of fighting myself, if you must know."

"What are you talking about?"

He returned to the bed, this time sat on the edge and looked down into her miserable pout. "I can't live with the terms of this marriage, Vanessa. Not any more."

A feeling of doom settled over her. Sobered, she fell still, didn't resist the way he leaned over her, planted an arm on either side of her reclining form.

Once again those eyes roamed over her, feasting upon the delicate sculpture of her face, the silky texture of her skin, the way her breasts rose and fell beneath the snowy white fabric of her gown.

"This was supposed to be a marriage for honor . . . remember? Friendly . . . genteel—"

"But it has been," she whispered.

He moved closer now, as if he was unable to contain his hunger for her any longer. She could feel her breath deepening as he whispered in a deep, husky voice, "But I don't want that kind of marriage with you. I want more than that. I want you . . . your passion . . . your children."

She sighed at the feel of his lips brushing across her

own, ever so lightly caressing every corner of her mouth. "Gabriel . . . " Her fingers slid beneath the collar of his coat, her face instinctively turning up into his, inviting him to taste more.

He did so, momentarily smothering her lips beneath his own, his kiss turning deeper and deeper until they were tasting fully from each other.

But then he stopped, drew away, left them both burning and breathless.

"I can't live with my own terms," he admitted, "and for this I refuse to punish you. No. It's my fault. I knew what I wanted when I married you, but I tried to fool myself and it didn't work. Now I'm stuck with terms that leave me restless in the night."

He got off the bed, buttoned his waistcoat around his swollen body.

"Gabriel . . . I'm afraid—"

"I know," he said, disappeared into the corner where his bags were left and brought out a plain black tri-cornered hat. "And I can only hope time will change you." He slapped the hat on his head and went toward the door. With one hand on the latch, he turned around, looked at her very directly and said, "I want this marriage to be on *my* terms but, unfortunately, at the present time, you're unable to live with them. And I'm unable to live without them. So why discuss it, eh? It just frustrates us both."

He opened the door, stepped out into the hall and whispered back over his shoulder, "*Bonne nuit, madame . . .* "

It shut behind him with a quiet click of the latch.

The sun was still flirting with the horizon when Vanessa was awakened by a commotion of scurrying soldiers, racing horses, the faraway pop of exploding muskets. She sat up in bed, glanced through the lace curtains at the figures moving on the front porch. The dull mist of early morning turned their blue coats to gray while their white britches looked too bright. Tri-cornered hats were all facing in the same direction, toward the gunfire, and then the place where several riders burst out of the woods.

She watched them charge toward the house with such fury it seemed they would go straight through the front door.

Will MacLeod reared his horse just short of the stoop, thrust his fist into the air and bellowed, "They fired, Gabe! Johnny's on the field! Let's fight!"

She spotted her husband, the only man in the group who wasn't in uniform. He was leaning heavily on the porch rail, his sleeves rolled up, his hair tussled. She noticed his side of the bed was unruffled. He hadn't slept here last night, if he'd slept at all.

A series of reports blasted from the distance as if to confirm Will's information.

"Not so fast, Captain," Horatio Gates barked at Will who was already turning his mount toward the gunfire. "I'm saving my mounties to turn the tide of battle. Let the foot soldiers take the field."

Gabriel jerked off the porch rail, an expression of angry surprise on his face when he looked at Gates. "But sir . . . we've come all this way."

"No arguments, Colonel. I'm not about to waste my best men in field fighting. You'll get your turn to fight."

Gabriel and Will looked at each other, their faces falling in instant disappointment.

Just then, the boom of an exploding artillery piece shook the tiny room, made Vanessa jump in her skin.

"Madam! Madam!" Mrs. Freeman called from the hall. "The fighting's begun!"

She rushed off the bed and hastened to the door. Her hands were trembling, could barely manage the latch. Another cannon roared at the morning and she could feel the vibrations in the floor under her bare feet. With a cry of dismay, she forced the door open.

"Jesus, Mary, and Joseph." Mrs. Freeman crossed herself in spontaneous prayer. "Hurry and dress yourself. We'll go to the cellar where it's safe."

"Are they that close?"

"In the lower fields . . . a mile off . . . come, child!"

A few minutes later she gathered in the kitchen with the other ladies. Polly Blaire had tears in her eyes, kept looking toward the dining room where her husband was. Vanessa had to nearly drag her through the cellar door.

"My Lord, preserve us!" Polly cried as they descended into the darkness. "They're so close! What if they storm the headquarters and take us prisoner?"

"Polly!" Vanessa reprimanded. "Have you no faith in our fighting men? Eleven thousand men stand between us and them!"

"But it's so hard to have faith sometimes!" she wailed, set her lantern on a row of cider barrels and sank to her knees against the wall. "Let's pray, ladies."

They did so, five of them, kneeling on the moist earth floor.

The sound of guns grew louder as the battle intensified. They could feel the earth shaking under their knees. Overhead, the sound of men's boots pounded, muffled voices spoke in sharp quick syllables, the door of the house slammed and banged.

Hours passed. The women huddled together, their backs against the wall. Vanessa swore she could hear all their hearts pounding, echoing off the cellar walls, a steady drum of fear.

No one spoke. They just sat there and listened to the sounds of war exploding all around them, confined in this cold damp hole with no way of knowing what was really happening up there.

Vanessa saw that Polly could hardly stand the tension

much longer. The woman was trembling so hard the curls on her head were bobbing. Vanessa moved over, put her arm around her friend and allowed her to cling with all of her dainty might.

Finally, the tears came in one quick burst. "Oh, God, but I hate the British! I hate this war! Why are they doing this to us? Listen to them! They're killing us! Why can't they go away and leave us be?"

"Hush, Polly," Vanessa soothed her. "We've tried everything else. They've left us with no other choice."

"Not war, Nessy! Not war! Why must it come to this?"

Vanessa held her, slowly rocked her back and forth, let her weep until her misery emptied itself.

The fighting continued late into the afternoon. The dampness of the cellar left the women stiff, achy, yet they tried to stitch, read, pray, anything to take their minds off the constant roar of guns. By dinner hour, Vanessa was the only woman still awake, her companions dozing on blankets spread over the earth floor. She rose to stretch, moved toward the cellar stairs to listen to the activity upstairs.

The first voice she heard made her heart skip a beat. An elegant French drawl, resonant with authority. "Most of his army has stayed in camp all day. He's just testing our strength."

"Damn him!" Gates cursed hotly. "He's got his chance for battle! Why won't he take it?"

"Because he has to weaken us, General," Gabriel explained coolly. "Without Clinton, his six thousand men can't make a stand against our army. Johnny's known this since about noon today. He's just trying to kill off as many infantrymen as he can."

"How the devil do you know that, Colonel?"

"I heard him," Gabriel replied smoothly, as if the General should know better. "I was only a few feet away from him when he said it—"

"WHAT THE DEVIL WERE YOU DOING OUT OF HEADQUARTERS?" Gates boomed, his temper completely lost now.

"Doing my duty, sir," Gabriel returned in a much sharper tone of voice. "I'm not a headquarters Commander. That's Moylan's job. I'm a spy, not a map maker."

"Damn you, Gabriel! You're downright insubordinate!"

"And you, sir, will claim a victory because of it!"

Silence. Finally, Gates remarked in a conciliatory tone of voice, "You're sure Clinton is nowhere near?"

"Positive. I had a report from a listening post just an hour ago and there's no sign of an army advancing from Albany. I tell you, General, he won't make it here in time to save John Burgoyne. Press on. That's my advice. No matter what happens today, drag him out to the field again tomorrow and that will finish off his powder, his men, and his food. The man's doomed and he knows it."

Vanessa realized she was clinging to the stairwell as she listened to this information, tried to realize that the Continentals might actually defeat the great John Burgoyne. The mere thought made her shiver in excitement.

The guns suddenly stopped and the house fell queerly silent. The absence of noise gradually woke the women. Huddled together in a small group, they made their way upstairs.

The kitchen was a mud-stained mess, the floor and walls splattered by the passage of too many soldiers. They did their best to tidy the room, then prepared a small stand of refreshments for the parlor where the wives could enjoy a brief reunion with their husbands.

Gabriel's mood was foul when he caught a moment with her in a quiet corner of the room. "If it was safe to travel, I'd send you to Valley Forge tonight. The fighting is too close—"

"Never mind fretting over me," she scoffed, reached up

to smooth his rumpled collar as if it might ease his mood. She felt genuinely sorry for him, knowing how hard Gates had been on him today. "I think the General is being unfair with you," she confided. "He won't let you fight . . . won't let you spy—"

"And how do you know that?"

"I have ears, Gabriel. I hear what's going on around here."

"Yes, well, Gates won't punish my men because of me."

"What do you mean?"

"I mean he brought them here under the auspices of fighting, but what he really wants is me . . . because he thinks I can lead him to the Archangel." He leaned against the wall, glanced through the room once, then resettled his attention upon the sympathetic gaze of his wife. "I won't let that happen. I'll resign and leave before I'll allow my men to be denied the battle they worked so hard to arrange."

He meant it. She could tell by the crisp, cold look in his eyes. "What are you going to do about this? How much longer can you continue sacrificing your own honor for this faceless spy?"

His stern gaze turned on her for an instant, made her shiver with its dark intensity. "Sacrificing my honor for others seems to be a pervasive theme in my life, eh?" He meant her.

Offended, she shrugged him off and walked away.

It took her a long while to fall asleep that night. The room felt cold, her bed empty, Gabriel gone off on some covert activity that was too dangerous for her to ponder.

She rolled over, closed her eyes, the guns of war still humming in her ears. The smell of damp cellar air seemed clogged in her nostrils.

By God! War was real today. It was death, destruction, fear. She was close enough to touch it. How could these young men run into those howling guns, actually hunger for the chance the way her husband did. What courage they had! And how much more awesome was this cause of liberty now that she'd watched men fight for it.

And die for it.

The rains began sometime during the night and dampened everyone's hopes for a quick conclusion to the months-long pursuit of John Burgoyne. During the days of foul weather, the British kept themselves busy building the Great Redoubt and hoping for the appearance of General Clinton. While the enemy waited and hoped, the Continentals took a much needed rest. All but Moylan's Horse.

Many of them, including St. Claire, spent days in Burgoyne's camp, returning to headquarters only long enough to give reports on the enemy's waning food supply. As September ran into October, Burgoyne's commissary conditions became critical. His supply of salt pork and flour, the mainstay of his army's diet, was almost gone. None knew where Clinton was or why he had yet to show himself anywhere in the neighboring countryside. Gabriel's listening posts patrolled the road from Albany twenty-four hours a day without any sign that Clinton was on the march.

Burgoyne was soon left with little choice but to wage the battle before his men were too weak to fight.

It came sooner than expected, in the form of snapping sniper fire from the distance while the ladies were feasting on a luncheon of ox heart and cabbage. General Gates threw down his fork just as Gabriel rushed into the room with a report.

The British were trying to advance from their redoubts, being held back by Daniel Morgan's riflemen. Thus far, the enemy had only managed to advance a few feet from their trenches.

A genteel lunch gave way to instant bedlam. Officers from every company and division streamed into the headquarters to await their battle orders. Gabriel, who knew every enemy position, plotted strategy with Gates over a detailed intelligence map. Meanwhile, Morgan's guns continued to pop in the distance.

Three companies of foot soldiers were sent to battle and told where to advance. While the women hurriedly cleared the table to give the men more room to work, Vanessa watched Gates's knobby finger point into the center of the battlefield.

"It must be a frontal attack, Gabriel, with enough firepower and mobility to cut down his forward flank. I need my cavalry now, Gabriel, and you're going to lead them." Vanessa's heart fluttered in her breast even though she could see her husband's eyes instantly brighten. His thirst for battle was about to be satiated.

Gates chuckled upon sight of his enthusiasm. "It was worth the wait, eh? Here's your chance. I'll give you three companies of mounted soldiers."

Vanessa cringed, struggling to hide her fear when she found Polly in the kitchen and quietly gave her the news. Not only would there be a battle today, but their husbands had just been chosen to lead the way.

Polly fell to her knees at once, begged the Lord to spare her husband, whose excited voice could be heard plotting strategy with his Colonel in the adjacent room. Vanessa crossed herself and muttered her own prayers while Gabriel prepared to confront the enemy he'd been chasing for so many months.

Within minutes, three units of cavalrymen assembled on the front lawn. They were heavily armed, horses restless, riders tense and alert to their Commander's every move as Gabriel strolled out the front door and hopped into the saddle of his own mount.

Gates came onto the porch, shielded his eyes against

the sun and inspected the troops. Gabriel waited for his nod of approval on a steed that pranced and fidgeted under him. It was a warhorse and it smelled battle. Like its rider, it was keen on the scent of war.

Gates came alongside her husband, grabbed the reins of his nervous mount and held it still. "Bring him down, Gabriel . . . cut him to pieces." Gabriel's dark eyes gleamed with fervor. "I tell you, if you force John Burgoyne from the field today I'll make you a Major General before the sun goes down."

Gabriel's arm snapped upright into a proud salute, a gesture that was immediately returned by Gates. No matter what animosity lurked between them, on one point they certainly agreed.

Liberty.

Vanessa stood in the doorway and watched her husband charge down field until he came to the forefront of his men. From his lips burst a battle cry that brought a thundering echo from those who followed, their roar peeling through the air as Benny Cooke's voice boomed, *"Move out!"*

Their gallop was fast and furious, so fearless as they charged toward the woods and the gunfire. The mere sight brought tears of emotion to her eyes and she knew she would never forget this moment for as long as she lived. Human courage never looked so glorious as it did now, with those three hundred horsemen pounding across a farmer's field, their coattails flapping and their flags billowing and their throats filling the air with battle cries. If Burgoyne knew the force coming at him at this moment he would surely flee the field because these men weren't just soldiers fighting for ground. No, they were fighting for their lives, their beliefs, their honor as human beings.

They deserved to win. To live. To come home victorious.

She watched Gabriel's black stallion leap into the woods. He disappeared from sight.

She rushed forward, clung to the porch rail and squinted for one last sight of him. But he was gone, swallowed by the woods and whatever destiny this day would bring him.

It came over her then, in a swift and powerful surge of yearning. What if he were to be cut down today, left to lie in a field full of dead? She might never look into those mysterious eyes again, hear that elegant speech of his, see the way the sun painted streaks of auburn through his glossy hair. In this single sobering moment, Vanessa realized something that seemed to startle her every sense.

She wanted him. God, how she wanted him in that moment, fiercely, completely, even if just for one more moment of life where she might touch him, see him, feel him! Never in her life had she wanted anything more than she wanted him at this moment.

And she knew why in a startling instant of perfect clarity.

She couldn't live without him.

It was the longest day of her life. She prayed constantly, fervently, never stopping until the moment she heard the commotion upstairs, the noisy shouts and whooping bellows and pounding boots. They all rushed to the cellar stairs and listened to a young man's shout rend the air, *"Burgoyne has fled the field. He's fled the field!"*

"Oh my God!" Polly cried, rushed halfway up the stairs, her face alit with utter disbelief. "He's fled? John Burgoyne?"

As if in answer, the gunfire began to wane in the very next moment, a new sound reverberating through the shaken house. Cheers of victory, chants of uninhibited joy, the thumping roar of hundreds of boots rushing through the house.

"I can't believe it!" Vanessa cried, hugging Polly in sheer delight as they added their own excited whoops to the noise from upstairs until a new sound brought them instantly alert.

Horses. Hundreds of hooves thundering from very close by. It was the cavalry. They were returning from battle. She and Polly flew through the cellar door, pushed their way through the crowd of exuberant soldiers and rushed onto the porch.

It was the cavalry alright, powder burned and dirt smudged but still riding proud on their nervous mounts. They were shouting at one another, already sharing tales of battle, comparing notes, slapping one another on the back. They looked so pleased with themselves, as if they couldn't believe what enormous champions they actually were.

But there was no sign of Moylan's Horse. She and Polly continued to cling to one another until that first sacred moment when the company flag appeared through the trees that separated the farm from the battle.

"There they are!" Vanessa cried and excitedly pointed at them. While Polly strained her eyes to see, Horatio Gates came up behind Vanessa.

The joy of victory was heavy in his whisper when he said, "How does it feel to be the wife of a General, eh?"

She whirled around, took one look at the beaming pride in his eyes and completely forgot protocol just long enough to give the General a delighted hug. He was surprised, his tired face splitting with a very pleased grin for just an instant before she was spun away to greet her dear friends of Moylan's Horse.

Benny let out a whoop of delight when he saw her, picked her up and spun her around until the entire field saw her petticoat.

"Benny!"

"Phewee! We whipped them good this time! Hell, they're all yellow-bellies when you see them up close. They started running the minute they saw us! We didn't even get a shot off and a whole unit turned around and ran!"

"Where is he? Gabriel—"

"He's here somewhere," Benny put her down and looked around.

"You mean you don't know where Gabriel is," Lauren teased the sentry who looked suddenly guilty.

"Well now . . . last I seen Gabe he was dragging some limey officer into the woods. I didn't follow. Guess I didn't want to see what he was going to do to him."

Vanessa grimaced. "Oh, dear . . . "

Robert and Polly spun past her, twirling in a victory dance. "We've won the day!" Robert bawled and Polly giggled with joy.

"You seen Gabe?" Benny asked Robert.

"You mean you don't know where he is?" the Lieutenant Colonel asked and continued dancing with his wife.

"Aw hell." Now Benny felt really bad.

"Since when do you lose track of Gabriel?" Francis asked, already disarming himself in preparation to become a doctor again. He would tend the wounded for the next three days, Vanessa knew, hardly sleeping until the last man was bandaged.

Benny looked faint with guilt. "I can't believe he got away from me," he muttered dismally, then added with a touch of anger, "You know it ain't easy following the likes of St. Claire! You try guarding his back . . . if you can *find* it! Why, I know fish who ain't as slippery as he is and I—" The Sergeant stopped in mid-sentence, his whole face blooming in relief as he stared at something directly behind Vanessa. "Where the hell you been?"

"Looking for my wife," came a smooth drawl from just behind her.

She spun around, looked up into a face that never appeared so spectacular as it did at that moment. "Gabriel—" she breathed, so consumed with joy to see him she couldn't think of a word to say.

And into her radiant welcome he flashed the broadest grin she'd ever seen on that ruddy face. Without a doubt, she knew she was witnessing one of the happiest moments of his life.

"I was wondering if I might have the pleasure of this dance," he asked softly, still grinning.

She let out a windy little giggle. "Here?"

"Why not? We've been known to dance in unheard of places," he replied, the double meaning in his words bringing back a memory of a long-ago dance on the front lawn of a house full of Tories.

While she was captured in the memory, his arm slid around her waist, a gloved hand ensnaring her own. He spun her around, fell into the same gliding step as Polly and Robert. Soldiers began to clap a beat and join the dance, a fife and drum added to the tempo. Music sprang into the air while General Gates beamed at their spontaneous celebration.

"Let the enemy hear our rejoicing! Bring out the drums. Sound the horns! This day belongs to liberty!"

As if in final tribute to the glory of the moment, the child within her stirred awake, fluttered ever so lightly. She sighed, blissfully aware of it, of how wonderfully redeemed she felt to have them all alive.

It took a few moments for her to realize the music was dying, fading away on the wind. Gabriel stopped moving, his attention fixed on something in the distance.

Everyone was staring at a small group of redcoats that came trotting out of the woods. They were carrying a banner, the brilliant colors of John Burgoyne. But it was the other flag that drew their attention.

A white sheet.

Silence. It fell over the field full of soldiers until they were all standing there as if suspended in some kind of mystical dimension.

The soldiers continued to ride toward the house, slow

and somber as they moved through the opening the crowd made for them.

They stopped at the porch where the flag bearer extended a long rolled parchment toward Horatio Gates.

The General took it, spread it open and read for a moment.

"Yes," Gates finally said to the flag bearer. "I will await his terms."

He turned toward the field then, seemed to momentarily savor the quiet of this moment.

And then he spoke, very calmly, but very deliberately, enunciating every syllable.

"John Burgoyne has offered terms for surrender."

No one moved. They just stood there staring at the hazy figure of the General who stood within the dusky shadows of the porch. It was as if they were unable to comprehend what he had just said.

This was too gigantic, a victory too enormous to be fully comprehended while standing out here in this simple farmer's field.

One of England's greatest Generals had just been defeated by a rag-tag army of rebels. A proud army of six thousand soldiers along with eight Generals and countless other officers would surrender their arms to American freedom.

Stunned, they watched the redcoats ride back into the woods. Silence followed them, a gesture of respect for this mighty chunk of liberty Burgoyne had just handed to a new nation called America.

A movement from beside her made Vanessa look up.

It was Benny.

He put his face in his big hands and wept.

22

Moylan's Horse arrived at Valley Forge on a cold November morning. Ice and sleet rained out of the gray winter sky, but it wasn't enough to keep the residents indoors once the company was spotted on the main road. They spilled out of their homes, lined the road to watch the proud passage of one of Washington's most decorated units. With their flags flapping proudly in the wet winds, Moylan's Horse paraded past in a whirl of triumph and glory, inspiring tears from the ladies and making many a gentleman toss his hat triumphantly into the winter sky.

Vanessa watched the spectacle from the window of her coach, the good cheer making her smile despite her nervousness. She was about to meet her husband's family and she would do so alone, without him. Gabriel had other business to attend to and promised to join her as soon as possible. He and Francis departed Freeman's Farm the same morning she did. As contrary as it was, Vanessa missed him. She didn't like being apart from him. Gabriel had become her security, her safety, her home.

The fanfare followed them to the St. Claire farm and did much to distract her from the apprehension she felt inside. Alain and Chloe St. Claire were as gracious as their son and coddled her from the instant of her arrival. Never did she meet two more warm-hearted and welcoming people, so open and friendly and excited about the impending birth of their first grandchild. Their easy natures slowly overrode her nervousness and she began to relax in spite of herself.

Alain St. Claire was still a handsome man at fifty, only a hint of gray in his thick shock of dark brown hair. Gabriel favored him in both his tall and powerful physique and the rugged strength of his features. But it was his mother who lent him his disposition. Chloe was an instinctively elegant woman, impeccably groomed, her petite figure fashionably attired. She was still a very beautiful woman with very crisp and aristocratic features and the most magnificent dark red hair Vanessa had ever seen. Always smiling, always cheerful, she was like her son in the way she never let anyone see the place where a beloved had been torn away. While Gabriel favored his father in physical appearance, his spirit betokened the influence of his mother.

Vanessa's first few days on the farm were too eventful for worry. News of Burgoyne's surrender had already reached this corner of the colonies and people came from all around the area to see the soldiers. Many hundreds more were building a camp five miles away in preparation for a long cold winter and citizens for miles around began to stockpile food, clothing, and firewood for the soldiers. The war had come to Valley Forge, not in the form of fighting, but bringing thousands of soldiers needing shelter for the coming winter. It would be a cold one, the local farmers predicted, and the winds of November were already strong and harsh.

Moylan's Horse was quartered in one of a pair of huge cattle barns at the far end of the St. Claire property. Unlike the soldiers in Washington's own camp, Gabriel's company would be on duty throughout the winter, scouting the area and maintaining its security against any possible incursion from General Howe in Philadelphia, only twenty miles away. Reconnaissance required a certain amount of autonomy, which was facilitated by the close proximity of the St. Claire farm, and Washington's permission to winter there came quickly.

But like the rest of Moylan's Horse, they were all a bit lost without their Commander. Weeks went by without word from Gabriel, no sign of his arrival as Thanksgiving waned into the holidays. Although Vanessa was comfortable and happy at the farm, not a day went by without a thought of him. She found herself warmed by any tale of his childhood, proud when a compliment toward his valor was granted to her in his stead. How cherished he was by all! And no man was more deserving than this champion who devoted his life to the liberation of the oppressed. He was valiant but not for his own glory. No, Gabriel was a truly selfless man, always giving yet taking so little for himself.

Sometimes, when he was spoken about so lovingly, a warm feeling would come over her heart, like the wrap of a tender hand. It was the same feeling she had whenever she thought of her mother or Danny.

Love.

Real love. The genuine kind that came from deep inner places where the spirit of a person lived. It was not of the body, nor of the mind. It was deeper than that.

She loved him. And as the days wore on without him, she became more and more aware of how her heart had finally begun to turn in his direction.

The weather became bitterly cold, the land flooded with waist-deep snow by Christmas morning and the heavy skies of dawn promised still more. A dull gray light greeted the family's rising, penetrated the stone farmhouse with a damp cold that made stoking hearths the first order of the day.

Gabriel had still not arrived and she had secretly hoped he could share this first Christmas with her. Despite the festivities of Christmas Eve, she spent most of her time watching, waiting, hoping.

Loneliness made her footsteps sound weary on the wooden steps as she made her way downstairs. The family was awake, their voices seeping out from behind the parlor doors. She stood outside for a moment to collect herself, forcing some semblance of Christmas cheer onto her face just before she pushed open the parlor doors and beheld a sight that momentarily startled her.

The room glowed with the light of a farm-grown Christmas tree that was decorated with what appeared to be a hundred tiny candles. It was a dazzling sight, so festive and pretty, obviously erected after she had retired the night before. If Chloe and Alain meant to cheer her, they were very successful. As she walked into the room, into the warm arms of Christmas, she couldn't help but smile.

How different this Christmas felt as she shared the embraces of her new family, their greetings so merry and open-hearted. During her childhood in Millbridge, there was always an element of restraint in the air, something ominous waiting just outside the merriness of the holiday. In a single moment, her father could spoil everything.

But he was gone, dead and buried.

There was nothing to fear now as she helped Chloe pour hot chocolate for all before they gathered around the tree and the assortment of gifts arranged beneath its decorated branches. There was something for all in the gay pile. Lauren received a handsome new robe with matching slippers. Vanessa was given a sterling vanity ensemble, a mirror and comb and a genuine boar's hair brush.

Her initials were etched into the back of the silver mirror in an elegant, swirling script. She had never seen a set so lovely, even after all her shopping days in Philadelphia and she was grateful for their kindness. When she thanked them, her embrace was particularly warm, conveying the deeper gratitude she felt to finally realize a normal family life.

But she said nothing, as usual, always avoiding any mention of her true past and instead rose to fetch their gifts.

"Where are you going, *chérie*?" Alain called just before she reached the door.

"Why . . . to get your gifts—"

"Wait a moment . . . there's no hurry—"

"Oh, but I can't wait to give them!" she said, pulled open the door and looked upon a figure in the shadowy foyer that made her come to a sudden halt. "Francis?"

"Merry Christmas," came his reply in a weak, tired voice.

Her heart instantly soared. Had Gabriel arrived after all? The Surgeon was favored with a particularly merry embrace, her eyes sparkling with joy as she gazed up at his sleepy face.

"When did you arrive?"

"Very late. You were long asleep before I got here."

"And Gabriel?"

"With Washington at the moment, much to his chagrin."

Gabriel was in Valley Forge! She wanted to shout for joy, and barely contained herself as she took Francis' arm and urged him toward the parlor. "Come . . . have some chocolate and see the tree."

This made Francis smile down at her in a very secretive way. "Oh, but I'm on important business this morning. Gabriel's orders, you see. I brought you his gift."

"Mine?"

He nodded, his expression turning suddenly solemn as

he regarded her more seriously. "He's been working on this gift for a long time and I tell you, we barely managed to get it done in time for Christmas. But first, tell me how you fare."

"Me? I'm fine!"

Francis took the cup of chocolate Chloe offered and smiled after her in thanks. She returned to the parlor and Vanessa noticed that everyone was watching. They looked away when they saw her notice.

Suspicion seeped into her warm mood.

They knew something. All of them.

"Francis? What's this about?"

He put an arm around her shoulder and turned her away from the open parlor door. His face conveyed a doctor-like calm as he slowly walked her toward the library doors. "You look well-rested and fit . . . not at all like a woman nearly five months along . . . "

Francis reached for the long brass lever on the library door, lifted it, pushed it open just a crack. "If you need me for anything, I'll be right outside the door."

It struck her then, as he was speaking, a peculiar scent that was strangely familiar. She stopped, looked around, clutched her shawl closer.

"What is it, Vanessa?"

"That smell . . . do you smell that? It's . . . familiar. Oh! Forgive me. Your secretiveness is making my mind run on—"

"The smell is coming from in here," Francis said, pushed open the door and let it swing wide. "Merry Christmas, Vanessa," Francis said softly, his eyes filling with emotion when he motioned her into the room.

She turned on the threshold and looked inside.

There was a woman standing next to the fireplace, tall and stately, blue-black hair showing only the slightest hint of gray. A pair of round violet eyes stared directly into her own perfectly matched pair. Elegant fingers were clasped together at her waist, ever so slowly wringing in anxiety, the way she always did when faced with something that frightened her.

Mother.

Vanessa felt her knees buckle. She slumped but Francis was there, holding her up, whispering words of encouragement that she could barely make herself hear.

Vivien Davis rushed toward her in alarm, her beautiful face momentarily distorted with concern, fear, confusion.

"Dear God . . . give me strength . . . " Vanessa whispered to Francis, to God, to whoever it was that doled out such benevolences. She closed her eyes, tried to suck in enough air, then quickly looked up again to be sure her mother was really standing right in front of her.

Yes. It was her mother.

But she couldn't believe it, just stood there letting the shock steal her voice, her wits, everything except a tiny place inside where a lost child longed for its mother's arms. It was a wonderful yet terrifying feeling, the same kind she used to have when struggling out of the painful grips of her father, and running into the sanctuary of her mother's saintly arms.

Every part of her was back there again, in her childhood, broken and beaten and discouraged, reaching out for the only refuge she had ever known.

"Mother . . . "

The mere utterance of that word brought tears of pain and joy to Vivien's eyes. It wrenched her heart just to look at her daughter again, after all these years of nothing but lonely memories. It was a miracle, this moment, brought about by the hand of a man who was determined to create something good from the wreckage of their lives.

"Nessy? My little girl . . . "

They stepped closer, reached for each other. Their fingers touched, felt one another, then groped together like the clutch of two stricken women caught in a terrible raging storm. Years of life passed between them, horrible memories of pain and death tempered with brief glimpses of the love and solace they could always find in each other . . . the three of them . . . just her and mother and Danny.

Vivien pulled her daughter close, freed her hands so they could slide over her beautiful young face in a moment of sheer rapture.

"Oh how beautiful you've grown . . . just like I hoped . . . and prayed . . . but never thought I'd see . . . "

Ever so slowly they melted together, held onto each other with all their combined might, their embrace racked by the same sobs of relief, joy, remembered pain.

They were not aware of the family standing in the doorway behind them, so still and quiet. Overwhelmed with emotion, Chloe pressed her face against Alain's chest so his blouse would muffle the sound of her tears. Francis inched out of the room and quietly shut the door behind him.

Vanessa couldn't remember going to the divan, nor did she have any idea of how long they sat curled together, holding each other and weeping until their tears were drained away.

Vivien began to tell the tale of how she had been freed from St. Peter's Home in Erie. It took months to settle the legal details of freeing her, but Gabriel was dauntless in his pursuit of her liberation. He lent the services of his own physician, Francis Stone, who conducted the examination that declared her mentally fit. In conjunction with the Millbridge physician who was aware of her husband's long addiction to spirits, Fred Davis was declared unfit to have committed her. But the final stroke of luck came with the event of his death. From that moment on, Gabriel bombarded the local magistrate with enough evidence to have her case heard again.

"Those were the longest weeks of my life . . . waiting to hear if the magistrate would allow your husband to come to Erie to make his arguments," Vivien reflected. Just remembering the anxiety she'd felt while confined in the jail-like hospital made her suddenly clasp her daughter tight against her breast. She didn't want Vanessa to see the terrifying effects of those years spent with the insane, cut off from the world, no hope of ever being free again.

"I was never so glad when word arrived that Gabriel would present his arguments on December the seventh. Oh! You can't imagine how happy I was . . . almost as happy as the day the wardens summoned me to say my daughter's husband was waiting to speak to me in the anteroom. It was a miracle! Someone found me . . . finally . . . after all those years!"

"But Father told me you were dead! That's why no one found you! No one had any reason to look!"

"Until you married a truly brilliant young man."

Vanessa looked down at his signet ring, felt a movement of something quite magnificent in her heart just then, like the great heaving motion a spirit felt when it was forever changed. "I wish he'd told me," was all she could say aloud, unable to reckon with how she was feeling about her husband at that moment.

"He kept quiet for good reason," her mother said in that gentle, melodious voice of hers. "What if the end result was disappointing? He did this for your own good and I agreed with him. However, your father was an enormous help in the end."

"Help?" The mere mention of his name spoiled Vanessa's mood. She looked up sharply. "What do you mean?"

"By dying he lost control over my welfare and it passed into your hands . . . according to your husband." Vivien saw a chilling hatred flash through Vanessa's eyes just then. "But we needn't think of him anymore," she hurried on. "He's gone . . . and may God rest his soul—"

"May God do nothing of the kind!" Vanessa hotly declared. "He deserves to burn in hell for what he did to you . . . to me . . . and Danny."

Vivien instantly tried to soothe her. "Don't think of it now . . . it's all over . . . there's no point—"

"It's not all over!" Vanessa cried, suddenly jerked off the divan and fell into a furious pace before the fire well. Back and forth she stalked as if driven by the sheer power of her mounting rage. "Sometimes I think it will *never* be all over for me."

Vivien stared at her daughter in a kind of horrified fascination. "What did he do to you? Tell me, Ness—"

The words blurted out of her mouth, spilled loose as if driven out of some dark corner in her soul. "First, he lied to me about you . . . told me you were dead. Other than beating Danny to death and trying to kill me, this was his worst crime. Only a demon could do such a thing, could so cruelly manipulate his own child. You don't know what a nightmare it was to live with him . . . all alone . . . like some terrible dream that wouldn't stop. It got so bad at times I didn't even feel human anymore. No. I don't know who or what I was except that I lived on hate . . . hate and the terror of waiting for him to pounce on me again. And he always did! Always found excuses!" Her eyes became wide and animated, as if infused with a kind of macabre thrill as she spewed these deepest, darkest secrets of her broken heart.

"Like kneeling at Danny's grave. On some days, it was a crime, on others he didn't care. That's how he made me live . . . as if there was an invisible gun to my head every moment . . . never letting me know if his finger was on the trigger or not.

"And all the while he drank more and more . . . the beatings got worse and worse. Sometimes I couldn't leave the house for weeks on end. I had no where to go. No one wanted to talk to me. They didn't want to get involved—"

Vivien burst into tears but Vanessa couldn't stop herself. She was crying, too, but she didn't care. It was as if some hidden plug inside her spirit had suddenly popped free, disgorged her blackest and most despicable memories.

"Somehow I managed to meet him . . . Gabriel . . . and he found all this out and the day I married him was the same day Father finally tried to kill me . . . over in the Morris' field. He put my face in the mud and held it there until I stopped breathing. The next thing I knew Gabriel was there . . . holding my head up . . . forcing the dirt out so I could breathe again. If it wasn't for him I'd be dead right now! You call my husband brilliant but to me, he's life itself . . . and I have done nothing but punish him for my father's cruelty. Yes! Over and over I punish my beloved Gabriel and I hate myself more every time I do it—"

She stopped then, a great heaving sob spilling out of her throat with enough force to make her slump to the floor, bury her face in her hands and weep in the most abject misery she had ever felt in her life.

She didn't know how long it was that she sat huddled on the floor, weeping from the guilt and the agony of so many terrible mistakes. It was only after her strength waned and her sobs diminished that she managed to finally see some clarity.

She'd never told all this to anyone before, not even herself. Putting it into words brought a strange cognizance to her life, the way it was then and how it would be now. As the rage slowly drained away, so did the madness, and when she finally looked up again, the world was perfectly clear.

It was really over. The little girl who once longed for a father's love now longed for someone else's, the only man who had ever wanted her, other than as someone to hurt.

Vivien slid off the divan, took her daughter in her arms

and just held her for a long, long time, the way she could have done after all those beatings if only she'd been there.

"I'm sorry, Mother . . . "

"Hush . . . it's alright . . . I'm here now . . . we'll help each other just like we used to . . . "

"I think I love him, Mother . . . "

"Let yourself, Ness . . . "

"I will, Mother! I swear it! I won't let Father stop me anymore!"

"Ah! Now you sound like my girl again!"

Vanessa looked up, watched her mother smile so softly, so beautifully, behind the quiet rain of her tears. It was the kind of serene joy one felt who looked upon their own redemption and realized that at long last, they were finally free.

Huddled beneath a pelt of fur, Gabriel rode into Washington's camp with his head bent against the wind, his mount plodding mournfully through the deep snow. Beneath the frozen brim of his hat he took a look around, at the soldiers' huts that were grouped into small clearings near any stand of timber that might block the howling winter winds. Men moved passed him, bent against the furious weather, ragged clothes flapping, feet covered in batting as they plodded through waist-deep drifts.

It was pathetic out here.

Even though each hut had a stone chimney, he could see that the dim interiors were hazy with smoke, the refuse of burning wood seeping through any crack in the walls of the wooden buildings. The fire wells were hastily built and poor, with insufficient drafts to ventilate the soldiers' quarters. Everywhere he could hear the harsh, hacking coughs of sick men.

The sight both shocked and disturbed him. He momentarily forgot his domestic disappointments, a profound sense of worry overcoming him as he headed toward the distant farmhouse where Washington housed his aides. For the first time since the surrender of John Burgoyne, he didn't feel so victorious anymore.

The Commander in Chief met him in the den of the farmhouse. Washington was dressed casually, in warm wool britches and knitted tunic, deep lines of worry momentarily melting from his brow when he chose to clasp Gabriel's hand instead of returning his salute.

"You served me well in New York, Gabriel. My thanks to you."

"The honor is mine, sir."

"Come. Sit."

He was motioned into a chair that faced the General's cluttered desk. There were no aides present and Gabriel was instantly suspicious. This kind of absolute privacy never occurred in military life.

Washington looked tired, his small eyes unusually dull and lusterless, seeming to sink alongside his long thin shaft of a nose. His lips were tightly set, almost stern when he looked at Gabriel.

"The news of Burgoyne's surrender was the only happy moment we've had in this valley since the snow began. But the victory in New York gives my heart cause to rise. The surrender of John Burgoyne will send a shock wave through Europe, you can be sure. I was never so delighted to confirm a rumor."

Gabriel looked up in surprise. "Rumor? I would have thought Gates's courier was on his way to you that very night."

"No, Gabriel. Gates has yet to write me a line of correspondence about the matter. I heard it elsewhere."

Gabriel was shocked at such blatant insubordination. He knew Gates was a political man but this was downright hostile behavior. "No man who serves himself belongs in a rebellion."

"Well said, Major General, and my sentiments exactly. But don't worry about Gates. I'll deal with him in time. For the moment, I have more pressing concerns." With only his head, Washington nodded toward the window and the camp beyond. When he looked back again, the General's suffering for his beleaguered army was so apparent it was almost palpable. Gabriel looked down at the snow-covered hat on his lap and felt as miserable as that sorry piece of felt looked just then.

"But at present, Gates is so enormously popular it would make me even less popular to reprimand him," Washington went on as if the change of subject comforted him. "So I'll hold my tongue and wait for a better time."

Gabriel nodded, pleased with the wisdom in the remark. "I've no particular affection for Gates myself."

This made the General's eyebrow rise. He leaned forward, rested an elbow on the desk and looked at Gabriel with a peculiar intensity in his eyes. "You have always been loyal to me, Gabriel. When I summoned you here, I did so with the hope this conversation would not destroy your faith."

"Sir?"

"Nothing could help me more right now than to make known the Archangel. The public is completely infatuated with this hero. Think of the support they'd lend me if I could prove how faithful he's been to me all these months. But how can I prove it if I don't know him?"

Gabriel sat back, steeled himself for a conversation that he knew was coming the moment he read Washington's summons. "Why is everyone so convinced I know him? I can assure you I have never met the man, but if I do, I'm likely to kill him."

Washington issued a short sniff, about all the laughter he could summon at such a moment. "You do yourself an injustice to think I promote you because of him." The

General rose, paced to the fire well and bent over the flames, slowly warming his hands. "From the very beginning, I knew you were an exceptional man. The Archangel only enhanced your worth to me."

This was well-spoken and Gabriel was almost inclined to believe him.

Washington stood upright, his tall frame partially blotting out the light. He looked at Gabriel from across the room. "I need to know who he is."

"Sir, I—"

"I need the people to rally around me, Gabriel," Washington insisted with a firm note of authority in his voice. Gabriel could see the General was serious about this. "And they'll do it if they know the Archangel's strength is mine."

"How can you be so convinced I know him?"

"Come now, Gabriel, no man gets as close to him as you do. For instance, on the night of the Swanson mission, I received two separate notes, in different handwritings, both bearing the same message."

"What does that prove? I was in the middle of a country green when that information was revealed. Although the immediate area was secured by my men, the Archangel could have been anywhere in the vicinity and I wouldn't have known—"

"And your scouts . . . probably the best in this army . . . couldn't find him?"

"The man is good."

"So are you."

The room fell silent. Washington was watching him quite intently as he said, "I had a long and very informative meeting with your Philadelphia ally, Jonathan Meeks. Our discussion concerned your dead brother Michael."

Gabriel could not contain a burst of black humor. "So you're resurrecting the dead too, eh? Jonnie has quite a following for his theory."

"What do you mean?" Washington asked, obviously surprised that Gabriel knew about this.

"My wife overheard Gates talking on the day we arrived at Freeman's Farm. It seems he's also wondering if my brother is still alive."

Washington didn't know how to respond. It disturbed him that Gates had the same theoretical information. How had he come by it?

"I respect your work, Major General, and your clear devotion to the Cause, which is why I will not press this matter on Christmas Day. But I urge you to rethink your position tonight and come back here tomorrow prepared to tell me everything you know about the Archangel." The General crossed the room, stood over him where Gabriel could see the troubled expression on his face. "My career is sliding and if I lose the support of our people, it could jeopardize our alliance with France. Please think this over, Gabriel. Whatever reasons you have for withholding information, balance them against what I've just told you. Return to me tomorrow at the same time. By then, hopefully, you'll see the merits in telling me what you know."

"And if I don't?"

"Then you will not leave here tomorrow."

"Talk or be confined. Are those my options, General?"

"I'm sorry, Gabriel . . . "

Gabriel said nothing.

"You are dismissed, Major General."

Gabriel left the room, shut the door quietly behind him and started down the hall. He stared at the floor, deep in thought, studying every twisted angle of the nefarious position he was in.

There was only one way to defend himself and he grew resigned to do it, no matter what the personal cost would be.

"Is it the infamous Commander of Moylan's Horse?" came a familiar voice from inside the lobby. Gabriel looked up into the wry smile of Stephen Moylan. "You look worried, Major General. What did Washington have to say?"

"Why don't you ask him yourself?"

"There's no need. We all know the trap you're in . . . caught in the middle of a race between Washington and Gates to find the Archangel and claim his exclusive loyalty."

"And who's side are you on, Colonel?"

"Neither."

"Always were in it for yourself."

Moylan's honor was pricked. Anger snapped through his eyes as he pushed Gabriel back against the door and snarled, "You have a problem, St. Claire. No one wants to tangle with you because you're too good. That kind of power never serves a man for long. Sooner or later, they'll make you talk about the Archangel or they'll ruin you. So you see, I don't have anything to worry about. You stole my command of Moylan's Horse but you won't steal my future post in Washington's Secret Service. You'll be finished by then! I've already promised Tallmadge to prove myself a better man, and it seems the circumstances will bear me out, eh?"

Gabriel threw back his head and laughed in delight. "Fool! What if I decide to tell something you don't know about, eh? Then what will you prove to Tallmadge? That you're an ass?"

Before Moylan could reply, Gabriel launched a forearm against his ribs that sent the Colonel sprawling to the polished lobby floor. The clatter brought several aides running but by the time they reached the lobby, the only trace of the master spy was a fine dusting of snow on the tiles, let in during his swift exit.

23

Vanessa had no idea what time it was when something cold nipped at her hand and brought her awake. The blanket was turned back, her shoulders feeling chilled. She glanced at the fire well and noticed the flames were still leaping hungrily at a large piece of kindling.

Strange, but she didn't remember putting such a giant log on the fire.

She sighed sleepily, closed her eyes and immediately saw a vision of her mother's face. Vivien was right now sleeping in the very next room. The mere thought brought a trickle of joy into her drowsy spirit, like the sprinkle of a warm rain. What a marvelous sensation, to feel so good from so deep inside. It was as if something dark and heavy had been removed from her spirit, and she was finally free for the first time in her life.

The fear was gone and how wonderful it felt to be without it. Yes, she felt changed, profoundly transformed, marvelously alive. There was nothing to be afraid of anymore. Fred was dead, her mother was back. They could start all over.

She smiled in utter bliss, just about to doze off again when a strange sensation made her eyes pop open.

Someone was watching her.

She lifted her head, reached for the lamp on her nightstand and slowly brought up the wick. While the lamp glowed to life, she hung there listening to the quiet of the night, too sleepy to discern what was making her feel so vaguely disturbed.

Then she saw it, on her hand, where the signet ring used to be.

A diamond.

She gasped, looked closer at the large round gem that was cut so exquisitely it sent a dazzling spray of blue light into her eyes.

Stunned, she almost didn't hear the voice that spoke softly from somewhere across the room.

"You didn't think I'd let you wear that signet ring forever, did you?"

She threw back the covers, leaped up, her eyes shooting wildly across the room until she saw him sitting in his chair on the other side of the bed. "Gabriel!"

"Merry Christmas," he whispered.

She crawled across the bed, stared into the shadows until she could distinguish the outline of his figure in the dark. Yes! It was really him!

Gabriel watched her face brighten with the most radiant joy he'd ever seen there. How beautiful she looked just then, draped in her pitch black hair, a white linen gown left open at the bodice just enough to reveal the soft white purity of her skin. Round orchid eyes filled with happy tears until they sparkled with a glory so spectacular it took a bit of his breath away just to look at her.

"I missed you," he whispered and could feel his body turn warm with want.

She sensed his emotion, seemed to absorb it as she sat back and pushed back her heap of raven hair. Full sensuous lips curled into a delicate, provocative little smile that he hadn't seen on that face for a long, long time. It reminded him of Millbridge, the Bordens, the Whig spy and Lieutenant Paul Graves.

"And I missed you . . . " she said, "especially today."

"Francis told me you were shocked and I'm sorry for that . . . It was not my intention—"

This brought her hand up to quiet him and he obeyed, falling very still on his chair, just watching her from the shadows.

For the first time in their marriage, Vanessa let her eyes travel over him without bothering to hide her admiration. No, she didn't need to hide any more, to fear, to pretend to hate the man who had somehow managed to become the greatest passion of her life. Yes, he was her passion, her love, her liberator.

How fine he suddenly looked, sitting in his easy chair the way he used to in Philadelphia. His long legs were casually sprawled, wide open to the eyes that wandered up the length of them, adoring every muscled curve so powerfully revealed beneath the snug white britches he wore. His waistcoat was open, the lapels flung wide as if he'd been sitting there relaxing for quite some time before she awoke. A General's purple satin sash snuggled around his slender midriff, the black leather belt of his saber riding low on his hips. He was comfortably nestled against the tall seat cushions, with his hands hanging off the chair arms, and she found herself marveling at the dichotomy of him just then: so much power in such a quiescent man.

By the time her eyes returned to the chiseled outline of his handsome face, she wanted him like she never wanted anything in her life.

"Don't apologize, Gabriel . . . not for anything about today. This was the happiest day of my life."

His eyebrow rose but still, he made no move to get out of the chair. He wouldn't, she knew, because he thought that giant wall of fear still stood between them.

"I'm glad for both of you. You deserve another chance . . . another life. But it will be a very different life in my home. My terms are peace."

"Yes," she sighed, emotion bringing a veil of tears over her eyes. For a moment, she lost sight of him in the blur. "How I want your terms . . . want to feel worthy of them, but after how horribly I treated you—"

"No . . . it doesn't matter now . . . what you did or I did. Believe me, I don't resent you for it."

How could he say that? She'd hurt him time and time again. Was there no end to this man's compassion?

She just shook her head, nearly speechless as she regarded that tall and majestic shadow in the corner of the room. "Why?" she asked, this single word seeming to burst out of a heart so full of love it almost ached. "You give me everything and I return nothing? Why?"

This made him laugh softly, the sound whispering through the room for a moment before he fell very quiet and still. Only his eyes reflected the intensity of his feelings in that moment, glittering from the shadows like a pair of jewels sparkling in the night.

"Why? Because I love you, Vanessa Davis."

He said it so matter-of-factly, she thought she might not have heard him right. She just sat there staring at him in a kind of dumbstruck wonder.

But he would leave no doubt in her mind, speaking in that deep calm voice of his that seemed to wrap around her very soul. "In fact, I'm so in love with you, I daresay it doesn't even matter what you give me in return. I don't seem to need your love in order to give mine. It comes freely from me . . . don't ask me why . . . but it does and it always will. No matter what you do to me, Vanessa Davis, I will always love you . . . only you . . . until I die."

The very earth seemed to pause around her, a long interlude of stillness falling over the world as his words touched her heart with the most mystical magnificence she had ever felt. Never in her life had she known what it felt like to be so profoundly loved by another person.

Her throat was choked with emotion, too tight to speak. Instead, she slowly slid off the edge of the bed, approached the shadows that enveloped him until she stood before him.

A hand that glittered with a diamond's light reached down, found the tie at the throat of his tunic and gently tugged it open.

He stiffened, his eyes rising into hers with a startled, unguarded question.

"What . . . "

A trembling finger brushed across his lips, touched him with a new boldness that both surprised and empowered her. He was no longer a threat. Oh no! His intimate confession made her feel so absolutely loved she could find not a flicker of hesitation in herself.

"No, don't speak," she whispered down at him, "just let me do what I never could before . . . because I was too full of fear and hate."

Tears of joy seeped from her eyes as she bent down and smoothed his hair away from his face. How magnificent it felt to touch him like this, while loving him so fiercely. Everything about him felt so enormously good to her, the soft texture of his thick hair, the rigid structure of his face, the fires of desire leaping like flames in his dark eyes.

"I'm not the same woman anymore, Gabriel . . . and I never want to be her again. I want to be the woman you created with your gentle hands. Come . . . it's time you meet her."

She lifted his face, kissed him tenderly, savored the manly taste of tobacco around his mouth, the faint trace of rum on his tongue. It was more than just arousal that pulsed through her body now. It came from a deeper place, in her heart, in that quiet little corner where she hid the most honest and sincere love she had ever felt for anyone.

Her kiss left him breathless, full of pleasure. It made her want to give him more, everything he deserved after being so heartlessly denied by the battered girl from Millbridge. She stood upright, reached for the lacings on her bodice and slowly unraveled them, holding his gaze in that seductive way that she knew so well.

With a flick of her fingers, her bodice opened, slid down the length of her arms. His breath caught in his throat at this bold unveiling of herself, the pink-tipped breasts that poised above him in all of their naked splendor. From within the enveloping wings of his chair, she could see his eyes turn dark with hunger, a kind of raw and primitive energy flashing between them as he slowly perused her pristine beauty. The way he looked at her made her tremble, but it was not from fear. No, it was pure pleasure, rising out of the soft flesh between her legs until her body seemed to swell with a warm, pulsing heat. One last swish of the hand found her nightdress lying in a heap around her ankles.

No one had ever seen her as intimately as he saw her at that moment and the desire in his eyes seemed to burn her in places so deep and private it made her shudder. Yet there was no mistaking the effect her beauty had on him, the passion in his eyes never quite so brilliant as it was in that moment.

She felt completely beautiful in his eyes.

Finally, he moved forward, his hands warm and firm as they slid over the soft curves of her hips and drew her nearer. Ever so tenderly, he kissed that place where his child was rounding her belly, his breath coming fast and hard and hot against her skin. "You were created for my eyes . . . no woman ever looked so beautiful to me as you do at this moment . . . "

She shivered, sighed at the feel of her fingers plunging into his thick dark hair, letting his warm mouth slide over her curves in that fiercely tender way of his that always made her feel so adored. "I cherish you . . . " she said, her voice nearly choked by the emotion in her throat. "How could I have been so wrong . . . to blame you . . . hurt you . . . what a fool I've been!"

"No . . . those are not the words I want to hear right now."

She knew what he wanted to hear and no force on earth would ever again stop her from speaking the truth, what she hid in that quiet corner of her heart reserved just for him.

She reached down, lifted his face and looked deep into his eyes. "I love you . . . " she whispered, softly, fiercely, "I love you so much, my beloved Gabriel, my liberator . . . "

Never before did she see such a splendid light pass through those eyes of midnight, such a quick and brilliant flash of a man's most poignant satisfaction.

Ever so slowly, he rose, lifting her in his arms, dazzling her with his unspoken joy as he carried her to the bed.

They slid across the coverlet, her naked body draped in his warmth, her face hidden beneath the shadow of his own as he leaned close to whisper, "I waited a long time for this . . . but somehow it all seems worth it."

She smiled at him, her eyes brimming with love, her ego soaring at his obvious pleasure. It made her greedy for more. She reached under his blouse, let her hands slide up the length of his lean, muscular torso. She felt his heart pulsing beneath her palm, his dark auburn hair tickling her fingertips as they slowly explored him. She closed her eyes and savored the delicious feel of him, how strong and male and vital he was.

It excited him. She could hear his breath come faster, harder, his voice seeming to moan out of his throat as he murmured, "I want all of you tonight, Ness . . . but I don't want to hurt you . . . the baby . . . "

"Hush . . . I'm fine." She proved it with a long and penetrating kiss, one that seemed to tap at the core of their long-suppressed desire, let it loose in a way that turned their love into a swift and furious dance.

It reminded her of that night so long ago, in the abandoned barn on Fleece Downe Road, when time lost itself in a kind of sensuous madness. Like then, she didn't remember undressing him, only that he was naked in her arms, that his body felt so warm and hard, his skin so full of life's warmth. She felt no shame, no embarrassment, no fear as she explored him in intimate ways and allowed him the same privilege.

They stoked each other from the inside out, their movements hastening, their lips sampling every curve and indentation of each other. She floated higher and higher upon some blissful cloud of passion, her love and his blending into an intimacy far too tender for the scorching fires it sent through their bodies.

"Gabriel!" she gasped, her head tossing from side to side as he ravished the delicate white skin of her breasts. "How could I have compared you to him? How? The way you touch me—"

"Is the way you deserve. Hate will never touch you again, Ness. I swear! Only love . . . my love . . . all of it . . . "

As if to prove his sincerity, he took complete possession of her then, joining his body to hers as deeply and completely as nature would allow. He didn't stop until she was full of him, a part of him, her body and his melting into complete oneness.

She gasped, her back arching and her eyes opening wide as she gazed up at him and seemed to look into his very soul. He hid nothing in that moment, every magnificent aspect of this man fully exposed to her view. She saw his love, his want, his needs, the pleasure that made him tremble in this most private embrace.

He moved within her and Vanessa wanted nothing more than to join him, to submit to his dance, to follow his lead. And so she did, letting his hands settle around her hips with a gentle grip, urging her body into perfect synchrony with his own. It was a dance of love, hers and his, both of them finally free to come into the fullness of life and become the bond that would forever unite them as man and wife. Together they climbed upon their own special peak, let it lift them high above anything that had ever stood between them, everything that prohibited them from being as close as they were now. Only the softest and most ecstatic moan escaped her lips when he once again brought her to nature's most intimate release and adored her pleasure as if it was his own.

While she shuddered against him, he kissed her velvety skin and whispered, "How you shine in my light . . . I adore you . . . love you . . . for all time . . ."

His arms suddenly clenched around her, his words choked to silence as his own release caught him in a fierce grip. The power of it stiffened him, made him moan aloud as he poured his love into her, let it fill her, strengthen her, heal her in those places where she was the most ravaged.

Peace came over them like a magical spell, melted them into the feather bed where they lay locked in each other's arms and the vibrant glow of two spirits in utter relief. They needed nothing at this moment but to revel in the complete contentment they had somehow managed to find in the tangled wreckage of what had long been considered a doomed marriage.

Not any more.

No man and woman were ever so united as they were at this moment.

A long and turbulent journey had finally come to an end.

She sighed, a long and blissful sound that made her feel as if the last dark wind of her soul was finally expelled. "I don't think I'll ever forget this day for as long as I live!"

Gabriel's face appeared above her, his skin gleaming golden from behind the scattered tumble of his long hair. She thought he looked wickedly handsome just then, bathed in the sweat of his manly passions, his body still weak from the drain of his intimate exertions. A soft, sleepy grin spread across his cheeks. "I daresay, no one ever surprised me with a Christmas gift quite like this before . . . and I rather liked the way you unwrapped it for me."

The mere memory of that steamy moment brought a flush of color to her cheeks. "No one on earth was as surprised as I this Christmas," she whispered. "I still can't believe she's here . . . "

She told him about that special moment of hers, all the while caressing him and nibbling at him in ways that were as luscious as they were grateful. "I don't know what made me say the things I said in there . . . but once done . . . I felt so different . . . so . . . relieved of whatever it was that haunted me for most of my life."

"Fear . . . violence . . . " he suggested softly, kissing the puzzled frown on her brow.

"Yes," she breathed, her eyes turning thoughtful as she gazed up into the face of her beloved. "It's what held me from you . . . made me afraid of what you made me feel . . . afraid that if I allowed it you'd become mean like my father did . . . turn on me . . . hurt me . . . "

"Betray you . . . "

"Yes."

"And now? What do you feel now?"

Gabriel watched her eyes soften with love as she studied him for a long, silent moment. "Right now I believe I trust you more than I ever trusted anyone in my life . . . trust you enough to love you like I never thought I could ever love a man."

She reached up, brought his face close, kissed his lips with an affection so real and intense, it renewed all the passion they had just realized. Burrowed deep within the warm blankets, they embraced, strained to be intimate again, to know each other now that all their secrets were revealed.

And they did, slowly, for as long as they wanted, until their sparkling new love made its own demands and left them once again shuddering in each other's arms.

Christmas night eased them into its warm arms and let them sleep long and peacefully, until the first rays of dawn began to filter through the curtains.

Vanessa woke first, lying cuddled in the arms of her sleeping husband, watching her new ring send a prism of tiny lights across his brawny breast.

She sighed, closed her eyes, wondered if she had ever felt so completely happy as she did at this moment.

Gabriel started to waken, in that sluggish way of his, draping an arm across his eyes as if to blot out the reality of morning.

"It can't be dawn already," he grumbled.

"Shall I fetch you tea?"

"No." His arm tightened around her, snatched her close. "I want you near for a few more minutes."

"Alright," she soothed, laid her head on his chest and continued to admire her diamond.

After a long moment, he said, "I've got to leave, Ness—"

"What?"

"I'm not staying."

Surely he was teasing. She lifted her head, leaned over him and swept the hair out of his face. "What are you talking about?"

He just sighed, closed his eyes as if he couldn't bear to look at her when he said, "It's either that or report to Washington today to be confined to quarters."

Her heart instantly dropped. He was serious. "But why?"

"The Archangel . . . " was all he said, no more explanation needed.

She let her face fall to his breast again so he couldn't see the bitter disappointment she felt at that moment. It made her want to wail aloud while he told her about his meeting with Washington, all the forces that were gathering against him because of his connection to the master spy who dogged his every step.

"But what of your command, Gabriel?"

"I'm deserting it . . . "

A kind of frozen pause fell over her. Ever so slowly, she lifted her head until she could see into his eyes, realize how powerfully they reflected her own stunned sorrow.

"I have no other choice, Ness. I can't work like this anymore . . . with everyone trying to pull something out of me that I cannot give. Please try to understand that it must be done."

"Where will you go?"

"To Philadelphia . . . into the underground . . . where I can do what I do best . . . spy on the enemy."

"Then you'll continue to serve?"

"Of course I will. I'm too devoted to our independence now . . . especially after watching Burgoyne fall. Now I know it's possible. Whether I'm in uniform or not, I'll do everything in my power to see us liberated from the Crown."

Just to see that righteous glint in his eye, hear the

determination in his words, brought a breath of doom across her lazy spirit. He would leave her again and after spending such an unforgettable night in his bed, she knew she would ache with loneliness for him.

As if he read her mind just then, he slid his hands up the side of her face, framed it in his big brown hands and whispered, "No, don't look like that . . . not after last night. Nothing will ever separate us . . . never again. I want you to listen to me very closely now, and do exactly as I say."

She nodded, mute with grief, her only strength found in their shared patriotism.

"Only you are to know how to contact me. You can reach me at the Blue Dolphin . . . through George Chaffe. I'll make the arrangements with him. I want to know when your time is near, do you hear? I want to come home then . . . be with you. Send a note to Chaffe but don't give your name or mine. Just say that your time is near. He'll know what to do then.

"As for my men, I want you to tell them that this departure is only temporary. I will come back and I will lead them again but only when I can stand among them in my own boots . . . not the Archangel's. I have to deal with this now . . . before it goes any further . . . but when it's done, I'll be back. Can you tell them this for me?"

She nodded again. "Gabriel, this will crush them . . . "

Sorrow filled his eyes just then. She felt devastated just to look at it, to realize that no one in Moylan's Horse would feel the pain of this departure more than he. "I'll give you the resignation letter. Give it to Francis and tell him to take it to Washington along with my sword. Tell him to care for my men as I would . . . and comfort them."

"What of you? Who will comfort you?"

"You will . . . every time I remember this—"

He started kissing her then, urgently, passionately, as if

already feeling the strain of being separated from her. She responded instantly, fueling his want with equal doses of her own, desperately trying to stave off the pain that wanted to mar what she now knew would be their farewell.

"Love me again," he whispered fiercely, breathlessly, "One more time."

Vivien Davis found her daughter in the kitchen, alone, beside the window, a forlorn gaze fixed upon the stunned company of soldiers in the backyard. She couldn't decide who looked more lost, Vanessa or those aimlessly wandering soldiers. It was as if a cloud of mourning passed over this farm the instant Vanessa made the announcement that Major General Gabriel St. Claire had just resigned his uniform.

Vivien felt her maternal instincts flood over her, made her rush to hold her child and lend her the special kind of solace only known to mothers and daughters.

"He promised to return and he will, Ness. He's a man of his word. He'll never disappoint you . . . "

This was no consolation, especially not when her body could still feel his presence in its deepest and most private places, while his scent still clung to her flesh, while her mind was too full of the memory of his lovemaking this morning. With separation looming over them, they drank from each other with a kind of frantic desperation that she recalled with a shudder of pleasure and a furious blush. To be separated from him now, in the wake of such an unforgettable night, impacted her like a cruel blow.

If she wasn't so angry she would have cried just then.

"Damn that Archangel! I'm not going to stand idly by and let him drive my husband off!" She turned, looked at her mother and whispered, "On our wedding day he said two spies had no business getting married. I aim to prove him wrong."

With that, she slid out the back door and headed straight for the officers of Moylan's Horse.

Although it took months to arrange, Vanessa and the officers of Moylan's Horse were finally granted permission to talk with Jonathan Meeks. The meeting took place outside the prison, on a cold February morning, in an old Quaker Meetinghouse on the outskirts of Reading.

Jon looked well despite five months of captivity. Although his face was overgrown with a shaggy blonde beard, his eyes still shone with the same alert vitality she remembered in him.

"Gabe's been to see me," he said and Vanessa's heart leaped at the mere mention of Gabriel's name. She hadn't heard from him since Christmas night. "Disguised himself as a preacher wanting to spread the word of God to his errant son." Jon grinned and pointed at himself. "We had a long talk. He knows I didn't betray him. I think we both figured out those two men Washington hired were double agents alright . . . working for Washington *and* Gates!"

"So that's it!" Lauren said, sank himself onto a prayer

bench and breathed, "That's why Washington denied their papers! He didn't want Gates to know what he was doing!"

"And all the while, Gates was conducting his own search," Jon added.

"Meanwhile, my husband is caught in the middle," Vanessa said, breaking their astonished silence.

Jon looked at her very directly for a moment, then said, "Washington offered me freedom if I'd find Gabe for him."

"Are you considering it?" she asked.

"No. That's why I'm still here. When Gabe wants to tell what he knows about the Archangel, he will."

"And what do you think he knows, Jon." Francis wanted to know.

"Everything."

They just looked at him dumbly, unable to accept his certainty.

It was Francis who finally leaned forward and asked in a clear, calm voice, "What is this theory of yours . . . about Michael . . . can you tell us? We just want to help him."

Jon moved closer, checked to be sure none of the guards were near enough to hear and said, "My suspicions began long before the war started . . . when I first met Gabe shortly after he arrived here. In those days, he couldn't speak English, nor did he have much reason to. Law books are written in Latin, which he could read very well, and many of his student friends knew French. Teaching him the language was mainly my idea at first, but Gabe became more and more interested in learning English.

"So I'd teach him and before long he could carry on a reasonable conversation in the language. However, there were days when he seemed to have completely forgotten everything I taught him and would just stand there mute when someone spoke to him, as if he didn't know how to respond. I used to wonder about these . . . er . . . memory lapses of his because he never struck me as being an absent-minded man."

They all agreed among themselves that this was not characteristic of Gabriel.

"Sometimes his accent would seem unusually heavy, as if he just stepped off the boat. As the years went on, it became even more strange that he could sometimes speak fluent and flawless English and other times stumble over the language.

"These memory lapses are not confined to the language, however. Martina will never forget the morning Gabriel forgot how to bake his croissants, which we all know are the finest in the neighborhood, from a family recipe he refuses to disclose. Well, Martina put out all the ingredients for him and watched Gabriel stand there and stare at the table in utter perplexity. He'd baked those croissants nearly every week for five years and he couldn't remember what to do! Martina had to coach him through it.

"This particular experience upset Tina, although there were others. We just couldn't understand why he acted this way until I began to piece together the story of his past in France, his identical twin, the game they used to play with their identities.

"Strange as it might sound, it certainly fit the way he acted at times. I began to wonder if Michael St. Claire really died that day or if he might have survived the gunshot."

"But why would Michael hide himself from a family who grieves him so bitterly . . . " Lauren questioned and Vanessa could see the Quartermaster did not want to believe what he was hearing.

"That's a question I've never been able to answer," Jon admitted, "but Gabriel had aims in espionage and was an early enthusiast of the rebel movement. Maybe he and Michael planned this Archangel scheme."

Francis shook his head and got off the bench as if he couldn't stand to sit while hearing such mind-boggling concepts. He was clearly agitated as he paced to and fro in the front of the tiny Quaker Meetinghouse. Finally, he turned around and defiantly announced, "No, your theory is absurd."

"Why? Because you don't want to believe Gabe has deceived us so well?" Jon countered.

"Just because he lapses into French, forgets a recipe, acts absent-minded now and again, is not enough reason to believe Gabriel could manage such a perfectly concerted identity switch in the course of his day-to-day life," Francis insisted.

"I'll tell you how he manages it, Francis," Jon said, got up and joined the Surgeon in the front of the room. "Gabriel St. Claire can mimic anyone. He can be a beggar or a high-society barrister. He can be whatever you want him to be at any given moment. How? By growing up with an identical twin and making a child's game out of switching identities!"

"Dear God!" Vanessa breathed, thinking that the room felt suddenly warm and fanning herself with a glove. "What you describe is madness, Jon!"

"Of course it is! Haven't you ever spoken to the St. Claires about the twins' little game?"

"No . . . I don't mention anything to them . . . about Michael or the Archangel. Gabriel forbids it."

"Because he knows how deeply disturbed they have always been by the way Michael and Gabriel played their game. It was a serious family problem."

She could stand no more, her head suddenly spinning with questions. Her husband. Who was he? Was he capable of doing something like this? "Francis . . . I must go—"

* * *

Alain St. Claire stood at the parlor window and tried to ignore the furious pace at which Chloe was knitting. Even though she spoke calmly and clearly, Alain knew the conversation was beginning to unnerve her.

"Of course it was just a game, *chérie.* They never meant any harm by it although it did bring us trouble as they grew older. You must understand, there were no physical differences between the twins . . . no special birthmarks or moles. They were the same height, weight, coloring—"

"Surely there was some way to distinguish them," Vanessa insisted as she plied her own knitting needles, "perhaps their tone of voice or some mannerism."

"But this was how they played their little game, you see, by mimicking each other's tone of voice and mannerisms. It was difficult to distinguish them . . . even for us . . . when they were playing their game." Chloe said with a nervous little laugh and continued knitting at a breakneck speed.

Vanessa stopped knitting and shared a curious look with her mother on the opposite divan. Vivien noticed Chloe's awkwardness and was clearly uncomfortable with this conversation because of it. The two women had become fast friends in the past few months, drawn to each other by the morbid bond of having each lost a son.

Vanessa hesitated to press the subject, not wanting to disturb either woman, but her worry for Gabriel was greater. It was March. She hadn't seen him or heard his voice since Christmas night. The yearning in her heart was overpowering, especially now that their child's birth was only a month away.

"Why are you all so interested in this subject lately?" Alain wanted to know, his dark eyes passing from face to face in search of an answer.

Lauren and Francis stopped playing chess in the corner of the parlor, their attention wholly focused on the conversation.

Ever since returning from Reading, they'd done nothing but argue about how to broach this subject with the St. Claires. Any mention of the matter made Chloe act visibly disturbed until Alain changed the subject.

"Just curious," Francis said with a shrug and feigned returning his interest to the chess game.

It was Lauren who made the decision not to let the matter pass this time. "No, it's more than that." Francis looked at him sharply. "This could have some bearing on the problems Gabriel faces with the military."

Chloe looked befuddled, stopped knitting and stared across the room at Lauren. "But how could it?"

Alain crossed the room and stood over the two men in the far corner. "I think the time has come for you to explain what's going on, gentlemen. It's not like my son to abandon his uniform and I've long been troubled by it. Why don't we go somewhere and talk in private—"

"No," Chloe said and everyone looked at her. "He's my son, too. I want to know."

The moment had come. Vanessa looked between Lauren and Francis, shared an unspoken agreement to spill the truth at long last.

Lauren transformed from a soldier to a lawyer, smoothly taking control of the situation. "What we discuss in this room must never leave it." He waited until everyone gave him a nod of promise, then said to the St. Claires, "Your son is somehow connected to the Archangel. I'm sure you've heard of this spy—"

"Of course," Alain said, "But I don't understand . . . what kind of connection?"

"That's what we're trying to determine. Now why don't you tell us everything you can about Michael's death?"

Chloe looked momentarily stricken. Alain joined her at once, sat on the arm of the divan and held her hand. "Such as?"

"Where exactly was hc shot?"

Alain pointed to his left cheek, just under the bone.

"Did the bullet exit his head?" Francis inquired as gently as he could.

"No. Gabriel was holding him. If the bullet exited, it would have injured him as well."

Francis studied the man for a long moment, as if assessing whether the St. Claires were under too much strain for further discussion. "Judging from my experience on the battlefield, I can say that facial bullet wounds are not always fatal. The amount of bone in the skull seems to provide some protection."

"Michael was shot at a relatively close range," Alain insisted, looking very unsure of what Francis was trying to say.

"How close?" Lauren interrogated.

"Ten yards."

"What kind of gun?"

"A fowling piece of some sort."

"Fowling pieces are not very powerful weapons."

Alain came to his feet. "What are you implying, son?"

"That Michael is still alive."

Chloe looked at Lauren in a kind of appalled horror.

"That's impossible!" Alain declared. "I carried him to the servants' quarters . . . laid him on the table there . . . he was dead!"

"No pulse?" Francis's voice was amazingly calm.

"None! Don't you think I would check?"

"Did you call a physician?" Lauren persisted.

"No! I couldn't call anyone! There was no time! For God's sake, Gabriel killed Louis in full view of a field of servants! They saw it all . . . were running in panic. It was only a matter of time before the entire countryside came running up to our doorstep. We had to go . . . immediately!"

"So you just left Michael lying there," Lauren concluded for Alain.

"No . . . well, yes . . . but I took a moment to pack some papers . . . clothes . . . "

"And bury Michael?"

"No. The servants did it."

"Then you never actually *saw* him buried?"

Vanessa cringed at Lauren's merciless questioning. Chloe hadn't a hint of color left in her face.

"No, but I saw his grave during subsequent visits to France."

"Is there a body in the grave?"

"Oh for the love of God! Of course there's a body in the grave!"

"Did you ever *see* it?"

"No!" Alain's face turned a ruddy shade of red. He was getting angry, nearly furious. "I tell you, my son Michael is dead. Neither of my sons would prevent us from knowing if his beloved twin was still alive. We were a close and loving family. Those bonds hold fast—"

"I'm sure they do!" Lauren cried, angry and frustrated. "But the facts lend themselves to well to Jonnie's theory."

"What theory?" Alain demanded.

"That the Archangel is your son Michael."

Chloe swooned, slumping weakly against the cushions. Vivien had to hold her up. The woman just stared at her, dazed and shaken. Ever so carefully, Vivien helped her off the divan and out of the room. Alain stared after them, too distraught with shock to do anything but watch her go.

"I can't believe this," he murmured at the back of the parlor door. "What you're saying is madness!"

"Yes, it's all madness, but now that it's out, we need to make it into sense." Vanessa struggled to get up, so heavy with child she could barely manage it until the men remembered themselves and rushed to her aid. She was panting by the time she found her footing. "Somehow we must determine if this is true."

"How can such a ridiculous notion be proven true?" Alain responded hotly. "Michael can't be alive . . . posing as the Archangel. I'll not believe it! But I will say this, it would not surprise me in the least if Gabriel was the Archangel. That is a theory that strikes me as being entirely plausible." He turned away from her, stalked to the window and scoffed at the yard beyond. "Gabriel could outwit a fox. I never doubted he was the orchestrator of the game. Yes, he could very well manage to convince everyone that Michael might be alive . . . might be the Archangel . . . just to throw suspicion off himself. I shall take the advice of *ma belle-fille* and make some sense out of this," Alain decided, crossed the room and let himself into the lobby where he immediately draped himself in his cloak.

"Where are you going?" they all asked at once.

"To Washington," Alain announced, coming to stand on the threshold of the parlor just long enough to point a finger at Lauren and say, "I'm going to prove you wrong, young man, and I know just how to do it!"

Vanessa sat on the porch swing, inhaled the first breath of spring that poured across the fields as a new day was born in Valley Forge. How still it was on the farm, the family and soldiers yet to stir, only the birds awake and singing from every crevice in this blossoming countryside. It was a peaceful moment for her, a quiet resignation taking root inside as another pain flashed through her abdomen.

Today her child would be born.

She smiled, undeniably glad about it, happy to put an end to this clumsy, lonely pregnancy and discover the graces of motherhood at last. By this time tomorrow, she'd be holding a baby in her arms, nurturing it, bundling it in all the tiny clothes she'd fashioned these many months. Until the pain passed, she clung to these thoughts and, while no one but mother nature could see, she grinned through the worst of it.

Besides, it was a blessing to be distracted from the anxious worries of the past few weeks. Alain St. Claire had indeed met with Washington but neither man was talking. Something was planned, she knew, but no amount of prompting could make Alain reveal anything except to ask her not to summon Gabriel home for the birth of his child. It was better to leave things be until this secret plan could unfold and she was asked to comply out of a sense of patriotic duty. Fearing she might be betraying Gabriel unwittingly, she attempted to learn the truth from the General himself but the meeting proved fruitless.

Washington learned, through Jonnie Meeks, that his scouts had betrayed him to Horatio Gates. He was deeply wounded by this knowledge even though Vanessa could see the General genuinely grieved the loss of the scouts. Now Washington was unwilling to trust anyone except those people closest to the situation, such as Jonnie Meeks and Alain St. Claire. He released Jon from prison and allowed him to join Gabriel in the Philadelphia underground, wherever that might be, and issued an order for Martina Meeks to be released from the army's custody to rejoin her Kingston relatives. Whatever plan they had in mind, Alain and the General made it quite clear that it would be the last effort. If this failed, the search for the Archangel would be permanently terminated. It was becoming too costly for all parties involved.

Vanessa agreed, especially now when another pain gripped her and told her the time had come to wake Francis. She went inside, moved through the house with quiet footsteps, leaned against the door to her mother's room and clenched her teeth against a new wave of pain. When would all the mysteries end, all the searches and the theories and the unanswered questions? Who would discover whom and what would he be? A spy, a Major General, a long lost brother, a father?

Vivien was already awake. She knew it was her daughter's time, almost felt a bit of the labor herself. They held each other happily, through another contraction, supported each other through the pain the way they had all their lives.

Ever so quietly, Vanessa tread into Francis's room, sat on the edge of his bed and gently shook him awake.

"Come, Francis," she whispered, "one of our mysteries is about to be solved."

Alain found his way into the loft, high above the noise and commotion of the soldiers on the barn floor. He pulled a candle from his pocket, wedged it between the planks and struck a flint. He had just enough illumination to write.

A small square of wrinkled paper and a lead stick were placed against his knee. He stared at the blank space for a long time, tried to dissuade himself from writing the message he and Washington agreed upon.

But it was too late to back out now.

The stick scratched across the page. Alain cleared a lump out of his throat and looked around, as if afraid someone might catch him. Of course no one was there. It was just his guilt. The stick moved again, a deceiving message forming on the page. He blinked his eyes, tried to see through the gathering tears. How it hurt to write this! He paused but only for an instant, his trembling hand suddenly spilling the words across the little paper, then adding a hasty signature. He hurled the lead stick across the loft, never heard it land.

Damn him and his bright ideas, Alain raged against himself. Why did he offer to do this, to be the one who wrenched out the heart of his own son? Why couldn't he let the search for the Archangel fend for itself? Why mix politics with dark family secrets?

Because that cursed child's game had haunted him long enough.

A few minutes later, the note was sealed and placed into the hand of a sentry for delivery to Washington. The General would see it sent from there. He walked through the barn, out into the yard, hardly hearing the usual invitations to drink that followed in his wake. Alain felt cold inside, numb, as if his own heart was gone.

He opened the front door and was startled by the noisy commotion that greeted him. Benny, Lauren, Will, and Chloe were clustered around Francis Stone, craning and pushing and exclaiming over whatever it was the Surgeon held. Chloe saw him in the doorway, broke from the group and spilled herself into his waiting arms.

"We have a grandson! Look! And what a little angel he is!"

Alain said nothing, felt a breath of joy scamper across his aching heart but it passed quickly, was only a memory when he pulled back the knitted coverlet and looked upon the tiny pink face of Gabriel's first child. Somehow, he managed a smile, took the boy and headed for the stairs.

"Alain?" Chloe knew something was wrong, stood very still on the landing and watched him climb the stairs.

He didn't answer her, just kept climbing until he rose above their silent, questioning faces.

Vanessa was sitting up in bed, her long hair neatly braided, her eyes closed as she dozed with a gentle smile on her lips.

"Francis," she whispered wearily.

"No, it is I," Alain said and sat on the bed. His grandson squirmed within his bundle of blankets, a tiny hand fisting just before it was thrust against his puckered lips. Vanessa turned, looked at the babe and smiled with a kind of awestruck radiance. "Isn't he handsome?"

"He looks just as Gabriel did when he was born," Alain said but his voice cracked. Just to look at the infant, see his shock of red-brown hair, brought back memories that choked him with emotion.

Vanessa's hand found his arm and gave it a gentle squeeze, as if she secretly understood who he was thinking about just then.

"And Michael . . . " she finished for him.

"Yes, and my beloved Michael."

"This is good because it makes me glad for the name I've chosen. Michael Gabriel. I hope it pleases you."

The message he'd penned in the barn flashed through his mind.

"Michael is alive. Come home."

The lump in his throat grew so big he couldn't swallow any more. At the very least, he thought, now the note wasn't a total lie. Michael was indeed alive, in this new son.

With the infant clenched in his arms, Alain leaned forward, laid his head on Vanessa's soft shoulder and sobbed as he hadn't done since his childhood.

As they had been informed, General Washington arrived at the St. Claire farm without his usual entourage of aides. He was dressed in civilian clothes, looking like any other middle-aged man as he strode across the porch. The moment he walked into the lobby, however, it filled with a palpable sense of greatness, honor, and distinction.

The officers of Moylan's Horse saluted him in unison. He returned the gesture and bade them all to be at ease as he took a place among them to wait for Gabriel's arrival.

He was coming home at last but not the way Vanessa

wanted it to be, with everyone so tense and nervous, so terribly sobered in the wake of Alain's revelation.

"It's the only way to get at the truth. If Michael is indeed alive, posing as the Archangel, Gabriel will know the game has been discovered because of the note. They'll both come home. I know them. They'll not continue the ruse anymore."

Vanessa felt the joy of seeing him again and presenting their new baby son being slowly smothered beneath the weight of this dreadful situation. She wanted to celebrate, be festive, dance with joy, but once again, the Archangel stole the glory.

Washington was only seated a few minutes before a pair of riders appeared on the distant road.

Alain and Chloe both looked at each other in a moment of utter shock, then rushed to the window. "Dear God . . . it's them!"

"Michael!" Chloe clasped her hands to her mouth, a rush of tears overwhelming her eyes as she strained to see the riders.

Vanessa's whole body tingled with fear as she rose, slowly walked to the window and stared at the riders as they turned onto the drive. It was only when they came within a few yards of the porch that she saw who the second rider was.

Jonnie Meeks.

"Mon Dieu!" Alain clenched his eyes and looked away. "What have I done?"

Gabriel's boots sounded against the porch, compelled Alain across the parlor, into the lobby. No one followed. They all sat there as immobile as stone statues, struck cold by the reality of their failed scheme.

The front door swung wide. Gabriel was standing there, dressed in plain clothes, a long black riding cape swishing to a halt around his booted calves. His eyes glanced once through the parlor, then settled full upon his father.

"Where is he?" Gabriel asked in French. "Michael—"

Alain felt his heart sink, a terrible sensation of doom assaulting his senses when he looked upon the urgent expcctancy on his son's face. Hope. It shone in his eyes like a beacon in the night, a light he must soon snuff.

"Père," Gabriel whispered, imploring his father to tell him what he wanted to hear even though he was already realizing the truth. Sorry tears filled his father's eyes. "But your note said—"

"I'm sorry, my son, but I had to do it."

"Do what?"

"Trick you."

All the hope died in Gabriel then, seemed to seep out of his spirit and dissipate in the air around them, leaving him to stand in some strange empty pocket of complete desolation. In that moment, he was the loneliest man in the world.

Once again, Michael died.

"Why? Why would you do this to me, Father?"

"Because I knew you'd bring him here if the rumors were true—"

"Rumors? About Michael being the Archangel? Is that what this is about?"

Jon let out a disgusted sigh, able to understand enough of their language to comprehend the sorry truth. "I told you there was something wrong, Gabe."

"I thought the same but I never imagined my own father would do such a thing to me. That's why I came. Because I trusted you, damnit!" Gabriel snapped at his sire in a cold, icy voice. He was angry now. Very angry. And hurt. "You owe me an apology!"

"Of course, I'm sorry!" Alain said vehemently. "Do you think I wanted to do this . . . trick you . . . deceive you so cruelly just to end a few rumors?"

"Oh, for God's sake!" Gabriel cursed in his native tongue again, spun around and glared at his mother as well when he said, "Let him die already. Why can't we just let him die so we can learn how to live without him, eh?"

Chloe rose, hurried to the doorway, alarmed at this unprecedented behavior from her son. She'd never seen Gabriel so angry before. He looked downright malevolent just then and she was struck by the sight of him in such an unusual temper. She never knew he could produce such a cold and impenetrable anger. It made him seem so inhuman just then, almost spectral. Lord, but he was a deadly man when it suited him!

"I'm so sorry," Alain was muttering dismally, "But a flicker of hope found me when this theory was revealed . . . that maybe our Michael was alive after all . . . even though I knew deep inside neither of you would do this to us—"

"Of course I wouldn't!" Gabriel growled.

Chloe could feel his pain just then, her heart breaking once again for the misery Gabriel had endured ever since that fateful day in France. "Perhaps this is why I wanted to stay that day . . . just a few more hours . . . to see my little one laid to rest. I saw him born . . . I should have seen him buried—"

Gabriel put up a hand to silence an argument he'd heard too many times before. "Enough. We cannot and will not see him buried in the ground, mother, but we can bury him here." He pointed at his heart. "In here we can all give him the burial we always wished for him."

Chloe burst into tears, ran into his arms where Gabriel embraced her tenderly, smoothing her hair and whispering to her in French until she calmed enough to be set aside.

With an abrupt turn, he strolled into the parlor, as if he needed to be away from the dark family secret just revealed. But then he saw Vanessa and paused in mid-stride.

She caught his dark gaze and let herself fall into it from across the room. They remembered their last night together, the bliss of it still very much alive in their hearts just then. But then his glance dropped and he noticed she was no longer pregnant, saw the small wooden cradle at her feet. He made a move toward her but she motioned him away. They could deal with their personal matters later.

Gabriel looked at his Commander in Chief, began to speak in a slow but determined voice, as if afraid he might change his mind if he didn't act now.

"Before you place me under arrest for abandoning my uniform, there's something you should know." He stopped, seemed to relax a bit in his long dark cloak and continued quietly. "Within three months of volunteering for service in Boston, I knew the kind of reconnaissance work I was capable of doing could not be done while in uniform. Not only was I saddled with military codes and regulations, but one could never be sure if the sentry hired to deliver a note would reach his destination before being bought by the other side.

"Military information channels are too untrustworthy so I began to send top-secret information to you through the civilian mails. I signed them anonymously but I knew my notes reached you because within time, you began to react to the information I sent. Once I had your respect, and your attention, I had to deal with the dilemma of getting myself, Gabriel St. Claire, linked to the anonymous note-sender so I might be stationed closer to the center of the action. How was this to be achieved?"

Vanessa's heart paused in her breast. Along with everyone else, they knew what he was about to say. Benny seemed to be holding his breath until it seemed the edges of his lips were turning blue. Lauren and Francis came halfway out of their seats, poised and staring at him in complete astonishment. Only Jonathan Meeks stood quiet and sure, as if he already knew.

"I created the name Archangel—"

"You," Washington exclaimed, but his voice was so soft it sounded more like a sigh. "How?"

"It was very simple. I sent information to you under the Archangel's signature, then immediately followed with the same facts under my own name. It took only a few months for you to link us together. Once done, you responded by placing me in the most critical theaters of the war. My goal was then achieved. I was now able to do what I do best . . . spy . . . in areas that had a great effect on the outcome of the fighting."

Francis stood upright, his eyes full of righteous indignation. "But how could you do this without any of us knowing?"

"Come now, Francis, you know I always spy alone . . . with one or two exceptions." He gave his wife a warm look just then. "Not even Benny accompanied me, would just wait for me at a designated place to be sure I got out safely—"

"But the Swanson mission?" Francis was not convinced. "We were all there . . . on the green!"

"Yes, but who paid any attention to what I was writing afterward? I penned two notes with the same information. One I handed to Benny and told him to have it sent by sentry through the normal military channels. The other note I handed to Steve MacLeod to post in town, through the private channels, which moved twice as quickly as the military routes. The note I hurried was signed by the Archangel . . . the one I allowed to travel more slowly was signed by me. I was doing this all along and none of you had any reason to question a particular note among the volumes of relays I send out daily."

"What about the note to Gates," Vanessa breathed aloud. "It arrived *after* you came to Freeman's Farm . . . and from the opposite direction!"

"I merely disappeared for a few hours while traveling

there . . . garnered a few scouts and sent a relay to Gates. It was deliberate. I wanted to throw him off."

Gabriel was telling the truth. A room full of stunned friends and family could only stare at him, awestruck by what he was saying.

To his closest aides and friends, Gabriel said, "I had no other choice but to work without your knowledge. If I told one of you, eventually you would all know. It had to be kept secret . . . until now . . . when this search began to grow more costly than I could tolerate. First, Jon was imprisoned because of it. My family was forced to endure the torture of these ridiculous notions about Michael. Last, my Commander intended to confine me, which meant I could no longer work. No. Keeping silent is a luxury I can no longer afford. I've known this moment would come for many months now . . . since I abandoned the uniform. I was only waiting for the right opportunity to speak."

Washington rose then, tall and proud at his great height as he looked at his errant General and said, "Why didn't you tell me this before abandoning your uniform, Gabriel?"

"Because there was one last thing I needed to do before I revealed myself. I had to know what was going on in Philadelphia, sir. That's my home," he said so matter-of-factly that the General seemed taken aback by it.

"But this is adequate grounds for court-martial!"

"No, this is adequate grounds for liberating a city, sir."

Gabriel looked his Commander straight in the eye and professed, "End my career if you wish, but I'll never stop fighting . . . I'll never stop feeding you information . . . and I'll never align myself with any other General in the Continental Army."

Washington was clearly moved by the forthrightness of this statement and how vehemently Gabriel delivered his allegiance. The General's brow furrowed in deep concentration as he crossed his arms over his chest and nodded toward Francis, "Summon my aides."

The ensuing scuffle did not cause even a ripple in the Commander's concentration.

Finally, in a gentle but firm way, he asked, "Why me?"

"Because you are a man of honor," Gabriel replied without hesitation. "Like me. And you fight for the people's sake . . . not your own. That's enough reason for me.

Silence gripped the two soldiers who faced each other in the center of the room. Gabriel was beyond question and the General knew it.

It was Will MacLeod who broke the silence and muttered, "But you were always so upset about the Archangel, Gabe!"

"It was all part of the cover, Will."

"What about that note you sent to Moylan," Benny asked, his great face looking childishly hurt by this great deception, "you know . . . the one about all men named Lucifer being the devil."

Gabriel looked at his sentry, the first whisper of a smile playing across his lips as he said, "Moylan was very close to the truth, wasn't he, Benny?"

The sentry's huge head nodded quickly but he still looked sorrowful. "You could've told me, Gabe. After all, I been your sentry for years."

Gabriel sighed at him. "I might have confided in you if not for your devotion to the bottle—"

"But you know I can hold my liquor, Gabe! I ain't the kind who gets to blubbering when I'm drunk!"

"The hell you aren't," Will retorted. "You're the one who told Stevie I was sweet on his girl—"

"I did not!" Benny defended. "I said you thought she was perty, is all. Besides, you ought to be glad Stevie ain't alive to read the letters you're sending that girl now!"

Washington put up a hand to stop the officers of

Moylan's Horse from another one of their famous rows. He gave his full attention back to Gabriel, along with a large bulky parcel just delivered by one of his aides. On top of the pile rested a familiar weapon that made Gabriel smile just to see it again.

His rapier.

"I'm going to do something now that breaks my long tradition with military discipline," Washington said and handed Gabriel the sword. "I'm going to forget your desertion . . . strike it from my mind as if it never happened . . . that is, if you're willing to resume your position, General St. Claire."

Gabriel looked relieved as he reached for his sword. "I will."

A cheer rang out among the officers of Moylan's Horse. Their Commander was back!

"But first," Washington quickly interrupted, "I want proof. If you are indeed the Archangel, prove it to me as we stand here now."

Gabriel thought this over for a moment, then motioned for Washington to follow him to the window. Once beside the panes, he slid the rapier from its sheath while quietly reciting a well-known verse, "Thundering wings, hooves of steel, a golden edge does his rapier wield . . . "

Washington's eyebrow rose with delighted intrigue as he took the blade and turned it into the light. Everyone rushed around him, examined it for some sign of the famous edge. For a brief, stunning moment, the sunlight flashed over the weapon and sent a bright ripple of gold down the edge. It was there, just on the cutting edge, barely visible to the naked eye.

They all gasped, staring at the owner of the blade with profound respect and a bright sparkle of excitement in their eyes.

Gabriel St. Claire was the Archangel!

* * *

"What Father wrote me was the truth, eh?" Gabriel said when they were alone in their room with their newborn son. Stretched out on the bed with the child between them, they watched him gurgle and fawn in the complete adoration of his parents. "Michael is indeed alive."

"Yes, he is," Vanessa breathed, reached across the child to delight his father with a warm and inviting kiss. Gabriel's hand slid along the svelte lines of her reclining body, as if savoring the luscious moments they would soon enjoy. "The Archangel's son!"

Gabriel smiled at her, enjoyed the sweetness in her violet eyes. In them he saw a tender history, two people caught in the complex web of their own private pains yet capable of finding clarity in a united life. "Were you surprised by the truth?"

"Very much so, although I always believed you knew more about the 'Angel than what you were telling us."

"And now you're convinced."

Something about his tone of voice made her feel momentarily unsettled. She rolled onto her stomach, looked at him curiously. "Shouldn't I be convinced?"

"All colichemarde blades have a golden edge."

"Gabriel!"

He reached up, put a finger to his lips and hurried, "Hush! The baby wants to sleep now—"

"Don't change the subject! Gabriel, if you've lied about all this—"

He grinned, pleased with himself. "Now, now, Lavender . . . where's your spying instinct, eh?"

"What do you mean?"

"A good spy never tells his secrets."

AVAILABLE NOW

Comanche Magic by Catherine Anderson

The latest addition to the bestselling Comanche series. When Chase Wolf first met Fanny Graham, he was immediately attracted to her, despite her unsavory reputation. Long ago Fanny had lost her belief in miracles, but when Chase Wolf came into her life he taught her that the greatest miracle of all was true love.

Separating by Susan Bowden

The triumphant story of a woman's comeback from a shattering divorce to a fulfilling, newfound love. After twenty-five years of marriage, Riona Jarvin's husband leaves her for a younger woman. Riona is in shock—until she meets a new man and finds that life indeed has something wonderful to offer her.

Hearts of Gold by Martha Longshore

A sizzling romantic adventure set in 1860s Sacramento. For years Kora Hunter had worked for the family newspaper, but now everyone around her was insisting that she give it up for marriage to a long-time suitor and family friend. Meanwhile, Mason Fielding had come to Sacramento to escape from the demons in his past. Neither he nor Kora expected a romantic entanglement, considering the odds stacked against them.

In My Dreams by Susan Sizemore

Award-winning author Susan Sizemore returns to time travel in this witty, romantic romp. In ninth-century Ireland, during the time of the Viking raids, a beautiful young druid named Brianna inadvertently cast a spell that brought a rebel from 20th-century Los Angeles roaring back through time on his Harley-Davidson. Sammy Bergen was so handsome that at first she mistook him for a god—but he was all too real.

Surrender the Night by Susan P. Teklits

Lovely Vanessa Davis had lent her talents to the patriotic cause by seducing British soldiers to learn their battle secrets. She had never allowed herself to actually give up her virtue to any man until she met Gabriel St. Claire, a fellow Rebel spy and passionate lover.

Sunrise by Chassie West

Sunrise, North Carolina, is such a small town that everyone knows everyone else's business—or so they think. After a long absence, Leigh Ann Warren, a burned out Washington, D.C., police officer, returns home to Sunrise. Once there, she begins to investigate crimes both old and new. Only after a dangerous search for the truth can Leigh help lay the town's ghosts to rest and start her own life anew with the one man meant for her.

COMING SOON

Tame the Wildest Heart by Parris Afton Bonds

In her most passionate romance yet, Parris Afton Bonds tells the tale of two lonely hearts forever changed by an adventure in the Wild West. It was a match made in heaven . . . and hell. Mattie McAlister was looking for her half-Apache son and Gordon Halpern was looking for his missing wife. Neither realized that they would find the trail to New Mexico Territory was the way to each other's hearts.

First and Forever by Zita Christian

Katrina Swann was content with her peaceful, steady life in the close-knit immigrant community of Merriweather, Missouri. Then the reckless Justin Barrison swept her off her feet in a night of passion. Before she knew it she was following him to the Dakota Territory. Through trials and tribulations on the prairie, they learned the strength of love in the face of adversity.

Gambler's Gold by Barbara Keller

When Charlotte Bell headed out on a wagon train from Massachusetts to California, she had one goal in mind—finding her father, who had disappeared while prospecting for gold. The last thing she was looking for was love, but when fate turned against her, she turned to the dashing Reade Elliot to save her.

Queen by Sharon Sala

The Gambler's Daughters Trilogy continues with Diamond Houston's older sister, Queen, and the ready-made family she discovers, complete with laughter and tears. Queen Houston always had to act as a mother to her two younger sisters when they were growing up. After they part ways as young women, each to pursue her own dream, Queen reluctantly ends up in the mother role again—except this time there's a father involved.

A Winter Ballad by Barbara Samuel

When Anya of Winterbourne rescued a near-dead knight she found in the forest around her manor, she never thought he was the champion she'd been waiting for. "A truly lovely book. A warm, passionate tale of love and redemption, it lingers in the hearts of readers. . . . Barbara Samuel is one of the best, most original writers in romantic fiction today."—Anne Stuart

Shadow Prince by Terri Lynn Wilhelm

A plastic surgeon falls in love with a mysterious patient in this powerful retelling of *The Beauty and the Beast* fable. Ariel Denham, an ambitious plastic surgeon, resentfully puts her career on hold for a year in order to work at an exclusive, isolated clinic high in the Smoky Mountains. There she meets and falls in love with a mysterious man who stays in the shadows, a man she knows only as Jonah.

Harper Monogram **The Mark of Distinctive Women's Fiction**

LORD OF THE NIGHT

by Susan Wiggs
A Venetian lord dedicated to justice suspects a lucious beauty of being involved in a scandalous plot.

ORCHIDS IN MOONLIGHT

by Patricia Hagan
Caught in a web of intrigue in the dangerous West, a man and a woman fight to regain their overpowering dream of love.

A SEASON OF ANGELS

by Debbie Macomber
Three willing but wacky angels must teach their charges a lesson before granting a Christmas wish.
National Bestseller

For Fastest Service
—
Visa & MasterCard Holders Call
1-800-331-3761

MAIL TO: **HarperCollins Publishers**
P. O. Box 588 Dunmore, PA 18512-0588
OR CALL: (800) 331-3761 (Visa/MasterCard)

Yes, please send me the books I have checked:

- ☐ TAPESTRY (0-06-108018-7) $5.50
- ☐ DREAM TIME (0-06-108026-8) $5.50
- ☐ RAIN LILY (0-06-108028-4) $5.50
- ☐ COMING UP ROSES (0-06-108060-8) $5.50
- ☐ ONE GOOD MAN (0-06-108021-7) $4.99
- ☐ LORD OF THE NIGHT (0-06-108052-7) $5.50
- ☐ ORCHIDS IN MOONLIGHT (0-06-108038-1) $5.50
- ☐ A SEASON OF ANGELS (0-06-108184-1) $4.99

SUBTOTAL ....$________
POSTAGE AND HANDLING ....$ 2.00
SALES TAX (Add applicable sales tax) ....$________
TOTAL: $________

*(ORDER 4 OR MORE TITLES AND POSTAGE & HANDLING IS FREE! Orders of less than 4 books, please include $2.00 p/h. Remit in US funds, do not send cash.)

Name ________________________________

Address ______________________________

City _________________________________

State ________ Zip ____________

(Valid only in US & Canada)

Allow up to 6 weeks delivery.
Prices subject to change.
HO 751